Playing the Changes

Playing the changes is a jazz phrase. Technically, it means improvising on an existing chord progression and, in jazz-speak, each chord is a change. Playing the changes of an existing piece transforms it into something new and more elaborate. This is no more than a basic skill, but jazz musicians use it to generate narrative, emotion, humour and mood, as well as a conversation with the other musicians and the audience. An advanced player will even change the changes while adhering to the deep structure of the original. For a while, our South African jazz life consisted of 'playing the changes' there.

Darius Brubeck at the Music Department, University of Natal, Durban, in the mid-1990s (photo: Paul Weinberg).

Playing the Changes

Jazz at an African University and on the Road

Darius Brubeck and
Catherine Brubeck

First Illinois printing, 2024
© 2023 by Darius Brubeck and Catherine Brubeck
Reprinted by arrangement with the authors.
All rights reserved.

1 2 3 4 5 C P 5 4 3 2 1
∞ This book is printed on acid-free paper.

South Africa edition published in 2023 by the
University of KwaZulu-Natal Press.

Library of Congress Cataloging-in-Publication Data
Names: Brubeck, Darius, author. | Brubeck, Catherine, 1936–
    author.
Title: Playing the changes : jazz at an African university and on the
    road / Darius Brubeck and Catherine Brubeck.
Description: Urbana : University of Illinois Press, 2024. | Includes
    bibliographical references and index. is
Identifiers: LCCN 2023057844 (print) | LCCN 2023057845
    (ebook) | ISBN 9780252046179 (cloth) | ISBN 9780252088261
    (paperback) | ISBN 9780252047442 (ebook)
Subjects: LCSH: Brubeck, Darius. | Brubeck, Catherine, 1936– |
    University of KwaZulu-Natal. Centre for Jazz and Popular Music.
    | Jazz—South Africa—History and criticism. | Jazz musicians—
    Biography.
Classification: LCC ML3509.S6 B78 2024 (print) | LCC ML3509.
    S6 (ebook) | DDC 781.65092/268455–dc23/eng/20231220
LC record available at https://lccn.loc.gov/2023057844
LC ebook record available at https://lccn.loc.gov/2023057845

For all those musicians, students and friends who made our jazz life in South Africa rich and unforgettable.

And, for our Brubeck, Morphet and Elmer families.

Contents

Foreword *by Christopher Ballantine*	ix
Acknowledgements	xvi
Abbreviations	xx
Preface	xxii
Prelude	1
1 The Mission	7
2 The Scene	23
3 Improvising Education	50
4 Durban to Detroit	77
5 The Jazzanian Effect	98
6 The Jazz Centre and Drinks at Five	128
7 Some Remarkable People	146
8 Off Campus and on the Road	193
9 Continuum	240
Coda	262
Appendix 1: Out-Takes	273
Appendix 2: Documents	277
Discography	289
Notes	291
Bibliography	303
Index	306

vii

Foreword

A story typically has multiple times and places of origin. Some of these can be unexpected, even confounding, but they can also sit happily alongside others that in hindsight seem always to have pointed to predictable outcomes. The narrative that Darius and Cathy Brubeck relate in this enthralling book is just such a story.

So, what are its origins? Surprisingly, one is the FIFA World Cup of 1978. As a visiting scholar that year at both the City University of New York and Columbia University – I was on sabbatical leave from the University of Natal (now the University of KwaZulu-Natal, UKZN) – I met Cathy at a neighbour's brownstone house in Prospect Park, Brooklyn, where my partner and I were living. With the World Cup in Argentina already in progress, the conversation soon turned to football. Cathy and I were delighted to discover a mutual passion for the 'beautiful game' and gleefully decided to get tickets for the final – or rather, for the broadcasting of the final onto a giant television screen at Madison Square Garden. So, on 25 June, in a sold-out arena, we and many thousands of excited fans were virtually transported from New York to the Estadio Monumental in

Christopher Ballantine, 1995 (photo: Paul Weinberg).

ix

Buenos Aires, where we joined the 72 000 people who were physically there to watch Argentina defeat the Netherlands in extra time. Of course, I had no idea that Cathy and I were laying the groundwork for what would become a long, deep and consequential friendship, nor that some notable features of that friendship were already moving into place. One of these features was that, when it came to football, Cathy and I would never agree. (Yes, she backed the winning team; I didn't.) Another was that where there was Cathy, there would also always be Brubecks. To the final she brought Dave Brubeck's manager, Russell Gloyd, and Darius's brother Chris – the first time I had met anyone owning up to that universally celebrated family name. I don't think I saw Cathy again or met any more Brubecks before we returned to Durban late in the year. But football disagreements notwithstanding, Cathy and I were keen to stay in touch.

If Madison Square Garden is one early – and totally unexpected – source for the story that follows, another is the Shakespeare bar in New York's Greenwich Village. At the beginning of 1981, I was back in New York, this time en route to Middlebury College, Vermont, where I had accepted an invitation to be visiting professor of music for the winter term. Cathy, Darius and I arranged to meet at that bar one wintry Sunday morning. There, for the first time, we allowed our imaginations to explore a radical and thrilling idea, even if it seemed to have only a remote possibility of a successful outcome. Framed as a question, the idea was: might our Department of Music in Durban be able to create a teaching post for which Darius could apply, so that he could establish Africa's first-ever university degree in Jazz Studies? (Privately, I relished the idea that this plan for jazz was mooted – incongruously! – in a venue named after William Shakespeare, who happens to be my favourite writer.) Our question had no easy answer. But I vowed to continue thinking about it. When I returned to Durban, I began discussing it with colleagues. And soon we resolved to make it happen.

For the Brubecks, despite the strikingly forward-looking, well-resourced and welcoming Department of Music that awaited them, what lay between the Shakespeare bar and the flourishing of the continent's pioneering jazz programme was a path that was long, hazardous and full of obstacles. This book describes these with gripping precision. Two of the earliest obstacles merit brief mention here. There was the anti-apartheid boycott, initiated by the African National Congress (ANC) in 1958 and adopted by the United Nations a decade later. Darius and Cathy took this obstacle seriously, discussing their plans with the ANC in exile and secured its approval to go ahead. The other obstacle was the stark fact that our young Department of Music had nothing even remotely resembling a 'jazz post'. Our only vacancy at the time was a job in music theory. So, we thought imaginatively outside the box and conjured some smoke and mirrors. Morphing the existing vacancy into a first-ever jazz post while remaining true to our commitment also to continue teaching music theory involved not just sleight of hand. It involved something close to the heart of jazz: creative

x

improvisation. As this book reveals, this would turn out to be just the first of a long line of schemes, subterfuges, manoeuvres and improvisations, all of which Darius and Cathy recount in exquisite and often hilarious detail.

The narrative also explains why the two of them chose to walk this difficult path and it shows that, the many obstacles notwithstanding ('an administrative nightmare' Darius has called it), the jazz programme delivered remarkable successes at astonishing speed. These included global recognition and fame, a stream of eminent local and international visitors (many of them wanting to perform on our stages) and successful tours by student groups to locations as diverse as the United States, the United Kingdom, Mozambique, Namibia, Italy, France, Germany, Turkey, Sweden, Denmark, Thailand, Peru, Korea and Australia. Perhaps the most legendary of these groups was the Jazzanians. When Darius and Cathy took this band to the United States in 1988, principally to perform at the National Association of Jazz Educators Conference in Detroit, I went along too. My job was to present a conference paper on *marabi*-jazz. But for me, the most unforgettable part of this pre-eminent conference was watching the Jazzanians perform and being deeply moved by the musical flair and creative brilliance they so confidently displayed alongside their international student peers, most of whom had access to resources and privileges of which our students could only dream.[1] From beginnings such as these, many of our jazz graduates went on, and today still go on, to become celebrated and influential music figures both in South Africa and abroad, as performers, recording artists, producers, teachers and researchers.

How all that came to pass is part of the riveting story of this book. Though its telling is marked by many moments of pride and joy, it seems to me that the book is in some ways too modest about the extent to which these achievements depended on the enormous personal investment of Darius and Cathy. They always went far beyond the call of duty. Cathy's role is emblematic of this. She is the story's unsung hero. Unsalaried and never more than a (notoriously) unofficial 'member of staff' – hence not technically a staff member at all – she effectively became both manager and mother to endless cohorts of jazz students, raising funds to cover fees and other expenses, establishing scholarships, organising gigs (also for members of the jazz staff) and, when necessary, taking care of other basic student needs, such as the provision of food, accommodation and musical instruments. This extended even to the opening of their home: the Brubeck house became a base camp for out-of-towners of colour, partly because during the jazz programme's early years the Group Areas Act still restricted where so-called non-whites could live and partly because even in later years appropriate accommodation was at a premium. It was also Cathy's unstinting efforts that secured for us the Malcolm Hunter Collection – a large, world-class collection of historic recordings (mostly 78-rpm records) and a library of hugely valuable but out-of-print jazz-related publications. Despite lively bidding from other universities in the world,

Cathy stayed as focused on her goal as any of the football superstars she so admires. She out-dribbled the opposition and scored. The collection is now a proud part of our Music Library.

These 'genesis' reflections also point in the direction of another source for this book's story, with an even earlier and broader prehistory. That source is better thought of as a cluster of origins: a set of rhizome-like roots whose vital connections remain obscure until one starts digging. The connections I have in mind link together discrete things, such as colleagues, institutional culture, place, time, apartheid, colonialism, capitalism, politics, freedom and music. In order to shed light on how those links are relevant to this book, I shall now say something about a personal journey of my own.

For me, at least, the birth of the Shakespeare bar jazz idea was timed to perfection. My very first journal article – fifteen years earlier, in *African Music* – had dealt with Tswana pipe music, an endogenous South African music genre. But since then, my publications had focused primarily on Western music, philosophically and in relation to society. Yet, by the early 1980s, for reasons both personal and political, my research interests were turning again to South African music, most notably to its jazz history.[2] Of course, no one knew that this would be apartheid's final decade. But, after the dark night and the upheavals of the previous two decades – the Durban strikes of 1973, for instance, known as the 'Durban moment', had shown that change was possible and inevitable – the anti-apartheid struggle now seemed to have extra resilience. Despite the ever-brutal and repressive weight of the state, the push against it was gathering momentum on a number of fronts (including academic ones). Its most significant new manifestation would soon appear – in 1983, to be exact – and would take the form of the enormously important civil society movement known as the United Democratic Front.

These circumstances, it seems to me, allowed music, research and activism to come together in ways that had remarkable promise. My earlier publications had shown music's transgressive potential, arguing that music could confront social injustice, support political transgression, break boundaries, disrupt too-settled identities, imagine integration, forge hybridity and direct sentiment towards more inclusive or cosmopolitan ends. And now it was clear to me that a study of the musical and sociopolitical history of South African jazz (in my view best referred to as *marabi*-jazz) could provide an ideal case study, with strong contemporary relevance. Globally, after all, jazz – a modernist music with potentially anti-hegemonic potential – had often been a harbinger of a vital historic mission. And perhaps nowhere was this truer than in my home country. What research into *marabi*-jazz therefore needed to investigate seriously was its repressed and largely forgotten history. Crucially, that would also involve a study of how the idiom's own complexly layered disputation of fixed boundaries had long enlisted it in the liberation struggle – so that, more than any other South African music, *marabi*-jazz had managed to work beyond and outside race thinking.

Of course, the apartheid state had done its brutal best to resist any practices that disputed 'race', especially after the implementation of the Group Areas Act of 1950. Notoriously, that had caused many of the best jazz players to flee the country, with the result that long before the 1980s it had become very difficult for the remaining, mostly part-time musicians to keep *marabi*-jazz alive. The hope we nurtured in the Shakespeare bar was that a university-based jazz programme, provided it was inspirationally led and well supported, would help to reverse that trend. In so many ways, then, the moment we found ourselves in – the early 1980s – seemed powerfully, inescapably serendipitous. The programme's home, moreover, would be our young Department of Music, committed as it was to a progressive and strongly anti-apartheid trajectory.

Some years earlier – in 1974 – I had accepted the position of professor and head of department. With the Music Department then still in its infancy, it was immediately clear to me that the position provided an incredible opportunity to help shape the department's development – to try to make it relevant to its social, historical, political and geographical location. That, in turn, meant that the department would need to look for ways of grounding itself in opposition to the apartheid state, and in teaching and research that strove for an anti-colonial and radically emancipatory mindset. It also meant that we would need to search for and appoint extraordinary staff. The goal was as explicit as that. And it is no secret that over the years we succeeded in securing a cohort of brilliant, progressive-minded colleagues: a wonderful group of people, who made unique contributions to these commitments in their teaching, research publications and performance activities.

We were also a diverse bunch. But this collegial diversity was healthy, not least because it fostered lively debate among our students. Never was this clearer than in the curricular choices our students made – freedom of this kind being one of the features of the varied degrees we were developing. And now we were adding Jazz Studies to the list! So, from undergraduate to doctoral level, a celebration of difference was everywhere. Though some students would tend towards conventional musical paths, others would choose to investigate musical genres such as the Zulu migrant-worker idioms, known as *maskanda* or *isicathamiya*, or penny whistle *kwela*, or other varieties of local popular music, or South African Indian music, or they would elect to produce compositions that sought integrations with the endogenous musics of Africa, or choose to focus primarily (and performatively) on African music and dance, or critically research music and capitalism. In one striking example, two senior undergraduates in Ethnomusicology, both white women who went on to become eminent international leaders in their fields, undertook their fieldwork research by becoming admired and respected members of a prominent, all-male gumboot (*isicathulo*) troupe of migrant workers living in Durban.[3]

xiii

Broadly speaking, then, that was the scene that awaited the arrival of Darius and Cathy Brubeck in 1983. Or rather, it was the more academic part of the scene. What about the practical, performance-based aspect our activities – an aspect that would obviously be of crucial importance to the intended jazz programme?

Darius knew that performance opportunities on campus were abundant, flexible and forward-looking and that, in our first decade, the Department of Music had built up an exceptionally rich and varied performance culture. Regular concerts, once or twice a week, began when we first opened our doors in 1972. As the years progressed, our programmes included – and these are just a few examples – performances of *isicathamiya* by Joseph Shabalala and his Ladysmith Black Mambazo, the jazz piano of Abdullah Ibrahim and Chris McGregor (alongside the classical piano of Jorge Bolet and Charles Rosen), legendary *marabi*-jazz swing bands, outdoor performances by Venancio Mbande and his Chopi Timbila Orchestra from Mozambique, musicians from other parts of Africa, *maskanda* festivals and concerts of classical Indian music. There were also modernist performances of characteristically subversive avant-garde or experimental music that called into question how we saw the world. These included works by composers such as Olivier Messiaen, Karlheinz Stockhausen, John Cage, Christian Wolff, Earle Brown, Ulrich Süsse, Nam June Paik, Gerald Barry, Mauricio Kagel and Kevin Volans – works often receiving their South African premieres – and improvisations and realisations by the Department of Music's own New Music Group, of which I was proud to be a member.

If the story told in this book has multiple beginnings, it also has a vital and vibrant afterlife. Following their decades in Durban, the Brubecks now reside in England, where Darius enjoys an illustrious career as a touring performer and band leader. Significantly, he remains on the staff of UKZN as an honorary professor. In South Africa, to which he and Cathy return whenever they can, their legacy is resoundingly evident. In addition to UKZN, several other South African music departments, and even some secondary schools, now have flourishing jazz programmes. This utterly changed pedagogical landscape has played a major role in revitalising jazz performance and jazz research in the country and created a host of related career opportunities. They also left behind, at UKZN, the most successful and thriving campus-based jazz and popular music venue in the country (the Centre for Jazz and Popular Music, established by Darius in 1989 as part of the Department of Music).[4] And as one cornerstone of its flourishing jazz programme, the department also boasts a jazz piano tradition so unique in its cultivation of recognisably distinct and exceptional keyboard talents – each different from others, several exploring mergers with other idioms – that it has been dubbed the 'Durban school', or more precisely the 'Brubeck school'. Many of the country's leading jazz pianists have emerged from it. The book speaks about several of them, just as it does about many who excelled in other jazz fields – in all, too many for the book to mention. But as I write this, some of the cited names randomly flood my mind, each with its own vivid memories. Among them are Andile Yenana, Zim Ngqawana, Mark Kilian, Melvin Peters, Neil Gonsalves, Sibusiso Mashiloane, Burton Naidoo, Nishlyn Ramanna, Nduduzo Makhathini, Kevin Gibson, Johnny Mekoa, Debbie Mari, Natalie Rungan, Victor Masondo, Feya Faku, Nic Paton, Lulu Gontsana, Lex Futshane . . .

The pages ahead offer the first detailed account of the Brubecks' exceptional and comprehensive achievement. As renowned literary scholar Professor David Attwell – one of the (initially anonymous) readers of the manuscript – wrote, the book 'is a marvellous archival record, woven together with clarity and flair, and a celebration of a huge, diverse community of artists both accomplished and in-the-making. The cumulative account of the careers made and the friendships forged in so many collaborations is moving indeed.' One must hope that this 'vital archival record', as Attwell called it, will prompt further study and research, especially now that the extensive Brubeck papers are in the process of being properly archived.[5] The recovery and precise telling of South African history, including its music history, is far from done. Crucially, in its contribution to the telling of that history, this book stands as a significant cultural document. Its testimony offers compelling and inspiring evidence of some of the ways that the country's young and still-troubled democracy is being built.

Christopher Ballantine
Professor of Music Emeritus and University Fellow
University of KwaZulu-Natal

Acknowledgements

We have so many people to thank and we hope that readers of this book will spend time recognising our grateful appreciation of the many.

This memoir would never have been written without constant coaxing from Darius's mother, Iola Brubeck, who kept everything (letters, newspaper clippings, programmes and memorabilia) we sent her from South Africa for 25 years. We wish she and Dave were alive to see that we did listen and did our 'almost-best' to quote drummer par excellence Lulu Gontsana, who always used this phrase when he intended to accomplish something.

We also want to honour others who died before seeing this book in print. First among those is Catherine's brother Jo, who read the entire first draft and, as a former subeditor, sent us numerous emails with corrections and suggestions. He also steered us through some political minefields. We kept notes from numerous conversations with Johnny Mekoa, Barney Rachabane, Zim Ngqawana and Don Albert before they died, and we are indebted to them for their wit, stories and oral histories. Another, no longer here, whom we should acknowledge is Margaret Daymond, a renowned literary scholar at the University of KwaZulu-Natal (UKZN) and a close friend. We stayed with her during our frequent research visits to Durban and benefited from her vast knowledge of South African literature.

Most definitely we want to thank Sally Hines (managing editor) for her excellent advice and guiding the book to print. All this was done in a very friendly and professional manner. Her swift responses made our task much, much easier. Any errors are certainly ours, rather than hers. We also thank Alison Lockhart for her careful editing; Susan Elliott for the layout and design of the book; Marise Bauer for the cover design; Judith Shier for the proofreading; and Christopher Merrett for the indexing.

This book was made possible by the very generous support of the Stellenbosch Institute for Advanced Study (STIAS). We really would not have reached our goal without all the patient help from the former director, Hendrik Geyer, as well as

Christoff Pauw, Nel-Mari Loock, Maria Mouton and Leonard Katsokore. We were also fortunate to briefly overlap with the current director, Edward Kirumira. Our thanks must also include the STIAS fellows we encountered during our residencies in 2017 and 2019 for their tremendous interest and support as well as all the convivial times. Beyond the overall patronage, the all-important space, time and intellectual stimulus contributed greatly to this work. STIAS is a brilliant and gracious setting for anyone who has embarked on a long-term project. Particular mention should be made of former STIAS fellows Stella Viljoen, who theorised that we had truly been engaged in practice-based pedagogy, and David Atwell and Derek Attridge, who were both in favour of emphasising the 'university narrative'. We were thrilled to receive encouragement from Joe Stiglitz, who liked all the personal stories. We were also inspired by Abdallah Daar, one of the most benevolent and humane individuals we have ever met. All of their general observations helped *Playing the Changes* remain a memoir, but also a record of the development of the first-ever jazz degree in Africa and the accompanying Centre for Jazz and Popular Music (CJPM), often simply referred to as the Jazz Centre.

Much of what we achieved at the Jazz Centre is due to the vision and flexibility of former University of Natal (now UKZN) executives, Piet Booysen, Chris Cresswell, Andrew Duminy, Michael Chapman, Ahmed Bawa, Bobby Mills and Bruno van Dyk. Additionally, James Trinder, Rodney Harber and Dennis Claude made an enormous contribution to the building and maintaining of CJPM. Rika Engelbrecht's groundbreaking research in the area of Library Science would not have happened without the jazz programme, which in turn benefited greatly from her methodology and acutely focused interest as music librarian in the extensive jazz collection housed in the Eleanor Bonnar Music Library at UKZN.

A university is a complex bureaucratic and hierarchical institution in which progress is not possible without the help of senior academics and administrators. We owe the very existence of CJPM to these people and CJPM is at the very heart of this book. And – more unusually – where would we have been without the attractive bar constructed and donated by South African Breweries, which remained a source of support through their special deals and prizes, adding commercial and professional flare to our activities.

We particularly want to recognise with gratitude our university colleagues Gerrit Bon, Ulrich Süsse, Mike Morris and Jürgen Bräuninger. In addition to his technical expertise, Jürgen and his wife Brigitte hosted us for countless delicious dinners with conversations about the university and the jazz programme. Furthermore, Christian de Haas (alias Fuzzy Roadstone) and Dale Wardell, both former students of Jürgen's, kept the shows on the road at the Jazz Centre with their skilful sound engineering.

And now, many, many thanks to our wonderful friends and associates who read chapters and made necessary comments. R.W. Johnson sent us relevant suggestions and expert criticism. We also appreciate Michael Gardiner's overall observations and contribution of insider knowledge and detail to our depiction of Johannesburg's arts and activism matrix. Sybilla Higgs gave us effective feedback and David Papineau stressed the importance of writing at least three hours a day. We tried very hard to emulate his example. Playing the Jazzanians' LP *We Have Waited Too Long* on his very superior sound system, Karel Tip reignited our appreciation of this amazing band and how central its members were to our jazz life. Mel and June Narunsky, former Durban residents, hosted regular jazz-listening and jazz-film-viewing nights at their home; their bountiful help increased our knowledge of both local and international jazz. Ben and Pam Pretorius continue to influence our thinking and they deserve a special place in our honours list. As does Zara Harber, who, throughout our association, was involved with the welfare of the jazz students.

We are also deeply grateful to those who helped us take many student groups on the road, both domestically and internationally – for example International Association of Jazz Educators (IAJE) executives and members, Dennis Tini, Richard Dunscombe, Bill McFarlane, Chuck Owen, Ron McCurdy, Bill Prince, Bob Sinicrope and Larry Ridley, as well as local individuals like Durban architect Paul Mikula, who, in addition to significant tour support, donated all the chairs and tables that still furnish the Jazz Centre.

We want to acknowledge our long-term relationship with the United States Information Service under successive ambassadors (Herman W. Nickel, Edward Joseph Perkins, William Lacy Swing and Princeton N. Lyman) and the Cultural Center staff, particularly Deva Govindsamy, at the United States Consulate in Durban. They were there for us in so many ways: financial and cultural support for student tours, visiting artists and lecturers and wise advice for our Fulbright and other scholarship students. We have named certain Durban-based officers in the text.

Our very close friends Colleen and Douglas Irvine provided endless accommodation and hospitality in Johannesburg while we interviewed former students and their home became a second home for us, where numerous conversations took place about our ideas and what we intended to include in the book. In this regard, we also thank Marianne Claude and Lettie Gardiner.

We are very grateful to Deborah Eagle and Nicole Verdelli for the long days spent in our home in England cataloguing and identifying relevant material as well as making pertinent observations about the content of our personal papers. And, in terms of archival help and caring encouragement, we must thank Dr Lizabé Lambrechts for having placed these papers in the Hidden Years Music Archive at the Documentation Centre for Music (DOMUS), Stellenbosch University. We have also sent official university and CJPM records to the UKZN Archives in Pietermaritzburg.

Glynis Malcom-Smith, whom we recognise later, supervised this with help from Thuli Zama, who kindly let us go through all our old office cabinets.

Former students filled in questionnaires, were willing interviewees and correspondents and provided insightful observations from their own experience of the time we were all together. For their great (and important) contributions, we acknowledge, in alphabetical order, Sazi Dlamini, Marc Duby, Andrew Eagle, John Edwards, Feya Faku, Lex Futshane, Kevin Gibson, Neil Gonsalves, Marc Kilian, Debbie Mari, George Mari, Victor Masondo, Mfana Mlambo, Nic Paton, Melvin Peters, Nishlyn Ramanna, Natalie Rungan, Rick van Heerden and Andile Yenana.

We are also very grateful to Chris Merz, Dusty Cox, Mike and Di Rossi and Jeff Robinson for sharing their opinions and memories. Ramoll Bugwandeen and David Marks gave us a lot of their time discussing the 'old days' and what made jazz at the university important for them.

We have of course credited journalists and photographers where relevant, but we would like to name George Nisbet, Don Albert, Anne Pretorius, Giselle Turner, Anthea Johnston and Lindelwa Dalamba, who were extremely engaged reviewers and critics, who tracked our progress and held us to high standards. Talktome Sandile Ngidi also helped us in recent years and we value his continued interest in *Playing the Changes*, the book and the documentary of the same title. The film-makers Michiel ten Kleij, Maarten in t'Hout and Jorne Tielmans followed us to Poland and South Africa, reconstructing the past and filming our renewed contact with key people in our lives. This was all set in motion by the film producer David Richardson and we thank them all for their impact on our writing. Thanks also to Rafs Mayet, who not only helped the film-makers, but also provided us with a choice of excellent photos. We are very grateful to Omar Badsha and the late Ted Brien as well. Paul Weinberg, too, must be thanked for his brilliant photographic portraits.

Professor Christopher Ballantine who has written the foreword to *Playing the Changes* is in a category all on his own, or rather bestrides many categories – from renowned author and scholar to an authority on South Africa jazz. He has been our guide, our mentor and our critic throughout our stop-start writing endeavours and we highly respect his judgement and are very proud to be his friends.

Finally, our profound and heartfelt thanks go to Glynis Malcolm-Smith (now Hartogh), who for seventeen years, worked with us on every aspect of our developing, developed and improvised programmes. She shared the good and the bad times, and put up with all our irregular demands, emergencies and impulses. We really couldn't have run the Jazz Centre without her passionate commitment to the students and to our entire project, of which this book is a memoir.

Abbreviations

ABRSM	Associated Board of the Royal Schools of Music
AJP	African Jazz Pioneers
ANC	African National Congress
BAT	Bartle Arts Trust
BMU	British Musicians Union
BP	British Petroleum
CJPM	Centre for Jazz and Popular Music
COSATU	Congress of South African Trade Unions
CRAN	Commission to Restructure Arts in Natal
DACST	Department of Arts, Science, Culture and Technology
DIFM	Durban International Festival of Music
DOMUS	Documentation Centre for Music
ECM	Editions of Contemporary Music
IAJE	International Association for Jazz Education
ICC	International Convention Centre
IFP	Inkatha Freedom Party
MAG	Music Academy of Gauteng
MANA	Music Association of Natal
MAPP	Music Action for People's Power
MOJO	Members of the Original Jazz Organisation
NAJE	National Association of Jazz Educators
NAPAC	Natal Provincial Arts Council
NBC	National Broadcasting Company

NCC	Natal Cultural Council
NDP	non-degree purposes
NGO	non-governmental organisation
NPO	Natal Philharmonic Orchestra
NPR	National Public Radio
NU	Natal University
NUDF	Natal University Development Fund
NUJE	Natal University Jazz Ensemble
NUSAS	National Union of South African Students
NYJF	National Youth Jazz Festival
PAC	Pan Africanist Congress
SABC	South African Broadcasting Corporation
SACP	South African Communist Party
SADF	South African Defence Force
SAJE	South African Association of Jazz Educators
SAMA	South African Music Association/South African Music Award
SAMRO	Southern African Music Rights Organisation
SRC	Students Representative Council
UCT	University of Cape Town
UDF	United Democratic Front
UDW	University of Durban-Westville
UKZN	University of KwaZulu-Natal
UN	United Nations
UND	University of Natal, Durban
UNISA	University of South Africa
USIS	United States Information Service
WEA	Warner Elektra Atlantic
WOMAD	World of Music, Arts and Dance

Preface to the
University of Illinois Press Edition

South Africa is known to the rest of the world for two things: music and its inspiring freedom struggle against apartheid. *Playing the Changes* covers 23 years (1983 to 2006), the years that we were there together, and they were mostly glory years for jazz and the 'struggle'; the two were intertwined as never before or since. We were deemed 'comrades', and motivated by our strong beliefs, just like many others ranging from Communist trade union organizers to Christian clergy. Today, streets and landmarks named after Nelson Mandela are found in many major cities throughout the world, and we were elated to be there in 1990 when he was released from prison.

We didn't start with a 'master plan' but, in retrospect, what we at first improvised worked. Jazz Studies now exists in every higher education institution in South Africa that has a music department. Beyond this, there are events and stories that resonate with challenges to the status quo and adapting to changing times.

The global impact of jazz as a liberalizing and unifying force is most urgently needed in societies struggling with top-down oppression. With our bands and students, we demonstrated this benefit wherever and whenever we toured. The distinctive jazz inflections of these South African and international musicians appealed to diverse audiences and cultures throughout the United States and in Germany, Thailand, Peru, Turkey, and beyond.

'These are the days of miracle and wonder,' sang Paul Simon. His blockbuster hit album, *Graceland* (1986), and his subsequent tours included many musicians in our own circle. International and exiled musicians Hugh Masekela, Miriam Makeba and Abdullah Ibrahim had powered anti-apartheid movements worldwide, and there were other musicians of major stature who left South Africa during apartheid. Their stories intersect with ours at various times and places. This jazz diaspora has had an incredible impact worldwide, but in our book we mainly wanted to celebrate and memorialize musicians who *remained* in South Africa and whose names will not be as familiar to international readers.

We are also concerned here with institutional history and memory. A celebrity culture doesn't favour the lesser known. The work of significant individuals, academic leaders and teachers is often bypassed. Events and processes and changes that incrementally contributed to education, racial inclusivity, the restructuring of institutions and arts councils and diplomacy are important elements in our story, and universally important.

A documentary, also titled *Playing the Changes* (directed by Michiel ten Kleij), which begins in Poland in 2018 and follows us to South Africa in 2019, will be making the film festival rounds. Although it doesn't replicate the book, we think it reveals the 'do it yourself' strategy that we emphasize in our personal memoir. Hopefully others will find a source of ideas and encouragement to take down a new road.

We are delighted that the University of Illinois Press is publishing an international edition of this book because it speaks to modern concepts of education and freedom of choice. We would like to acknowledge director Laurie Matheson and her colleagues at the University of Illinois Press. Many thanks to them and to author Dale Cockrell for initiating this connection. Dale overlapped with us at the then University of Natal and is now Professor Emeritus of Musicology at Vanderbilt University and a Research Associate of the University of the Free State (South Africa).

Catherine and Darius Brubeck
(Rye, East Sussex, UK, February 2024)

Prelude

Darius

Poland 2018

Moving carefully in the dazzling light, I stepped off the stage at the Radio Szczecin concert hall to embrace a beaming, well-dressed, elderly woman, who had stood up from her seat next to Cathy, my wife, at a front-row table. She had been at the first concert of the Dave Brubeck Quartet's 1958 tour. Speaking through an interpreter, she told me that she went backstage with a group of fans to see my father and tried to get as close to him as possible but, sadly, when she saw what a beautiful woman my mother Iola was, she knew she didn't stand a chance. Turning to Cathy, she said that she didn't remember a lot about the concert except 'the two little boys'. My brother Michael was one and the other was me. We had been pushed onstage by the Polish tour manager, who wanted to demonstrate that the great Dave

Darius in front of a billboard in Szczecin, November 2018 (photo: Cathy Brubeck; Cathy Brubeck collection).

Brubeck from America was not afraid to bring his family to communist Poland. Even at the age of ten, I knew that once in front of an audience one was supposed to do something, so I went to my father at the piano and Joe Morello stood up and beckoned Mike to the drums. We played 'Take the "A" Train', well known in Eastern Bloc countries as the theme music for Willis Conover's 'Voice of America' short-wave radio broadcasts. So, my first public performance took place in Szczecin and here I was again, 60 years later, beginning a concert tour with my own quartet. When your father's name is part of what defines a particular era and is known around the world (a fate I share with, among others, Mercer Ellington and Ravi Coltrane in jazz and Jakob Dylan and Sean Lennon as singer-songwriters), you're always asking yourself what point you're making in the same field.

Earlier in 2018, I had been invited to Szczecin to play 'Take Five' with the Lincoln Center Jazz Orchestra – an honour – but what made this trip remarkable was a VIP tour of the Solidarity Museum.[1] Most of the museum is literally underground in Solidarity Square, now a memorial park on the site where pro-democracy demonstrators were shot by Polish and Soviet police in December 1970. Its grey, undecorated cement exterior and hunched, low-profile shape reminded us of the Holocaust Memorial in Berlin. It is a narrative museum like the Civil Rights Museum in Memphis, where you 'walk the walk' in semi-darkness to a soundtrack of historical news reports and environmental sounds. Here, the subterranean journey begins in post-war, occupied Poland and ends with full sovereignty in 1989. The first vitrine contained a short-wave radio c.1956 (the year 'Voice of America' began broadcasting jazz into Eastern Europe) and a Dave Brubeck concert programme. These iconic objects spoke for those times. I now understood the special attention we were getting 60 years after the United States State Department tour and the importance of jazz in this historical timeline. The Poles themselves attributed even greater impact to the quartet's 'cultural exchange' tour (Cold War terminology) than its most ardent proponents in the United States Information Service (USIS) dared claim. As in South Africa, jazz engaged people on levels beyond fandom. This doesn't mean that all Polish jazz fans were political activists, but they were longing for a more open society. The museum walk included video clips of speeches and Soviet propaganda, anti-Soviet demonstrations, strikes and rallies, newsreels showing uprisings and state violence, Solidarity negotiations and even scenes suggesting nostalgia for that era. The last room featured four foreign heads of state who helped to free Poland: Ronald Reagan, Margaret Thatcher, Mikhail Gorbachev and Pope John Paul II – not remembered by Cathy and me as champions of freedom and human rights – but, given the national narrative of present-day Poland, they obviously belonged there.

The Darius Brubeck Quartet was followed by a film crew from the moment we arrived in Szczecin, giving us an aura of modern-day celebrity. A documentary about our tour was a chance for the film-maker to explore how jazz is still linked to histories of social change. Michiel ten Kliej, the director of the documentary film *Playing the Changes* expects it to be on the film festival circuit in 2023 and 2024. Cathy and I had engaged with cultural diplomacy throughout my career in South Africa, but if we were still 'diplomats', what country did we represent now? Does retracing my father's 1958 tour and introducing university jazz education in South Africa during apartheid really form a connected narrative?

Jazz music is universally associated with ideals of freedom and struggle against oppression. The rationales and modalities of oppression and expressions of freedom are specific and extremely different depending on local circumstances. 'Black and Blue' and 'Strange Fruit', as sung by Louis Armstrong and Billie Holiday, respectively, are laments about racist cruelty in the Deep South; Charles Mingus's 'Fables of Faubus' mocks the Arkansas governor's resistance to integration; and Duke Ellington's 'Black, Brown and Beige' implies an unusually affirmative take on black history as overcoming prejudice while maintaining identity. Songs make easy examples, but the oppositional character of jazz does not depend on words. The very sound of jazz, the pervasive aesthetic of individuality, improvisation and continuous reinvention defies definition and control by authority. The music itself is global. Jazz musicians *from* everywhere *go* everywhere, jazz festivals are tourist attractions on every continent and the United Nations (UN) celebrates International Jazz Day on 30 April every year. Proclaiming jazz as 'the music of freedom' sounds like a cliché these days, but it is still true. The intriguing thing is how this manifests in radically different societies where it is clear that the music matters.[2] For example, the association with freedom is concretely historical and specific for people who live in Poland and South Africa.[3] Fortuitously, for the film project, my journey as a musician started in Poland as a ten-year-old and arguably culminated in South Africa. The performance of jazz in South Africa under apartheid and in Poland under Stalinist Russia was about the music, but it was often a consciously political gesture – *playing the changes* that people yearned for.

South Africa, 1983

I have a long association with South Africa. I taught at the University of KwaZulu-Natal (UKZN) for 23 years, during which time Cathy initiated and managed tours for professional and student musicians, raised funds and organised special jazz projects and events. She was born in England and arrived in South Africa in 1942 as the six-year-old daughter of a Royal Air Force officer. She grew up listening to jazz and watching numerous movies of the era. She became a prominent student activist at the University of Natal, where she studied English and Political Science. Cathy was working for the Duke Ellington Orchestra and was based in New York when we met. We went together to South Africa in 1983 to establish a Jazz Studies degree programme at what was then the University of Natal (Durban campus: hence UND) and later it became a model for many South African universities with music departments.

It was a time fraught with challenges. Black students still needed permission to attend white universities and many potential students didn't have the standard entry requirements or any funds. Improvised solutions included allowing talented performers to attend classes and it took some years to prove that this was a viable route to official qualification. In retrospect, we were ahead of the transformation curve.

South African jazz has its own deep tradition and style, originally a hybrid based on dance-band era swing and an indigenous urban style known as *marabi*. Like African-American jazz music, it has significant traces of church music, imported European concert music and African traditional music. It is both cosmopolitan and down-home. Jazz acknowledges and transcends race. The joyous vibe I encountered in certain situations in South Africa was what I imagine it felt like in Kansas City or Chicago in the 1930s and 1940s. But, sadly, a crucial difference was that South Africa's best-known stars were overseas, while the local scene sometimes seemed stranded in the past.

The National Party, which had been in power since 1948, introduced increasingly oppressive measures over time, but the 1950s were still recalled as a kind of golden era by the black musicians I associated with in the 1980s and 1990s. Records, photographs, newspaper articles and even a few films attest to this. In broad strokes, the notorious pass laws, 'white-by-night' curfews and the mass bulldozing of urban black and mixed-race settlements all but erased the economic and societal basis for jazz culture. Broadcasting was controlled by the government and ghettoised by language. Jazz that was correctly perceived as appealing to urban black audiences was

Cathy and Darius at Dave and Iola Brubeck's house in Connecticut, December 1982 (photographer unknown; Cathy Brubeck collection).

replaced by rural, 'tribal' indigenous music, which the authorities considered more appropriate for the 'natives'. All of this, in the long run, seemed to have enshrined jazz in popular memory as the music of struggle (as it certainly was for musicians!) and the sound of the good times before the cops broke up the party. Some of the best (and soon to be most famous) jazz musicians, notably Chris McGregor's Blue Notes and members of the cast of *King Kong*, managed to leave South Africa to pursue their art in exile.[4] Their distinctive style and intensity made an impact on the development of modern jazz in the 1960s and beyond, particularly in England, showing that they were much more than adept imitators of American jazz. International acclaim enhanced the exiles' mystique back home, but life abroad certainly wasn't easy for them.

Crossing over the Atlantic and crossing over into popular music, a few South African jazz artists became international stars. I remember watching Miriam Makeba perform 'The Click Song' (Qongqothwane) on TV with Harry Belafonte's band when I was thirteen. Hugh Masekela's 'Grazing in the Grass' was a *Billboard Magazine* number-one hit eight years later while I was a student at Wesleyan University. At some point, the evocative piano stylings of Dollar Brand (as Abdullah Ibrahim was then known) wafted into my world. Hugh Masekela, who moved to New York to study jazz after a period in London, was a worshipful acolyte of American masters like Miles Davis. As Masekela told America's National Public Radio's 'Morning Edition' in 2004, 'Miles was a funny guy. He said, "Listen, I'm going to tell you something. You're going to be artistic because there's thousands of us playing jazz, but nobody knows the shit that you know, you know, and if you can put *that* shit in *your* shit, then we're going to be listening." '

Masekela and the others came from a rich musical environment and their 'shit' was distinctive and appealing. Like bossa nova from Brazil or Afro-Cuban jazz, it was yet another tributary and it *was* jazz.

When we arrived in Durban, even the best musicians, like guitarist Allen Kwela, were leading a shadowy half-life, respected within their close communities, but impoverished and invisible in the media. There were some gigs to be had, but it wasn't a livelihood. Arguably, formal jazz education at a university might not have been as needed when there was a strong township and downtown scene but, after a generation of apartheid, it was the way forward for aspiring musicians. I was often told by self-taught musicians that they encouraged their young followers to enrol at the university. They had never had the opportunity to study music formally and were in favour of a music education for the next generation. University offered this training in an environment that conferred legitimacy on jazz as serious music and as a career path.

During our jazz life in Durban, we met many of the remarkable people who helped keep jazz alive. There was also a multi-generational community of fans and record collectors who were well versed in the American jazz classics. Aficionados in black townships often formed Sunday jazz clubs, the meetings of which were later advertised on the radio, and I attended a few. They were essentially record-listening sessions held in garages, backyards or even simple community halls.

World-renowned South African musicians like Miriam Makeba, Hugh Masekela, Abdullah Ibrahim and trombonist Jonas Gwangwa (leader of the Amandla Cultural Ensemble, the African National Congress's official artistic group) returned in the 1990s when the freedom struggle was considered to have been won. In fact, they had helped to win it. Exiled ANC leader Oliver Tambo told Jonas Gwangwa, 'We'd been out here for some 20-some-odd years . . . trying to talk to the international community about our struggle. But here Amandla does it in two hours.'[5]

Cathy and I had no idea that the freedom struggle might end during our time in South Africa. Initially, I signed a contract for two trial years. I felt strongly committed to the mission, but whether setting up a jazz course was to be a singular adventure or lead to a whole new career was a completely open question. It was a move away from building a career in my father's world to the unknown. We departed from a freezing, nearly snow-bound John F. Kennedy Airport in New York and stopped to refuel in Sal, an island in Cape Verde, because South African Airways was not allowed to fly over Africa's airspace. We landed at Jan Smuts Airport in Johannesburg (now OR Tambo International Airport), went through the usual immigration formalities and boarded the final flight of our long journey. Tired and excited, we descended the metal stairs to the tarmac at Louis Botha Airport in Durban (later replaced by King Shaka International Airport), engulfed by the silver-grey glare of mid-morning and the hot, humid coastal air smelling of jet fuel and the sea. Professor Christopher Ballantine was there to meet us.

1

The Mission

> **Darius Brubeck appointed university lecturer: Jazz 'first' for Natal**
>
> Darius Brubeck, son of one of jazz's all-time greats Dave Brubeck, has been appointed lecturer in jazz at Natal University, Durban.
>
> The 35-year-old musician – the most famous of the Brubeck sons with an international reputation of his own as a keyboard player and jazz musician – is likely to arrive in Durban in late January, in time for the beginning of the academic year in mid-February.
>
> Mr Brubeck's appointment to the newly created jazz lectureship is . . . another 'first' for the Department of Music at Natal University . . . This is the first time a professional jazzman has been appointed to a South African music department.
>
> Natal University's head of the music department, Professor Christopher Ballantine, said: 'I think this appointment meets a real need. There is an enormous amount of talent in South Africa – particularly in the black communities. Jazz musician Dollar Brand has often said the future of jazz lies in South Africa. But these young musicians have nowhere to turn for their jazz education.'
>
> — *Daily News*, 8 December 1982

Darius

This press announcement from the *Daily News* is a good place to begin, but needs some personal perspective. My formal education did not make me an obvious candidate for a jazz post anywhere. I entered Wesleyan University in Connecticut for an Ethnomusicology major and completed the full undergraduate curriculum. I also wrote a thesis for an Honours degree in the History of Religion, which turned out to be useful, both academically and socially, in Durban. Through Ethnomusicology and History of Religion courses, I acquired some background in anthropology, philosophy and non-Western religious traditions. These wider interests gave me something to talk about besides jazz chords. Inevitably, in South Africa every conversation turned to politics, which I had not studied, but Cathy and her academic-activist friends helped me see the bizarre contours of the political landscape.

My interest in Indian culture led to contacts in the Durban Indian community. The Moon Hotel, owned by the Bugwandeen family, advertised itself as 'the home of jazz'. This unlikely home was situated next door to a neighbourhood mosque in Clairwood, on a noisy and gritty industrial and wholesale strip along the old two-lane South Coast Road. Ramoll Bugwandeen, who ran the hotel, was impressed that I had brought with me records by a cross-section of Hindustani and Carnatic artists. South Africa has the largest Indian population outside of India and two-thirds of them live in Durban. When *bansuri* (North Indian flute) virtuoso Deepak Ram joined the music faculty at the University of Durban-Westville (UDW), a nearby campus designated for Indian people under apartheid, we formed a hybrid Indo-jazz group, which I named Gathering Forces. The creation of UDW was a rare example of racial classification benefiting a community because, as an 'Indian university', UDW had a mandate to support Indian culture. Deepak was as much a student of jazz as I was of Indian music and our interaction influenced some of the student musicians around us. Indo-African-jazz hybrid groups, notably Mosaic, which included some of our best music students, flourished in the 1990s. Such a fusion may have been inevitable, given

Darius and Deepak Ram at Hindu Temple, Durban in 1993 (photo: Cathy Brubeck; Cathy Brubeck collection).

that Durban was indeed a musical mosaic on the shores of the Indian Ocean, but the arrival of Deepak and our performances together proved to be a catalyst for this musical fusion.

There are two prequels to the main story. My first visit to South Africa was as a member of the New Brubeck Quartet in 1976. This was a quartet of Brubecks under my father's leadership. It included my brothers Chris (trombone and bass) and Dan (drums), and I played electric keyboards. After seeing American news coverage of the Soweto uprising,[1] my father, Dave, a staunch proponent of Civil Rights in the United States and of anti-racism, wanted to cancel the tour, but his agent had already signed a contract while we were playing in California and there would have been legal consequences. Dave was able to impose certain conditions and was assured that we would not perform in racially exclusive venues. He further insisted on hiring an African bass player, transforming a white family band into a 'mixed' group, and demanded a local black opening act. The promoters, Graham Wright and Beryl Benn, engaged the extraordinary duo that went by the name of Malombo. (This programme was accepted in Johannesburg and Cape Town but, ironically, the management of the Playhouse Theatre in Durban decided it couldn't allow mixed audiences, so we cancelled the Durban performances.) This trip was the start of my long association with the South African jazz scene. Advocates of a complete cultural boycott were disappointed that Dave hadn't cancelled the whole tour, but musicians and many activists were glad we were there. The UN-supported boycott, backed by organised labour, took a more rigid stand in the 1980s.

The first jazz musicians I met – at the rehearsal in the old Coliseum in Johannesburg – were Victor Ntoni, our acoustic bass player for the tour, and the duo Malombo – electric guitarist and multi-instrumentalist Philip Thabane and his nephew, Gabriel 'Mabi' Thobejane, who played an elaborate array of indigenous percussion instruments. I also met Don Albert, who came to interview Dave. Don had started out as an alto and baritone sax player and then became an internationally recognised jazz critic who, in later years, reviewed many of my performances. He organised a workshop at the Johannesburg Jazz Club, and later we visited that unique institution Dorkay House, founded by Father Trevor Huddleston in 1954.[2] It housed the African Music and Drama Association and enabled rehearsals and instruction for aspiring jazz musicians.

The unforgettable singer Thandi Klaasen was part of the Dorkay scene of influential musicians who stayed in South Africa and, with very little support, kept jazz alive. Thandi had been disfigured as a result of acid being thrown at her by a love rival many years previously. However, she always told audiences (and me) that she was still beautiful and belted out songs in a passionate style. (I later saw film footage of Thandi as a pretty, young star and better understood the gothic drama of her life.)

She could still really sing and her courage and presence helped her maintain headline status. I was privileged to share billings with her in the many festivals that sprang up in the late 1980s and 1990s.

In 1976, I also met the late, legendary tenor saxophonist Duke Makasi, with whom I would later play all over South Africa and in Harare, Zimbabwe. Duke went through life with a vague and dreamy air but, when he needed something, he was quite single-minded. Once when the Brubeck/Ntoni Quartet was on its way to play at a concert at Natal University, he remembered that he hadn't brought his pyjamas and insisted we stop so that he could buy some. The rest of us were focused on getting to the sound check but, at that moment, for him the pyjamas were the highest priority. He was in pyjamas the last time I saw him. In 1993, Cathy and I went with Victor Ntoni and Lulu Gontsana (the quartet's drummer) to visit Duke in Soweto's perpetually overcrowded Baragwanath Hospital. He was unconscious on a gurney in a corridor and never knew we had come. I still regularly play Duke's tune 'Years Ago', a romantic ballad of wistfulness and regret. That song carries a different sadness for me now.

Cancelling the Durban Playhouse concert meant we had some tourist time so, before flying back to New York, Dan, Victor, Cathy (who was Dave's assistant on this tour) and I took a highly memorable drive down the 'lovely road' of Alan Paton's novel Cry, the Beloved Country into the newly minted and theoretically independent Xhosa homeland of Transkei, which was artificially created by the National Party government. We headed south to visit Victor's wife in Umtata (renamed Mthatha in 2004), which meant crossing a new 'international' border. There was a brand-new, first-day border post on the only road south and I discovered that I had left my passport in Durban. Victor took charge of the situation, addressing the young border guards, who were dressed in crisp white uniforms just out of the box. In his resonant voice and formal isiXhosa, he explained that we, as 'people from overseas', didn't need visas for the Transkei. Africans were used to having to produce papers for everything and so Victor let them examine his South African passbook, but convinced them that white foreigners were exempt. Fortunately, their training hadn't yet included the usual purpose of showing a passport. We went on our merry way and checked into the new Umtata Holiday Inn. When we went downstairs for drinks, we were amazed to hear someone playing the piano in the style of McCoy Tyner, as heard on John Coltrane's famous quartet recordings. This was one of South Africa's future greats, Durban-born Bheki Mseleku. We spent the evening with him after his shift ended.

Once back in the United States, it seemed impossible to leave South Africa behind. Bheki Mseleku was in the United States the following year as a third member of Malombo on a tour organised by Cathy. Victor, with help from my father, came over to study at Berklee College of Music in Boston. Through Victor and Cathy, I met more South Africans in the United States: exiles, artists and politicos – from acclaimed artist Bill Ainslie and Market Theatre producer/director/playwright Barney Simon to photographer Peter Magubane and musicians Hugh Masekela and Thembi Mtshali, then based in New York. And, related to my future return to South Africa, I met Christopher Ballantine, who was already a friend of Cathy's. He was then the head of the Department of Music at the University of Natal and it was his idea to introduce a degree in Jazz Studies. He later told Cathy:

> What I remember is that from the very beginning, being absolutely sure that this is what we had to do, that we had to get Darius and you, that we had to create a jazz environment. This was a new department. The first students came in 1972, so we were the new kid on the block in music departments in the country. I took over as head in 1974 and, from that moment onwards, I mean my whole *raison d'être* for being in South Africa when I came back from the UK after five years there was what I was going to do here was going to be politically relevant. You know, I was a child of 1968. I came back a Marxist. I was at Cambridge University and took part in the anti-Vietnam War march – the famous one to the American Embassy in London in Grosvenor Square. I was going to do whatever I could, short of actually ending up in prison, to do my little bit against apartheid. And we had already started to do that in terms of the staff that we recruited. People who could do things differently and could issue a challenge.[3]

Meanwhile, back in Connecticut, I continued working with my father and building up my own fusion quintet, the first Gathering Forces, with my brother Dan on drums. My other brother, Chris, was establishing a funk-rock fusion band in New York and the three of us made two albums backing guitar legend Larry Coryell. We made brief forays into the avant-garde, Lower Manhattan loft scene and then I unpredictably did a coast-to-coast tour with Don McLean, whose songs 'The Day the Music Died' and 'Vincent' were worldwide hits. This tour paid well and allowed me to pick up some of the lore and outlook of a different professional environment. Don gave me a new spruce-top Washburn acoustic guitar at the end of the tour as a keepsake and I still have it. Gathering Forces played at Seventh Avenue South (New York City), the ideal venue for the kind of fusion music I was playing in those days. During this time, I also wrote arrangements for my father to use for guest appearances with symphony orchestras. In short, my career was active, but what was it about really? I didn't know at the time that I was modulating into a second life in a new key.

My second visit to South Africa took place in July and August in 1982. Cathy and I decided to visit her mother, Dorothea Shallis, in Pietermaritzburg and, once arrangements had been made, it made sense to tie in some performances. Evan Ziporyn, who later became world-famous as a clarinettist and composer, was already in Cape Town, having travelled from Bali to Pakistan to Tanzania and down south overland with Cathy's daughter, Alexandra.[4] Evan had met Marc Duby, already a highly rated acoustic and electric bass player and, through Marc, connected with inventive Cape Town musicians Nic Carter (guitar) and Lloyd Martin (drums). Together, we appeared as the Darius Brubeck Jazz Ensemble for a run of seven concerts at the Peoples' Space Theatre in the centre of Cape Town. Winston Mankunku made a memorable guest appearance. He was a major artist, South Africa's greatest tenor sax player, with a national following, but painfully shy. Evan and Marc continued in versions of Darius Brubeck ensembles, which appeared in Swaziland and Johannesburg with the amazing Tony Moore on drums.

Press coverage was never a problem in those days, either for publicising concerts or for getting reviews. It became clear that internationally isolated South Africa welcomed overseas 'stars' – and that is what I was made out to be. Even my liking for wine featured in two press stories. We still joke about 'Darius Brubeck Knows His Wine' printed in bold type above a picture of me holding a glass of wine in 'Scene around Cape Town'. (This was the day we met Gyles Webb at Stellenbosch Farmers' Winery, a year before he established his now world-famous Thelema estate.) A welcoming case of wine was subsequently delivered to me while I was giving one of my very first lectures. Pictures and versions of my life story appeared in all the major dailies. Stories highlighting my father's name and using phrases like 'keyboard wizard' made me more than a little self-conscious, as well as anxious about the level of expectation. I didn't get this sort of attention in Connecticut!

Cape Town audiences liked us, but I was quite relieved when the reviews came out. The *Argus* reviewer called our show 'riveting jazz', while the *Cape Times* reported: 'Brubeck jazz a gourmet's delight'. In Johannesburg, Don Albert wrote, 'Don't miss this original Brubeck' in the *Star*. There was praise aplenty, but the one headline I'll never forget was in *Die Burger*, the national Afrikaans-language newspaper: 'Goed, maar Geen Towenaar' (Good, but No Wizard). Yep, that's me, but I never said I was one. Acknowledging this truth has shaped my whole approach to education and performance: make the most of the talents you have.

We visited Chris Ballantine when we reached Durban. 'This is fortuitous,' he exclaimed because he had just put in a motivation to fill a vacant post in music and, although it would not be designated as a jazz post, he could use that vacancy to bring in someone able to initiate a degree in jazz. Chris took us on a campus tour of the University of Natal and talked to us seriously about my applying for the new post.

Applying seemed okay as a show of friendship and support, but I didn't expect to get the job without a Master's degree. I was not an experienced teacher, nor had I graduated from a top-rated jazz programme such as North Texas State or Berklee

College of Music. But supposing I did get the job, should I take it? Economic sanctions against South Africa were in place and many nations, even long-term allies like the United States, eventually supported these sanctions. As mentioned earlier, the UN supported (but did not actually enforce) the cultural and sports boycotts called for by the ANC and the Pan Africanist Congress (PAC), South Africa's main political movements in exile. There was considerable inconsistency in policy and practice. The point of these sanctions was to discourage international sport competitions and visits by famous entertainers, actors and musicians. Cathy said we should consult her exiled political friends and contacts in New York and London before deciding, so we met with these people to discuss whether boycotting South Africa applied to my situation. We even visited the ANC mission attached to the UN in New York. At these meetings, we learnt that despite some activists calling for an academic boycott, the people we spoke to believed that the South African government couldn't survive indefinitely and that the ANC felt nearer to taking control of the state. They also believed that state institutions like universities were valuable assets to be transformed, rather than destroyed, and that cultural change would light the way to political change.

The exiles we met all liked jazz and believed in its transformational effect. Much to our surprise, word came in November that the university had approved my selection as a junior lecturer. Chris Ballantine phoned me in Wilton, Connecticut, to get my answer. Up to this point, a commitment to South Africa was a hypothetical question, but now we had to decide. I must admit that I really wanted to go. This was a turning point in my life. Supporting the anti-apartheid cause and an unprecedented opportunity to design a programme not only at a university, but within a country on a continent that didn't yet offer a degree in jazz, really appealed to me. The decisive factor was that Cathy would be with me and we could commence our double act.

Cathy and I are from very different backgrounds, yet our interests are well matched. We read Shakespeare's plays together and discussed Bob Dylan with the same seriousness. Our separate experiences of 'hippiedom' in the United States during the 1960s and 1970s contributed to our flexibility. We loved jazz and all kinds of music, and our aspirations were adventurous rather than materialistic. Suddenly, we were looking at a future together completely unlike the past. I had travelled the world, but never held a full-time job before. Going to South Africa seemed right for both of us because it perfectly suited who we were. I said 'yes' to the job and we said 'yes' to each other. We married on 1 January 1983 and arrived at the Department of Music in Durban on 14 February, Valentine's Day.

> In Sweden, everything works but nothing is possible and in South Africa,
> nothing works but everything is possible.
> — Kajsa Claude (in reply to the question of why she had chosen
> to live in South Africa, rather than her homeland, Sweden)

Catherine

'Many people have told me that Americans drive on the right side of the road, but I see that *you* are capable of driving on the left side.' This statement came from a well-dressed black male hitchhiker we picked up on one of our very first car trips in the Transkei in 1983. Exchanging glances in the front of the car, we wondered why he had become nervous and unresponsive after Darius told him that he was an American jazz musician teaching at the University of Natal. Did he think Darius would be determinedly American and insist on driving on the right? Did he now doubt what many people had told him or was this encounter with versatility an amazing one-off? We later speculated that he would relate this experience to others as we, likewise, have singular tales to relate ourselves. They turn on the axis of South African paradox, exceptionality, tragedy and humour and often reveal soulful and special qualities about the people we met and the jazz life itself.

We had come to South Africa to be on the left side, politically speaking. These were the days of international boycotts, but also the early days of exiles preparing for change. Many of these people told us that the time had come for transforming institutions from within. Jazz, after all, was on the side of the struggle and we could help with the struggle for jazz. In November 1982, Darius signed a contract with the University of Natal for two years, which turned into almost a quarter of a century of improvisation.

The hip slogan shown in the photo was invented by Ben Pretorius, the original co-owner, with Billy Mthembu, of Pinetown's legendary Rainbow Restaurant and Jazz Club, when it was threatened with closure in 1985. It was used later as a chapter title in Gwen Ansell's admirable book, *Soweto Blues: Jazz, Popular Music, and Politics in South Africa*.[5]

Driving from Johannesburg to Durban in 2018, I feel connected, despite years away from student life in both Pietermaritzburg and Durban and more than a decade away from the time I spent fund-raising, organising and managing music groups in the fragile, edgy and bountiful jazz world. Connected by roads, places and people – Peter Brown Drive, Archie Gumede Place, Alan Paton Road, Chota Motala Road, and hearing Chief Albert Luthuli in a magnificent speech in the mid-1950s declare 'Durban belongs to me'.[6] The current names of streets and roads dramatically indicate the change in political geography from when I was growing up and from the years

Ben Pretorius (far left) and musicians march to new Rainbow premises, March 1984 (photo: Omar Badsha).

Playing in front of 'the Struggle' banner, March 1984 (photo: Omar Badsha).

when I was national secretary of the Liberal Party, which, in Pietermaritzburg, often worked with the Congress Alliance.[7]

I always felt music was essential to a good life. My father had played the violin when he was young, had a good singing voice and told me he had gone to a Duke Ellington concert in London in the 1930s. My direct links to jazz start over half a century ago with the pretentiously named African American Music Appreciation Society, which was based in a university lecturer's rondavel and influenced by the unusual fact that Pietermaritzburg boasted a renowned jazz discographer. Malcolm Hunter was his name and he was often asked by critics, record companies and journalists from around the world to identify an unnamed bass or horn player on a scratchy-sounding 78-rpm record or even on an early vinyl LP that neglected to name all the musicians. A number of us, seventeen or so years old, sat on the floor listening to him talk about the greatness of the American jazz originators, principally from New Orleans: Buddy Bolden, whose trumpet, according to jazz mythology, could be heard 40 miles across Lake Pontchartrain; King Oliver, who was Louis Armstrong's mentor; Jelly Roll Morton, the self-proclaimed inventor of jazz and the suave Duke Ellington from Washington who, like Bach, had written hundreds of compositions. Later in the 1950s, we discovered there were live musicians, black and white, around us in South Africa, playing this music called jazz. As in the United States, their sounds and souls often had a protest edge, an awareness of the injustice and inequality that determined their place in society. For someone eager to explore beyond the boundaries of convent Catholicism and the boy-meets-girl-movie superficiality of the 1950s, this was a revelation.

It was certainly a provincial life in Pietermaritzburg but, through jazz and politics, the movies and Shakespeare, I found it easy to connect to the bigger universe of England and the United States. I'd played Hamlet at school and Juliet at university and, all the while, tried to persuade whoever would listen that Louis Armstrong was a great and important musician.

Later, when I was living in London, political friends arranged a week's work session with Bertrand Russell at his home in Wales. It was the severe winter of 1961. Russell (aged 89 at the time) was very involved in the Campaign for Nuclear Disarmament and had spent time in jail for his sit-down protest in Trafalgar Square. While in jail, his mail had amassed and there were literally trunks full of letters on disarmament, philosophy, mathematics and politics to reply to. Under the direction of Russell's American secretary, Ralph Schoenman, three of us had the task of answering this correspondence, which also included a lot of fan mail. We all got snowed in with Russell and his wife and celebrated seeing in the New Year together. He opened some very fine dry champagne and toasted each one of us and, raising his glass, said, 'Death to Macmillan'. This was quite shocking and yet compelling. It felt as though we were just talking as peers, until he would say something like, 'When I mentioned this to Gladstone . . .'. Here was someone who was already in his mid-thirties at the time of the Boer War. He didn't like many people and so I naively asked whether there was anyone out of all the famous people he knew whom he really revered. He replied, 'Joseph Conrad, for his broad vision' and then he accentuated the merit of prolonged and dedicated commitment to a cause. I took this to heart.

In 1983, when Darius started teaching, we proposed that the university buy the Malcolm Hunter Collection for the music library in exchange for free university tuition for his grandchildren. The university agreed and I was able to get temporary paid work in the library, unpacking and organising the approximately 2 000 LPs and 8 000 78s, as well as filling large cupboards and bookcases with jazz journals and books. The Music Department librarian, Rika Engelbrecht (Piano Licentiate from Trinity and Royal Schools), enthusiastically and creatively devised and wrote up 'Recorded Music Collections' for her Master's degree in Library and Information Science, with special reference to this collection. I believe the University of KwaZulu-Natal, to this day, has the most comprehensive jazz library in South Africa.

WEA Records' headquarters in New York, July 1977. Back (from left): Chris Brubeck, Philip Tabane, Darius Brubeck, Dave Brubeck, four unknown executives from WEA. Front (from left): Gabriel Thobejane, Cathy Brubeck, Peter Davidson (Malombo's manager). Behind Cathy is Herbie Mann and behind Peter Davidson is Bheki Mseleku (photo: unknown WEA staff photographer; Cathy Brubeck collection).

My special jazz engagement with the university and beyond had taken off, although my entrepreneurial career had begun much earlier. In 1977, working with their manager Peter Davidson, I arranged various performances in the United States for Malombo, which, unusually for the group, was joined by a very young Bheki Mseleku. I was thrilled to introduce them on stage at Carnegie Hall in New York City as part of that year's Newport Jazz Festival and arranged for them to appear in the half-time break at a showcase football match between the original New York Cosmos and Benfica, from Lisbon, Portugal. Eusébio, born in Maputo and often hailed as the first great African footballer, was there; Pelé was there and Jomo Sono, a recent South African addition to the team, was there – playing for Cosmos. This team was then owned and promoted by Warner Music Group Corporation, whose label Warner Elektra Atlantic (WEA) had also just released Malombo's album *Pele Pele*.[8] (The name has no connection with the footballer.) Herbie Mann, the famous jazz flautist, then working for WEA Records, was also there and I felt elated that I had united two of my greatest passions – football and jazz.

During my New York/Connecticut years, I was in close contact with bassist Victor Ntoni and singer Thembi Mtshali, who were both working with Hugh Masekela and, through these friends and others, kept up contacts in South African music and political circles. I remember the horror, anger and sadness as Victor, Thembi and I watched reports about the murder of Black Consciousness leader Steve Biko. What could we do?

Darius and I were often asked why we went to apartheid South Africa at a time of boycott and strife, so I'll make the answer part of this story. We met in New York in 1976 on 29 April, Duke Ellington's birthday, at a celebratory Ellington Is Forever concert that I had organised. While working as a conference organiser for the stewardship section of the executive council of the Episcopal Church, I had suggested we present a concert featuring Duke Ellington's *Liberian Suite*. I knew this music from my student jazz club days and it would perfectly match the stewardship office's fund-raising efforts for a college in Liberia. Making this connection launched me into the American jazz world and I worked closely with Mercer Ellington (Duke's son) for a good while after this major event, which also featured famous jazz artists like Charles Mingus, Sarah Vaughan and Dave Brubeck. Dave arrived with his sons and that's how Darius and I met. Darius was very interested in South Africa and my long-standing political and music connections – and me. I remember, however, that we mainly talked about Bob Dylan.

Two years later at a cafe in Greenwich Village, Chris Ballantine, who was visiting New York City, discussed his dream of introducing jazz studies at the University of Natal and, out of this conversation, an opportunity to do something new, exciting and hopefully musically and politically worthwhile finally emerged. Of course, there were intervening steps but, in 1982, a post (in music theory) was vacant and advertised and Darius applied for the job. The hidden agenda was to launch a comprehensive study of jazz, with the certain knowledge that most of the potential students would be black and poor. Contrary to what was generally believed overseas, it was never totally illegal for black people to attend the major English-medium universities, but the apartheid system made it extremely difficult and a black candidate needed a very hard-to-get permit from the Minister of Bantu Education. Normal integration was still a long way off.

The only way there was going to be a jazz course was for us to personally follow up word-of-mouth leads and for Darius to attend and/or play at every conceivable gig as a means of advertising the new opportunity 'on the hill'. It was difficult for mostly part-time musicians to keep jazz alive and, 40 years ago, it was extremely difficult and complicated to establish trust and communication with musicians living in distant townships. We had to entice potential students and cultivate our own funding sources. Nearly all the candidates we managed to persuade were poor and, in most cases, didn't meet university entrance standards. 'Smuggling' students into courses, which they were ostensibly taking for non-degree purposes proved a good way of circumventing administrative barriers and financial requirements and of pushing the limits.

Music staff wondered what I was doing, as I was so often on campus, but had no official status. Looking back, it was very unusual indeed for both of us to be so involved with the welfare of jazz students, forming numerous bands, looking for gigs and setting up tours. I now wonder how we dared to establish an extensive extramural operation that caused consternation and confrontation, as well as administrative confusion. Some staff objected to my presence and found it extremely odd that Darius would have his wife as his assistant. It would not have been conceivable or possible without support from others in the Department of Music. Chris Ballantine assured us that he knew, when appointing Darius, there would be a second person on board. Apparently, he had pointed this out to the selection committee as an advantage in appointing Darius. Luring and enlisting students from all over the country, some already semi-professional musicians, was essential for the creation and success of the jazz programme and I did a lot of it. Gradually, colleagues recognised this role and also came to see that Darius performing with professionals and students was not only good for publicising the university and the department, but it was also fieldwork – a way of teaching while subsidising the students financially. And, conversely, it helped Darius to improve his own playing and to learn the South African repertoire.

It took months to get a phone in 1983 and, with no phone in our campus cottage, I was given a space in the Music Department library and the right to use the phone to set up gigs and locate people countrywide who might apply for the jazz course. I think this paved the way for my ongoing involvement. From this office, I organised Darius's speaking and playing engagements. Newspaper advertisements and official notices were limited and unlikely to reach potential candidates, so I was acting as a recruiter, guardian, guarantor and promoter. I never lost the latter role and added many other developmental and public relations tasks along the way.

Darius, meanwhile, was teaching music theory and gave extramural and evening classes in jazz. Ulrich Süsse, a colleague and composer, told us about the doubts that other staff had. When the post was originally advertised, Associate Professor Gerrit Bon had phoned him in Germany to ask whether a jazz musician could teach theory. Ulrich said he had no idea and Gerrit asked him to ask his contacts in New York City. Gerrit, who later became the head of department, also became one of our most progressive and supportive allies. Jazz education was still relatively new in the United States, so doubts about its role and impact were not unusual. By and large, music lecturers were interested, if not directly supportive, and we felt an instant rapport with Kevin Volans, who was teaching composition. Today he is known and acclaimed worldwide, but I was delighted to recount to him my clash with his family's business in Pietermaritzburg. As a student there, I was part of a street protest against Volans Dry Cleaners, which had separate entrances for 'Europeans' and 'Non-Europeans', despite the clothes, once deposited at the relevant counter, being tossed into the same work basket. Kevin was a young boy at the time and was of course unaware of the Volans name being associated with our student demonstration. I don't remember why we particularly targeted the Volans shop because the practice of separate entrances for white and black people was the order of the day everywhere in South Africa. However, here we were, decades later, sharing the absurdities of South African life. Ultimately, the name 'Volans' would evoke the beautiful sounds of South Africa worldwide.

Early on, I collaborated with Darius on his first radio shows for Radio Port Natal. Port Natal was another name for Durban and Darius was offered a regular series presenting jazz soon after we arrived. Every week, we visited the home of Mel and June Narunsky for listening and viewing sessions, which helped with compiling music for the radio series and, also indirectly, the jazz course. Mel had run an excellent jazz record shop (Recorded Music Specialists) in central Durban in the 1950s and he arrived at Darius's office early in 1983 to introduce himself. Mel and I knew many of the old 'jazzers' from my Pietermaritzburg student days, so this meeting was inevitable. Our friendship and association remained strong and, when the Narunsky family left South Africa for Israel, Mel gave me his copy of an old 1943 movie *Reveille with Beverly* (a precursor of the 1987 film *Good Morning Vietnam*), which included famous clips of jazz bands – for example, Duke Ellington and his orchestra playing 'Take the "A" Train' on an actual train. Naturally, we gave this film a special showing for our own seventeen-piece big band (Natal University Jazz Ensemble) and all the jazz students.

Professor Geoffrey Durrant, the head of English at the University of Natal, Pietermaritzburg, had given my 1953 portrayal of Hamlet a generous and enthusiastic review and so, when I began student life in 1955, I studied English Literature, albeit with proselytising forays into the world of jazz and song. One of my all-time heroes was Paul Robeson, the black American actor, singer and international peace activist, who was blacklisted by the American government for his campaign of friendship with Russia. From the age of eight, I hoped to come across a South African equivalent of Robeson and instead found that for most whites, black people didn't count. I believe my admiration for Robeson influenced my choice of Political Science as a second university major. In any event, I didn't become either a musician or politician, but both interests have stayed the course. My first marriage was to the South African literary critic and academic Tony Morphet. After this marriage ended in 1967, I moved to New York City and got a job with Seabury Press, which had just published Alan Paton's *Instrument of Thy Peace*. Between 1967 and 1976, I led an exciting, cosmopolitan life in New York City – part hippie and full-time single parent to Alexandra. She and I experienced a range of activities from live jazz, rock and classical concerts to travelling all over the country, where I had many friends and contacts through my countrywide conference organising for the stewardship division of the Episcopal Church. My move to working in the music world followed the hugely successful 1976 Ellington Is Forever concert and led to my association with the Brubeck family. I married Darius Brubeck shortly before we went to South Africa.

Our first year in Durban was jam-packed with foundation work and public relations. We needed to find students, money and an effective way to launch the study of jazz at the university and fortunately it seemed that everyone wanted a bit of the Brubeck lustre. Darius, in a letter from South Africa to his mother in 1987, wrote that 'Dave Brubeck is at least as well known here as the Pope'. There was so much coverage about Dave composing a mass for Pope John Paul II's appearance at Candlestick Park in San Francisco that one might think His Holiness was coming to America to hear the music. Dave was featured on 'Zulu TV' (TV2) four times in our first couple of years and, of course, everyone knew 'Take Five'. At an early gig at the University of Zululand, we witnessed people actually dancing to 5/4 time. Audience members got up and imitated instrument playing as they danced and this was often seen at the Rainbow Restaurant and Jazz Club concerts as well. It made us feel welcome and we realised we could advertise jazz education just by showing up. Requests to attend municipal, consular and alternative high-flying events flowed in and, in the spirit of contact and conquer, we accepted almost everything, especially chances to speak or perform. The local Toastmasters Association, along with many other unlikely societies, all endured or enjoyed hearing a lecture about the importance and relevance of jazz music. There were hundreds of these missionary opportunities and we took them all. Invitations to premieres, notably the inauguration of the Natal Philharmonic Orchestra (NPO) in 1983, the Durban International Film Festival and various arts and quasi-political associations were eagerly accepted. As we were minor VIPs, even the owner of a local supermarket, Mr Buxton, personally guided us through all the groceries in his store!

The weekly jazz programme for Radio Port Natal, which Darius and I scripted and he presented, led to more correspondence and invitations, and this recognition transitioned into public awareness of the new jazz education opportunity. All this additional exposure justified the university giving me space to work while Darius taught piano, music theory and aural perception and began devising a jazz syllabus for the following year. In one of her early letters, Darius's mother, who had lived with music all her life, asked, 'What is aural perception?' – and well may she have asked. I asked Darius and he didn't strictly know either! Basically, it was ear-training in the British system of music education.

In between classes and responding to letters from wannabe song collaborators, Dave Brubeck fans, people in prison and those wanting Darius to play or just appear at their events, we drove up and down the country, mainly to Johannesburg, and persuaded established and potential musicians to join the jazz programme in Durban. It was on one of these trips that we met three people who were to prove essential allies and indeed very, very important in our lives: Johnny Mekoa, Lulu Gontsana and Barney Rachabane.

2

The Scene

Darius

Travelling up Durban's West Street, the main drag from the beachfront, one passes the Victorian City Hall, which is flanked by the old station, now converted into a vast shopping complex and the imposing, well-landscaped civic buildings on one side, with the historic and classy Royal Hotel, where Mark Twain once stayed, on the other. This is all in a subtropical setting. The city of Durban lies between the Indian Ocean and the university, high up on a ridge that separates the city from the hinterland. The Esplanade, a peripheral highway, is bordered by a strip of park and a marina on the harbour side. Architectural gems of art deco high-rise buildings line the town side of the Esplanade, which merges into the old South Coast Road that leads through the industrial docks and warehouses and southern suburbs towards the old airport and ultimately into farmland. It is hard to look south here because the glare of the sea, the tin roofs, oil tanks, tarred roads and factory parking lots, housing projects, isolated private houses and shanties, mostly painted bleached-out pastel colours, in an almost treeless landscape, makes you squint. Take your bearings by the ziggurat-like Memorial Tower Building, at the centre of the university campus, which rises above the dark mass of foliage on the Ridge, and a searing light reflected by the golden ball on the dome of Howard College, the oldest building on campus, steers you west towards the Berea, as the slope rising to the Ridge is known.

Many of the older commercial buildings along the central axis of Durban still have a leftover, colonial look – colonnaded walkways with intersecting arcades, decorated loggias and balconies, even though garishly painted signs at street level shout out unheard-of prices for designer brands and other products. There is no preservationist plan at work here, apart from generations of families preserving leases against new arrivals from everywhere else.

Heading inland, we pass what was, until 2012, the largest mosque in the southern hemisphere on Grey Street, paradoxically hard to notice because it is so immense. Lacking any obvious grand entrance, it seems like just another city block with its own warren of arcades, cardboard signage and shady colonnades. Other city streets converge on all sides and multi-lane ramps appear, with gigantic overhead signs guiding you north, south or onto the N3 freeway that takes you up the Berea, on to Pietermaritzburg, the Natal Midlands and to Johannesburg, seven hours' drive away. Or, at the last second, you can slip into the other face of Africa on one of the littered side roads that takes you under the ramps into a hectic network of smoky, shaded blocks of taxi ranks, bus stops, informal shops and stalls selling *muti* (traditional medicine) ranging from benign herbal remedies to weirder items like desiccated monkey hides displayed on sticks like Goyaesque lollipops for Titans. This area is known as the Warwick Triangle. There is a huge Indian market selling bulk quantities of spices, intricately carved and inlaid Kashmiri screens and furniture and, yes, aisles and aisles of astonishing plastic junk from China. This area is a transport hub – a noisy, congested no man's land full of smoke, blaring music, legal and illegal trade, life and menace.

Inevitably, you see the nests of the homeless and transients who had to spend the night because they missed the last bus or didn't have the fare. It doesn't feel safe. Beyond this junction, the neighbourhoods get better, greener, more private and orderly, as you literally rise in the world. At the very top of Berea Road, before it disappears over the Ridge, the open sky is dramatically framed by the impressive, high arch of the suspension bridge spanning the freeway. To get to the university campus, take the Toll Gate Bridge off-ramp, but instead of crossing over the freeway, turn left on Ridge Road. This road is like a roller coaster, with alternating deep dips and steep climbs. When the traffic suddenly stops for some reason as you are climbing, you have no choice but to balance on an overheating clutch, with one hand on the handbrake, anxious not to roll down backwards. People do it every day. I did it every day. The last and deepest dip before campus is the intersection of Ridge Road and King George V Avenue. For a second or two there is nothing to see but lush vegetation and blossoms. This intersection is always in deep shade from overhanging trees, cool and dark as you descend out of the blinding sun. A gentler gradient on King George V ascends once more past Queen Elizabeth Avenue on the right and up to the crest of the hill and the boom gate with a guardhouse that marks the main campus entrance. This journey was our daily commute for several years until we moved over the Ridge to a house on Queen Elizabeth Avenue in the green suburb called Manor Gardens. Most of the academics we knew lived there, in family houses architecturally adapted to precipitously sloping lots with tropical gardens and crazy, near-vertical driveways.

During our first years, the Music Department was situated in a substantial, pseudo-Tudor, double-storey house outside the official campus entrance. It was surrounded by huge, old trees, flowering shrubs and flowerbeds. A colleague pointed out that the daily collection of battered, downmarket academics' cars parked in front and along the side of the building didn't suit these grand surroundings.

A new single-storey block on a narrow strip of level ground was behind the house and it accommodated most of the Music Department offices. The main lecture/recital room and a fine and substantial library was in the main house. My first office in this annexe was equipped with a good sound system (no computers in 1983), invitingly empty wooden shelves and both a Steinway baby grand and an upright piano in a room with large windows and a glass back door, opening to jungle-like, subtropical foliage down the steep slope. The view through and over the banana, avocado, papaya and palm trees and blooming bougainvillea and hibiscus offered glimpses of suburban houses and blue rectangles of swimming pools, some high-rise buildings to the north along the Ridge and, further away, across a major road, another low ridge covered with shacks.

By the 1980s, many informal settlements had risen from the wreckage wrought by the notorious Group Areas legislation that regulated who could live where. A whole local community, Cato Manor (or, in isiZulu, Umkhumbane) was destroyed.[1] (A jazzy musical set in Cato Manor, *Mkhumbane*, written by Alan Paton and Todd Matshikiza and staged in 1959, featured some musicians and actors I was destined to meet.) Established communities were cleared out, but over time shacks made of all kinds of salvaged materials began reappearing under the trees, a colourful but sad reminder of life beyond my comfortable setting. After-hours it was very quiet in the annexe. Sometimes, I had the sensation of being watched. When I looked up from my work, I would indeed see a vervet monkey or two staring at me through the glass. At times, whole troops of them jumped noisily on and off the roof to raid the fruit trees.

To begin with, Cathy and I were billeted in one of the staff cottages. These were situated on a shady slope below the main university buildings, about ten minutes from anywhere I had to be on campus. The cottage had a kitchen, bedroom, bathroom and lounge/living room, with a small veranda in front and a patio outside the kitchen door. Nic Paton, grandson of Alan Paton and soon to be a jazz student, visited us not long after our arrival. I directed him on the phone to go via 'Princess Ellis Avenue'. I was not used to local accents and this was exactly what I heard the woman in charge of staff accommodation tell me was our address. (Who was Princess Ellis?) Nic eventually found our cottage, which overlooked Princess *Alice* Avenue! Nic and Cathy thought this was hilarious.

The matron of 'Princess Ellis' fame recommended that we engage Julia Zondi to take care of our house cleaning and laundry. This seemed practical and affordable, and my scruples were somewhat assuaged by the fact that Julia was described by the matron as 'a friend'. All hesitation vanished as soon as we met Julia, who was the personification of warmth, kindness and responsibility. Julia worked for us everywhere we lived in Durban for the next 23 years and became a close friend. She met my parents when they visited and always asked after them, became friends with Victor Ntoni and all the musicians in our circle, the students who came to stay with us and with Cathy's daughter Alexandra, who was living in the United States, and Alexandra's children, our grandchildren. We also saw a lot of her husband Wallace, who was always very formal and enjoyed (so he said) polishing our brass trays and candlesticks and imparting surprising scraps of information – for example, a warning to us to beware of pickpockets at Orly Airport in Paris. Julia was Wallace's second wife, which was normal according to traditional Zulu custom. Wallace had children with both of his wives and they all got along just fine. We were sometimes visited by members of their extended family and got involved in their family matters.

At first, we were never cold in the staff cottage because we had moved in at the height of summer, so different from Connecticut in February where there had just been twenty inches of snow. However, sometimes I arrived at my own lectures soaking wet from sudden showers. We weren't allowed to stay in the cottage indefinitely and went house-hunting whenever there was a gap in my schedule. By the time we moved out, in August, the cement floors felt cold and we slept with blankets. In Durban, a house, even a working-class one, if in a white area, was not just a free-standing domicile, but often very substantial, with garage, servant's quarters, walled garden, patio, toilets for staff and maybe a swimming pool. Such a place was our house in Peace Avenue in Lower Morningside, which is where we moved to. There was no swimming pool, but it had an outdoor pizza oven we never used and productive fig and papaya trees in a terraced garden falling away towards the sports stadium complex between us and the sea.

Wallace Dube and Julia Zondi, Durban, 2008 (photo: Darius Brubeck; Cathy Brubeck collection).

It was not convenient for the university and not considered a good neighbourhood because of stadium noise, traffic and, it was whispered, some of the houses weren't really owned by whites. There was a general sense of the area having seen better days, but we liked it for its open views to the sea. We installed Julia in the large

The Scene   27

garden room and, a year later, Marc Duby took over a basement room in the garden, parking his classic yellow VW Beetle on the street. It was too old and noisy to steal. We still had plenty of space, which was good because the house would eventually fill up with black students who weren't allowed to live near the university (or legally in any white area) even if they had the money, which none did. Peace Avenue was an ironic misnomer for our hectic household.

Feb 26, 1983
Dear Iola & Dave,
Well, Darius has had a hectic first week and right now is up in his grand office practicing on his grand piano . . .

We still haven't found a car, but have high hopes of a 1976 Peugeot 404 station wagon for R1 750 . . .

I think we will have to wait for months for a phone, so I had better give you Darius's office number. Not having a phone is inconvenient, especially since I have to make arrangements for Darius giving a concert . . . We might go with The Abbey Theatre which would be possible in April, but the hunt is on for a horn player. Anyway, to make phoning around a little easier, the Dept. of Music is giving me an office to make calls from . . .

Dear Mom & Dad,
As you already know, I've been extremely busy with teaching, and usually need to work at night to keep up . . .

When a troop of around 20 monkeys charged up the hill, I was reminded that I was in Africa even if I was in an air-conditioned office reading Schoenberg for a theory lecture the next day.

Apartheid really works in its own terms. It does keep people apart . . . On the brighter side, the most popular group in SA at the moment is the multiracial band called Juluka. Cathy and I went to see them at the Student Union which sponsored a special concert to welcome the 1st year students. The response was totally beery, boisterous . . . students in hot, hot weather, predictable. But what they were cheering and yahooing over was a band of three whites and three Zulus singing very revolutionary lyrics . . . So, there we were in this rock concert as South Africa's white youth whooped and drank to its own downfall.

The white band leader was the extraordinary Johnny Clegg, known in Europe as *le Zoulou Blanc*, with whom I would later be associated as a cultural activist in the South

African Music Association (SAMA). He was deservedly a legend by the time he died in 2019. We met on the road several times and two of my former students, Concord Nkabinde and Neil Gonsalves, were in his band for five years.

Cathy remembers my coming home to our staff cottage one day during my first week of teaching and announcing that I was so happy. Lectures were in Room 2 in the big house and piano lessons and small classes took place in my office. On my first day of classes as a junior lecturer, three smartly dressed first-year girls punctually arrived at my office. (The days of neat, punctual students weren't over yet.) This was my inaugural aural perception class and I wasn't very certain about what I was supposed to teach, so I started with questions, asking them things they were likely to know, like what sort of birds made those whooping sounds in the morning. Well, this did have something to do with aural perception. The girls were prim yet friendly and one of them brought a bird book for me to the next class. We struggled a little with each other's accents, which was relaxing because it was mildly funny. One of the girls lived in Pinetown, a suburb of Durban. 'What's it like?' I asked. 'S'nahss,' she answered sweetly. This was my first conversation with Carol Muller, later professor of Ethnomusicology at Penn Arts (United States) and author of scholarly articles and books on South African jazz and indigenous music. Her good friend and classmate Janet Topp (later Fargion) is now lead curator of world and traditional music at the British Library. I've reconnected with Carol at academic conferences in Europe and Carol and Janet's academic distinction in fields that were novel at the time is indicative of the kind of music department Chris Ballantine was building.[2]

In this early period, I was also supervising Marc Duby for a Master of Music degree, which gave me full-time access to a graduate assistant and a live-in bass player when he moved into Peace Avenue. Happily, there were innumerable other gigs for a bass player of his quality. My first undergraduate jazz students included Richard Robinson and Rick van Heerden. Kevin Gibson, still in high school at the time, came to classes as often as he could and easily kept up with the others. Melvin Peters was already a postgraduate student in music education, so he only took piano with me, but I later co-supervised his Master's thesis.

Nic Paton had just finished his compulsory stint in the South African Army; he was a saxophonist in Major George Hayden's Entertainment Corps band and enrolled at the university in 1985. Reminiscing recently about these days, Nic recalled that Richard was always a bit 'hot-headed' and described him as 'very English somehow'. (They had known each other from school days in Johannesburg.) Nic recalls Richard as being 'rude and demanding' when he told me that I 'wasn't qualified', 'just the son of a famous man' and that Cathy did more work than I did – and that I was 'incompetent'. To give him his due, Richard was a hard worker who contributed a lot more than was required when I was setting up the big band. He felt that his education was costly and what he was getting in return wasn't good enough. We have long since reconciled, but I bring this up to acknowledge that he was partly right, not at all unreasonable according to his expectations of a Berklee College of Music by the Indian Ocean. A few more reactions like this could have scuppered the whole endeavour before it gained momentum. I wasn't qualified in a traditional sense and wasn't sure what would be possible from one week to the next.

Nic's attitude was the polar opposite. As he correctly remembers, there was 'no guitar teacher, no sax teacher' and yet he was 'thriving in an improvised learning situation'. I scrambled to make good on commitments as best I could, arranging lessons with Sandile Shange and Allen Kwela, neither of whom had taught before and didn't really take to it. They were both amazing guitarists and Nic praised us for 'engaging with things as they were: no teachers, no traditions, no feeder system'. He saw that I 'improvised the course, from day to day'. Richard thought we were conning everybody, but Nic thought that creating a 'scene' as a learning process was a great way to develop a locally relevant programme.

> ### Letter to Dave and Iola Brubeck, 30 May 1983
> One favour you could do for me is start collecting all the music instruction material your publishers send you, ie. guitar books, sax, drums, and published arrangements to send over the cheapest way . . . I don't know whether Alexandra told you that Evan (Ziporyn) won the nomination as a visiting musician for 6 weeks and we hope that he takes it up early in 1984 . . .

It is impossible to tell a story about those years in South Africa without acknowledging that people were (and still are) identified by race. I will refer to Indians and Africans and coloureds, but Kwame Anthony Appiah is right in insisting that 'racial identity is a biological nonsense . . . yet socially, we use these things all the time as if there's a solidity to them'.[3]

There were practical as well as habitual reasons for taking 'race' into account – for example, language, in the case of isiZulu and isiXhosa speakers. I was teaching in their second language. I asked myself how well I would perform if the lectures and all the written materials were in French. In fact, spoken English was not much of a problem, but *written* English was often inadequate. Very few African music students would have passed courses solely assessed on written essays and exam questions. That was just the way it was and allowances were therefore made. Is this discriminatory? Strictly speaking, yes. African students were identifiable by name. On the other hand, Melvin Peters, my first jazz piano student, is of Indian descent, therefore 'an Indian' in local parlance although he comes from a Christian family with generations of English names in their ranks. Being 'Indian' is an indispensable part of Melvin's story, as we will see.

Aren't all South Africans 'African' by birth, irrespective of race? That hopeful and morally sound way of thinking was central to the Rainbow Nation ideal, still a few years in the future, but already espoused by the University of Natal.[4] Everyone in our personal, professional and social circles resisted or at least disagreed with apartheid, but that didn't mean we could magically avoid its consequences or disavow our own whiteness – race applied to us too. No one *we* knew was living 100 per cent within the social strictures of apartheid, but what Kira Erwin refers to as 'differential management' prioritised the needs of whites in white areas and imposed inconveniences on everyone else, resulting in frustrations, lost opportunities and relationships of dependence that colour-coded and reinforced differences in social rank.[5] It is now nearly 40 years later and racial distinctions haven't melted away, although some very young South Africans I've spoken to recently believe this has happened. I won't argue with them. It would be true if enough people believed it.

Yeoville

In the 1980s and early 1990s, Yeoville, a suburb of Johannesburg, was still noticeably Jewish and despite being officially designated a white suburb, was by then one of the first 'grey areas' in Johannesburg after the forced removals of the 1960s. The mixture of black people and European immigrants and its proximity to the city meant that this area was a centre for anti-apartheid activism with a vibrant counterculture on display in the record stores, bookshops, cafes and bars along its main roads. The iconic art deco Piccadilly cinema, synagogue and public swimming pool were landmarks of note. Nelson Mandela himself found refuge in a white comrade's house, when he was on the run in the 1960s and, as a present-day tourist website points out, Yeoville was 'a place of understanding and freedom'.[6] Cathy and I were friendly with Eleanor and Ronnie Kasrils, a self-described 'Jewish boykie from Yeoville', who later became deputy minister of defence under Mandela and then minister for security services in Thabo Mbeki's government.

Cathy's brother, Jo Shallis, worked for CBS News as an assistant producer, covering the violent confrontations between the state and the liberation forces. He lived in Yeoville in a neglected but not unpleasant apartment building. Jo was a bachelor and loner, which accounted in part for his fearlessness on assignments, but also for his spartan lifestyle. He always lived in flats that were short on home comforts, but located in cheap, interesting neighbourhoods. Our other connection with Yeoville was through Cathy's circle of Pietermaritzburg friends. Rather than accepting Jo's hospitality, we had a standing invitation to make Colleen Taylor's home our base in Johannesburg. Colleen (originally Cook) and her husband Mike had managed to buy a former boarding house in Hopkins Street. It was a large, square building with a labyrinth of hallways and bedrooms situated on a side street, a block or two from the synagogue. It had a *mezuzah* on each doorpost. The Taylors took delight in the comings and goings of musicians, academics and political comrades and there was always room. The Taylor family, though neither black nor Jewish, were the epitome of what Yeoville was all about at that time.

Rockey Street was home to Art Kelly's Rumours, a jazz club, and Colleen liked to go there for the music and just to hang out. Art Kelly was himself a bass player and was often seen standing bleary-eyed in front of his club, smoking a cigarette in the sunlight after hosting an all-night jam session. Yeoville in the mid-1980s was rough, but in a friendly way. Gradually, the village atmosphere turned slummy rather than cheap; the economy spiralled down to just rough and these days it's considered dangerous. The Taylors, Rumours and even the synagogue have all long since gone.

One of Colleen's brothers, Allen Cook, was in London working for the International Defence and Aid Fund for Southern Africa.[7] He was one of the most learned and ardent jazz fans and collectors I had ever met. Her other brother, Jasper, went one further by becoming a professional jazz trombonist, good enough to become the only permanent white member of the African Jazz Pioneers (AJP), led by alto saxophonist Ntemi Piliso. Colleen managed this group for a few years, starting in 1989.[8] Although their official launch was as late as 1983 (accounts vary slightly), Ntemi started rehearsing at Dorkay House in 1981 and the music itself was from the 1950s and early 1960s. The band specialised in a playing style called 'township jazz' by whites and *mbaqanga* or simply 'jazz' by black people.[9] This style was implicitly political without a word sung or spoken because it revived a style of music and social dancing that grew out of racially mixed urban communities that flourished before apartheid destroyed them. For a time, the AJP was the semi-official band of the anti-apartheid movement at home and abroad.

The AJP played at Rumours while Colleen managed them and one night her whole family came to hear them. Colleen's daughter, Adrienne, who was excited that her uncle Jasper would appear on stage as part of a famous band, asked if she could bring a friend from school. The Pioneers roared through a set that had everyone in a packed club on their feet applauding, whistling and shouting. Adrienne's little friend, who had never seen or heard such goings-on, had only one question: 'Which one is your uncle?'

Gigs galore

Beginning my performance career in Durban, I was, most Sundays, either a leader or a 'special guest' at Maitre Pers or the Albany Hotel. Maitre Pers was a restaurant a few steps down below street level, but not truly a basement venue because it had windows. The Albany Hotel, on a side street opposite the City Hall, had less of a jazz history, but was a decent venue trying to get in on the action. Both were right in the centre of town and presented established regulars like vocalists Bobby Minter, who was a manager at Beacon Sweets factory, and Anita Zucker, who often sang duets with Ronnie Madonsela. Saxophonists Milton Johnson, Phil Harber and Basil Metaxas, trumpeter Des Kerdachi and vibes and clarinet player Johnny Williams were featured and usually accompanied by Willie Ellison (bass) and Gerald Kerdachi (drums). There was another Kerdachi brother, Simon, who for decades was the resident pianist at the Oyster Box Hotel in Umhlanga. They were all long-established, popular and good Durban jazz musicians. In addition, I should also mention the big band Music Unlimited, led by trombonist Mario Monteregge and many good pianists like Les Dolly, Noel Bothma,

Clipping from *Natal Mercury*, 18 March 1983, describing Durban as a 'Mecca for Jazz'.

Joe Delew and John Drake. Mike Mazzoni, another notable Durban musician, was one of our early drum teachers. All these musicians contributed a great deal to Durban's jazz community and I am grateful to them for their generous interest in my arrival, their support and the many invitations to 'sit in'. They helped the jazz programme by organising gigs and bands that hired students and so both town and gown energised the jazz scene.

Maitre Pers and the Albany hosted what was essentially a white jazz scene, but they were not racially exclusive. The white musicians I met were not against playing with black musicians, but apartheid circumstances largely precluded this. The Albany was licensed as an 'international' hotel and therefore exempt from racial laws. Although Maitre Pers flouted these laws, it was considered too small an infraction to matter. As in other places in Durban and elsewhere, black and white musicians could play together on a casual basis without police interference, but this wasn't a widespread practice. Maitre Pers was an upscale restaurant during the week that catered for a middle-aged, white clientele, so no hotbed of radicalism there. I guess it was tacitly understood that hiring and advertising a black band was out of the question, but if black musicians came to play, as far as I could tell, the customers didn't care.

Catherine

Durban was described in a newspaper headline as a 'Mecca for Jazz',[10] despite the historical and easy association of jazz and alcohol. The owner of Maitre Pers was Danish, so no Mecca there – instead, slightly inebriated customers requesting the same songs over and over again. 'Indiana with bongos', one patron would repeat and repeat until Darius played the standard '(Back Home Again in) Indiana' minus the bongos, which the fan attempted to simulate right on the piano lid. For those who want to remember the 'Indiana with bongos' fan, his name was Austen Pikey. Darius worked out that he was thinking of a 1949 Dave Brubeck Trio record that featured Cal Tjader on bongos on one track ('Body and Soul'), but not on '(Back Home Again in) Indiana'.[11]

Darius

Maitre Pers was where I first met and played with guitarist Sandile Shange, beginning for me a very special jazz partnership. I also accompanied the excellent and flamboyant jazz singer Ronnie Madonsela a few times and met Brian Thusi, a terrific trumpet player and subsequently founder of a community music school in Umlazi. Kevin Gibson (now one of South Africa's top drummers), came often to Pers, while he was still in high school.

All the regular musicians were part-timers who loved to play, but made their living from day gigs. Willie Ellison manufactured kitchen cabinets; Barry Taylor, another bassist, was a commercial fisherman. John Drake oversaw maintenance at the university's Medical School. Another jazz pianist, Joe Delew, owned amusement arcade outlets on the beachfront. Phil Harber, also at the top end of this spectrum (musically and financially) ran a textiles factory. He later enrolled at the University of Natal as an adult student when he retired from business. Special guests included many Brits, mostly transients who had gigs in the tourist hotels up and down the coast. In the late hours after the dinner service ended, jazz devotees came to drink and listen. I don't underestimate the value of playing lots of standards, but I knew I wasn't going to reach many potential students in this setting and nor did it feel very African.

During this same time, township musicians James Mbambo (guitar), Theo Bophela (keyboards), Clarence Kumalo (drums) and Agrippa Magwaza (bass) were members of the Keynotes, an enduringly popular band based in KwaMashu, a township twelve kilometres north of Durban. Agrippa Magwaza had played with Winston Mankunku and Abdullah Ibrahim when he was still known as Dollar Brand. The Keynotes frontline featured Dalton Kanyile and Gerry Kunene on saxes and sometimes Brian Thusi on trumpet. Brian was a multi-instrumentalist who enrolled at UND and then went on to do a PhD at the University of New Mexico. Years later, Theo Bophela, then quite elderly, enrolled at UKZN.

Beverage companies hired jazz musicians for ubiquitous product promotions, especially in or near African townships. Sunday jazz clubs based in shebeens (unlicensed pubs) and garages were regularly visited by brand reps, often spreading their goodwill with guest stars like Victor Ntoni in tow. It was through sponsored concerts and competitions promoting Smirnoff Vodka, Martell Brandy, Amstel Lager, Castle Milk Stout and Gilbey's Gin that I got to play with out-of-town jazz musicians like Ezra Ngcukana (tenor sax), Dolly Rathebe (vocalist), Stompie Manana (trumpet) and Johnny Fourie, who described himself as a 'detribalised Afrikaner' and was generally considered South Africa's greatest jazz guitarist.

Breweries and distillers were well aware of the black consumer market and how to reach it. Several members of the Keynotes, whose players were among our earliest jazz musician friends, were full-time 'booze-reps' employed by Gilbey's. We jokingly referred to the group as 'Agrippa and the Alcoholics', as they enjoyed sharing and partaking of their product while performing in Gilbey's branded wear.

The Keynotes and others, like bassist Sipho Gumede, often played at the Rainbow Jazz Club, which opened in 1981 and became a boisterous, multiracial haven for many musicians defying the oppression in South Africa in their music. These were violent and difficult times and the struggle for a post-apartheid future was intense and dangerous, destroying many lives in what was then Natal. The Rainbow was a hub for community activists and local political networking, but noted most of all for Sundays' joyous revelry and good music: revelry with meaning and purpose. Ben Pretorius

Ben and Pam revisit the Rainbow, 13 April 2019 (photo: Jorne Tielemans; still from documentary *Playing the Changes*).

and Di Vlotmann (later Rossi) established MOJO (Members of the Original Jazz Organisation) to further the cause of jazz and, although it didn't last long, it inspired the jazz community to work together and to recognise that their cultural role was also political. There was often a connection between 'nation-building' and 'cultural work' as understood in that era. Articles relating to and photos of musicians, and close associates who are still with us, and sadly many who are not, are pieces of the mosaic of South African jazz history. Ben and his wife Pam are still an important constant in our lives, very good friends that we look to for realistic updates about business and politics. Pam was a wonderfully caring presence at the Rainbow and bravely dealt with the many complications that came with presenting jazz musicians during apartheid. She still maintains a high-flying career as a human resources consultant.

First concert

I met alto sax virtuoso Barney Rachabane in 1983, when I was booked for a four-night run at the Garden Restaurant in Johannesburg's swanky Carlton Centre. He had been hired to play with me on the recommendation of Izio Gross, the Brazilian resident pianist. Sometimes Barney was referred to as 'a little giant' in the local press. His head was barely higher than mine when I was seated at the piano, but I knew immediately that I was playing with a world-class alto saxophonist. Barney had serious bebop chops (reviewers compared him to American saxophonist Sonny Stitt for his technical fluency and energy), but his personal sound and embellishments, especially his trademark shrieking octave leaps, were unmistakably South African. He was like no one else I had ever played with and, luckily, I met him just in time to invite him to play in my first real concert in Durban. This meeting began a musical association and friendship that lasted until he died in November 2021.

My first show at the Abbey Theatre in Durban sold out and a second was added. The front page of the *Daily News* featured individual shots of me, Barney, Marc Duby and Nelson Magwaza from KwaMashu.[12] Although I had been gigging around town, this was my first opportunity to choose a line-up since the Cape Town concerts the year before.

Our first concert and the front page of the *Daily News*, 20 April 1983.

The Times, a weekly campus newspaper, promoted the Abbey shows under the headline 'Campaign against Varsity Racism in Full Swing'. I was glad to be perceived as a campaigner, although it only then dawned on me that I was leading a 50-50, black-white quartet. This same quartet went up to the University of Zululand near Empangeni to give a concert for drought relief, played at the Executive Hotel a few times and appeared at the Mangosuthu Technikon and the Africa Arts Festival. These concerts, some of which also featured Ronnie Madonsela, were all in Umlazi township, south-west of Durban. At the time, not many whites ventured into black townships. In an article titled 'Jazz Fundis Rejoice' for *Africa Today*, Themba Blose wrote:

> Listening to American keyboard wizard Darius Brubeck in concert is like going on a jazz pilgrimage that takes you in the space of one session from superb renditions of the good old standards to a dazzling performance of contemporary, mostly self-penned tunes . . . But honestly, the response at the Bhekuzulu Hall in Zululand University is probably the most wonderful an artist can expect from an audience.[13]

The quartet, plus Gabriel Thobejane on African percussion and Sandile Shange on guitar, that played Zululand went on to record a maxi single, 'Tugela Rail'. To this day, it's as close as I've ever come to a hit. The piece is reminiscent of the South African countryside, with long passages of undulating sameness broken up by steep, dramatic climbs. Going to Zululand from Durban involves crossing the Tugela River, the southern border of what was the Zulu Kingdom. We passed a railway siding named Tugela Rail on the way to Empangeni. It was little more than a station platform and had a general dealer and a mosque surrounded by miles of sugar cane and I took a photo. I loved the way the sound of the words seemed to fit the music. Recording it with these musicians naturally gave it an authentic African feel.[14] We recorded my father's hit 'Take Five' on the flip side and this LP resonated with a large black audience.[15]

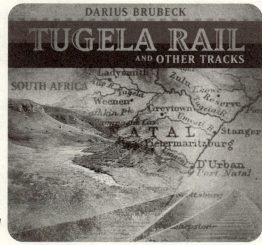

Cover of CD *Tugela Rail and Other Tracks*.

In the early 1980s, Durban had an eclectic and younger white alternative arts scene for which the Hermit Vegetarian Restaurant, with its tiny upstairs theatre, was a focal point. The Hermit was a venue for singer-songwriter musicians, stand-up comedy and small-scale plays, but I don't think jazz was presented there until the proprietor, Tam Alexander, invited me to give it a try.[16] The small stage was suitable for duos and I played Fender Rhodes electric piano with Sandile on guitar, Marc Duby on bass and Evan Ziporyn on clarinet while he was in Durban as a visiting lecturer. Another notable guitarist I played with at the Hermit was Allen Kwela. Cathy organised a Sandile-Allen-Evan gig that ended spectacularly in a punch-up between the rival guitarists. These Hermit engagements, however, went on for a long time and I recall that we also had a themed series featuring a different Jazzanian band member every night. (There will be much more about the Jazzanians later.) Occasionally duos became trios, with Marc on bass.[17] The Hermit vibe, a little edgy, was a refreshing change from the nostalgia scene that Cathy once memorably described as 'jazz shmazz'. At the Hermit I was reaching a different age group some of whom, especially Tam, were involved with the End Conscription Campaign and the United Democratic Front (UDF).[18] At that time,

Marc Duby, Allen Kwela and Evan Ziporyn at the Hermit Restaurant, 1984 (photographer unknown; Cathy Brubeck collection).

who else would patronise a vegetarian restaurant? They weren't jazz fans as such, but very liberal and welcoming.

Any account of my early years must include the Natal University Jazz Ensemble (NUJE). This was meant to be a typical college seventeen- or eighteen-piece big band, but I called it an 'ensemble' because I didn't know whether we could assemble the personnel required to play traditional big band arrangements. In 1983 and 1984, there weren't enough jazz students to fill the sections. Happily, after some haggling with management, the NPO allowed its members to play in our university big band, if they wanted to. I had to really persuade the NPO management that this was good and necessary 'outreach' for the NPO and it certainly benefited our students to be in a band with trained musicians. Trumpeter Rob Sayer and trombonists Ron Minor from the United States, Bill Stuart (United Kingdom), Phil Cousineau and Serge Filiatreault (Canada), made significant contributions and Rob Sayer gave me photocopies of several big band arrangements.

A few university students from outside the Music Department, a Physics professor (Don Bedford) and musicians from the wider Durban area completed the line-up.[19] This was fantastic because students, who were seldom good readers, would be sitting next to experienced players, who were there basically for the love of playing, and teaching by example. Sometimes I felt self-conscious and nervous about having no prior big band experience, but I forged ahead anyway with what I knew was fundamental to

First NUJE, with guest soloists Evan Ziporyn and Barney Rachabane, Howard College, UND, 1984 (photographer unknown; Cathy Brubeck collection).

jazz education – and just fun. In some ways, a university ensemble is like a university sports team. Being in the band meant you were (at least potentially) good enough to represent the university. Coming to rehearsals was something you could do, mostly with the same people, every year. This was the best way to improve musicianship, reading and precision, get instrument-specific, informal but important tips from more advanced players, while learning the repertoire and unwritten conventions, ranging from jazz phrasing to rehearsal etiquette. The ability to write and direct arrangements for instruments other than one's own largely comes from this experience. Due to its uniqueness at the time, the NUJE was a huge success. We travelled to Pietermaritzburg and to townships around Durban and even travelled by bus to Johannesburg. Our scrapbooks are full of reviews and announcements and the big band became a good advert for what we were trying to achieve with jazz studies. Student players of real quality gradually replaced orchestra players. For several years running, the NUJE gave concerts in the Victorian bandstand in Durban's beautiful Mitchell Park, helping to establish a regular series of jazz concerts for other groups too. The important thing was that the university *had* a big band and we were therefore similar in structure, if not yet quality, to the famous university jazz programmes in America. Two of our first guest stars with the big band were Allen Kwela and Barney Rachabane.

Our collection of newspaper clippings shows that, in these first two years, I had close to a hundred gigs, leading and playing in different groups while teaching and maintaining a presence on radio.[20] I was frantically busy, but all these activities both promoted and extended the jazz scene and attracted more students. My active entry into 'the arts' meant public recognition from within many different communities. In the highly collaborative field of jazz, success is dependent on other musicians and year after year I had the best of luck in finding them and their finding me. My Durban debut as a serious musician, rather than just another jammer, was a dramatic example of this.

Acronymania

It was through another important contact, sound engineer Dave Marks, that Cathy and I became involved with broader activist groups. Under successive states of emergency, practically all large gatherings – from funerals to rock concerts – were potentially explosive. Some were broken up as 'illegal gatherings' or, even if not deemed illegal, they were targets for police sabotage or harassment. Other gatherings were shunned or even attacked by left-wing groups bent on asserting their authority on behalf of the masses. A few outdoor concerts became sites of violent clashes. Recalling one such incident in 1987 when he was contracted to work the Lion Lager Road Show (sponsored by Lion Lager, a South African Breweries brand), Dave Marks told me:

I still have a 'scar that shines' [a line from folk star Syd Kitchen] on my cheek. The bottles rained down on the sound platform. I tried to keep the music going by playing a cassette. Eventually it got too bad . . . I had to try and duck backstage . . . so the crowds formed a 'shield' of umbrellas around me and shuffled me into the dressing room pantechnicon. The concert was at Kings Park Stadium that holds 75 000 people. The concert featured Brenda Fassie, Hotline, Harari and some supporting acts. Apparently 4 people died.

And what about South African acts touring overseas at this time? Should Johnny Clegg, for example, be barred from working at festivals in Europe? The British Musicians Union (BMU) thought so. I remember discussing this anomaly with Dennis Scard, a BMU official, on one of my trips to London. He bluntly said, 'We can't just lift the boycott for whoever says, "we're the good guys" – you either boycott South Africa or you don't.' Point taken, but well-meaning people (including me) were on both sides of this argument.

It didn't take long for Johnny Clegg and Dave to see, from different perspectives, the dilemma of fighting apartheid through music while being politically aligned to the cultural boycott advocates who would stop them from doing so. Clegg got a committee together, as one did in those days, and set up SAMA, so that musicians could, as he often used to say, 'speak with one voice to the international community'. It wasn't crystal clear to me *why* we wanted to do this or to *whom* we needed to speak – my talk with the BMU in London came later – but I sensed this was the crowd I belonged to and it was exciting to claim a recognised political role *as a musician*. Along with Dave Marks, Victor Ntoni and a large number of 'comrades' (we were all comrades now), I attended a launch event at the Market Theatre complex in Johannesburg. It was exhilarating to share the space with current pop stars, black and white, and raise our fists to 'Nkosi Sikelel' iAfrika', the ANC anthem, led by Sipho 'Hotstix' Mabuse, with people who could really sing! (My uncle, Howard Brubeck, in California wrote to me that he had seen this on the nightly news on American TV.)

Dave Marks soon convened a group of similarly minded comrades in Durban and we launched the Music Association of Natal (MANA), another great acronym, and set about finding out what we could make it do. MANA was accepted into the fluid network of anti-apartheid community structures with all its proliferating acronyms.[21] MANA's general aims were more parochial than speaking with one voice to the international community. There was recognition in certain quarters that an independent arts scene was beneficial to the city as a whole and city councillors, notably Ros Sarkin, Peter Mansfield and later Mike Sutcliffe, were approachable and indeed approached us, usually through the newly formed Durban Arts Association, of which I was also a board member. We began to enjoy some success by co-operating with the City Council and its officials instead of ignoring them. Anyway, how would they know we *weren't* speaking to them unless we spoke to them? In 1991, MANA picked up further political gravitas and responsibility by assisting with the formation of the Natal Cultural Council (NCC), which was an initiative of COSATU (Congress of South African Trade Unions, founded in 1985). Mi Hlatshwayo, union activist and aspiring dramatist and I were elected chair and vice chair at the founding meeting. Thus, MANA was positioned to sponsor talks by distinguished returning exiles – for example, Barbara Masekela in the 1990s, a meeting at City Hall with Paul Simon in 1992 regarding the controversy over *Graceland* and public discussions (too many) about the UN boycott, which, like Brexit in the United Kingdom in 2016, was an ever-present, divisive and awkward topic. Closer to our original aim of representing musicians' interests, MANA and the Durban Arts Association formalised street busking, so that musicians worked predetermined territories and hours. This sounds almost Stalinist in cold print, but musicians wouldn't have followed the rules unless they had benefited from doing so.

Because MANA was allied with COSATU, we even made a short-lived attempt at setting up a musicians' union. I advocated this, but it was never going to go anywhere. Musicians complained to MANA about what they called 'the venue problem' (lack of locations for casual work) and attended meetings, but didn't join. This was particularly true for black musicians for whom the investment of membership dues and the cost of attending meetings were beyond their meagre incomes. Apart from the professional NPO, employed by the Natal Provincial Arts Council (NAPAC), there was no 'shop floor' to organise, so, quite correctly, MANA continued to be an association rather than a union. The only paid-up members I knew, although there must have been others outside Durban, were a handful of my Music Department colleagues, some of Dave's business contacts and members of the Durban Folk Club.

Sometimes meetings were quite procedural, with minutes and resolutions and reports from subcommittees, but often they were simply gatherings of Dave's contacts, with no agenda beyond getting together for news about the music industry and local politics. These topics were closely related when it came to giving concerts in city parks and organising music around events during Easter weekend or the July Handicap, Durban's premier horseracing event. Durban was a tourist city and it wasn't terribly hard to submit plans and obtain budgets through Durban Arts. Seen from a transactional perspective, we gained influence over programming in return for doing work that city politicians didn't know how to do. This meant we could bring in musicians from the townships for *maskandi* competitions and present local choirs and various other music groups.[22] Dan Chiorboli, a percussionist, successful businessman and former pro footballer, who went on to produce World of Music, Arts and Dance (WOMAD) festivals in South Africa and organise Durban's Fan Zone entertainment for the football World Cup in 2010, was very active in these projects. In a relatively brief time, we were able to punch above our weight through our affiliations with organisations that backed non-governmental organisations (NGOs) like the Natal University-based Culture and Working Life Project and reach out to other similar organisations, notably MAPP (Music Action for People's Power) in Cape Town. In terms of a larger but still local picture, MANA gradually emerged as a quasi-official alternative to the government-backed NAPAC.

NAPAC was one of the four South African performing arts councils. It was founded in 1963, with four departments: Drama, Opera, Music and Ballet. Its main facility was the Playhouse. (Ironically, this had been the venue booked for the New Brubeck Quartet concerts in 1976 that refused to countenance our contractual provisions for mixed audiences and for incorporating Victor Ntoni and Malombo in our shows.) In years to come, my bands, including Afro Cool Concept with Victor, would be a main attraction at a few historically pivotal concerts presented there.[23]

Renovations to the Playhouse were being completed just as Cathy and I arrived in South Africa. ProSound, the sound reinforcement company that Dave Marks ran in Durban, was installing the sound system. Dennis Claude (lecturer in Architecture at the University of Natal) was responsible for the acoustic design of the concert hall. Members of the press, politicians and some of my Music Department colleagues were given a 'hardhat tour' before the formal opening.

Until the mid-1980s, arts funding was no more political than city council budgets for planting flowers along the highways. It was 'nice to have' after higher priorities were met, without significant journalistic scrutiny or public debate. Publicity around the gradual tightening of the UN cultural boycott changed public perceptions about the importance of culture. Activism focused on the state-sponsored arts establishment was a surrogate for the wider struggle, with wild swings locally between co-operation and denunciation, approval and disdain, experimentation and stolid conformity. 'The arts' emerged as a symbolically charged and fiercely contested area of public policy – even for people who, in the words of Herman Charles Bosman's character Manie Kruger, 'knew as much about art as a boomslang'.[24]

As often happens in South Africa, I was soon taking part in an argument in which I identified, partly, with both sides. Many people we knew, although critical of the way NAPAC was organised and of the colonial mindset it epitomised, were nevertheless stakeholders in some way. I had, at least hypothetically, a vested interest in the Playhouse as a potential arena for creative involvement and we all wanted to live in a city that had world-class cultural facilities. And, eventually, controversy notwithstanding, the Playhouse was unveiled as a performing arts complex that would do any city proud.[25]

In 1987 a public letter was written to the City Council by a committee of artists and university colleagues from the University of Durban-Westville and the University of Natal. The *Sunday Tribune* abridged and reported it in a way that made this group seem determined to dismantle NAPAC, as if *that* would help anything. My subsequent letter to the editor on 22 March 1987 conveys a sense of the growing tensions around arts funding.

It is regrettable that the *Sunday Tribune* (15 March) didn't print in its entirety an open letter to Durban City Council re: funding of the arts.

The letter I signed (along with 22 others) was not a petition to the council to withdraw (your word) all of its subsidy from NAPAC (or Durban Arts). It indeed urged the council to increase funding for the arts, but at the same time reconsider automatically granting an allocation of R800,000 (roughly 80% of the city's arts budget) to NAPAC.

The main point is to have the recipients of money, in this case NAPAC and Durban Arts, consider in turn whether their programs 'meet the cultural needs of the greater Durban community'. As a board member of Durban Arts myself, I welcome the challenge, but your article put nearly everyone on the defensive, which is not conducive to discussing a very proper and important matter. Furthermore, in these tense and sensitive times, the huge caption 'NAPAC doesn't cater for blacks' appeared to at least one NAPAC representative as a reckless, harmful, and unfounded charge of racism. No name-calling was intended or even implied. The use of public money should constantly be reconsidered, and for that reason alone public and open debate ought to be welcomed by those who administer it.

For centuries the history of official patronage has been a conflict between the establishment and the 'Salon des Refusés', the latter trying to get the former to move ahead. In South Africa the conflict has unique ironies. For example, NAPAC puts on a tribute to Andrew Lloyd Webber because it can't obtain the rights to *Evita* (or any other musical he wrote) in the very same year that Paul Simon records a Grammy Award-winning album with Ladysmith Black Mambazo. South African musicians on this album (some of whom are presently touring the world) performed on our City Hall steps (thanks to MOJO, an independent organization that was funded by Durban Arts), but not one of them, to my knowledge, has played the Playhouse. Ladysmith Black Mambazo are best-sellers, in their own land (have been for years) and now around the world, but the arts establishment in South Africa has yet to recognise them.

Various factors led to the beginning of transformation at NAPAC. One of these was a reduction of the state subsidy because the South African economy was contracting due to domestic unrest and international sanctions. NAPAC itself was trying to respond to mounting pressure from political and cultural organisations and needed an entity with whom to negotiate, a 'mass organisation' capable of conferring legitimacy. MANA, on behalf of musicians, and NCC as a larger organisation could work with NAPAC. This made sense, given the times.

Official discussions, chaired by Chris Ballantine and billed as the 'Democratisation of the Performing Arts in Natal', lasted from August 1990 to February 1991. The next phase was CRAN (Commission to Restructure Arts in Natal), which ran from 1992 to 1994. (Some of us called it CRAP, Commission to Restructure Arts in the Province.) I remained involved and gradually became more familiar with what was at play and the pressures and prejudices that affected all sides. CRAN business was mostly conducted in a formal atmosphere of respectful incomprehension. Every time I entered the building housing the modern conference rooms at the refurbished Playhouse across the street from City Hall, or sometimes the administration centre around the block on Aliwal Street (yes, two multi-storey buildings for NAPAC), I couldn't help thinking: Where do we start?

On one side of the table sat salaried NAPAC staff in charge of guaranteed budgets to manage every kind of resource one could imagine – human and physical – and on the other sat a delegation of MANA and/or NCC for whom I was often, reluctantly, appointed the main spokesperson. NAPAC people saw themselves as hard-working, qualified through training and experience and mostly open-minded. They were basically civil servants in the arts sector who felt undeservedly cast as the bad guys. Their institution was an easy target for 'rolling mass action', under fire from white as well as black intellectuals. I got the impression that as individuals, their main concern was that we all understood that ending up on the wrong side of history wasn't their fault. They were doing their jobs, keeping facilities running, managing a full symphony orchestra, opera and ballet, while justifying their existence by staging shows that middle-aged, white audiences wanted, like *My Fair Lady*, which, in theory, anyone could attend. Their funding didn't depend directly on the box office, but it did depend on keeping the politicians in the municipality and ultimately in the national government happy. If attendance dropped off, funding cuts would follow, but salaries were covered – in contrast to, say, the Stable Theatre, also in town, which had to pay its own way or it would fold. NAPAC provided a secure environment for many employees but, as a Playhouse theatre manager commented to me as a meeting was breaking up, 'Is it so terrible that I can ask someone to go get a ladder?' My strongest sensory memory of these late afternoon meetings is the cool blast of air conditioning and the odour of cleaning fluids, while cleaners and caterers and front-of-house staff prepared for another evening of Culture.

One of our students, Feya Faku, was thrilled to be invited to join the trumpet section led by his teacher, Michel Schneuwly, the Swiss principal trumpeter of the NPO, for a piece that called for extra brass. Michel considered Feya's technique and reading to be at a professional level, a powerful validation for Feya, especially since the music had nothing to do with jazz.

This would be Feya's first classical concert. Late that evening I got an apologetic phone call from Feya asking me to come and pick him up. On the way back, I could see he was upset. He said that no one in the orchestra had talked to him, or even given him instructions. He played his part, which should have been a personal milestone that merited encouragement. But, when it was over, no one thought to offer him a ride home, so he had to call me. Feya is an extremely sensitive person and was so hurt, he said he would never do it again. The classical musicians were probably oblivious of the fact that Feya didn't own a car like the rest of them and they obviously didn't understand how difficult and expensive getting around town at night was for a black person. They certainly didn't see his vulnerability and bravery for going in the first place. Transformation means a lot more than simply not being racist and this incident demonstrated that there was still a great distance to go.

Getting back to negotiations – I sat with NCC people, who mostly had no knowledge or experience of managing budgets. I was always uneasily aware that I was speaking on behalf of people who knew the system was unfair, but didn't know how it operated. Getting paid to perform had usually meant being hired by white people, probably *these* white people. Community groups occasionally attempted to put together a show or concert with a cast of part-timers, with predictably uneven results. Such productions were allowed space and sometimes small sums in the Arts Council's annual planning, but these interactions mostly reinforced a fear that untrained amateurs were aspiring to take over Durban's equivalent of New York's Lincoln Center, infecting an otherwise thriving institution with the virus of failure.

Personally, and historically, I had more in common with the secure and privileged people sitting across from me. I think NAPAC just wanted to know what we (NCC/MANA) wanted, so that they could deliver it – or not. Why didn't we use this opportunity to just ask for it? My thinking was that without massive restructuring, we would *always* be asking and they would always be deciding. What was really needed was a truly radical paradigm shift. Written in 1987, this passage by Njabulo S. Ndebele describes exactly what the problem *really* was:

Even those who hate apartheid with all their hearts, insist that the need for the maintenance of European culture in South Africa is not negotiable. Instead, change means drawing the oppressed into this culture and making its benefits available to all – to some extent. While apartheid insisted that the oppressed would develop better alone, liberals insisted they would develop better within the prescriptions of European standards. They insist on wanting to draw the oppressed into an already sterile, derivative cultural environment.[26]

Cathy and I often went to orchestra concerts, which were held on Thursday evenings. Outside of formal discussions, I had to put up with snide comments, like this one from a symphony patron, who asked, 'So what must we do now, go on Thursday nights and listen to natives playing bongos?' Dan Chiorboli, a MANA member and 'native' of Italy, is the only one I ever saw playing bongos. What kept me coming back for more meetings I didn't totally enjoy and only half-believed in was outrage at the lack of support for the arts outside this 'derivative cultural environment' and the concentration of power and capacity within it.

NCC and MANA were not *against* having a symphony orchestra, *against* having a world-class opera stage, or even opposed to revived musicals, if other shows for other interest groups were staged on an equitable basis. It was the gross inequality of opportunity, representation and cultural capital on display in a publicly funded body that had to change. In the end, research commissioned by CRAN and our committee members' comments and detailed recommendations were bound together in a book, replete with illustrative graphs of survey data and organograms for province-wide arts administration but, to my knowledge, the report wasn't utilised. It was only years later, around 1994/1995, as the democratic era arrived, that restructuring really did take place. More than 200 employees were retrenched (admittedly not happy days for them), a new board of directors of NAPAC was put in place and three main areas of operation were identified: Education, Development and Performance. There was more outreach from the centre and a gradual increase in interest and engagement from the peripheries. Programming broadened noticeably year on year. I think that provision for the arts is still too centralised and its administration too hierarchical and entrenched, but a quick look at the Playhouse Company (founded in 1998) website reveals a completely new soul inhabiting the old body. I'm not convinced that the long hours my colleagues and I invested in talks made this happen, but maybe we did play a start-up role.

Cultural activism had a long moment throughout the nation and I was propelled into ever-more political forums as grass-roots organisations received funding from the European Commission, church groups and foreign embassies. Government-to-government aid had been suspended during the apartheid era and foreign aid went directly to NGOs, especially in the trade union arena. I learnt more about this by attending a large conference of cultural organisations in Cape Town. Everyone spoke earnestly about what the future should look like and what we, as comrades, could do in the meantime.

At cultural conferences I networked with people who would become part of the arts, trade and foreign affairs establishment in the subsequent democratic government and these proved to be important connections for jazz and the future Centre for Jazz and Popular Music (CJPM). These gatherings brought together 'cultural workers' like the distinguished activist/oral historian Vince Colby. Colby was the driving force behind the District Six Museum and an expert on the history of the coloured community. He had a friendly but commanding presence and was a huge jazz fan. I experienced a surreal moment in Cape Town when sitting in a pub with a crowd of comrades after a hard day's work on 'new South Africa' when Vince stood up and shushed everyone, so that he could hear the radio that was playing behind the bar. The voice that rose over the obliging hush was mine, talking about John Coltrane on my 'Profiles in Modern Jazz' series, pre-recorded on the SABC (South African Broadcasting Corporation). Apparently, Vince never missed a single programme.

Conferences were run according to rigorous parliamentary routines. There were always a few people who knew the etiquette and the rest of us caught on. Debate was channelled through a chairperson, addressed as 'Com Chair' and everyone was addressed as Comrade-plus-first-name or sometimes by title, as in 'Comrade Reverend'. Typically, subcommittees were formed to work out positions on agenda items that would be raised in a morning session (meaning that only the delegates who proposed the item would have had time to think about it). After morning tea, subcommittees would go to sessions termed 'workshops' with an appointed facilitator. The facilitator was a person who knew something about the given topic and who perhaps had attended a workshop in facilitating. They were often very good at this. Standard equipment for workshops was a white board, sheets of paper and indelible markers. Whatever was decided in an hour about an issue – for example, local content in music broadcasting or how to support grass-roots cultural organisations in rural areas – would be reported to a plenary session and, if actionable in some way, debated and passed with amendments from the floor. Resolutions relating to the New South Africa's problems and priorities were made around the country in this way. 'Workshop' was the prevailing buzzword and forum. For all its obvious shortcomings, this felt like and indeed *was* democracy. However, such activity gradually waned after the first election in 1994 as foreign aid budgets went once again directly to government.

There was a sunny period of euphoria when the transfer of power took place and eagerness on all sides to make it work. For the first few years, CJPM was asked to contribute to the new nation's image abroad by sending staff/student bands overseas, which was always a thrill for us and the students who got to go, and there were many other forms of co-operation. I was even invited to put myself forward as a candidate for the National Arts Council and was flown up to Johannesburg to be interviewed by a panel chaired by Albie Sachs,[27] in itself a great honour. But then I was asked if I was still an American citizen, which of course I was, and if I would be willing to renounce my citizenship, which I was not, so that was the end of that. Cathy was asked to run as an ANC candidate for the Durban City Council, but she turned it down because we were intensely busy with jazz and cultural exchange projects, many of which were supported by the new government and foreign embassies.

Moments of national joy and fellowship were still possible when Cathy and I returned to South Africa in 2010 for the football World Cup, but the spirit of 1994 couldn't and didn't last. In 2022 the political news isn't about upliftment, but factional struggles and corruption within the ruling party. The ANC may indeed rule until, in the words of former president Jacob Zuma, 'Jesus Christ comes again', but speaking as a former comrade, I no longer see those democratic dreams we all worked for.

3

Improvising Education

> We need to explore jazz because, longer than any other music in the 20th century, it has mattered to people. Millions of individuals from a broad spectrum of communities the world over have played, listened to, fought over, and in all manner of ways, identified with jazz. And it is for that reason that this consequential music demands our attention.
> — David Ake, *Jazz Cultures*

Catherine

When we first arrived in Durban, there was a lot of jazz activity in South Africa, which was largely ignored by institutions of higher learning. In addition to a few announcements from our university about the new course, we had to actively search for students and persuade them to apply. We quickly realised that most potential applicants had zero money and there were then no loans or bursaries available for jazz students. The only way to attract attention, students and money was to do everything that came our way – a total onslaught, a jazz blitz to find known and young musicians and donors. We approached local shopkeepers, family members, overseas and South African foundations and we named potential students they would be sponsoring. We improvised as we went along, offering non-existent funds and accommodation in the belief that we would have all this in place by the start of the academic year. I recently looked at an old ledger book where all monies raised and paid out were listed and it shows a precarious hand-to-mouth existence.[1]

Darius accepted all kinds of gigs in all types of venues – paid, badly paid and unpaid – with the aim of persuading musicians, of whatever age, to come to the university. Music literacy would broaden their skills and potential. He wrote newspaper columns, compiled and hosted two series of jazz programmes for SABC and Radio Port Natal and through these, and numerous speaking engagements, appealed for support around the country. I remember one hilarious mismatch where he treated the Toastmasters

Association to an intense discourse on the need for jazz education in Durban and the bewildered members of this all-white Dale Carnegie-style speech-makers' organisation pledging their individual allegiance to the cause.

Sheltered by a university salary, we could do this, but we needed others to come on board without feeling exploited. With early bands, we opened supermarkets, launched clubs, closed clubs, played at grand weddings and, sadly, too many funerals. The immense contribution made to jazz and jazz education by members of these bands will be evident later. Significant players became students (real and provisional), part-time teachers and sometimes both. Our efforts to bring an opportunity to study to the attention of already-established musicians produced results, but not always those we had in mind.

Bill Evans's house

In 1983, most of South Africa's well-known and successful black artists still lived in small box houses in deprived townships far away from the cities and this was brought home to us in a touching, revelatory manner at our first home gathering with other professional musicians.

Close to the beginning of Darius's very first term at the University of Natal, the Students Representative Council (SRC), in alliance with Radio Port Natal and the End Conscription Campaign, organised a big multi-genre, multiracial concert on the university's rugby field. The newly formed Darius Brubeck Quintet was on the programme and it included two of the then only three jazz studies students, saxophonist Rick van Heerden and bassist Marc Duby. Additionally, the band featured an exceptional local guitarist, Sandile Shange, as well as Nelson Magwaza on drums. Nelson was also the drummer with the group Peace, one of the concert headliners led by Sipho Gumede, the former co-leader of the popular band Sakhile.

Concerts involving performers and fans of all colours, though technically illegal, were not unknown and enforcement of so-called petty apartheid was sometimes half-hearted and certainly inconsistent by the early 1980s. The SRC was trying to do something both righteous and sort of permitted. However, the police arrived, as they often did, sporting camouflage and guns that made them extremely conspicuous and they stopped the concert.

After some confrontation and distress, members of Peace and the Darius Brubeck Quintet retreated to our small staff cottage. With a few beers on hand and an opportunity to further the education cause, Darius gave an impromptu lecture – at least 40 minutes – about the American pianist Bill Evans and I played his compilation LP *Spring Leaves*.[2] As an earnest and enthusiastic fledgling jazz teacher, hoping to encourage a few enrolments, Darius held forth at length on the greatness of Bill Evans, his inventiveness and his place in jazz history, the improvisation that his rhythm sections were famous for, the influence he had, particularly on people like Chick Corea, and how he had created a pianistic idiom, a modal vocabulary and new harmonic abstractions. These were the kind of things one could learn as a registered student of jazz. Everyone listened attentively and at the end of this impassioned tutorial, Darius encouraged questions. After a longish silence, Nelson Magwaza asked, 'Did Bill Evans have a nice house?' Of course, we really had no idea, but Darius said, 'Yes, he did'. A humbling lesson for the teacher on this day of confusion and South African drama.

In roughly one-and-a-half decades, we raised more than a million rand for tuition, accommodation and living expenses. This was in part due to performances and tours by student bands, which in turn attracted more students and more support for the programme.

Whether contracting with others for student concerts or generating concerts for the many newly formed bands, I sometimes deducted 10 ten percent, which was used for some specific project or entity, such as the NUJE. A 1985 contract with the Natal Performing Arts Council, for example, lists in addition to individual fees, R100 for the ensemble. It sounds very little, but it helped to pay for sax reeds or transportation or indeed meals.

For years, we called upon every source of funding we could, with tenders and proposals. In a letter to Darius's mother in 1987, I proudly announced that we had received R2 500 from the *Daily News* Goldpot (established by that newspaper for community efforts) to hire a bus for our students to participate in a national youth music festival. Along with this more formal event, I also mentioned adding an extra gig at a hypermarket. This we did outside, in a very windy Boksburg, with all our sheet music flying off the stands until we used some of the money earned to purchase clothes pegs in the same hypermarket.

This was also the year that the Natal University Development Foundation wrote a letter to potential donors saying, 'We are exceptionally proud that our Jazz Band led by Darius Brubeck, has been invited to perform at the highly prestigious National Association of Jazz Educators Conference to be held in Detroit from 7–10 January 1988'. We were proud of the possessive *our* and that the university was beginning to take notice.

Our constant and sometimes pathetic appeals for student support didn't fall on deaf ears, even when our approach was rather naive. 'What if the music stopped?' appeared often in our solicitations. In 1990, we stated in one of our simple but truthful begging-bowl letters, 'Ten talented students studying jazz this year have no money . . . as you know it takes R12,500 a year to study at this university'. (This figure included fees, accommodation, travel to and from Durban and minimal pocket money.) Two students (McDonald Setlotlo and Aubrey Skalkie) would not have been able to register at Natal University without the help of scholarship money. Their marks were so good that the head of Music advised them to change from a diploma to a degree. McDonald was an outstanding saxophone student and the top jazz student in his year with an average mark of 80 per cent. An example of recycling success was that former student Cyprian Cebekhulu, a saxophonist, who had previously benefited from our fund-raising efforts, was their teacher at the Mmbana Cultural Centre.

Darius's promotion to associate professor status in 1989 gave him more power within the institution of the university. While formal study hurdles and administration battles still existed, our projects were periodically financially supported directly by the vice-chancellor's office. Our jazz ensembles, including the big band, were often asked to perform at official high-level university functions and were kitted out in NU JAZZ T-shirts, paid for by the University Development Fund. These auspicious events included graduation ceremonies and, notably, Chris Merz (the second lecturer in jazz to be appointed by the university) conducted the big band in celebration of Nelson Mandela receiving an honorary doctorate. The programme featured a new arrangement by Darius of Dollar Brand's 'Mannenberg'.[3]

The scholarships we had a role in establishing and the financial support we engineered were major factors in attracting good students. The Ronnie Madonsela

Ronnie Madonsela (centre) with Marc Duby (left), Nelson Magwaza and Barney Rachabane, Executive Hotel, Umlazi, 1983 (photo: Rafs Mayet).

Scholarship for Jazz (1985) and the Phil Harber Scholarship (1991) were both established after the deaths of these jazz musicians. In the case of the former, there is a very unusual story that combines both tragedy and farce.

The Ronnie Madonsela Scholarship for Jazz

Backing up in time to 1983, to a cinema in a somewhat dodgy and rundown area, the Durban International Film Festival was previewing *The Last of the Blue Devils*, directed by Bruce Ricker. It documents a reunion of musicians celebrating the famous Kansas City jazz scene of the 1930s and 1940s.

Ronnie Madonsela, South Africa's best-ever male jazz singer and the two of us were guests at this private screening. We knew Ronnie and, in fact, I had known him in the early 1960s before leaving for the United States in 1967. He was not someone you could forget. He sang with white bands in white venues, posh and shabby, in the early 1960s when all the apartheid strictures were firmly in place. He was a world-class performer and he knew it. No doubt that helped his bold defiance of curfews and the white/black divide. Everyone loved his personal scat technique and his extroverted personality and, of course, he was often a featured singer at the Rainbow Restaurant and Jazz Club, the first restaurant that catered for black people in a so-called white area. It was situated close to the large Pinetown bus terminus and taxi rank, a perfect meeting and eating place for workers and political activists from the surrounding

A crowd at the Rainbow, 1984 (photographer unknown).

townships. In 1983, Ben Pretorius, who was a great friend of Ronnie's, introduced regular Sunday jazz concerts at the licensed Rainbow, his own brave social and cultural assault on apartheid. At these concerts, during a period of low-intensity war between the ANC and the Inkatha Freedom Party (IFP), supporters of both factions socialised and enjoyed the music, clearly regarding the Rainbow as a neutral zone.

One night in 1985, early morning really, certainly hours after midnight, we received a call from Ronnie's second wife, asking if we knew where he was. She sounded very anxious. We didn't know and, in any case, we knew he was quite a midnight rambler. Once fully awake, we thought it strange that she was hunting him down and calling people at unreasonable hours. That made us anxious and we started calling around. Some hours later, Ben called us with the terrible news that Ronnie's body had been found. Where? How? Why? The jazz community was thunderstruck. It was a shocking death and it hit hard. Not only was his death the loss of a distinctive talent, but it was also the loss of a person admired by many people, black and white.

Ben immediately proposed a major memorial concert to help his family. This is a common South African tradition that both celebrates the artist and contributes to the money, usually very meagre, available for the funeral and for the family. Top musicians from all over the country wanted to participate, sponsors were found, Durban's large and beautiful City Hall was booked and we all rallied in support of his wife and family as more details emerged.

Ronnie had been stabbed, rolled in a blanket and then set alight. It was horrible and there were as yet no suspects or explanations. Ben and Jerry Kunene, a much-respected Natal sax player related to Ronnie, endured a traumatic time at the morgue identifying the body. They were determined that he should be buried as Ronnie Madonsela and not as an 'unknown'. Gradually suspicions about his wife and her sons began to surface and, as these whispers circulated, musicians started dropping out of the proposed benefit concert.

At the funeral, which was scheduled for a date before the benefit concert, a member of Ronnie's original family came forward with some *muti* (traditional medicine) to throw into the grave because many believed this would help find the killer. Mourners noticed that Ronnie's wife tried to prevent this. Shortly after the funeral, she and her two sons were arrested for murder and found guilty. Her early morning calls to us and others were clearly attempts to establish an alibi. Julia Zondi, who worked for us and had witnessed the wife's reluctance to engage with the *muti* tradition at the funeral, triumphantly exclaimed, 'See, it works!'

Ben and the concert committee meanwhile, despite public announcements and newspaper articles about supporting the family, made a creative and hasty U-turn. The Ronnie Madonsela Scholarship for Jazz became the phoenix rising from Ronnie's ashes. Money already collected was immediately diverted from the suspected murderers and musicians were re-engaged to honour Ronnie and his love of jazz. I wish he knew that the scholarship bearing his name has helped some of South Africa's greatest young musicians. Another kind of *muti* perhaps. His legacy continues with the annual concerts held on behalf of the scholarship.

The second significant scholarship commemorated Phil Harber, who was an older student, living his dream of studying music after retirement. We were immensely grateful to his wife Zara and his family for their generous sponsorship following Phil's death in a car accident. I mention this not only because of the financial benefit, but also because this scholarship reflected advocacy in the community. Together with the Harber family (Zara, acclaimed journalist Anton Harber and Stephanie Millar), we organised a major concert in the Natal Playhouse and musicians from Johannesburg and Durban launched a scholarship in Phil's honour.

Long before these two scholarships were established and topped up by either the Harber family or by holding annual 'Jazz Jols' (party-type concerts), we had knocked on

NUJE sax section, UND, 1990. From left: Karendra Devroop, Janet Colepepper, Stacey van Schalkwyk, Phil Harber, Mfana Mlambo (first recipient of the Phil Harber Scholarship) and S'thembiso Ntuli (photo: Ted Brien; Cathy Brubeck collection).

many doors. Darius and I asked literally everyone we knew for money – individuals, shopkeepers, charities, family, friends, trusts, companies with social responsibility programmes and foreign consulates. We needed more and more support for the growing number of students who arrived – invited or spontaneously – on campus or on our own doorstep. Many of the black students weren't eligible for housing and only about 5 per cent could produce Matric exemptions for degree course acceptance. Funds collected were used for both private off-campus theory and language tutoring as well as lodging, meals and travel expenses.

When Music Department numbers were still relatively small, all students – classical and jazz – were required at the beginning of the year to gather in one room for scheduling courses, ensembles and individual lessons, as well as a briefing on procedures for practice room and library use. This long planning session was chaired by the head of department, who on one memorable occasion, announced a welcoming braai (barbeque). After particularly emphasising that new jazz students, even diploma students, should join the wind band and encouraging them to attend the Music, Culture and History lectures, Professor Gerrit Bon asked for questions and suggestions. Immediately, a new jazz recruit, Thami Mtshali, put up his hand and earnestly said that everyone should bring three pieces of meat to the braai and that way there would be enough for those who couldn't bring any. There were certainly going to be changes for the predominantly white, well-educated music fraternity and, for many years afterwards, Thami's intervention kept us mindful of essential requirements. Later, in 1990, Zanusi bass player Thami represented MANA, NCC and MOJO at the first Zabalaza Festival in London. This festival celebrated the coming of a new dawn in South Africa. And, in 1992, the NU Jazz Connection recorded his ominous sounding composition 'Tributes'.

In an email response to our questionnaire for former students (9 May 2019), Mark Kilian remembered his first orientation meeting:

> There I was sitting next to a black guy twice my age from my very own hometown, Benoni, Johnny Mekoa. Next to me on the other side was a coloured guitarist from PE [Port Elizabeth], Ruche Walton who went on to become one of my very best friends and still is. In front of me was an Indian girl pianist Chloe Timothy with whom I'm still friends and next to her was a black sax player also from PE, Zim Ngqawana, who also became a good friend. Next to him was Allen Paul, a white bass player from Kenya who I still am in touch with to this day. Then, when all the teachers introduced themselves, I thought I was sitting at the United Nations! It really blew my mind and it really felt like something I had always craved but didn't even know it. I was so incredibly happy and excited to be a part of this . . . I had grown up, like most

white kids in South Africa, without having had the opportunity of making friends with 'non-white' kids . . . There were no black kids at our school, none at the ice rink or sports fields. None in the pools we swam in. None at the movie theatres or play parks or restaurants. None in the buses we took and not even would we see non-white kids walking in our streets. We did, however, see black workers walking in our streets, going back and forth from their jobs as maids or gardeners in our white houses and did sometimes form strong bonds with the live-in 'maids'. But they weren't allowed to sit at our dinner table or indeed even drink or eat out of our plates and cups . . . Making friends for the first time with folks from across the racial divide was perhaps the highlight of my university career . . . Just about every week and sometimes even every day, there would be protest marches on the university campus and invariably the security forces would come onto campus to break these up. It was very surreal for me because just before I came to university, I was in the security forces and now I was on the other side. The worst thing happened during a mass protest on campus, in 1988 I think it was. The cops broke their formation and started chasing us with sjamboks [long, stiff whips], cattle prods, and firing teargas all around. A fleeing young student girl fell in front of me and in a second there were four cops on her kicking her and sjambokking her. I tried to help her up, but they set upon me. I avoided going to jail that day, but boy did that sjambok hurt.

Darius

Politics on campus

For me, just having a day job was a new experience, never mind learning how to navigate a complex institution. I had guidance and support from Chris Ballantine, along with many new friends already adept in the customs and procedures of academic life. Being an outsider, literally foreign with my American accent, gave me extra leeway in terms of testing limits, sometimes ignoring rules, without seeming too insubordinate or troublesome. There was less internal resistance to innovation than one might have expected. Official documents from the 1980s show that the university resisted implementing apartheid policies, but it was still effectively a 'white university'. I was, in a modest way, helping the university achieve its stated policy.

In 1983, Natal University (NU) was divided into two main campuses, one in Pietermaritzburg, about 78 kilometres inland, and one in Durban, where the Music Department was located.[4] Like all university employees, I was indirectly working for the government in a job that gave me the status and means to oppose it. (This irony also applied to my freelancing at the SABC.) Our circle included faculty who were working in areas such as human rights, organised labour, public health, mass-literacy

Music Department staff, c.1984 (photo: Ted Brien).

projects and so on. The SRC and the National Union of South African Students (NUSAS) were highly politicised and subject to harassment by the apartheid regime. Both symbolic and directly practical actions, disruptive or charitable, were plotted and initiated on both campuses. Conservative members of the university community, and there were some, expressed their unrealistic yearning for a happy campus dedicated to scholarship and sport, free of politics, but opposition to opposition inside the ivory tower was reactive, peevish and feeble. Activists – from student leaders to senior academics – were popular, influential and by now relatively safe on campus. This was new. Before I had arrived, there had been a history of extreme harassment, arrests and even assassination. And yet, it was not long before I was personally caught up in the struggle between university and state, when I was invited to play at the Concert for Academic Freedom on 16 May 1983. The *Daily News* reported on 17 May:

> Angry reaction has followed the breaking up of the Concert for Academic Freedom at Natal University in Durban by police on Saturday night. The crowd of about 6 000 was given 20 minutes to disperse before the arrival of a squad of 30 policemen in camouflage gear, with guns, sjamboks and teargas canisters. The audience, a cross-section of the Durban community from little children to domestic workers, dispersed peacefully after they were told that the concert was an 'illegal gathering' under the Riotous Assemblies Act.

I am quoted further down the page, saying that the police action 'showed a deep authoritarian streak, a tendency to show power for its own sake'. Cathy has already described the aftermath in the 'Bill Evans's house' story, but this police action was also an acute reminder that the deployment of aggressive force was always an option for the state. However, life was not about heroically manning barricades. We could say what we liked, despite the police reacting to what they considered an illegal gathering. Sometimes they stormed onto campus and raised hell with the students and at other times it seemed okay to do almost anything. Another Concert for Academic Freedom took place a month later without incident. Unless directly involved, we carried on teaching during various forms of mass action until the overwhelming noise made by circling helicopters made this impossible. When this happened, we would all go outside to see what was going on. Intimidation in these instances caused 'illegal gatherings', which might not have otherwise occurred. It seemed the default mode of police power was repressive tolerance.

I first grasped the extent to which Africa had different standards of political dialogue when Chief Mangosuthu Buthelezi, chief minister of the 'homeland' of KwaZulu and leader of the IFP, came to speak on campus at the University Forum. (An invitational lunch-hour talk took place every week in the largest lecture theatre on campus, Shepstone 2.) On this occasion, a group of students occupying several rows started heckling Buthelezi almost before he could say anything. He read from his prepared script with dignity. (I think it was something about extending education into rural areas.) Despite my inclination to side with left-wing students, their rudeness made me uncomfortable. This was a forum, not a political meeting. Why not let an invited guest of the university say what he had to say? The heckling coalesced into a rhythmic chant of 'stooge, stooge, stooge', referring to Buthelezi's role as a leader of the Zulu 'homeland' established by agreement with the National Party. This was too much for the chief minister's handlers, so they formed a protective phalanx around him and escorted him up the stairs of the theatre, past the rows of chanting students. The University Forum was open to anyone and quite a number of adult black men were present to hear the words of the man who, as chief minister, spoke for their king. Such disrespect for any older man, never mind the king's emissary, was not to be tolerated and scuffles broke out as the room emptied. The men, followed by some students, exited the room into the wider space of the Shepstone concourse. The university security guards tried to hold back the students, then a contingent of Inkatha men arrived (or had been waiting all along) wielding sticks and sjamboks. This was about to go very badly for the students when a dozen or so blue-bibbed cleaning and catering staff, including women, entered the fray to protect them. These were unionised workers, natural opponents of Inkatha. Once Gatsha, as the students taunting Buthelezi called him, and his party were in their vehicles, the usual white Toyota van for the protection team and a ministerial Mercedes for their principal, the Inkatha men came back inside to attack clusters of demonstrators and really beat up the ones that broke away, chasing them down the echoing concourse. But, as the field of action widened, the explosive energy dissipated. Students scattered or simply disengaged, taking their books and walking to their next lecture as they did every day. The panting Inkatha tough guys regrouped near the stairs to the exit. The blue bibs melted back to their specific workstations and campus security guards checked and locked up the lecture room. I had just witnessed a massive brawl and the most remarkable part was how quickly it evaporated, as if I had dozed off and just woke up from a troubled dream. When I related this drama to Cathy, she seemed unperturbed, even amused that I was still huffing and puffing about Gatsha and violent Zulu nationalists on campus. 'Leadership means wielding power,' she said. Thought of this way, it was a draw on the day. Both sides demonstrated their capacity to mobilise; the chief didn't get to make his speech and some young men had been 'taught a lesson', but were proud to have done their part. The workforce, by siding with the students, demonstrated that the students weren't just a bunch of rebellious kids. As for white people, it didn't seem to be our business and no one cared what we thought about it. The campus itself was not a target for either side and routine and order returned in minutes.

62   Playing the Changes

Dr Piet Booysen was appointed vice-chancellor and principal in 1984, the same year that Jazz Studies was officially offered as a new degree. I grew to really respect him. He was serious, modest, confident and consistent – ideal qualities for a leader in volatile, troubled times. He listened, but would not be pushed or pulled by aggression or guile. A former rugby forward, his large stature was befitting of his authority. He wasn't light and nimble and didn't try to bedazzle or belittle with erudite repartee, but he was as solid as a boulder. In his inaugural address, he stated: 'It is our firm belief that this university must be open to all those who meet our academic criteria for entrance, irrespective of race, colour or creed'. From the jazz standpoint, academic criteria would require serious adjustment to *really* achieve this openness, but insisting that the University of Natal was not a white university was significant.

In Natal, the policy of apartheid assigned Indian students to the University of Durban-Westville, a few miles inland from Durban, and black students to the University of Zululand, so that they could supposedly benefit from studying with their own 'population group'. Exceptions to this scheme were allowed with ministerial permission, wherever a university designated for one group did not offer the course of study applied for. As the first and only university in the jazz field, this loophole meant anyone from anywhere in South Africa could enroll in our Jazz Studies programme. Piet Booysen made a further statement on the university's racial policy at the end of the 1980s:

> If not always, then certainly for a long time now, it has been the firm and unequivocal policy of this university that the admission of students and the appointment of staff should be at the discretion of the university and that only academic criteria and individual merit should apply in exercising that discretion. Race, colour and creed should be of no account in admitting students and appointing staff. Despite this policy, over the years we have been subject to governmental controls regarding the admission of African, Coloured and Indian students. In the last five years there has been some relaxation in the governmental control of our admissions policy. Although ministerial approval for admission of black students is no longer required, the minister still has authority to define our admissions practices in relation to racial quotas. While we applaud the fact that he has elected not to exercise that authority, we continue to protest the legislative potential for ministerial controls of the admission of our students. In practice, however, we now admit students of all races on academic merit.[5]

This leads me back to 1983, to the first time I needed my academic gown. Academic dress was the prescribed attire for a march led by the world-famous author Alan Paton in Pietermaritzburg against the Quota Bill, more formally known as the Universities Amendment Act. On the occasion, Paton said:

> The proposed Act, in section 9, lays down the requirements of a quota system to be applied to all students not of the ethnic group for which the university is classified . . . not only is a quota to be stipulated for each university, but also for the courses the student may take. The quota is to be stipulated by the Minister of Education . . . It is abhorrent to expect the University to administer it.[6]

In a related speech at the university in Pietermaritzburg, he said:

> What the future holds for the University of Natal, who can tell? What does the future hold for our country? No one can tell that either. That a new dispensation is coming, becomes more and more certain. But how will it come? It is my prayer that it will not come through violence and destruction, for most of our institutions would perish, including our university. I do not belong to that school of thought that believes everything must be destroyed in order that a more just dispensation may be brought into being. Therefore, I hope – I may even see it – that our university will become an open institution. That it will be a painful part of our evolution I have no doubt, but who expects the future to be painless?

My future that day was not painless. Taking his seat in the row behind me, Paton poked me sharply in the back with his stick and growled, 'You have a rather strange idea of five minutes'. He thought I was Michael Kirkwood, an English lecturer, who was about my height and we both had longish dark hair. Kirkwood had given a rather long and, in Paton's opinion, unnecessary speech. More general pain was indeed to come. Successive states of emergency in 1985 and 1986 were meant to frighten off organised political challenges to the government and suppress flare-ups of violence in the townships. The so-called De Klerk regulations of 1987 were directives via the Ministry of Education and Culture calling on universities to enforce a clutch of contentious security laws. I remember attending a mass protest meeting in the Student Union and a remarkable university document states: 'It is not often that all participating bodies of a university i.e. students, staff, Senate and Council agree on an issue. But in this instance, all are united and fully concur.'[7]

I remember telling the dramatist-journalist Rob Amato, 'The West is having a nervous breakdown over South Africa. It's like having a schizophrenic in the family.' I was referring to the dual sense of normality and anomaly. South Africa in the 1980s was propped up by Western powers as a bulwark against communism in Africa. In most respects, except democracy itself, South Africa and its institutions resembled modern liberal democracies. With its relatively independent judiciary, free and critical press and public debate about the future, the democratic family of nations *wanted* to include South Africa, but were increasingly losing patience with apartheid and disingenuous attempts to reform or rebrand it. States of emergency inevitably undermined favourable perceptions and revealed how things really were. And yet, there was hope. Everyone I knew was eager to help South Africa. I wrote an article for the American *Jazz Educators Journal* (December/January 1988) on teaching jazz in South Africa. I was addressing international jazz educators as colleagues with a shared culture and similar values who had never experienced anything like the violence and poverty or the openness to possibilities that existed in Natal. In turn, their positive response resulted in long-lasting support for jazz education in South Africa and many special opportunities for South African students. The International Association for Jazz Education was a model of networking that was adopted successfully in South Africa as jazz education began to spread around the country. This organisation was the impetus for many international exchanges, connections and indeed lifelong friendships.[8] An abridged version of the article is reproduced here.

> The observation that jazz symbolizes triumph over oppression may have a familiar if distant ring. For many in South Africa it represents the living hope of a non-racial society and creative participation in international culture. South Africans know and understand enough jazz to be original, but still reverently acknowledge and emulate masters of the American tradition. The good news is that there is a lot of eager talent here. However, there is plenty of bad news too.
>
> Music education (of any kind) is scarce in white schools and non-existent in black schools so relatively few music students make it to university. The university is required by law to *only* admit students holding a 'matric' certificate (the equivalent of a high school diploma), which further limits the field.
>
> A sub-standard and segregated educational system for South Africa's black majority has been further reduced by chronic 'unrest' resulting in frequent school closings. It is rarely possible for an African student to actually complete 'matric' in 4 years. Anyone with serious musical aspirations can be forgiven for thinking they might as well stay at home and practise. It is not unusual or surprising that the better players can barely read music or cope academically, while applicants who look better on paper have had little practical experience in jazz. Then, there's the question of money. Not all whites are rich, not all blacks are poor, but university is very expensive. Jazz students are at a double

Improvising Education   65

disadvantage in receiving financial aid, because top priority is given to assisting students in technical or professional fields and grants in the arts and humanities (such as they are), are awarded on the basis of academic achievement . . .

Finally, I am sad to report that being fortunate enough to enrol in Jazz Studies does not guarantee the student will receive good or even adequate instruction on his or her instrument. The land is full of inspired players, but inspirational teachers in the jazz field are rare indeed! Furthermore, most students have problems adjusting to a rigorous university music curriculum . . .

Teaching in a third world context

In cold print the programme looks deceptively 'normal' for a small department: ± 100 [music] students, 23 involved in jazz, 11 full-time staff (1 jazz teacher). My big band plays charts your bands play, and I use the Aebersold series in Jazz workshops . . .[9]

'Recruiting', too, sounds like a normal activity, but it certainly isn't in this divided society . . . I frequently meet people who play an instrument, can't read music, but 'want to learn'. The university can't admit them, and there aren't any other institutions offering preparatory courses in the province. I encourage these prospective students to do what they can and stay in touch. It can take years between the first meeting and a successful application. For the extraordinarily tenacious who, against all odds, pass the required Grade V theory examination, there still remains the whole issue of 'matric'. By this time the student is probably old enough to apply for a 'mature-age exemption', but digging for proof of passes in a minimum of 4 high school subjects from years ago and in some cases a burnt-down school, makes it a long weary journey for both of us to get to the first jazz class.

The Natal University Jazz Programme

I find myself fighting bureaucratic battles for a few months of every year. Fortunately, university authorities are, more and more, wrestling with the disparity in education that apartheid has engendered . . . Students mostly have no money. Let me be very explicit: I don't mean 'not enough money', I mean NO money. Students, of course, have to live somewhere, they have to eat, they have to get to and from university 5 days a week, buy at least one notebook and so on. Often that means that those coming from outside the Durban area move in with me, until I can find free or very low-cost accommodation for them elsewhere. Eventually the student will start working in town (fortunately 'gigs' aren't hard to come by) and those with initiative and promise might get help from private business or supportive individuals that we have canvassed.

White students might struggle for funds but seldom had a problem meeting the university entrance requirements. They are more attuned to the demands of student life, such as following a prescribed routine, budgeting time, preparing assignments, and, of course, dealing with an English-speaking environment.

South Africa has one of the least flexible conscription systems in the world. All young white males are expected to serve in the armed forces. The choices are jail, exile or joining what are seen as the forces of oppression, even if all that means is putting on a uniform and playing in a marching band . . .

Jazz students are remarkably accepting and free of racial hang-ups, but for black and white alike, these few years together at university may be one of the few times in their lives in which racism, in one form or another, isn't calling the tune . . . Behind the scenes is an ongoing course in crisis management. As I write this, Admissions has lost a student's transcript and two students won't have beds because the ones they borrowed have to be returned. Much more seriously, a graduate student may be fleeing the country in a matter of hours because his deferment was refused. (He may also have all the big band alto parts with him) . . . and the only available sax teacher just emigrated to France . . . But the music has to tell its own story, and it does. The musicians, whatever their technical limitations, play like it really matters, surely, a definition of 'soul'. Jazz in South Africa is a cause, a way of life, an example. When you go to the Rainbow Restaurant on a Sunday afternoon and hear good original South African jazz, see people mixing freely and easily, and feel the great 'vibes' this creates, you could almost think South Africa is a great country.

In 2022, such a *cri de cœur* for a university jazz course seems disproportionate, given mass migration, famines and atrocities in Africa and Asia, populist attacks on liberal democracy in the West, war in Ukraine and the failure to keep the worst impulses of capitalism in check. And now, having survived a pandemic that nearly killed me and one of my brothers and did kill three times the number of Americans that died in the Vietnam War, starting a jazz course at a university doesn't seem such an existential issue. Nevertheless, at that time and in that place, it was a worthy cause and transformational both for students and public platforms beyond the campus. Starting from around 1988, when the above article was published, the trajectory was ever upwards.

The Department of Music

All departments were reviewed from time to time by ad hoc committees of senior academics from other departments. The review report typically included data like the number of students on the course, completion rates, staff-student ratios and findings based on interviews with staff. This report (which I only saw in 2019) was an accurate description of the department I joined. Here are some telling excerpts.

> **Review report: Department of Music (9 December 1982)**
> Professor K. Knight, Professor R. Sands, Professor P. Scholtz (Convenor)
> The Committee interviewed all the members of the academic staff in the Department of Music. The points listed below summarize the views of the staff members . . .
> l) Direction and Objectives.
> Opinions were generally divided on the direction the Department should be taking. It was felt by some staff members that the Department had achieved a high standard and reputation at the level of research, and that this was acknowledged both in this country and overseas. Others felt that too much emphasis was placed on Ethnomusicology and the socio-political context of Music . . . The polarization was expressed in the following terms:
>
> Group A
> i) The Department is unique in South Africa.
> ii) The first Department to concentrate on Ethnomusicology.
> iii) This direction was in line with the needs of the community.
> iv) There was a high level of awareness and thinking about music – it was an academic department.
>
> Group B
> i) Inordinate stress on politics rather than on music.
> ii) There was a division between academics and performers.
> iii) Musical performance was undervalued and therefore the level of musical performance on instruments and on voice was very low.
> iv) The area of Music Education and the Department's influence at school level need to be developed.
>
> 2) Teaching Duties and Responsibilities.
> Some felt that the freedom of the lecturer was valued far too highly, and this meant that serious gaps could be left in the students' musical education.

> Others felt it was desirable because it created possibilities for innovation . . .
> Many . . . felt that a more equitable distribution of the workload amongst the
> staff members was desirable . . .

The desirability of a more equitable distribution of workload could be from any
departmental review of any university since the Middle Ages, but the division of staff
into groups A and B reveals some typical tensions in South African universities at
that time. Of course, there were some who had feet in both groups, but nevertheless
generalisations can be made.

Group A was aligned to the long-term vision of Chris Ballantine. He was not
interested in building another neocolonial outpost of European culture, especially not
one, given its location and resources, that was unlikely to achieve distinction. What
the department did have was a gem of a music library, an electronic music studio,
which was then the only one in southern Africa and the first Ethnomusicology course
in South Africa – and Chris was committed to introducing the first degree in Jazz
Studies, which was why I was there.

Members of Group B related to traditional music departments that exist in
universities everywhere. Firstly, classical performance, composition and music theory
had to be taught to the highest level possible. (This is exactly what Njabulo S. Ndebele
is referring to as a non-negotiable position, in the quote from *Fine Lines from the Box* in
Chapter 2). Academic specialisations, such as Ethnomusicology and Music Education,
were add-ons. By and large for Group B, 'Ethno' was about 'folk music', which was
interesting for collection, classification and analysis. The training of music teachers
was considered sufficient if lecturers imparted immutable knowledge set by Royal
Schools (officially, Associated Board of the Royal Schools of Music – ABRSM) or
UNISA (University of South Africa) syllabi. Fortunately, the reality in our department
was quite different and these courses were dynamic and modernising influences.

Instead of delivering the expected march of progress, with the late nineteenth
century at the apex, Chris's Music, Culture and History syllabus included classes on
the Beatles, Indian classical music, Tswana pipe music and Chopi *timbila* music, as
well as readings from texts by critics imbued with theory – even *Marxist theory*! The
report mentions an opinion that 'serious gaps could be left in the students' musical
education as a consequence of "too much freedom" '. There were concerns that
admitting jazz students would lower academic standards and one person in group B
actually said that 'jazz would ruin the pianos'.

I was, for the most part, welcomed as a fellow performer despite being part of
the experimental thrust and therefore not clearly in or out of either group, but it was

increasingly clear that most colleagues wanted and expected a full-time Theory teacher. Things eventually came to a head in a staff meeting, prompting this letter:

April 12, 1984

Dear Colleagues

It is evident that some of you hold the view that my appointment to this department should have solved what we are now referring to as the 'Theory Problem'. Further, at our last staff meeting, the most controversial part of the discussion seemed to be the re-designation of my post to 'Lecturer in Jazz' in order to clear the way for a 'Theory Specialist'.

This raises the question of what my job actually is and whether I am doing it. I came here with the specific understanding that I would be starting a 'Jazz Studies' course, which I have done. It was also made clear that my duties would include some lecturing in Theory, which I have also done. I did not apply as a 'Theorist' and would not have applied at all, if it had appeared that my primary responsibility would be to teach theory. It seemed reasonable to me that the Music Department would want me to share the theory assignment while setting up the new course, and I also assumed that staff members who had time in any given year would naturally have to devote some of it to the basic curriculum . . . I also wish to point out that re-designating my post scarcely alters my own situation and commitment, as I have seen it from the beginning.

Sincerely,
Darius Brubeck

Chris protected me by taking the blame for convincing me to join staff on this understanding, but then I was challenged by colleagues to produce evidence that there would be lots of jazz students. 'You said there'd be armies of jazz students. Where are they? How many have we auditioned for next year?' The truth was that Cathy and I were still searching for students and ways to fund them. Meanwhile the jazz degree course had been approved for rolling out in 1984. The official announcement, which I drafted and Chris, as head of the department, approved, was like announcing a 'grand opening', proclaiming intentions rather than facts, but it was also a strategic attempt to bring in experienced musicians and redefine admission criteria. Part of it read as follows:

Admission: prospective students for the jazz studies course who feel they do not meet the department's published admission criteria are encouraged to apply nevertheless, submitting an audition tape and information relevant to their application, such as practical experience . . .

Darius Brubeck, lecturer in jazz in the department, leads the team of instructors.

Having 'a team' to lead was more a wish than a reality, but we soon became a team, consisting of Marc Duby as a graduate student-teacher and local musicians appointed on a part-time basis, including members of the newly formed Natal Philharmonic Orchestra. With the help of these musicians, our big band, the Natal University Jazz Ensemble, became a local hit and Cathy saw to it that it earned money for the students too.

From the very beginning, we believed that even self-taught South African jazz musicians could become temporary teachers and advertised that we needed part-time staff. This raised our profile in unexpected areas. I knew our transformative and progressive intentions were taken seriously when an aspirant for a part-time teaching job handed me his application form, which included the following information:

Current or past employer: ANC
Type of organisation: Liberation Movement
Position held: Guerrilla.

During our interview I learnt that he had indeed introduced cadres to the theory and rudiments of music.

Our publicity and performance campaign paid off and prospective students started arriving, often late for registration, in ever-increasing numbers. Their need for practical help, advice and academic support was overwhelming. Finding black students places to live and giving them money for bus fare were essential parts of keeping the momentum going. For the first six years, nothing was regular.

Some of the new recruits were slightly older professional musicians taking an immense leap in the dark. Many didn't know about universities and that applications should have been made in the previous year. It was exceptional if they arrived *before* the deadline for registration had passed. Some were afraid to show up before the last minute because they didn't have the required deposit. Often those who could cover the nominal application fee had nothing more and didn't want to risk the deposit in case they weren't accepted. Cathy and I, sometimes with the help of sympathetic friends, worked out a modus operandi of getting letters from various sources, such as friends, pastors, foundations and businesses, promising further payment after registration.

I needed to convince the university that new students without academic credentials could become legitimate students and should be recognised as such in the system. In principle, a registered student was eligible for fairly comprehensive academic support and financial credit. A 'real student' (our terminology) could apply for a student loan at the finance office and receive bursaries donated by charitable endowments and churches – in some cases, long-standing scholarships. Real students could also apply for student housing on campus and a meal deal, instead of relying on raised funds or generous support from friends, sympathisers and us. For others, becoming a student was achieved through negotiation, grinding effort and, I must confess, a little deviousness. This was before computers were common, so sending memos through the university post, phone calls and scheduling meetings made stalling easy. By the time full payment was due, we would have got the money from somewhere and, once it was done, it was done and the student was in the system. In addition to dancing around administrative rules for the benefit of exceptional people, we were also under pressure to recruit qualified students to show that a jazz course was viable.

Only a few of those registered didn't make it, but it was never easy going. I remember interceding with Gerrit Bon, when he became head of the department, on behalf of a student who had failed to meet one of the department's basic requirements – something unarguable like attendance. My plea, which included citing the practical difficulty of getting to and from campus from a poorly served township, was that black students needed more time to get used to coping with rules and deadlines. Gerrit assured me that black or white made no difference to him and that he treated everyone the same. I said, 'Fine, but that's what we're hoping to do in the future. For now, it doesn't work.' He got it and we cut 'disadvantaged' students a lot of slack in the department. Gerrit, who is a good friend, has lived in Australia for many years now and, in a Zoom conversation, he said:

> I think there was a golden age – of collegiality and student dedication. Rick [van Heerden] and Richard [Robinson] practised scales until 4 a.m. I had fifteen years of happiness. I remember Prof. Clarence [the vice-chancellor] actually walked over to the Music Department to apologise and discuss complaints about not having two [instrument] lessons a week . . . there was personal compassion and patience . . . this made the jazz programme work – not applying or sticking to the rules . . . students made such a contribution. I remember Nic Paton playing Handel on soprano sax for an exam – that was what making music was.

However, chaos was impending in the serene, shaded enclave at our end of campus. For a department accustomed to training small classes of future academics, music teachers and classical performers, the new informality in the workplace was, for some, disruptive and irritating. Not so for Chris Ballantine, who found the informality refreshing. In an interview with Cathy, talking of these new students, he said:

> They were different. Marc Duby said, 'They've got ears like saucers, like they hear everything', which I thought, 'God that's wonderful'. It was also evident to me from the way that jazz students would never call you 'Professor', it's just, 'Chris, hi, howzit?' . . . and I think that began to rub off on other students as well . . . Having them in seminars, they were just very open and fresh and much more egalitarian – they brought a very different kind of vibe . . . these were our first significant numbers of black students.

Jazz was responsible for a lot of distracting traffic in the office block behind the Tudor mansion and knots of students congregated in the polished-wood foyer or sat on the staircase outside the library. When it came to registration for courses and deciding on the progression of jazz students from year to year, it was hard to square my good intentions with order, fairness and continuity. I often found myself arguing that certain existing rules shouldn't apply to jazz students when it was clear that a rigid application of these rules would result in the exclusion of some of our best and brightest – Lulu Gontsana, for example. He was one of South Africa's best-loved jazz musicians, but would never have qualified as a real student. As a drummer and a repository of jazz knowledge, he was indispensable to the whole programme, which depended on ensemble playing as its most effective means of education. Although he couldn't read or write music due to an eye problem, he knew where every jazz record in the library was and what was on them.

Even students who met entrance criteria struggled with courses assessed solely on the basis of written assignments and exams. I discussed this situation informally with department colleagues and was encouraged to take it up with the very supportive dean of Humanities. Raising the subject of admitting students without Matric points was a risk because the dean ultimately would have to condone this or shut the door. As dean, Professor Andrew Duminy proved to be wise, good-humoured and yet formal. He coined the verb to 'ad-hoc'. We ad-hoc'd along to keep students who were already in the university afloat, but Prof. Duminy didn't really like doing things this way. The problem of students who couldn't deal with written English at university level was soon resolved by creating a diploma in Jazz Performance. (There was precedent in that classical students had a diploma option if they didn't want to write loads of essays.) The university admission hurdle was formidable, but Prof. Duminy proposed that courses be taken for non-degree purposes (NDP).[10] The rulebook allowed for NDP admission 'at the discretion of the head of department and the lecturer'. This provision was indeed the thin end of the wedge. The next step would be converting NDP courses into credits for a diploma certification and then ultimately for degree purposes, if desired, but this would take a few more years. Meanwhile, I could hold auditions and exercise discretion in admitting students. I remember Prof. Duminy wistfully saying he wished there was a way of auditioning potential History students. We still needed to chase after external funds since NDPs were not centrally fundable. This was a serious impediment, but the NDP format nevertheless opened the path to university training and, finally, qualification. Formal recognition that this process could lead to a degree was achieved in 1989.

As a way of filling out the jazz content in the degree syllabus, I introduced an optional course called Theory and History of Jazz for the Bachelor of Music students. This was essentially studying jazz history via tutorials, lectures and listening sessions in my office. Specialist courses required a certain number of contact hours and, as I was the only lecturer in jazz, this was both exhausting and rewarding. I had not yet learned the pedagogical and practical wisdom of making students do a lot of the work, so I read an enormous amount and wrote copious lecture notes, thus also taking my own knowledge to a much higher level.

I was an experienced orchestrator, but my big band jazz-arranging skills were rudimentary. I covered the basics using old books by Russell Garcia and Bill Russo taken from my father's library, books that he had used himself. The programme was growing and needed a second full-time jazz lecturer, preferably a saxophonist and someone trained in formal jazz pedagogy. I was rushing around trying to cover all bases and maintain a tolerable level of performance myself. Fortunately, my first few students were inclined to be tolerant, helpful and engaged with the whole attempt to carve out a jazz curriculum. However, I'm sure they sensed I was in over my head.

Basically, a degree curriculum should look like other degrees in the same field. However, UND's music degree was complicated because we were a diverse and progressive department. For the four-year jazz degree, we started with a generic music template with a core curriculum of Music Culture and History, Music Theory, Aural Perception, Practical Studies, Jazz Workshop for two years, followed by Jazz Performance for those in senior years. Specialised courses were also required for third- and fourth-year students.

Every undergraduate in Music was required to participate in a departmental music ensemble. This is one of the reasons it was important to create the Natal University Jazz Ensemble as soon as possible. When Gerrit Bon was head of Music (1983–87), he directed the Wind Band, which must have taken courage, because apart from the jazz band, there was only an odd assortment of brass and woodwind players. He invited Johnny Mekoa and Zim Ngqawana to take part, if they were willing. They thought they might as well gain the experience for a year, so they attended rehearsals. They could read music, but this was such different music that they often got lost trying to follow parts with long rests and no chord symbols or bassline to rely on for place-keeping. Either Johnny or Zim told me that one day Gerrit abruptly stopped the band in mid-flight and said, 'How come it sounds right?' They had bailed out on the written parts and just kept playing through a passage where nothing was written for trumpet and saxophone. Both had grown up playing by ear and so they just played lead and a harmony part, like New Orleans musicians.

Thami Mtshali and Henry Zwane were both trombonists in the Wind Band. They regarded each other as rivals, rather than as section mates and, when Thami developed some medical problems that caused him to miss a rehearsal or two, he went to Gerrit to complain that Henry used witchcraft to keep him away. Lulu also took up the Wind Band challenge. A percussionist who can't read is a disaster waiting to happen. Nothing is more obvious than a cymbal crash at the wrong time and a percussionist can't 'ghost' a part like singers in a congregation, who join in without knowing the hymn. Lulu and Gerrit just laughed at his mistimed entrances, but Lulu had such an amazing memory that he never made the same mistake twice. (I witnessed this when Afro Cool Concept played with the Natal Philharmonic Orchestra in 1994.) Lulu memorised the music the band was learning and, by the time the rest of them got it right, he did too.

Written exams are always a mine of misinformation. I taught a jazz module in Music, Culture and History that consisted of four lectures on general jazz history, starting with New Orleans and then two lectures on the set work, Miles Davis's *Kind of Blue*.[11] Music exams in each module required students to identify recorded excerpts lasting less than two minutes and to respond to essay questions. Students were meant to identify the musician or composer, the style of music, the approximate date and country of origin. Some answers I still remember are that the famous solo trumpet introduction to 'West End Blues' was performed by Lance Armstrong. A 'country of origin' answer for the Miles Davis excerpt was 'Colombia'. I puzzled over this but, when I took the record back to the library, I noticed the bright red label, Columbia Records. By this logic, Miles,[12] Thelonious Monk and my father were all 'Columbians', not to mention their compatriot, Igor Stravinsky. An answer explaining the African-American roots of jazz stated that 'many Africans went to America to work as slaves'. How should I mark this?

I walked students through Duke Ellington's 1940 big band composition 'Harlem Air Shaft' using a graphic showing musical events like solos and entrances photocopied from Mark C. Gridley's *Jazz Styles: History and Analysis*.[13] Some sections and the final ending were closed off by a muffled cymbal stroke, a common punctuation device in those days. For one of my students, every other sentence, including the final sentence of her essay, ended 'with a cymbal clash from Sonny Greer'.

I'll return to Lulu, who hadn't even finished high school, for the most insightful and profoundly felt opinion that I ever read. I forget the exact wording of the question, but I invited students to write everything they knew about the musical evolution of Miles Davis. Some wrote several pages referring to Miles's apprenticeship with Charlie Parker in the bebop era, his moving on to develop a unique voice as leader of quintets featuring saxophonists Sonny Rollins, George Coleman or John Coltrane, the collaborations with arranger Gil Evans leading into his modal period and *Kind of Blue* and then onwards into inspired explorations with his new quintet in the 1960s and his ultimately launching the fusion era.[14] Here is Lulu's entire essay as I remember it:

> Miles came with his first Quintet and that was hip. Then he came with his Quintet with Wayne, Herbie, Ron and Tony, and that was some hip shit.

My interpretation: the earlier quintets produced definitive performances of the repertoire and conventions of jazz as of the mid-1950s and 'that was hip'. Miles later regrouped with a very young line-up of Wayne Shorter (tenor and soprano sax), Herbie Hancock (piano), Ron Carter (bass) and Tony Williams (drums) to make a series of albums that were unconventional and brimming with sophistication and 'attitude' and that indeed was 'hip shit'. I would have given Lulu's essay full marks, but alas, an external examiner would have thrown it out.

I adapted some of my lectures in Jazz Studies for Music Culture and History. This was a breakthrough. From now on, every single BMus student got six Jazz History lectures from me about the origins and development of jazz. I added optional jazz modules to Music Culture and History 2 and Music Culture and History 3 as alternatives to, say, Serialism or Organology. Including jazz in the core curriculum began a trend that, in later years, would be regarded as 'transformation'. Certainly, this was a game-changer for jazz students, but for everybody else too. For jazz students it was a *leveller* – a chance to show that they too came with special competencies and background knowledge. For thoughtful classical students, adding jazz raised questions about the relevance of what they were learning about their own culture. Music Culture and History opened new pathways to understanding all kinds of contemporary music and didn't divide music into 'serious' and 'light'.[15] All music students encountered jazz in an organised, respectful context and it was 'as serious as your life', to use Dizzy Gillespie's famous phrase when asked if jazz was serious music. Music Culture and History also helped white students to understand that those from other 'population groups' were not just being invited into a white space to learn about European culture.

Mark Kilian, now a successful film music composer in Hollywood, describes entering that multiracial space as a new arrival:

Quite honestly, everything at UND was so new to me I just absorbed as much of it as I could. I was influenced by just about everything and everyone I came into contact with. The teachers were all incredible and, in some ways quite 'other worldly' to me. I had never met people like that before. Academics. Half of them were foreign and all of them were incredibly smart. It was really quite something to have an American, a German, a Marxist, a Brit and a black lecturer. And all of them are the reason I have the life I do today. But I was also influenced by many of the students too. I remember late night impromptu jam sessions workshopping tunes and changes in the practice rooms with Johnny Mekoa, Zim Ngqawana, Rick van Heerden, Victor Masondo, Kevin Gibson, Lex Futshane and others. I learnt so much from those guys – even just hanging out with them in the university residence, where we'd sit around and play records and chat about jazz and the meaning of life.[16]

4

Durban to Detroit

Just being exposed to that much knowledge
is what I will always have with me.
— Victor Masondo

The trip to the USA gave us all a sense of the degree to which jazz music
education had established a proper legitimate status and place in
American culture.
— Andrew Eagle

And now, we are here.
— Lulu Gontsana

Darius

There was a karmic wind at our backs during the late 1980s. A trip to the Montreux
Jazz Festival in Switzerland in July 1987 exemplifies the perfect timing and serendipity
of those years. I was asked by the *Weekly Mail* to cover the festival for their arts section.
I would not be paid for this, but the newspaper had a deal with Swiss Air and our
stay at the Grand Hotel Suisse Majestic on the shore of Lake Geneva was taken care
of. I was also entitled to the talismanic press pass, which granted access to non-public
areas and free tickets to everything for Cathy and me. We could even enter the very
exclusive musician's bar. (Members of the press were on an invitation-only basis, but I
had credentials as both *musicien* and *journaliste*.) South African music (not all of it jazz)
was brilliantly represented that year by Hugh Masekela, Joseph Shabalala and Johnny
Clegg.[1]

As an experienced manager, Cathy knew it would be pointless and unprofessional
to make a last-minute bid for a concert by my group in a top-tier festival, where most
of the artists were signed to major labels, but a duo might just slot in somewhere
on the fringe. With all our own expenses covered, we decided we could afford to

take Sandile Shange with us. Sandy had been a regular member of my quintet for around three years and we had often played as a duo at the Hermit. We loved his playing and his compositions, and our intention was to also further his reputation and career.

The New Brubeck Quartet (Dave Brubeck and his three sons, Chris, Dan and me) had recorded *Live at Montreux* in 1977 and many of the same people were still running the festival, including Claude Nobs, the founding director.[2] He put us in touch with Swiss businessman and music entrepreneur Robert Trunz, who would later set up the B&W Music and MELT 2000 labels that released many recordings by South African artists. Robert was launching his New Festival at Quincy Jones's nightclub, Mr Q's. Quincy Jones is a superstar producer, known for his jazz, pop and orchestral arrangements.

We were pleasantly surprised to find that Robert was eager to present me and glad that adding a Brubeck name to his line-up enhanced the prestige of this new venture. Coming from South Africa at a time when Paul Simon's *Graceland* was a mega-hit must also have helped.[3] Furthermore, Quincy Jones was an ally of the anti-apartheid movement, so there was this timely political convergence. Added to all this, both the main and New Festival were featuring guitarists – for example, Stanley Jordan, who was very hot in the late 1980s. Guitar stars John McLaughlin and Paco de Lucia treated the festival audience to the musical equivalent of a 'buddy movie', supporting, challenging and kidding each other, and exulting in sheer prowess. It was one of the best concerts Cathy and I ever attended, and Sandy felt he had landed in guitar heaven. Lower down the bill, Norwegian guitarist Terje Rypdal's band was on before our duo set at Mr Q's, but they sort of flopped because the music was over-amplified for that kind of venue.

Mr Q's was located at the Platinum, a very fancy bar in the casino that overlooked Lake Geneva. This ultra-chic, very sophisticated ambience was nothing like the hippy Hermit, but it was the right size for Sandy and me. I saved the review from the *Montreux Jazz Chronicle* of 16 July 1987, which praised our set as '*un grand moment de musique pur*' (a grand moment of pure music). Sandy was singled out as a 'real discovery'.[4] Robert Trunz set up an interview and short performance for us with Radio Suisse Romande. We were delivering for his new venture and I was, of course, thrilled that things were going so well for us.

I also revelled in my temporary role as journalist, entitled to record interviews with Dizzy Gillespie, Hugh Masekela, Joseph Shabalala and Michael Brecker (all of whom I knew personally) and I was myself interviewed by European journalists about my life in South Africa. Cathy and I went to as many concerts as we could. One evening Johnny Clegg came up to our hotel room to decompress and drink wine with us on our balcony after his amazing show. With our years of experience in the music business, we could tell that *le Zoulou Blanc* was on the brink of superstardom in Europe and told him so. The rest, as they say, is history and I admire Johnny for staying in South Africa and engaging in the anti-apartheid struggle when he could so easily have moved on.

Commenting on the brazen advertising and product placement outside the casino building and along its corridors that resembled a massive duty-free shop, the late Paris-based jazz critic Michael Zwerin observed that Montreux looked more like a jazzy 'sponsor festival' than a sponsored jazz festival. In those days, record companies were powerful multinational corporations and WEA used the festival as its European sales conference, showcasing its artists and latest signings. Every performance was recorded on video and multitrack tape and was therefore potentially a new album. Swatch (a new brand back then) and many other European companies were making their presence felt – even book publishers. A Naomi Campbell lookalike in a canary-yellow catsuit presented me with an advance copy of the book she had just written when I stopped at a publisher's display near the press pen. It was in Italian, but that didn't stop me from accepting it.

The idea of forming a student band that could travel overseas was inspired by a fortuitous encounter in Montreux. Performances were running almost around the clock and one morning Cathy and I heard an American collegiate 'stage band' playing on a deck outside the huge casino. We talked about what it would mean to our students, the Music Department and the university profile to have a similar opportunity. Cathy discovered that Richard Dunscomb and Bill McFarlin, president and executive director of the American National Association of Jazz Educators (NAJE), were staying in our hotel and when she saw them sitting together in the lobby, she approached them about the possibility of a Natal University group playing at one of their gatherings. I was more reticent, but she got their attention.

Catherine

With the great student talent we had in 1987, I felt we could broaden our horizons, go abroad and give as many students as possible the benefit of international workshops and master classes. Like us, the NAJE, which had brought some of the top students from the United States to participate in the Montreux Festival, was also busy extending its international profile. Hearing about this, I asked if we could bring South African students to their next annual conference. With trepidation, we also asked whether they could provide sponsorship and financial support. Cautiously, they promised an invitation to their January 1988 gathering in Detroit and some support, provided we did the rest.

'The rest' turned out to be a lot: making and sending a demo tape, paying for flights if accepted, buying winter clothes for minus-degree weather and fund-raising

CAMPUS

The Jazzanians - from Durban to Detroit

A band of nine music students from UND known as The Jazzanians performed by invitation at the prestigious National Association of Jazz Educators Conference in Detroit in January.

I spoke to Andrew Eagle, guitarist for The Jazzanians, about the trip. To Andrew the main object of the tour was educational with exposure to American Jazz circles they would never otherwise encounter and to American culture in general. Also the band was a showcase of what's going on or could go on in South Africa and could encourage some interest in South African homebrew Jazz.

There were no political motives attached to the tour although it was seen as an ideal opportunity to project the image of a future South Africa and highlight the University's stand against apartheid and commitment to a more comprehensive culture. The visit to America implicitly strengthened the case against academic boycotts by drawing attention to Darius Brubeck, the American founder and leader of the University's jazz programme. But according to Andrew, attitudes seem to be changing and the band was very well received.

Comparing the jazz scenes he found that American standards are much higher. "We would struggle to compete in the mainstream jazz arena, it is so much more advanced. Students there are technical masters of their instruments by the time they're twenty."

Andrew found America and especially New York "culturally mindblowing". "New York is so cosmopolitan, there are such diverse nationalities and yet it seems to have a kind of unity. In South Africa we go on about the problem of diversity but it's not a problem - it improves New York so why can't it work here?"

From here the band will undergo a few changes. It is a student band, and so as some finish studying they leave and are replaced. "It is the concept of the band that continues as the members change". But Andrew promises us some concerts fairly soon when they are reorganised, and "we will possibly be recording later in the year - 'there is an album in the pipeline' - they all say that!"

"Jazz in South Africa is a cause, a way of life, an example. When you go to the Rainbow Restaurant on a Sunday afternoon and hear good original South African Jazz, see people mixing freely and easily, and feel the great vibe this creates, you could almost think South Africa is a great country."
Darius Brubeck

An article in the campus newspaper, February 1988.

for meals, daily expenses and accommodation outside of the conference dates. On the one hand, we knew that history was on our side; we could tap into the many social responsibility programmes that companies based in South Africa were engaged in, particularly those that had to explain their presence in a country despised worldwide. On the other hand, the task of raising a budget of around R100 000 was huge and it meant maximum and continuous effort from the moment we returned to Durban. Thirty-five years later, this amount seems so little, but many around us thought we were out of line, out of control and out of our minds. We wanted to present the strongest student band and also include Chris Ballantine in the touring group. He could give a paper at the conference on the historical context of South African jazz and the rest of us would describe and demonstrate the role of jazz education in South Africa, as well as the need to develop it further.

While Darius was extremely busy with his full-time teaching job, I launched a full-time fund-raising and public relations campaign. Here is a typical letter of appeal.

Natal University swings into the American mainstream

Jazz is a natural medium of cultural exchange between the United States and South Africa. The opportunity that is presented here will strengthen ties between South Africa and the United States and enhance our standing as an educational institution.

Two staff members and nine students of the Department of Music at the University of Natal have been invited by the Executive Director to attend the very prestigious National Association of Jazz Educators Conference to be held in Detroit from 7–10 January 1988. This is the first ever invitation of its kind.

The Conference theme this year is 'Jazz, an International Language', with particular emphasis on the 'Third World'. South African musicians are bound to be a major attraction.

The invitation to perform is a signal honour for our university as it is normal practice for students to audition to appear. Our musicians are a line-up of which we can be exceptionally proud; a student band able to play original compositions, mainstream and South African jazz. Their talent is being developed at the only university in South Africa, probably the only one in Africa, that offers degrees in Jazz Studies. Furthermore, some of these students intend following teaching careers in South Africa.

The impact of all this will be immeasurable:
- mass-media exposure in the States and in South Africa

- students will share an international platform with the best of their American counterparts, performing for delegates from universities throughout the US and other countries
- opportunities to canvass for more scholarship money for students to study in the United States and at home.

The visit is an ideal opportunity to project the image of a future South Africa and highlights the determination of the University to resist apartheid. Jazz has a long history in South Africa and symbolizes racial cooperation, freedom of expression and egalitarianism. It is also recognized world-wide as a uniquely Afro-American art form and represents black cultural achievement on an international scale.

Jazzanians on campus building rooftop, 1988. From left: Zim Ngqawana, Johnny Mekoa, Melvin Peters, Lulu Gontsana, Victor Masondo, Andrew Eagle (missing: Rick van Heerden, Nic Paton and Kevin Gibson) (photo: Ted Brien; Cathy Brubeck collection).

Versions of this letter were adapted according to the potential donor. I approached airlines and the United States Information Service for what I described as a very special opportunity and unique enterprise. I wrote many letters and I offered airlines photographic promotion and free performances for their events and Swiss Air took up the cause. Both the airline and the USIS saw an opportunity to fulfil a mutually beneficial cultural and educational role. Once these big operators were on board, it became easier and the university itself donated R10 000 from a special discretionary fund. Concerts, fund-raising and publicity exercises were focused on the stated goal. This was four years after the police broke up racially mixed performances on campus. The time was right. We had a dream and it came true. Swiss Air provided business-class flights, the University of Natal conference budget supported Darius and Chris (who was also helped by the Human Sciences Research Council) and the USIS sponsored a cultural tour of the United States for the students. Dave and Iola Brubeck and their friends accommodated everyone for the days between the conference and the USIS tour and many individuals in South Africa contributed to the funds needed for this big trip – for some band members their first time on a plane. Notably, Ben Pretorius of the Rainbow handed over a cheque, as did Henry Shields, the subsequent founder of the first National Jazz Festival in Grahamstown. Later, our supportive, advisory and working relationship with Henry resulted in gigs for many university-based musicians and the creation of workshops and lectures at the Grahamstown Jazz Festival, which in turn encouraged jazz education nationally. We were also generously supported by SAMRO (Southern African Music Rights Organisation), Gallo Africa, Foglar Sound, the Hersov Trust and the Oude Meester Foundation for the Performing Arts.

The Jazzanians, as the band was named, performed locally as much as possible and that money was put towards incidental expenses. The band name references 'Azania', which was one of the names that the Pan Africanist Congress movement had touted for a new South Africa. At least four of us claimed to have come up with the name and now I don't remember who ultimately got the credit.

Many donors contributed to this multiracial endeavour as a sign of their political dissent and their desire to change the status quo. We were consciously breaking with apartheid norms, but also complicating left-wing agendas, so we just had to succeed. Anti-apartheid activists didn't want to convey a picture of happy South Africans living fulfilling lives and we didn't either. In South Africa we obtained endorsement from the United Democratic Front, as well as from the Black Caucus in the United States Congress and I hope it is not too much to claim that this was because we delivered a message of tolerance and togetherness. Without these significant endorsements, the dream would have faded. On his return from the 6 000-strong NAJE conference, Chris Ballantine reported back to his sponsors: 'South African jazz as a mirror of social behaviour may be the only working model of multi-racial democracy that this country

84 Playing the Changes

has produced. Jazz education and cultural education generally should therefore be a top priority. The results and rewards might well be astounding.'[5]

Darius

---

23 August 1987

Dear Mom & Dad,

. . . it so happens that this year's NAJE theme will be 'Jazz in the Third World'. Naturally they were fascinated (rather than repelled) to learn what we were doing in S.A., took lots of notes, and promised an invitation to the conference.

The next break was that almost as soon as we got back from Montreux, Dr Bill Prince, a major figure in the Jazz Ed. scene was due to arrive on a USIS sponsored visit. We organised a very full schedule for him culminating in a benefit concert for the scholarship students in which they played a set as a group before Bill came on as a guest star with my group. He seemed to be genuinely knocked out by their performance, and of course I had seen to it that he had had lots of contact with the students during the week he was here. He said we *must* go to the NAJE and perform. He could offer full-tuition scholarships in the US to some of my students then and there and felt that other educators in the states would also be impressed with the talent and original 'African sound'. He even transcribed a couple of arrangements to use back home in Florida.

I think I should sketch some of the implications for me:

1) I will never feel good about leaving this place unless I know the program will survive . . .

2) I'll get students into programs in the States who really can't go any further here . . .

3) I may be looking for a second full-time teacher in the jazz course for next year if, as seems likely, the dept. will allocate the post Gerrit Bon is vacating (to become head of music at Cape Town) to another jazz specialist.

4) It would be an unforgettable triumph for the university and jazz ed. in this country in general . . . The coverage on this side would be huge, and the real point is that jazz was the one thing that could do it. This might even encourage greater investment in scholarships and arts programs – particularly music with some relevance to African values.

My letter goes on to ask if we can bring a student band to their house for four or five days in January. In the event, Juliet Gerlin, who replaced Cathy as Dave's personal assistant, and her husband Bob generously offered accommodation at their nearby home too. Our campaign must have been going well, but the next letter shows me – probably both of us – close to burn-out. The Jazzanian project was taking place on top of an abnormally high teaching load, gigs, radio shows, rehearsals, meetings and writing.

20 September 1987
Dear Mom,
I've been ordered to bed for the rest of this week because an X-ray taken yesterday revealed a small patch of pneumonia . . . Have had virtually a month of fevers, bouts of exhaustion, apparent recovery and relapse. So now, I am officially sick and can stay home reading back-issues of *New York Review of Books*.

I think the group could win over *any* audience . . . they will be so well-rehearsed by Jan.

The USIS people are getting more involved since I talked to you. They have begun thinking of making this an 'exchange visit' meaning that they will pay for and help organize a cultural program – i.e., visits to a few US cities – for the students, that could possibly include master classes as well as sight-seeing and going to concerts. Just this morning we got a call informing us we had a budget to do a video of the student band which they [USIS] will use to persuade Washington to spend money on them. Which is great, but like so many things it ends up entirely on Cathy to find out who can make a video and when and where we can shoot it.

Realistically it is still possible we won't go, but I only say that because we don't have any money yet . . . USIS can pay for everything for students on their tour but not *my* travel & expenses (because I'm a US citizen). I would prefer [local] business to contribute as much as possible for all kinds of reasons. I'm glad the one experience of 'overseas' for these students won't be restricted to a glimpse of New York, a rehearsal period in Wilton and 4 days in Detroit – all in January!

Thanks for offering shelter and please pass on thanks to Juliet too. It really is very generous.
Love Darius

Frank's Coats

The final weeks of classes, rehearsals, gigs and a hectic round of planning meetings rolled on as our departure date approached. Cathy already had some donor cash on hand, so we went to Frank's Coats to prepare for our winter journey. This unique enterprise acquired bundles of winter coats donated by charities in Europe and then sold them at ridiculously low prices in Durban for people to use in Europe. Most of the profits then went to South African charities. We joked about the incongruity of sending coats to subtropical Durban as we all tried them on in the sticky heat of Frank's huge, poorly ventilated warehouse in town. And yet, one might wish that all foreign aid schemes were so ingenious and simple. I still use the full-length German overcoat I bought there and wore it in 2018 on our trip to Poland, 31 years later. Zim Ngqawana said, 'I'm from Port Elizabeth, so I know about cold.'

We said, 'You don't know about the sub-zero cold you get in Detroit, especially when the wind blows.' We all left Frank's with real bargains.

By now I was fairly used to the timetable and tasks of my day job. We pushed through the final round of exams, marking and tabulating results. The end of term is like cashing up and accounting on a grand scale. Students can go home as soon as they have finished writing exams, but staff are required to work until the university officially closes for the holidays and expected to return to work straight after New Year. Cathy and I were busy liaising with students, parents, the United States Consulate and contacts in America about the forthcoming trip. I was additionally dealing with administrative niggles about taking leave that I hadn't yet earned. This unusual break with rules led to an academic skirmish when I came back late in January, which was quelled by the dean of Humanities, who grasped that the big adventure merited an exception.

Most of the band went home to their families for Christmas and met up again for the trans-Atlantic trek, but Lulu and Zim stayed with us at Peace Avenue. The four of us went to the British Middle East Sporting and Dining Club for a midday Christmas lunch and Zim's 25 December birthday, followed by a walk on the beach.

Black Caucus

In the era of international sanctions against South Africa, our well-publicised visit to the United States was a political and reputational risk for all parties, except the university. For UND, this was a chance to fly the flag abroad. However, helping us was a tricky one for the USIS and for Ambassador Ed Perkins, who had final responsibility. It was not American policy at the time to make South Africa look good and opponents of the National Party were suspicious of America's motives. For John Dixon (in charge of Cultural Affairs) and others we worked with at the consulate in Durban, the emphasis was on giving the students a meaningful and varied experience.

The NAJE was also taking a chance. Would a South African presence at the launch of the IAJE (International Association for Jazz Education) during the final and transitional conference of the NAJE attract protests? Would we ourselves be accused of breaking ranks with anti-apartheid movements around the world or, were we, as a multiracial group, auguring a post-apartheid nation?

We heard indirectly that our invitation had even been debated and ultimately endorsed by the Black Caucus of the United States Congress. I imagine that the late John Conyers Junior, whom we would later meet, was consulted by the NAJE board. Representative Conyers was the co-founder of the Black Caucus and a strong advocate for jazz and the conference was taking place within the district he represented.[6] The Jazzanians were ultimately given a free pass. In my experience, jazz often stimulates unusual alliances.

Jazzanians itinerary – band, Darius & Cathy, Chris Ballantine

Dec 27 – 28	All take charter bus to JNB – stay over airport Holiday Inn 2 pm US briefing, 3 pm Swiss Air Press conf.; dep. 5.55 pm Swiss Air via Zurich
Dec 29 – Jan 3	Wellington Hotel (55th & 7th) – appear on NBC TV
Jan 3	Greenwich, CT – rehearse w Dave Brubeck for 4.30 performance Congregational Church; 7 pm dinner and meeting w community leaders (high level business) discuss SA – return to NYC or Millstone
Jan 4 – 6	Millstone (Brubeck House in Wilton) rehearsals – stay with Brubecks, Bob & Juliet Gerlin nearby, CB in NYC
Jan 6	dep JFK 5.50 pm for Detroit
Jan 7 – 10	NAJE Conference, Renaissance Center, Westin Hotel
Jan 10	performance Michigan Coalition for Human Rights – downtown Detroit, meet community leaders, discussion of SA life
Jan 11	departure; band goes to Washington, continues USIS tour of DC, New Orleans, Orlando (Epcot) Jacksonville, NYC to fly home)

New York City – Wilton and Greenwich, Connecticut

We arrived at John F. Kennedy International Airport and checked into the Wellington Hotel near Carnegie Hall in mid-town Manhattan in New York City on 29 December 1987. The Wellington Hotel lobby is always overheated and overcrowded, with lines of tourists checking in and out and luggage everywhere. Cathy had chosen it because it had the art deco look that epitomises mid-century midtown – and it was a good deal. It also has (to this day) a cafe, where a good breakfast is served with prodigious efficiency by a team of Colombians (not Columbians) who manage an ever-present queue, seat you, take your order and bring it ASAP, refill your coffee and, just as deftly, bring your bill without being asked.

All of New York City was decked out with majestic, corporate Christmas displays up and down the avenues and supplemented by humbler efforts in the residential cross-streets. New Yorkers seem to unite every year in making the festive season bright. The pages of the *Village Voice* overflowed with adverts for clubs like Sweet Basil, Fat Tuesday's and, of course, jazz shrines like the Blue Note and the Village Vanguard. Famous musicians who toured for most of the year were home for the holidays. It was hard to commit to anything, given our South African rand budget, but it was exciting just to be breathing the same air. I remember Cathy and I going to a bar where the legendary Hank Jones was playing warm-hearted solo piano surrounded by appreciative customers standing with drinks in hand. We organised a group trip to hear Monty Alexander and Clark Terry on New Year's Eve. We all sat conspicuously at a long table perpendicular to the stage and Monty came over to say hello. When introduced on stage, the ageing Clark Terry informed the adoring audience that the 'the Golden Years suck!', a sentiment which we now understand! He managed to keep going, however, until he was 94. Our very close friend Sarah Papineau (ex-South Africa and England), who was working at the UN, hosted a party for us at her downtown apartment, which gave everyone a sense of New York living. On another night we introduced the band to sushi at an upmarket but affordable Japanese place that Sarah had recommended. Apart from the morning after we arrived, our days were free and between Cathy's and the USIS's orientation talks, everyone gained some useful knowledge of the city's history and geography. In fact, Cathy knew far more about the city than I did, since she had lived there for nearly sixteen years.

On that jet-lagged, dream-like first morning, we were picked up by limousines before dawn and driven to the Rockefeller Center to perform live on the National Broadcasting Company (NBC) television channel. All were impressed and uplifted by the scale and decor of the building with its famous, sparkling ice rink outside and most of all by the quickness and organisation of the NBC production staff. Lulu recounted being offered a choice of bass-drum pedals and snare drums. Despite such attention to detail, we were set up and sound checked in a matter of minutes. Not surprisingly, unfavourable comparisons to the SABC became a theme of later conversations. 'Here they treat us like artists,' concluded Lulu.

On 3 January, we all decamped to Wilton, Connecticut, to decompress and prepare for the next phase of the journey. At this time of year, Wilton is a veritable winter wonderland and the South Africans must have felt as if they were figures in a traditional northern Christmas card. The discreet charm of Wilton is best appreciated by taking a leisurely drive along its narrow and hilly winding back roads that spread and interconnect like strands of a spider's web between the main routes. Rounding every bend, a perfectly sited red barn, a frozen lake bordered with dark pines, a clapboard house outlined in fairy lights, deer silently foraging in the snow and colourfully gleaming Christmas trees could be glimpsed through glowing windows. One of the band members observed that the houses didn't have high walls around them. This had never struck me before as in any way remarkable but, in South Africa, affluent suburbs consisted of defensively walled compounds and properties in poorer areas were protected by chain-link fences.

Dave let us all clear his driveway as an exceptional privilege for foreign guests – as shown in the photo below, with Johnny, Andrew, Zim, Kevin and my brother Matthew and me wielding snow shovels. Band members went tobogganing down the steep slope behind the house, sliding out on to the frozen pond.

Jazzanians shovelling snow, Wilton, Connecticut, January 1987 (photo: Cathy Brubeck; Cathy Brubeck collection).

There was plenty of room to set up the band for rehearsals inside Dave's huge double-volume studio/living room. My parents, with help from Juliet Gerlin, coped brilliantly with the large group of excited students at their house. After listening to them rehearse,

Dave wrote a piece called 'Jazzanians', which he often played with his own quartet and which my brothers and I still play.

Based at Millstone (as we called my parents' house) and the Gerlins', which was also on Millstone Road, we played our first concert in America at the Congregational Church in Greenwich, Connecticut. A few snippets are shown in the CBS TV documentary about the Jazzanians (more on this later in this chapter). The church hall was crowded beyond its capacity, with people sitting on the floor. Johnny, Andrew, Nic and Victor sang 'Let it Roll Mr Brubeck' in close harmony, à la Mills Brothers within the chorus of Count Basie's 'Sent for You Yesterday' and, of course, the audience loved that spontaneous adaptation. Dave then made a cameo appearance with the band and they played my arrangement of his hit 'In Your Own Sweet Way'. The church community was extremely generous, plying us with food and drink at a special reception and yet more winter clothes. By this point, the students knew they really needed them.

Detroit

The annual jazz educators conference began on 6 January 1988. It was held at the massive Renaissance Center, a futuristically styled, enclosed 'city within a city' of skyscraper hotels, exhibition spaces, shops and restaurants on the riverfront in downtown Detroit. As we ascended a gleaming multistorey escalator with luggage and instrument cases, seeing the famous Rufus Reid with his bass on the downwards escalator opposite us was a thrilling sight! We had certainly arrived. The Westin Hotel lobby was strewn with typical musician clutter, horn cases on chairs and long, heavy coats draped over baggage, as we waited to check in as a group sponsored by NAJE. High up in our room, Cathy and I looked down on the Detroit River and the eerily inaudible and miniscule stream of cars. We could see the reflection of countless Christmas decorations in the frozen river and the lights of Windsor, Canada, on the other side. The band gathered at one of the hotel restaurants for a communal dinner and Cathy distributed some of the donated dollars for conference meals. With an awesome attendance by musicians, teachers, performers, students, exhibitors, music publishers, media and guest stars, we were certainly going to make separate choices of concerts and activities from then on. When we were seated, Lulu stood up and everyone fell silent. He spoke in isiXhosa in deliberate cadences. Those who understood the language made quiet interjections of agreement or encouragement and then he sat down to quiet, dignified applause. In accordance with the Xhosa tradition for marking major occasions, he had recited a poem that narrated our journey, thanked people who had helped, especially my parents and Cathy, and concluded with, 'And now, we are here', the only line delivered in English.

When the time came for the Jazzanians to perform, the band played music composed by its members, as well as the core South African repertoire that brought people to their feet back home. The enthusiastic brassy sound, exuberance, musicianship and, of course, the overarching South African struggle narrative made them a major hit at the conference. I was thrilled and proud to see enthusiastic smiles on the faces of respected jazz musicians like Larry Ridley, members of the Art Ensemble of Chicago, as well as students in the crowded room. Our original NAJE contacts were there, as was Bill Prince, who introduced me to Mike Rossi, of whom more later.

Catherine

After our performance, we were once again apprehensive when Darius was approached by Joseph Jarman, a member of the avant-garde Art Ensemble of Chicago. This band was cutting edge and their motto was 'Great Black Music: Ancient to the Future'. I had whispered to Darius, 'This is going to be hard'. We expected a confrontation about being in the United States and window-dressing South Africa when he asked, 'Who is the director of the group?' – but all he wanted was a Jazzanian T-shirt. This incident was in direct contrast to Nic Paton's telling us about meeting the Dirty Dozen in New Orleans during the Jazzanians' USIS-sponsored tour:

> Well, when we were taken to meet the Dirty Dozen, how shocked they were that we had whites in the group. They had not computed *at all* that there were going to be white people, that made me doubt their Black Consciousness credentials; not to know there were whites and blacks having conflict in South Africa! Anyway, I remember it was so awkward in the room. I mean no one knew what to do in that situation . . . these musicians were saying, 'Who are these guys?' . . . I remember they just basically took all the black guys and started playing and we were just standing there. It was a very, very awkward situation.

Nic experienced a more familiar form of racism in the South when he and Andrew Eagle went for breakfast:

> The white waitress came to us and said, 'Y'all from South Africa? Well, I just want you to know we're praying for you down there. We just pray that you put God's order back in the country.' She just took up the wrong story . . . there was a total misunderstanding . . . She assumed that if we were South African and white that we were on the same side. We just had to say, 'Well, what are you going to pray for?' It was an unpleasant ending to a nice breakfast.

Darius

We didn't leave the Renaissance Center until our departure on 10 January, except for a house concert, informal discussion and potluck feast hosted by activist and distinguished academic Ron Aronson,[7] on behalf of the Michigan Coalition for Human Rights. His house, in a modest residential part of downtown Detroit, was quite a contrast to the towers of Manhattan and the fields of southern Connecticut. The students were asked about South Africa and apartheid and we spent a few hours engaging more personally with American scholars and musicians, which was not often possible at the enormous conference. This was just a 'hang'. Andrew Eagle recalled

> a very interesting and thought-provoking discussion about American citizens who risked prosecution because they refused to pay taxes that were funding covert illegal operations against elected governments in Central America . . . I was transfixed and disturbed on the drive to Ron's place at all the empty crumbling sparsely populated houses. Detroit felt like a post-apocalyptic place with the city hollowed out. It made me think the USA had had some problems on the same scale as SA.

Chris Ballantine remembers with amusement that when it was time to leave,

> Johnny started to make a big speech and then called on 'the beautiful Melvin Peters' to say something. However, he didn't let Melvin in but carried on and on himself (saying how affected he was by the experience and all the acceptance – a sentimental Academy Award speech) until Victor Masondo interrupted and said, 'Just cry Johnny'.[8]

A second major TV appearance came later. CBS opted to make a short documentary as part of *On the Road with Charles Kuralt*, a regular 'Sunday Morning' feature, with Billy Taylor narrating. Billy had interviewed me and other band members in my hotel room, but our TV segment opens in New Orleans, where the Jazzanians were hosted by the USIS. Charles Kuralt provided a moving introduction and closed with a reading from Alan Paton's *Cry, the Beloved Country*, noting that Paton's grandson Nic was one of the Jazzanians in the film. It was aired in the United States in February 1988, giving us another publicity splash. Thanks to YouTube, one can still see Billy Taylor's interview and highlights of the Jazzanian tour.[9]

Our complex and challenging campaign to get the Jazzanians to the United States would not have materialised if the timing had not been perfect. Not only was the political climate (1987–89) ready for the Jazzanian message, but the resulting changes elevated jazz education to flagship status at the university and made other institutions eager to add jazz to their course offerings. Favourable winds, far outside our control or even comprehension, drove us on. International businesses in South Africa needed to advertise their non-racist credentials and, on a smaller scale, locals wanted to show their progressive colours as well. Cathy had received donations from many sources and, tremendously important, the Swiss Air tickets. The Cold War was still on, so the United States government had a strategic interest in introducing South African students to the best aspects of American life. After the fall of the Berlin Wall, USIS support for culture continued, but the emphasis was shifting more towards commerce and technology. Paul Simon's *Graceland*, released in 1986, was a global hit that placed South Africa on everybody's music map, surpassing even Miriam Makeba's peak popularity in the 1960s. Furthermore, *Graceland* included jazz musicians such as Barney Rachabane, who was part of the music scene we were in. This further amplified awareness of our platform in international terms. In 1992, the Brubeck/Ntoni quartet Afro Cool Concept opened for Paul Simon's Graceland show in Durban.

The South African government, ever more desperate to improve its image abroad, hadn't tried to stop the Jazzanian tour, which they might have done a couple of years earlier. 'Freedom' concerts on campus were now tolerated or ignored. We were anxious not to convey an 'all is fine in South Africa' message, but certainly our band demonstrated hope and racial integration, an image that few Americans had of South Africa at the time. It appeared that stopping our tour from taking place by denying students passports would have had more negative impact than any denunciations of the system we voiced while safely overseas. Verbal condemnations of apartheid were becoming more and more regular and expected. The Jazzanians was a diverse group of music students attending the *same* university, showing no sign of racial hierarchy or animus. Their statements on camera were full of optimism and camaraderie, rather than resentment or victimhood. While we saw ourselves as an example of what might be possible after apartheid, the plain truth was that the band was already more than 'possible'. By 1988, apologists for the system were tying themselves in knots in the deluded belief that apartheid could be sufficiently reformed to allow white control of the state to continue indefinitely. Concurrently, 'adapt-or-die' scenarios were being explored.[10] Secret negotiations with Nelson Mandela in prison and between high-ranking government and ANC officials were ongoing and sometimes not all that secret.

Internationally, South Africa was at a tipping point and constantly in the news. The global popularity and clear messaging of South African music encouraged belief that change would inevitably lead to positive outcomes for all.

Catherine

After the tour

Our first student tour overseas had been an emotional and politically charged journey, but ultimately a successful one. We had joined the universal jazz family and that family helped us. The IAJE later organised donations of instruments and books. Jamey Aebersold donated copies of his entire Play-Along series and subsequently Dave and Iola Brubeck continued to host waves of touring student band members in their Connecticut home. Our fifteen minutes of fame helped us gain a more permanent, stable situation at the university and the uncertain status of some jazz students would soon become a thing of the past. With the help of the Jazzanians and successive bands, we had increased the value of performance in the syllabus and without knowing it had a name – the value of 'practice-based pedagogy'.

Was there any discord? Of course, there was and, as recently as May 2019, mention of the band the Leftovers appeared on Facebook, reminding us to revisit this story. In a discussion with Nic Paton about the 'schism 'caused with those who didn't 'make the grade' (his term), we re-examined the criteria that led to choosing the group that would make that 1988 tour. Nic said, 'That's one of the things that cuts against my inclusive sense of things. I find it very hard to exclude or to fail or to otherwise make someone left-over.'

Some decisions had been difficult. Darius chose the Jazzanian musicians based on seniority and being the best players on each instrument. Selection in these categories was relatively easy because of the strength of certain players and he also considered those that were already playing together. On the other hand, we were required, by both NAJE and the big sponsors, to have a majority of black South Africans in the band. This was a difficult one because here we were purporting to be free of colour consciousness, but we had to be colour-conscious in order to create an anti-racist platform. A couple of good white players were left out and some took a long time to forgive us. We, too, had to live with regrets, despite feeling we did the best we could.

There were also practical considerations: money and the number of rooms that the NAJE was prepared to sponsor and even allot to us because of the huge number of conference applications. On the lighter side, a poll was taken among the Jazzanians to establish who would share rooms because we had to submit names very early on. Jocularly, I think, I got a couple of votes, including one from Chris Ballantine. In the event, he shared with Melvin Peters and ultimately all the students had to take turns sharing with a ferociously snoring Johnny Mekoa. Nic even spent a night in the bathtub to get some sleep. It was important that the group bonded politically and socially, as well as musically, and these factors also influenced the choice of candidates for this pioneering adventure.

Darius pointed out to disappointed students that no university anywhere in the world transports its whole jazz programme to another country and that simply being enrolled or being proficient on an instrument or having money weren't criteria. The buck had to stop somewhere and despite the authoritative axe, it certainly wasn't like that recent 'jazz education' movie *Whiplash* either. We selected the Jazzanians in terms of what they could *collectively achieve* and felt that in terms of creating an exportable repertoire, every person in that unit was necessary. Darius didn't think he needed to justify his choices because the boundaries were clear to him, if not to the Leftovers. It wasn't a field trip; we knew the band had to perform at the highest level possible. The standard of college and even high school jazz in the United States was very high and this benchmark was largely unknown to our students.

The Leftovers, whose name was in part humorous, played some highly original and, to my ear, postmodern music and remained a feature of the jazz life on campus for a while. Like the Jazzanians, its members dispersed in all directions. Two of the original members, Bheki Mbatha (trombone) and Vee Sabongo (sax), later taught in Johnny Mekoa's school and Mark Grimshaw (trumpet), one of the leaders, is now the Obel Professor of Music and Sound Knowledge at Aalborg University in Denmark and is also a published writer on sound in video games and related high-tech sound design. Another talented, interesting and individualistic 'left-over', Hamish Davidson (sax), famously said to Zim Ngqawana when Zim telephoned him some years later to do a gig, 'Music is no longer my problem'. Although on a different premise from Hamish's reflection, I would say the problem is all the other stuff one deals with before the music starts. If I didn't already know this then, I very soon acquired the knowledge.

The university jazz programme really took off in many ways following the Jazzanian success and fund-raising for the trip had set the bar high. We had estimated that we needed R85 079 to take twelve people to Detroit and we did it. Donors realised that supporting us produced something visible, educationally worthwhile and politically progressive. This book can't just be about the Jazzanians, but we find ourselves coming back to them repeatedly because this first overseas trip by a student group was such a significant, defining and influential event. Both *Drum* and *Pace* magazines, which had predominantly black readerships, ran feature articles in February 1988 and April, respectively, and these kinds of articles, together with continual press coverage, had an immense effect on increasing the numbers of jazz students. I have listed a few highlights from the first three years following the Jazzanian tour. The most significant was the creation on campus of the Centre for Jazz and Popular Music (more about this in Chapter 6).

1988
- Zim Ngqawana and Victor Masondo invited to study at University of Massachusetts. Zim spends a semester there.
- 30 students (majority black) now studying jazz at UND.
- The Jazzanians record the album *We Have Waited Too Long* for Umkhonto Records (a division of Gallo).[11]

1989

- Jazz education now widely accepted in South Africa.
- Brubeck and Ntoni pack the Baxter Theatre (Cape Town) for six nights of jazz history lectures and a concert with Winston Mankunku and Ezra Ngcukana sponsored by University of Cape Town (UCT) Adult Education Department.
- UCT commences Jazz Studies course; Pretoria Technikon appoints jazz musician to head 'Light Music'; Rhodes, Wits and other institutions put greater emphasis on jazz.
- University of Natal creates the Centre for Jazz and Popular Music (CJPM) with Darius Brubeck as director and one part-time assistant (Glynis Malcom-Smith) and agrees to waive matriculation requirement for newly instituted diploma in Jazz Performance. (Darius also appointed associate professor of Jazz Studies in Music Department).
- CJPM supports extramural instruction for would-be jazz students, continues raising money for undergraduates, organises concerts, assists students and professional musicians in arts and technical fields.
- CJPM arranges sponsored workshops around the country with Ezra Ngcukana in Durban and as far afield as Waterford College (Kamhlaba) in Swaziland (eSwatini) with Victor Ntoni and Duke Makasi.
- Michael Rossi teaches saxophone and jazz studies at UND for one semester on an American government Fulbright grant.
- The Brubeck/Ntoni Afro Cool Concept with Duke Makasi and Lulu Gontsana play at first-ever Jazz Festival within the Grahamstown National Arts Festival and includes performance in Nolutandu Hall. The quartet also plays the Afro Jazz Festival in Harare, Zimbabwe, and has conference with ANC Regional Cultural Committee about cultural programmes in South Africa.
- Melvin Peters (Jazzanian pianist) awarded Master's of Music degree in Jazz Performance and his quintet wins the national Carling Circle Competition.

1990

- Zim Ngqawana returns to the University of Massachusetts on full scholarship from Max Roach.
- Johnny Mekoa becomes first black South African to hold BMus in Jazz Studies.
- Melvin Peters joins faculty at University of Durban-Westville.
- Marc Duby joins faculty at Natal Technikon (later renamed Durban University of Technology).

- CJPM gives professional help for establishing jazz festivals in Durban, Grahamstown, Port Elizabeth and Bloemfontein.
- CJPM organises Abdullah Ibrahim workshop for students in Howard College and sold-out concert in Durban City Hall. Proceeds to Ronnie Madonsela Scholarship Fund.
- CJPM hosts Barbara Masekela (ANC Head of Department of Arts and Culture) for an address to Durban musicians on the cultural boycott.
- Brubeck/Ntoni Quartet with Barney Rachabane and Lulu Gontsana invited to international New Orleans Jazz and Heritage Festival, which National Public Radio recorded (released by Roots Records in 1990; subsequently on CD by B&W Music in 1993 as Brubeck/Ntoni Afro-Cool Concept, *Live at the New Orleans Jazz & Heritage Festival.*[12])

5

The Jazzanian Effect

Johnny Mekoa – trumpet
Andrew Eagle – guitar
Zim Ngqawana – alto sax and flute
Nic Paton – tenor and soprano sax
Rick van Heerden (not on album) – tenor and alto sax
Melvin Peters – piano and electric keyboard
Victor Masondo – bass
Kevin Gibson (not on album) – drums and percussion
Lulu Gontsana – drums and percussion

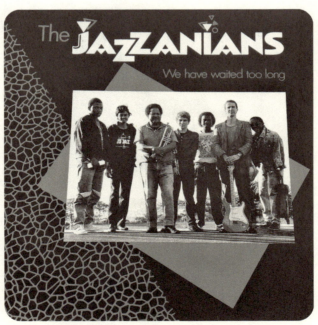

Jazzanian album cover of *We Have Waited Too Long*.

Darius

The band adopted its name out of allegiance to the struggle and a love of wordplay. The name 'Jazzanians' comes from Azania, the ancient Greek designation of the south and eastern coastal region of Africa, hence Tanzania.[1] A press reporter in the United States mistakenly called us the 'Jazz Onions', no doubt mishearing a South African accent. When Victor Masondo read this, he could hardly stop laughing long enough to say, 'We didn't come 8 000 miles with such a name!' Over 35 years later, the musicians on this journey are still identified as former Jazzanians, although the band lasted less than three years and made only one record, a vinyl release on the long-defunct Umkhonto label. We are in touch with all those still alive.[2]

Melvin Peters

Melvin was finishing a Music Education degree when I joined the department. He was already a relatively advanced pianist with good technique and a definite talent for improvisation. In response to our questionnaire for former students in April 2017, he recalled:

> Indian students had to attend the then University of Durban-Westville. In terms of the laws at the time, this university was set aside for students of Indian origin. So yes, technically I was doomed to go there . . . The only time we were permitted to attend UND was when there was a course not offered at UDW. I was fortunate that I was allowed to attend UND after I received special permission from the Minister of Education. I'm not sure how my father motivated for this . . . Studying jazz really did change my life. It opened up a whole new musical world, which probably would have remained dormant. I think what was also crucial was the timing of when I was introduced to jazz formally at university. I realised that I had discovered a genre where I could express myself as I felt, interact with my fellow musicians in ways I didn't know were possible, and connect with members of the audience on a very deep and personal level. Apart from developing the skill of improvising, I was also able to develop other skills, like composing and arranging . . . I enjoyed the challenge of developing my own personal voice. Whilst at university, jazz started to become more than a consuming passion, it became a way of life.

Melvin was allowed to study Music Education at the University of Natal and Professor Gerrit Bon encouraged him to continue studies at UND for his Master's in Music degree while taking jazz piano lessons with me. He became very good very fast, especially notable for his consistency, speed and ability to stretch out on solos, and it all seemed to come so easily. He sailed through exam recitals and won competitions with several bands, then helped others pass exams and win competitions by accompanying them. He always seemed relaxed and happy to be playing and everyone wanted to play with him. I remember Cathy once quietly asking me, following one of Melvin's stunning displays of pianistic prowess, if I honestly thought I had taught Melvin *anything*. It was a fair question but, fortunately, I didn't have to play better than he did to help him develop further. Like all jazz musicians, he learnt from multiple sources and experiences away from the hierarchical master-pupil relationship. Melvin further wrote:

> I spent many hours listening to Oscar Peterson's records . . . I loved his energy, passion and ability to swing. In my student days as a beginner jazz pianist, I modelled my playing on Oscar Peterson . . . I recall hearing Chick Corea in the late seventies, and in the early eighties, I heard Lionel Pillay.[3] The latter was quite significant, primarily because he was someone from the same community as me. I was aware of his journey in jazz, and soon realised that I had a role model closer to home.

Note the importance of hearing 'someone from my own community'. Neil Gonsalves, who grew up in Durban and is currently the director of the Centre for Jazz and Popular Music on campus and a former piano student of mine tells nearly the same story about the importance of hearing Melvin himself play.

Melvin continued:

> The church was an important institution in my development. I started playing the organ in church at the age of eleven. This . . . afforded me the opportunity to play in front of people, which invariably gave me the confidence I needed. As part of my journey, my playing in church also developed my affinity for chords/harmony. So, when I was introduced to formal jazz piano lessons, I already had a strong feel for jazz harmony, which Darius Brubeck was able to build on and indeed take to the next level.

He became the first jazz lecturer at UDW in 1990 and continued until 2001 when UDW's Music Department became a casualty of countrywide 'rationalisation' of higher education. (UDW was folded into UKZN in 2004). He took a year off in 1998 to attend Harvard University on a special abbreviated programme and joined the Dave Brubeck Quartet on stage at Symphony Hall in Boston for a memorable blues piano battle that, in Dave's words, 'brought the house down'.

Referring to the Jazzanian tour, Melvin said: 'The absolute highlight was meeting Dave Brubeck on our trip to the US in 1988. He was one of my musical heroes, so it was surreal to meet him face to face, and even have the opportunity to stay in his home.'

Melvin was declared a 'Living Legend' by the eThekwini Metropolitan Municipality (greater Durban) in 2010 and is currently the music director at the Anglican St Paul's Church in Durban.

Rick van Heerden

Rick van Heerden arrived from Harare, Zimbabwe, via Rhodes University in Grahamstown (now Makhanda), South Africa. In 1986 he became the first South African student to earn a Bachelor of Music in Jazz Studies. In response to our questionnaire (10 May 2019), he wrote:

> I had been fascinated with jazz and jazz-related music since the age of fourteen. At Rhodes, Norbert Nowotny gave me my first opportunity to learn and play the music extramural, but I dropped out of Rhodes. When the UND Jazz Programme opened, I leapt at the chance to complete my degree and actually become a Jazz graduate! It was something I really wanted to do. At UND I played with musicians with considerable ability and felt that I was really engaging with the music. But I also benefited from the inclusive and progressive vibe in the Music Department generally . . . Suddenly I had a sense of what it was like to be an active musician.

Rick and I had an active musical relationship because he was a member of my first South African quintet (which also featured Sandile Shange). This quintet played extensively and even went on tour to Namibia. He was more than just 'fascinated with jazz' and was developing an original, expressive style, improbably but effectively situated between African inflection and Paul Desmond's cool lyricism. His student career was not straightforward and I have kept this letter from Rick for 34 years.

Golden Stairs Rd
Marlborough
Harare, Zimbabwe
Friday II July, 1987

Dear Cathy and Darius,
Events took a revolting turn for the worse when I returned from our idyllic weekend in Grahamstown to discover that the SADF [South African Defence Force] had turned down my application to join the Permanent Force. This would have meant my having to report to Phalaborwa to spend two years with

the 7th South African Infantry Battalion. I got back to Joburg just before five on Monday afternoon, and there was a message at home from Major Roe of the Light Horse. Luckily, I phoned him straight away, and he informed me that the SADF 'psychologist' (read psychotic) who processed my interview and the questionnaire that I had to complete, had rejected me on twenty-seven counts. I have little doubt that this had to do with the fact that I tried to avoid army registration (I was eventually registered by a military cop who arrived at my door one morning) and that at the time I was living in a house with an activist tradition (it was the dreaded security police who tipped the military off that I was not registered). Another guy who was in my position was rejected on two counts, and Roe managed to talk Pretoria into admitting him to the band, despite the fact that this guy had spent three months in a drug rehabilitation centre, and despite the fact that he fooled around on the questionnaire and was cocky in his interview. So, Pretoria definitely had something against me in a big way. Such is the level of paranoia among the authorities that even someone as tame as myself is regarded as suspect, MUCH more so than a certified dopehead (which I also am, of course, but I doubt they know about that, although who knows in South Africa even the walls have ears!). Anyway, fuck them all. If they aren't prepared to have my professional skills for four years, they certainly aren't going to have me as unpaid cannon fodder for two. So, I booked onto the first flight to Harare on Tuesday morning, and here I am. I had to act quickly because Roe was expecting me on Tuesday morning when he was going to make a last-ditch attempt to get me into the band, failing which he had to put me on a train Monday afternoon, and I'm grateful to him for levelling with me. I'm also lucky that I had bread from the Grahamstown gigs with which to pay my airline ticket and that I wasn't stopped at the airport – only a few days ago, a student who was on his way to the WCC [World Council of Churches] conference was arrested on the tarmac at Jan Smuts just as he was about to board.

So, that's the latest from my end. If I could have predicted all this I would have opted for Master's, but that's the way things go. Now I must accept my new set of circumstances and make the most of them. Of course, the mood here is mellow and laid back in total contrast to SA (the State of Para Noya, as the one *Weekly Mail* columnist calls it!), and I reckon there's plenty of opportunity here if you're prepared to take the initiative and you don't expect too much money. To set myself up here, I must ask you a few favours . . . [lists books he needs, etc.]

The Jazzanian Effect   103

> That's all I can think of at the moment, but it's likely that I may need more help from your end. At any rate, I'll write again in due course to let you know how things are going. I'm sorry to heap all this at your door, but as you can imagine, my departure was necessarily rapid, and I would not have been able to tie up things that end, and I'd be very happy if you could help me out. My parents are predictably distraught about the whole thing, and Ann is going to join me in the long term. I've left behind a few debts, and I'll miss the jazz, the records and books, and many loved ones, who almost without exception have been, or would be, entirely supportive of my move. I won't miss the tension and the whole political morass. Fuck apartheid, fuck white intransigence and bigotry, and fuck the SADF! Up with jazz and everyone's common humanity!
>
> Thank you both for a wonderful last gig, and a wonderful last weekend in SA. Please convey my fond regards to Marc and Spaceman Sandile . . . and my love to both of you.
> Rick

In an interview for this book, he said he was grateful to have been 'living the dream' for so many years. I asked him to explain this in more detail, and he said:

> By 'living the dream', I mean my dream of being a jazz musician, doing gigs, playing sessions and touring. Throughout my teens and into my twenties and thirties it was the only thing I really wanted to do. In early 1987 I returned to South Africa to register for a Master's in the hope that this might keep the SADF off my back. It didn't. I avoided an August call-up by going back to Zimbabwe, and then joined you all in Durban in December for the Jazzanian tour. I was still technically registered at UND at the time. Thereafter, I abandoned the Master's while waltzing to-and-fro across the border and between Joburg and Durban. I reregistered for the Master's in 1992.

Rick ultimately settled in Grahamstown/Makhanda and taught music at St Andrews College. He retired at the end of 2022.

Kevin Gibson

'I didn't have anything to do with jazz before I got a motorbike,' explained Kevin when we asked him about his background in our interview on 30 May 2019. He continued:

> I had no idea who Miles Davis was before Darius. I remember our first gig. I remember going up to the library and listening to *Live at the Plugged Nickel*.

And hearing Tony Williams (drums) and thinking 'Jeez. Here I was playing "God Didn't Make Little Green Apples" '.

In the first couple of years, we didn't have a drummer good enough for viable workshops and jazz ensemble classes and we really needed Kevin. He started coming to my extramural classes in the second half of 1983. The following year I established a course called History and Theory of Jazz, thereby building up the jazz contact hours and demonstrating that a full curriculum could be managed. Kevin came to these classes too and started popping up at gigs around town, particularly at Maitre Pers, at first as a very attentive young member of the audience, but gradually he started playing too. I asked him to join my quintet while he was still in high school, which worked if rehearsals didn't clash with his water polo team practices. He was an extraordinarily fast learner and could have easily registered for a degree. He decided on a diploma instead, but never finished it. As should be clear from Rick van Heerden's experience too, the conscription dilemma facing white youths in the 1980s was constantly a threat. I told Kevin that my Vietnam-era stratagem of claiming student deferments until the draft system changed had worked for me and that he should do the same. But as he later told us:

> I started to believe that conscription was not going to end and I just wanted to get it over with . . . I thought, Well, this is it; if I finish the diploma, then I am eligible for the army. So why not just get this army thing out of the way? The day before I was going to go and sign up for it, the scholarship through you guys from Bill [Prince] came through. That was a life-changing decision! But the other thing [army] was quite serious because I'd gone and auditioned, and I had correspondence that they were expecting me.

Kevin managed to get himself to Boston in the United States and to pay for a Berklee Summer Course in 1986. How could this *not* be better than hanging around in Durban worrying about the army? In 1987, Bill Prince, the first United States-sponsored teacher to visit us, offered him a scholarship in Florida. Any opportunity to go to the United States to study jazz was like a gift from the gods and accepted without question. So, Kevin went to America with the Jazzanians on a student visa and stayed in Florida when the Jazzanians passed through Orlando as part of the tour sponsored by USIS. Rather than join the army when he came back to South Africa, he just kept moving around so that he couldn't be found, but this was a risky game.

Kevin has a successful career and lives in Cape Town. An excellent sight-reader as well as being a technically superb and creative player, he is one of South Africa's 'first-call' drummers for every kind of music.

Nic Paton

Nic Paton heard about the jazz course from his father, Jonathan Paton, who was a good friend of Cathy's from their university days. Nic was and still is an intense, truth-seeking person, a tireless self-improver, who is currently learning Chinese, so that he can read about the Tao in the original and who, for the last several years, has set himself the task of learning a new instrument each year. As mentioned in Chapter 2, he had already served in the army Entertainment Unit band led by Major George Hayden.[4] There was no jazz sax teacher at UND, but he made the best of the opportunity, winning praise from Gerrit Bon for his exam performance of a Handel sonata transcribed for soprano saxophone, as described in Chapter 3. His was an 'example of real music-making' were Gerrit's exact words. Nic is a full-time composer, mostly outside of the jazz field, but jazz and the groundbreaking music course at UND fired his creative journey as a musician. He remains an insightful raconteur and special friend. In our interview on 20 March 2018, Nic told us that he wanted to study jazz because it

> represented a higher achievement than the rock I had been interested in, with greater depth and complexity. Also, its improvisational nature appealed to me far more than the idea of reading the 'correct' notes as in classical orthodoxy. The jazz course created a subculture of education, passion, mutual learning and political resistance. The strictures of the classical orthodoxy did not apply, and I felt like there was a camaraderie and friendship in the music making. The university was a doorway on the world for many of us and created a hub where educated and under-educated could meet, where traditions could be kept alive.

At university Nic objected to being fed Theodor Adorno (Frankfurt School) by Chris Ballantine, whose Marxist analysis clashed with his evangelical Christianity. 'What did the Bhekis and the Vusis of this world have to do with Adorno?' Nonetheless, he contributed greatly to the ongoing debates about elitism in music studies. His heart and mind (and faith) were aligned to a new South African culture, and he was an early advocate of the importance of 'world music'. Summing up the Jazzanian trip, he said:

> Wilton was maybe my favourite experience. Victor and I stayed at Juliet and Bob Gerlin's. Woke up in the morning to the snow, blueberry muffins and then we went off to the Brubecks' and saw the lake and Dave's composition studio in the middle of the lake.

Victor Masondo

'Nothing lies beyond the reach of prayer except that which lies outside the will of God' appears at the bottom of Sibusiso Victor Masondo's emails. He grew up in a church environment. His father, who had been a minister in one of the many community churches in KwaMashu and played guitar, died in 1983. Victor had finished school by then, but felt depressed 'just staying at home doing nothing'. He came to my office and I was encouraging, but told him he had to meet minimal requirements, such as learning musical notation, first. Marc Duby gave him private lessons, taking him from zero to Grade VI theory in less than a year, a signal achievement for both teacher and pupil. In an interview, Victor said that before the lessons he couldn't even *spell* the word 'theory', let alone apply theory to making music.

Masondo's church, Assemblies of God, paid for him to register for the three-year diploma in Music Performance. He continued bass lessons with Marc, had master classes with Victor Ntoni when he came to Durban, and piano lessons with me. With solid backing from his church and his family, he was in a far more stable situation than many of his peers, but the geography and logistics of apartheid were still a major challenge, as he remembered:

> My church, Assemblies of God, paid all the fees upfront. I remember it was a whooping R9 000 for all three years. Then, as time went on, I managed to do some gigs to get money for things I needed most . . . Sad moments were really moments that created character in me, like being so broke you cannot even afford a sandwich and you need brainpower.

Victor spent many nights in the 'Prac Block', a long, low wooden shed (literally designed for 'wood-shedding' as Americans call hardcore practice) near the campus Student Union. It was divided into separate rooms and was an illegal home-from-home over the years for many students. It was against university regulations to spend the night there, but KwaMashu was far away and transportation was both expensive and unreliable. Richard Robinson and Rick van Heerden, who had digs in town, used to stay late too, competing in *dagga* (marijuana) fuelled marathon practice sessions. I often gave workshops in the Prac Block in the early years because the drums and amps were stored there and meeting there was easier than schlepping equipment around campus. I often found traces of 'informal occupation'.

Victor was awarded the first-ever diploma in Jazz Performance and Cathy and I attended a large, joyous party given by his church and family in KwaMashu. There was even a video made – a costly extra in those days. Victor's receiving a university qualification was a major event for his whole community. My mother said in a letter to me that the video brought tears to her eyes because she had also been the first in her family to go to university.

Victor radiated unmistakable star quality, which allowed him to take giant steps from graduation to arranging for Miriam Makeba and playing in a specially formed

International Jazz Orchestra, led by Dizzy Gillespie. I was frustrated at first with his slow progress on piano, but I shouldn't have been. The perceptive thoroughness with which he grasped principles of harmony and voicing made him a sought-after arranger in an astonishingly short time. His bass playing was 'in the pocket' because of his Gospel roots. His style also references the way electric bass in Africa really is a bass guitar – a lead or counter-lead. Paul Simon zeroed in on this style when he started researching *Graceland* and found a master in Bakhiti Khumalo. Victor was soon playing sessions that Bakhiti would have played had he not been on the road with Paul Simon. In their student days and for a few years beyond, Nic and Victor often played together. They were both very committed Christians and eager to use their upskilled jazz chops in the service of the Lord and their ecumenical, anti-apartheid values. In our interview on 20 March 2018, Nic reflected:

> You know there was that class of geniuses like Melvin Peters and Kevin Gibson and I would say possibly Rick . . . they're all the people that had the technical chops that I couldn't quite get to. And so, in a sense they were in a slightly different class . . . Victor for me was a friend and we had a lot in common. [Now when] I drive past Main Road and past Mars Music and there's a picture of Victor in the window as a sponsor with Yamaha, you know, a big name, he's like *the* guy! He was a phenomenal person just in terms of his openness, lack of bitterness, his kind of *joie de vivre* . . .

Andrew Eagle

Jazzanian guitarist Andrew Eagle already had a degree in Psychology when he enrolled for a Bachelor of Music degree in Jazz Studies. Zim Ngqawana and Andrew used to busk together on the beach as a sax-guitar duo, sometimes earning better money than people doing booked gigs. They could work as often and for as long as they liked. Unlike Kevin, Andrew did believe in the 'perpetual student' strategy for avoiding the army and he was also active in the End Conscription Campaign, which was gaining momentum on campus. Nevertheless, he immigrated to England in 1993, just in case. He is now a top consultant at a clinical psychology unit of a London hospital, but still composes, records and plays part-time. He joined my quartet for a performance at South Africa House (South African High Commission in the United Kingdom) on Trafalgar Square for a UKZN scholarship benefit concert organised by the university's alumni organisation in the United Kingdom. Andrew has also recently released two albums, which he recorded during visits to South Africa. In our interview in October 2021, he summarised the shared jazz experience:

> What got me really interested in jazz was hearing Abdullah Ibrahim play in Pietermaritzburg and also hearing Darius play with his band. If memory serves,

Barney Rachabane was on alto. I particularly loved 'Tugela Rail' and still do. It felt exotic with a great groove, but with a structure and some harmonic complexity too.

Stephen Dyer was my next-door neighbour and childhood friend, and he studied music at Durban, which planted the idea in my head. I commuted from PMB for the first year and then moved into an infamous digs called Bedford behind the university, next to Cato Manor. I still remember I paid R17 a month for my small room with a leaking roof made of corrugated iron. There was only one place in the room I could sleep where I wouldn't be rained on when the heavy rains came.

As I write, I am reflecting on what Darius and Cathy brought to the table: a deep pedigree in jazz and a conviction that you could make a serious proper career in music. And that was the aim of the course to really raise the bar and to aspire to something more – to see it as a valid and legitimate professional role and livelihood. I sensed that they wanted something more for the students – a way out of poverty and reduced expectations and aspirations. A ticket to a normal good life. An idea that jazz and music could be a proper career.

It was a unique experiment to try to introduce some rigour and systematic learning into a system so full of natural talent and exuberance, but with such inadequacies in the education system for black people. But it wasn't easy fitting in to the strictures and structures of a classical music department, where you couldn't just bypass the standards and requirements of the university institution.

This is also not to say that there weren't some tensions . . . and familiar South African questions about ownership and authorship of the culture. And I think people did ask questions about whether the Jazz course was trying to impose a formal Western culture on the 'native culture' with little understanding of the history and deep intelligence of that culture. But, on the whole, this was for me a creative tension and it produced creativity and professionalism.

It is easy to underestimate Andrew's importance to the Jazzanian project. His relative maturity made him a co-leader with Johnny Mekoa and he was able to assist us in practical ways. Musically, he blended in a smooth, intelligent pop (think Steely Dan) sensibility, widening the appeal of the group. His playing reminds one of African guitar styles because he always finds a little rhythmic and sonic niche where his instrument can be heard supplementing the density and dynamic dominance of the horns with a precise riff. His presence and approach conveyed that we were a cool, contemporary band that white youth could be interested in too, not just a township jazz revival band with a fashionable political agenda. His sophisticated composition 'We Have Waited Too Long' was the title track of the Jazzanians' album.

Johnny Mekoa

The leader and frontman of the Jazzanians was the formidable Johnny Mekoa. It was Johnny's robust, extrovert presence that made the Jazzanians an outfit to be reckoned with. We first met him in 1985. Victor Ntoni invited him to join us for a meal at a hotel coffee shop in Johannesburg when we were up there for a gig. Johnny was uncharacteristically quiet on this occasion, but soon it was clear that he wanted to quit his day job as an optical dispenser (I never learnt how he entered that trade) and study full-time in the coming year. Although two years older than me and a 'name' in the diminishing ranks of township jazz exponents, he was willing to sacrifice income, status and the comforts of home to pursue formal study. Johnny's wife Margaret was a highly qualified nurse who often did contract work in the United Kingdom and he also had a support system through extended family and beyond. Unique among the African students we had so far enrolled, he had passed enough courses at secondary level to qualify for a mature-age Matric exemption. He coped reasonably well with Western classical music history at Natal despite considering it to be of little personal value and hazardous to his grade-point average. Having passed the courses, he was very proud of showing that he knew about *Ars Nova*, Palestrina and Alban Berg. However, at the time, he thought that Music, Culture and History 1, 2 and 3 were hard graft and of little relevance.

Johnny had the open, rounded tone and the declamatory power of Hugh Masekela and took a lot from classic hard-bop trumpeters, especially Freddie Hubbard and Clifford Brown whose repertoires he knew as well as the township music of Victor Ndlazilwana, leader of the Jazz Ministers. My full tribute to Bra Johnny will come later, as our association continues way beyond the Jazzanian years.

Zim Ngqawana

When I mention that I'm writing about this period to people in the South African arts or media world and even beyond, they always want to talk about Zim. Zimasile Ngqawana (1959–2011) was the second arrival (in 1987) of a very important group of musically talented friends, which included Lulu Gontsana, Feya Faku and Lex Futshane, all from New Brighton township near Port Elizabeth (now called Gqeberha). Like Johnny, he had some real-world experience under his belt as a former member of Pacific Express and was informed and critically sophisticated about jazz. I first heard about him from Andrew Tracey, head of the International Library of African Music at Rhodes University and the doyen of ethnomusicologists in South Africa. Tracey was an ardent believer in Zim's talent and organised a benefit concert in Grahamstown to help him get to Durban. Zim had prepared for this by doing his music grades on flute as a part-time student at Rhodes. He excelled on this instrument having had lessons from 'Aunt Ann' (Ann Catt from Port Elizabeth) and his composition bearing that title was often played by the Jazzanians. He could read music and understood enough music theory to start straight away.

Having Zim and Johnny in the same band for a while was tricky, in an artistic sense. Johnny brought a lot of his distinguished past and reverence for 'the greats' with him and Zim leaned towards a future music that he would later create and influence. For the time being, respect for age settled the question of who would dominate in the Jazzanians and Zim fully committed himself to playing in older styles as an essential part of his education, but it was obvious to musicians close to him that he was destined to open pathways to a modern South African jazz identity. This realisation wasn't long in coming to Zim himself when, following the Jazzanian tour, he found encouragement, support and opportunities to study in the United States. As his career and artistry developed over the years, our relationship eventually encompassed much more than belongs in the story of the Jazzanians. Cathy and I will both write more about Zim later.

Lulama Gontsana

The advent of Lulu Gontsana (1960–2005) was another extraordinary gift to our jazz programme because he was another experienced professional. Lulu was truly indispensable to the success of the jazz course, yet he was 'unofficial' from beginning to end. His presence complicated the whole question of what a student was or should be.[5] He was one of the most truly independent people I have ever known. I remember a poignant conversation about how he was going to survive: 'My parents said they had nothing to leave me, so they taught me two things: to have good manners and to take care of myself.' Lulu's conduct exemplified both these character traits. He was an invaluable companion on road trips, very low maintenance and quick to volunteer to go with me to pick up people or equipment or to accompany us as we did other chores. He had a knack for learning layouts, usually leading the way in unfamiliar spaces from festival backstage areas to unknown neighbourhoods. Being helpful in these ways was in line with the kind of 'good manners' he had learnt at home. He could also switch on a different personality when we needed to get through a crowd or if it seemed like we were being approached by people with questionable intentions. The image of Lulu as protector will seem laughable to people who remember him, at about 5 feet, walking beside me at over 6 feet, but he had township street smarts and adopted body language that made him appear in his own words like 'just another *tsotsi*' (gangster) – an extraordinarily well-dressed one, who specialised in particularly colourful and wide-shouldered jackets.

Lulu hadn't come directly from New Brighton. Duke Makasi invited him to play with Spirits Rejoice in Johannesburg in 1981 and Cathy and I met him in 1983 when he was playing in Brazilian pianist Isio Gross's trio at the Garden Restaurant in the Carlton Centre. The next time I saw him he was at the Albany Hotel in Durban, accompanying American jazz organist Richard Groove Holmes. (I was at that gig as a Radio Port Natal interviewer.) I don't remember exactly when I invited him to join us in Durban, but it must have been after the Ronnie Madonsela Scholarship was established. Soon, he was living in the little wooden dormer-window room upstairs in our home on Peace Avenue. He was like an undemanding stray cat that knew he could always come back when he sometimes drifted away to Johannesburg or Port Elizabeth for work. Lulu spoke a sort of jazzy English, calling everyone 'cats'; for example, the guards patrolling the campus were referred to as 'security cats', but he was noticeably ill at ease with actual felines. One day we came home to find Lulu trapped between two of Marc Duby's purring Burmese on the stairway to his room at Peace Avenue, unable to move until they did. He said he was 'showing them I'm not afraid'. He went to university with me, set up the drum kit and played in the ensembles that Kevin Gibson wasn't covering. He also started getting gigs, of which there was no shortage in those days, partly due to Cathy's entrepreneurial skills.

It wasn't immediately obvious that the Jazzanians needed two drummers, but Kevin was very accommodating, especially since he was planning to study in America. There was also a 'racial' element. Cathy and I, in terms of USIS priorities, needed to showcase a predominantly African band. However, this was far from being the only reason Lulu remained in Durban. In addition to his value in a class as part of the rhythm section, he was the drummer for Afro Cool Concept. Lulu had a head start of several years in absorbing jazz repertoire and style and was already friends with all of the musicians I worked with during those years. He had a repertoire of 'township' beats and traditional Xhosa rhythms that Kevin learnt from him. We recorded *We Have Waited Too Long* in Durban in 1988 with Lulu as the sole drummer because Kevin was in Florida.

Blending styles

Like in any large jazz group, there were cliques that pulled in different directions, but they also overlapped and balanced each other. The deep, hard-core jazz guys – Johnny, Zim and Lulu – exercised a strong gravitational pull on Melvin. (By the time Rick came into the band, its overall direction was pretty much settled, but he was a jazz guy too.) Victor and Melvin had a strong church music background (as do many very famous musicians). Nic (who also played guitar) and Andrew (who was also a good keyboard player) had connections to and influences from the South African pop and rock world. There was in South Africa at this time an explosion of creative white-resistance rock, as in America during the Vietnam era. Nic and Melvin both appreciated classical music too. So, all in all, these different strands came together.

The identifiable *South African jazz* element, which would be special and representative in the United States, mostly came from Johnny. Johnny, Zim, Victor and Lulu produced the gritty, urban-core, down-home aspect, but versatility and variety of style and sonic focus came from the others. We were working towards that versatility by taking input from all the members. As the official 'jazz educator' and convenor of the group, I was careful to avoid pushing a purist jazz agenda. Cathy and I wanted our show in Detroit to be unforgettable, different, powerful! I was overall guided by one of my father's stories, one I would later hear directly from Cuban piano great Chucho Valdés himself. (Dave had advised Valdés and members of the legendary Irakere group to play their own music.[6]) Hugh Masekela told me that he got the same advice from Miles when he came to New York in the 1960s. In the 1940s, my father's mentor, Darius Milhaud, told him to stick with jazz. Many great talents went to America seeking to drink from the source, approaching jazz with eager humility, but when they succeeded there, it was because of the music that they brought with them. This thought was never far from my coaching of the Jazzanians.

In Detroit, Zim and Victor caught the eye of prominent jazz educators, mainly Dr Fred Tillis from the University of Massachusetts. This was great for them and what we had hoped for, but it also made life complicated. Both were offered scholarships to study at the University of Massachusetts (Amherst). Victor declined because he felt he could do more in the struggle back home. Although more of a peacemaker than a militant, he and we saw how important this was in Natal, where conflict between different black factions was escalating. Zim, on the other hand, voiced both musical and political militancy, which especially appealed to Max Roach. Zim had grown up in an atmosphere more aligned to Black Consciousness than to the inclusivity of the old ANC. In any case, through his acceptance at the University of Massachusetts, he had very close access to one of the founders of modern jazz and often stayed with Max Roach in New York when he wasn't at Amherst. Zim was always very sure he was more than just a student learning to be a musician; he would be a disciple, then a visionary artist and ultimately proclaim guru status in his own right. He returned to the United States for a further period, thanks to Max Roach, and several letters from Iola and Juliet Gerlin refer to sending food parcels to Amherst or inviting Zim to concerts when Dave played anywhere nearby or when Zim himself was in New York.

A beneficial consequence for our university jazz course was Zim's friendship with Chris Merz, who was a graduate student and part-time teacher at the University of Massachusetts. Encouraged by Zim, Chris applied for our department's sax post as soon as it was available and he had a profound and lasting impact on the development of the jazz programme as it entered its next phase, a two-man show with Chris teaching full-time along with me.

> Queen Elizabeth Avenue
> June 11, 1988
>
> Dear Mom,
> Our big news post-tour is that Zim is definitely going to the Jazz Workshop summer course at U. Mass (Amherst). We left not knowing whether enough money could be raised, but Durban Arts came through with a substantial grant & various private individuals came forward in response to an article run in the *Daily News*. We're very excited for him . . .
> Darius

Because of the Max Roach connection, Zim ended up at Wynton Marsalis's jazz camp in Sand Point, Idaho after the University of Massachusetts workshop adjourned. Meanwhile, Cathy and I made a deal with Umkhonto Records, a new Gallo subsidiary, to fund a studio recording of the Jazzanians in Durban. I remember answering the phone at some ridiculously early hour to hear Zim asking, 'Do you know where Sand Point is?'

'That doesn't matter', I replied. 'Do *you* know where it is?' Getting Zim back from the States in time to record and booking the ever-engaged Victor for the recording sessions was a major logistical hassle. We really didn't have money to throw at the problem or even a flexible recording budget. Somehow Cathy handled it.

> August 11, 1988
> Queen Elizabeth Ave.
>
> Dear Iola and Dave,
> I know I won't get very far as it is already the end of the day and your son will be home exhausted from teaching and practicing a few duo numbers for an appearance at a Melvin Peters special. In addition, he has a gig tonight with the great Mankunku (South Africa's foremost tenor man) at the Rainbow. All of this sounds very normal, but every aspect of these supposed normal activities has been full of stress these past weeks. For example: the Winston Mankunku gig venue changed because of a difficult political situation on the campus of the University of Durban (Westville) and this change, as you can well imagine, snowballed into lots of changed arrangements and double and triple work.

114 Playing the Changes

> Another difficulty: Zim is not back from the States, which has affected Melvin's concert and the Jazzanians' rehearsal and recording sessions. Not to mention our having to pay for reverse calls from Sandpoint, Idaho at 3 am for a few nights running. Therefore, no sleep and quadruple sets of worries. Victor Masondo has become so famous in SA that he is the first call bass player both here and for exiled SA musicians. This next week is the ONLY week he can record, so Zim just has to come back.
>
> . . . Anyway, it's not all Zim's fault because he didn't know the recording status . . . except that he should have put us in the picture much sooner, rather than on the day his flight was due to leave New York City. I am still a little worried that he won't get here although I have checked this end that he is booked on a new flight. I could go on and on and some of it would be very familiar stuff to you although mostly from days gone by. Bye for now, C.
>
> PS from Darius: Well, I've got to eat my cornflakes now. All I've got to do today is bring Lulu's drums to work, give a workshop, play two-piano pieces [with Melvin] in a lunch-hour concert, prepare for a big-band rehearsal at 5, and start recording an album [with the Jazzanians] tonight at 8. And this is only Monday! Love, Darius
>
> PPS from Cathy: Zim arrived, and the recording is proceeding . . . I was glad Z saw you and especially Juliet despite Max Roach agenda. Sounds like he'll return [to the United States] in Jan!

There was no question that 1988 was the Jazzanian year. We were going into 1989 with momentum, an opportunity to develop a venue and base of operations and a realisation that, in words borrowed from one of Stevie Wonder's songs, we had reached 'the higher ground'. Things were certainly on a new level, yet routine and stability remained elusive. On our travels we found that rather than regarding South Africa as a 'pariah state' that deserved to be punished, everyone we encountered was hoping for the best, even though *what* would be best was hotly debated in every quarter. I really love Nic Paton's review 35 years later:

> That time in our lives was extraordinary, extremely special. We did what we did out of an inner urge to express a life we imagined. We had faith that it meant something, and it did. I remember Darius and Cathy Brubeck and their (quasi) spontaneous enactment of a crazy dream, endlessly hospitably sharing the treasures of the Brubeck tradition. Chris Ballantine for his pulsating, urgent, insightful, dynamic reflections on it all. And all the players.

The Jazzanian Effect 115

Nic Paton at Jazz and Folk for Free Concert 8/6/86 (photographer unknown; Cathy Brubeck collection).

Photo op on UND campus, 1988 (photo: Ted Brien; Cathy Brubeck collection).

Those no longer with us: Johnny Mekoa, bigger than life, Afro-brassing it; Zim Ngqawana stolidly pursuing a point on his/our/the event horizon; Lulu Gontsana, a consuming firestorm of rhythmic passion; Melvin Peters, a quiet, eloquent genius; Kevin Gibson on an endless reserve of pristine melody-rhythm. Bra Vic 'what and whats' Masondo, the celebrated one who never allowed bitterness any foothold; Andrew Eagle, such a great synthesiser of folk and jazz, of lived reality and theoretical reflection; and neo-Bopper Rick van Heerden, who was always at least two notes ahead of where I wanted to be. All the boudoir Marxists and dharma bums of the University of Natal Music Department, 1984–88 and way beyond – Viva!

The jazz programme at UKZN became world-famous in the post-Jazzanian period, thanks in part to the American teachers who brought their creativity, expertise and personal dedication to the ideals of jazz education. For the first five years, I was *the* jazz guy on staff, responsible for everything from ensemble classes, where students learned how to play the changes to lecturing in music history, individual piano lessons, the

Flautist Stacey van Schalkwyk, saxophonist Janet Colepepper and pianist Connie van Heerden (photo: Ted Brien).

big band and more. I invited South African players to give workshops, but while these were inspirational for students, they were no substitute for weekly lessons, nor did I have a colleague with whom to share responsibility for the burgeoning jazz course. I really needed a sax teacher.

Saxology

In an undated letter, my mother, Iola said:

> I think Chris Merz and others who are in touch with your students are your best bet for a sax teacher. Obviously, you need to get young guys just out of school before they have the responsibility of family, and who are looking for a little adventure and a different way of life. That's how Stan Kenton and Woody Herman and all the bands organized their bands with young kids who were eager to play and were willing to put up with being 'on the road' in exchange for the experience. Either that, or an older guy who wants a different way of life and who wants to check out South Africa, but I doubt an older person would want to stay.

Dr Michael J. Rossi

Bill Prince introduced me to Mike Rossi during the Detroit conference as one of his star pupils, a recent graduate from Florida Atlantic University working on a Master's of Musical Arts degree at New England Conservatory of Music. Bill must have given him a positive account of what he had experienced in South Africa a year earlier because Mike was very eager to come. Cathy and I warned Mike that day-to-day teaching wouldn't be at the level he might expect at a university in the United States, to which he replied: 'I am a very compassionate person'. He had to be because he told me later in an email that 'weekly big band rehearsals were always a challenge in having enough brass players. The band sounded awful at the beginning but greatly improved throughout the year. I think that was one of my proudest moments, how they came together with very little skill.'

Hearing that Mike was taking tenor saxophone lessons with Jerry Bergonzi, who had been in the Darius Brubeck Ensemble in the 1970s and moved on to become a member of the Dave Brubeck Quartet in the 1980s, further convinced me that Cathy and I should work on getting him to Durban. Of course, I didn't remotely have the power to hire Mike by fiat, but applying for a grant at the United States Consulate and another starburst of right-place-right-time magic that seemed unfailing in those days resulted in Mike being invited as a USIS Cultural Grant-Specialist in Jazz for five months in 1989. His life-changing visit (for us and for him) was validated by his coming to Durban as my leave replacement. I did indeed have some leave due, but with Mike on board and the new Jazz Centre to establish, I stayed in Durban and we worked together. I was demonstrating that it took a minimum of two staff to maintain a flagship jazz programme. Sax players typically 'double' on other instruments in the saxophone family, often playing orchestral woodwinds too, such as flute and clarinet, so one teacher can teach several instruments. I knew that creating a completely *new* post wasn't going to be easy, but I was determined to make my case to the university.

Off-campus, it was great going out to the Rainbow or the Moon Hotel, where customers were literally awestruck by Mike's intense and daring improvisations. Having played with Bergonzi in my pre-South Africa days, I knew what the take-no-prisoners Boston 'Italian tenor' ethos was all about, but unsuspecting Durbanites had never encountered such prowess and swagger at a Sunday afternoon jazz gig. 'It sounds like he's trying to blow that horn straight,' exclaimed my sometime-drummer and great friend George Ellis. Audiences treated him like a rock star.

Musicians weren't the only ones impressed. During a break between sets at the Moon Hotel, Mike leaned across the table, lowering his voice to ask me if I knew

Natal University Jazz Ensemble conducted by Mike Rossi, UND campus, June 1989. Standing, from left: Thami Mtshali, Mpumulelo Thusi, Bheki Mbatha, Mark Kilian, Johnny Mekoa, Andrew Eagle, Sazi Dlamini, Mfana Mlambo, S'thembiso Ntuli, Susan Barry, Phil Harber. Middle, from left: Lex Futsane. Kneeling: Lulu Gontsana, Mike Rossi, Zim Ngqawana, Feya Faku (photo: Di Rossi).

that dark-haired woman sitting in the front row. I certainly did. She was active in the Durban Arts scene and MOJO that fund-raised and co-sponsored our annual fund-raising Jazz Jols. Her name was Di Vlotmann. It was she who introduced Cathy and me to Ben Pretorius just as the Rainbow was getting started. Di and Ben had been a couple in the past, but she was currently single. I introduced Mike to Di before we started the next set and an avid, sometimes histrionic courtship ensued. Within a few weeks Mike had proposed to Di in private, but re-proposed, again on bended knee, on a double date with me and Cathy. He was madly in love and stayed in Durban for as long as he could, so I was surprised when he turned down a firm job offer at the Music Department. He was determined to go all the way to Doctor of Musical Arts so, instead of taking the job, he went back to Boston with his South African bride. In 1995, Mike became the first recipient of the Doctor of Musical Arts degree in Jazz Studies from the prestigious New England Conservatory of Music.

In 1999, I was due for a sabbatical (now ten years after Mike's first visit), so I again applied to have him as my replacement for eleven months, this time funded by Fulbright, and I really did go away (to Nottingham University). The Rossis (now a family of four) stayed at our house in Manor Gardens while we were away, then the South African College of Music at UCT offered him a full-time position in 2000. Like Cathy and I, Mike and Di came as a couple to build a life together in South Africa. He retired from his post as professor in Jazz and Woodwinds in 2022. He and I have recorded CDs, co-written a book and performed together many times, sometimes with my brothers Chris and Dan, in South Africa, the United States, England, Germany and Italy.[7]

> 'Did you pack your bag yourself? Are you carrying anything for someone else?
> Are you carrying any weapons or sharp instruments?'
> 'Well, I've got my soprano sax here.'
> — Mike Rossi at an airport check-in counter

Mike directed the Natal University Jazz Ensemble the first time it provided music for a university graduation ceremony. This is a long and elaborate affair, requiring a large temporary stage and I thought it would be a good idea for us to go down to the Sports Centre and check out the set-up. There was enough space set aside for the band, but no chairs. When it came to large-scale operations of this kind, UND was systemically like most large organisations in South Africa. Black employees did the physical work under the supervision of an Indian staff member, who took orders from a white guy in a small office at Buildings and Grounds at the other end of campus, who was answerable to one of the deans. I guess that the person on site was explaining his inability to *personally* do anything about chairs when Mike's voice echoed through the vast hall, 'I don't care who you have to ask, we need fucking chairs!' The big band got chairs and a tradition of having the band at Humanities graduations was established. The film-maker Michiel ten Kleij told me that interviewing Mike was like meeting 'a character in a Martin Scorsese film'.

Thanks to the Rossis, UCT was an ally, rather than a rival, when it came to taking over the running of the South African Association of Jazz Educators (SAJE). With Mike and Di (who, like Cathy, excelled at organising events and conferences), this network of institutions, musicians and students became more active and capable than ever. The five of us (counting my assistant Glynis Malcom-Smith) had a shared sense of how things should work, which opportunities to pursue and what our guiding values had to be. Around the time of my retirement from UKZN in 2006, the centre of gravity in jazz education had shifted towards Cape Town, but because of a long history of co-operation and reciprocity, SAJE remains the international face of jazz education in South Africa.

Chris Merz

Chris Merz was a different kind of American, a Midwesterner; modest, quietly spoken, community-minded, churchgoing and slyly humorous. When he and his wife Jill arrived in 1991 in steaming Durban, they had just flown from Cedar Falls (Iowa) to Chicago, to New York City, to London, to Johannesburg and finally to Durban. He was wearing a suit and tie to make a good first impression. He certainly impressed and influenced many of the students, as former student Mfana Mlambo's high praise, during our interview in Durban in April 2018, makes clear:

> With every session I had with Chris Merz, I told myself afterwards that I wouldn't mind studying with him for the rest of my life . . . CJPM created a family . . . Cathy was holding it together . . . it was organised . . . the university jazz programme got the word out about music education . . . I graduated from the door [this refers to Mfana being the doorman at Kippies' jazz club in Johannesburg and hearing the Jazzanians there].

Chris Merz was the first full-time lecturer in the sax post. He replied to our advertisement because he and Zim Ngqawana had become friends at the University of Massachusetts. There were a few other candidates, but we were impressed by his audition tape and his recent Downbeat Award for Best Student Arranger and the selection committee felt he really wanted *this* job rather than just wanting *a* job. Chris played all the saxes and flute, but unlike Mike Rossi, his main instrument then was alto sax. He told me that he had started out as a drummer, but when he heard Paul Desmond on a Dave Brubeck Quartet recording, he switched to sax. Having grown up in Iowa,

Chris experienced the long twilight of the territorial big band tradition by going on the road with Russ Morgan and his Orchestra (by then led by Russ Morgan Junior). Later, as a student at the University of Massachusetts, he was taught by modernist and world-music-attuned mentors Yusef Lateef and Jeff Holmes. As part of my overall plan for developing the course, Chris took charge of the NUJE and we shared practical workshops and lectures. In his response to our questionnaire, dated 6 October 2017, he recalled one of his proudest moments:

> One of the greatest thrills of my life was taking part in the graduation ceremony at which Nelson Mandela received his honorary doctorate from the University of Natal. Darius and I played some duo tunes beforehand, and I conducted the jazz ensemble in the ceremonial music. Mandela gave a particularly stirring speech, after which he left the podium and walked within 10 feet of me. My brush with greatness . . .

Chris and I played together often in various 'straight-ahead' jazz groups and he knew hundreds of standards. As a young and gifted composer, player and teacher, he embraced the past as well as the future of jazz. He was a member of the NU Jazz Connection, our follow-up 'official' band after the Jazzanians, and was also featured in the latest version of Gathering Forces, my Indo-jazz fusion mini-orchestra in the 1990s, which was built around collaboration with Deepak Ram.

Replying to a questionnaire we sent to former staff, students and friends, Chris shared some observations about the jazz scene, as he experienced it, from 1990 to 1994:

> Things seemed well integrated by the time of my arrival. I never got the sense that there was any segregation at all. Most of the bands and all of the audiences I remember were integrated. I sensed more friction between musicians who played in the more pure township style vs those that sought to integrate an American concept into South African music. This friction seemed to only exist between black musicians. I never got the sense that black musicians didn't want me (for example) to integrate the South African sound into my playing and composing. But it seemed that some older, more traditional musicians frowned upon younger black musicians introducing American harmonic concepts into the local style. I heard this from Duke Makasi and Ezra Ngcukana in particular. Both had a very advanced harmonic palette and felt pressure from their peers to play in a more traditional style. Interestingly, I felt more criticism from the white community for the kind of music I was playing. It seemed to be perceived by some as both too derivative and not African enough. This puzzled me somewhat.

Chris had enough time in Durban to establish other musical partnerships; notably his quintet Counterculture with Feya Faku, Melvin Peters, Lex Futshane and Vince Pavitt (drums). They recorded the album *Art Gecko*. Counterculture's intentions, as stated in his liner notes are 'so different from anything else currently happening in South African jazz that Counterculture seems like an appropriate label'. The name of the album, *Art Gecko*, was funny because Durban was famous for its art deco buildings and also abundant in geckos. His liner notes further read: 'The mainstream post-bop groove is offset by the harmonic motion which is a departure from typical hierarchical structures. Movement between chords is regulated by coloristic concerns and varying degrees of tension.'[8]

'Ja. Well. No. Fine,' as they used to say in Durban. But Chris was not only there to pass on what he had learnt; he was ambitious and growing and he injected some new and lasting energy into the jazz course and the local jazz scene. I was surprised that he wanted to leave in 1994 when things were going well, but he just missed home and there were other personal pressures. He was well ensconced in his preferred life in the Midwest when I asked him to join me in Nantes (France) for another version of Gathering Forces in 1997 and we have always stayed in touch. He recently wrote:

> Looking at a Wikipedia article on South African jazz, I am delighted to see many of the students I worked with listed among the significant performers. These include Neil Gonsalves, Lex and Feya, Andile Yenana, and Concord Nkabinde. In so many ways, I learned how to teach while working with these students. I owe them, and Darius and Cathy Brubeck, a great debt.

Chris Merz has been the director of Jazz Studies at University of Northern Iowa since 2002.

Bryan Steele

Bryan Steele (1994) and Dustan (Dusty) Cox (1995–96) came and went in relatively quick succession. I remember Bryan telling me and Deepak at the Jazz Centre that he answered our job advert because Jerry Bergonzi showed it to him and said, 'Go work with Darius.'

'Yes, *guruji*,' Deepak said, folding his hands, acting the role of a disciple. That's not how it really works with academic musicians, but the connection with Jerry was reassuring. Bryan was good-looking and slim, a stylish dresser with shoulder-length black hair. He was a regular at our Wednesday late-afternoon sessions at the Jazz Centre. He perceptively called them 'over-the-hump parties', which is exactly what they were for a good many academic staff members, who queued up for Glynis's bar regardless of who was playing. Like Chris, Bryan soon became involved with interesting local musicians like the Indo-jazz group Mosaic and George Mari's band Error Nine. He played with me, of course, and made a guest appearance with Afro Cool Concept when we performed with the Natal Philharmonic Orchestra.

According to Bryan's website: 'The position [at UND] afforded him the chance to collaborate and be influenced by some of the country's best composers and musicians . . . the beginning of Steele's continuing love of African music'.[9]

Dusty Cox

Dustan Cox (he prefers Dusty) applied while he was a teaching assistant at University of Northern Colorado, one of the most famous jazz programmes at the time. He came with his wife Mitos, who was a highly trained singer and vocal coach. According to an old joke between jazz players, singers are 'people who like to hang out with musicians', implying that singers are *not* musicians. Dusty was an impressive, indeed multi-award-winning tenor man and composer, but Mitos (of whom I had no prior knowledge) also had a huge impact. Dusty was a very important teacher, band director and colleague. Mitos, who met Dusty while they were studying, was very definitely a fine musician and knew how to write for and direct a jazz choir. This was the beginning of the Natal University Voices ensemble that channelled groups like Manhattan Transfer. Mitos came along at just the right moment for Natalie Rungan, one of our best-ever student vocalists. Natalie took over NU Voices when the Coxes left, thus starting a succession that has kept NU Voices (now called UKZN Voices) going. After Natalie, it was directed by Debbie Mari, a lecturer in Jazz Studies, who is also an excellent singer and my former piano student. UKZN Voices has recently combined with the Pop Voice ensemble.

Dusty taught a few exceptionally good saxophone students, one of whom, Paul Kock, eventually became the sax teacher until he emigrated to Australia. Bernard Ayisa, another of Dusty's impressive students, is introducing jazz into schools in Ghana. According to a recent email, Dusty is still in touch with both of them, as well as other former students, but my impression was that he didn't have as easy a time as his predecessors. I had another period of leave in 1995, so he had a heavier than normal load for a few months. He was carrying a lot of student debt that was never going to be paid off, given the ever-declining foreign exchange value of the South African rand. His mother and sister needed support too. His father had been killed in Vietnam, leaving Dusty to grow up on army bases and low-rent housing in the Midwest and feeling he had to take care of his family as soon as he could. Bottom line, he had taken the job when circumstances were different, but now found he couldn't afford to stay in South Africa after all. I remember him explaining all this and apologising with sincere regret, concluding with, 'a man's gotta do what a man's gotta do'. It seems odd to me now that this hollow tautology seemed sufficient and final. It doesn't seem right

Dusty and Mitos Cox, CJPM, 1995 (photographer unknown; Cathy Brubeck collection).

NU Voices, CJPM, 1995 (photo: Ted Brien; Cathy Brubeck collection).

that someone whose father was killed on active duty had to pay for an education in the first place. On the other hand, his mother and sister needed him. I think he took a quick-buck job dealing cards at a casino while taking care of family responsibilities and then went back into music. I heard from him again when he landed a good job as a lecturer in jazz saxophone at the University of Adelaide, where he is now.

Having to find yet another sax teacher was a real setback for me. The process of advertising and filling posts was a grind of staff meetings, listening to audition tapes or videos and, at the final stage, a telephonic conference call with the selection committee and more meetings after that. This was an imposition on other people's time and a second jazz specialist would do precious little for them. Successful candidates didn't always accept the job, so we had to go through the whole process again. Meanwhile, my teaching load doubled, sax students were left treading water and relations with colleagues were strained ('Why is jazz so special? Are we going to have to go through this every two years?'). I understood why this wasn't a good situation for staff, but I simply had to have another instrument teacher and argued for this by citing student numbers and international fame and glory. American musicians did great things when they were in Durban and proved hard to replace locally. It was just too bad they

Ezra Ngcukana (middle) with a class on UND campus, 1997 (photographer unknown; Cathy Brubeck collection).

didn't stay. They had been to good schools, learned from great teachers, completed demanding curricula and, unlike many locals, were self-confident and adaptable. Yes, they hoped to prove themselves as artists too, but they didn't see teaching as a demeaning, temporary 'day gig'. In former times, most of our local students thought of themselves as potential stars, not teachers, but later as programmes expanded around the country, this changed and today, ex-students from UKZN and other institutions lead courses throughout South Africa.

American graduates viewed teaching as an elite but overpopulated field in the United States. They often desperately needed a first job *somewhere* and would go wherever there was one. I am pleased to say that working with us in a relatively small jazz outpost did give them greater visibility as teachers and performers. Our international tours and connections ensured this. However, most people aren't born to be ex-pats.

Ezra Ngcukana

The very special Ezra Ngcukana, who is described in more detail in Chapter 7, also taught for a semester while on leave from BP (British Petroleum). He introduced even more South African standards into the workshops and was a proponent of the modern, Eastern Cape, Coltrane-influenced style.

Jeff Robinson

Jeff Robinson (also American), who took over Music Education when Elizabeth (Betsy) Oehrle retired, was, fortunately for us, a very proficient saxophonist and instrument teacher, and he contributed greatly to the jazz programme, in addition to his real job in Music Education. Now retired from teaching, Jeff maintains a long-standing musical partnership with Melvin Peters and they regularly perform together, creating a lot of themed concerts.

Jeff also directed NUJE for periods when there was no official sax teacher. CJPM worked hard to bring in teacher-performers, who were funded through various exchange programmes and Jeff, who had developed a strong relationship with a consortium of Nordic universities, graciously shared his connections with us. They were interested in our jazz programme and South African music in general. At CJPM, we hosted a contingent of amazing Swedish conservatory students from Gothenburg University, who came to experience international fieldwork and they proved to be invaluable teachers.

Students came from Norway, the United States and Canada (and one from France) simply to join our courses. Their presence raised the general level and it is well known that jazz and sport have this in common: play with people who are better than you and you get better. Foreign students *always* had better early training and they were in Durban to gain experience. Our students, some of whom were still learning how to read music, were admired by the foreign students for their authenticity and passion. I think the strongest *educational* rationale for CJPM was and still is facilitating such connections and exchanges and this continues today under Neil Gonsalves. Saxophone is currently taught by another American, Salim Washington, who is a full professor on the permanent staff.

6

The Jazz Centre and Drinks at Five

Hello Central, Give me Doctor Jazz.
— Joseph 'King' Oliver (1885–1938)[1]

CJPM was an institution that created a scene –
maybe it should be the other way around.
— Mfana Mlambo

Catherine

The story of the Centre for Jazz and Popular Music begins in 1989 with many formal exchanges between Darius, the vice-chancellor, Professor Piet Booysen, and the deputy vice-chancellor, Chris Cresswell, about staff and student needs at a time when institutions, programmes and people had to confront extremely challenging political and economic realities. Personal leverage was a big factor because Gerrit Bon, newly appointed head of the South African College of Music at the University of Cape Town, wanted Darius to join him there and start a second Jazz Studies programme. Chris Ballantine and Darius had several meetings with Chris Cresswell, and Mike Morris (then a research fellow in the Development Studies Unit) advised Darius to make establishing a centre a condition of staying at the University of Natal. UND granted Darius's request for a dedicated jazz centre. A further very important special concession was normalising the presence of non-matriculants in jazz courses. This achievement in the development of the programme put us at the starting line of a broader process of institutional transformation.

The institution had acknowledged and advanced the study of South African jazz and its contribution to the local and international political and cultural arena. The crusade to develop a new model of learning had a healthy mix of humour, passion, problems and achievement, reflecting the improvisational aspects of the music itself. Professors Booysen and Cresswell, working with Professor Andrew Duminy and

The Jazz Centre and Drinks at Five   129

Professor Beverly Parker (now head of the Music Department) established guidelines for the new centre and an advisory committee. This committee included professors Duminy and Parker and Dr Michael Spencer of the History Department. Darius was appointed director and was now doing two jobs for the price of one. However, he was also promoted to the rank of associate professor.

The first advisory committee meeting estimated the cost of adapting and altering the accommodation in Shepstone Building. It was envisaged that once the CJPM was established, Darius – with the help of the Natal University Development Fund (NUDF) – would seek additional support from donors. Competing requests for help from NUDF meant that we were also encouraged to do our own fund-raising by the advisory committee. We were greatly helped by Bruno van Dyk, the executive director of the UKZN Foundation, who not only advised us, but also initiated performance projects overseas that would help us raise money. The university's point of view was that the Jazz Centre represented a changing climate in academe.

The university allocated a large, unused concrete space, home to feral cats, under the modern Shepstone building and over time paid for turning it into a performance venue with offices for Darius, me (as volunteer fund-raiser and project manager) and the only paid CJPM member of staff, Glynis Malcolm-Smith. Acoustic panelling was generously donated by Environmental Panelling Systems, but a further R50 000 was needed to cover the costs specified in our close friend Dennis Claude's acoustic design. (Dennis was a senior lecturer in the Faculty of Architecture.) Such was the enthusiasm for the Jazz Centre that some university staff (namely, Rodney Harber and James Trinder) went far beyond their official duties to ensure that we were ready to roll both aesthetically and legally. Rodney Harber, also of the Faculty of Architecture, designed and supervised the conversion of this derelict storage area into a public venue. James Trinder, who oversaw Campus Affairs, navigated the project through innumerable practical and administrative obstacles, including pacifying Muslim students who objected to the sale of alcohol near their proposed prayer facility in the same building. In response, Trinder organised the creation of a substantial place of prayer in the large parking lot across the road from us. In 1992, one of the peak jazz education years, the university allocated nearly R100 000 for improving the building. This remodelling included office space for visiting artists and a permanent base for the world-famous Joseph Shabalala, who was made a fellow of CJPM. (As the leader of Ladysmith Black Mambazo, Joseph was also trying to set up a Ladysmith Black Mambazo Academy in northern Natal.)

Glynis Malcolm-Smith was more than the ideal person for the job of administrative assistant and she was later promoted to programme administrator. When Darius and I interviewed her for the job, the Jazz Centre was no more than a little office at the bottom of the Shepstone building escalator. I told her that her job might involve illegal trips to African townships and described the unorthodox methods we were using to encourage and maintain student enrolment of all races. She replied, 'It simply makes no difference to me.' Her devout Catholicism translated into a humanitarian approach to all people and conflicts. Back then, Glynis was a widow raising two adolescent boys, which meant flexible hours were important to her and her availability on evenings and weekends was important to us. Subsequently, as her sons Gregory and Andrew left school, and did sterling work at the Jazz Centre as well, Glynis became CJPM's superpower, doing everything from complicated university administration to making sure there was sufficient toilet paper for our public events. I don't think Darius and I have ever come across a person so willing and capable and dedicated to the success of our many unusual activities. She was an attractive, blonde, bridge-playing suburbanite with an outgoing personality. Glynis had worked for Laurie Schlemmer at the esteemed and controversial Institute for Social Research and came with a network of campus friends who were administrators and secretaries for various deans. This was a huge plus because Darius and I were lost in this field and often needed to short-circuit the system. Wherever Glynis turned her attention, difficulties melted away because she knew how to access those that really mattered on campus.

Glynis recently wrote to me about her twenty-year journey with us, about the good and sad times and reminded me about our big band trip to the Carlton Hotel in Johannesburg and said that 'Zara and Phil Harber [in their early seventies] sat at the back holding hands, and that the middle of the bus had a detectable aroma of Durban poison [marijuana] wafting past. My introduction to JAZZ'. As our work relationship and friendship grew closer, we called her GMS because of her double-barrel name and the TV show GMSA ('Good Morning, South Africa'). GMS made friends easily with all kinds of people – from students to professors and delivery men to South African Breweries and Standard Bank executives. On the gig-getting and project-organising front, she replicated everything I did and was soon supervising large projects herself. The students loved her. Piwe Solomon (bass

Cathy and Glynis Malcolm-Smith selling CDs at a concert presented by Jazz at the Nassau, Cape Town, 8 December 2013 (photographer unknown; Cathy Brubeck collection).

player for the 1990s' student band Ba'gasane) told us recently that Glynis would be 'the first person you would tell if something bad happened and the first to help. She had that motherhood thing.'

With assistance from the university's Public Affairs Department, we had a grand opening in 1993, with representatives from South African Breweries, Environmental Panelling Systems, the Bartle Arts Trust, USIS, PG Glass and the Durban Arts Association, all of which had made important contributions in cash or kind. We had, by this time, engineered many activities and projects, but an official event gave us an opportunity to thank and recognise all the sponsors and patrons. We invited all the university top brass. The handing over of the pub was supervised by the South African Breweries community relations manager, Obed Mlaba, who later became mayor of Durban and then South African high commissioner in London. He was a good singer, giving a rendering of 'Stars Fell on Alabama' with one of Darius's many band formations. Sadly, like so many of our special ANC contacts, he left office under questionable circumstances.

So, Darius, Glynis and I ran a licensed club with a custom-made bar paid for by South African Breweries. We had to raise R5 000 for the liquor licence and obtained one in the name of Professor Piet Booysen, vice-chancellor and, now, licensee! Our relationship remained good with South African Breweries, who often donated raffle prizes and sponsored discounted drinks. In addition to producing and presenting special concerts, Darius later initiated regular Wednesday evening jazz sessions we called 'Trios Plus' where, over a drink, academics often mingled with colleagues from other departments and were able to invite their visiting lecturers and friends to share in the jazz ethos. By the mid-1990s, the Trios sessions were known for outstanding jazz performances by local and international groups. Music enthusiasts could relax and enjoy the vibe for a couple of hours and, with the original very low entrance fee of R3 and reasonably priced drinks, the crowds grew and grew. Showing up for 'drinks at five' was a popular social and cultural activity for both town and gown,

Cathy with Dave and Iola Brubeck in Monte Carlo for a Dave Brubeck concert, 1995 (photo: Darius Brubeck; Cathy Brubeck collection).

as was the annual fund-raising Jazz Jol (inaugurated in the mid-1980s), which moved to CJPM from its former primary venue, the Moon Hotel. Over the years, the Jazz Jols raised an enormous amount for the Ronnie Madonsela Scholarship.

Additional support

In 1987, Darius's parents donated a significant amount to the Ronnie Madonsela Scholarship, which had to be sent via the Urban Foundation in the United States, and this supported Johnny Mekoa, Beki Mbatha and Vusi Sabongo, who would have had to leave the university without this help.

Other major donors included the Hexagon Trust, the social responsibility arm of Union Carbide and, with the help of Reverend Peters (Melvin's father, who was on the board) and my former brother-in-law Mick Morphet, we received R25 000 for two years running. Many individuals generously supported our programmes and these included the musician Carol Ann Weaver, who both fund-raised in Canada and donated her earnings from a recording she made. A Canadian sax student even sent money for music stands long after she had left Durban.

Additional operations

We were inundated with requests from national and, very soon, international musicians to perform at our venue. Student bands now had a fully equipped rehearsal and showcase space. Furthermore, as was the intention, jazz colleagues could pursue their own artistic goals, along with creating and teaching ensembles. With only a small administrative budget from the university, we had to make ends meet by earning income from our own productions, venue hire and commissions on booking bands. Glynis and I became managers and agents, known for our ability to take student and professional bands around the world. For example, we took five staff/student bands to international jazz education conferences in the United States. In 2000, Glynis took UND and UCT student brass players to Australia to participate in the huge band at the Opening Ceremony for the Olympics. Brian Thusi helped to train our UND trumpet players for this prestigious event.

We also organised various university bands, playing American and South African jazz for performances worldwide – from Turkey to Peru.

The uses of the CJPM were many and increased on almost a daily basis. There was time and space for regular Music Department teaching, course ensembles such as NU Voices and student and professional band rehearsals, meetings and functions and, on Saturdays, the free music school (UKUSA) organised by Betsy Oehrle, a long-serving innovative and distinguished Music Department education specialist. Her enormous and successful undertaking was funded by the Swedish International Development Cooperation Agency (SIDA).

Glynis raising the South African flag at the Olympics in Sydney, September 2000 (photographer unknown; Glynis Malcom-Smith collection).

The Jazz Centre became a favourite launch pad for music festivals and even companies that wanted to put on promotional events. We hosted and arranged entertainment and catering for departmental gatherings, weddings, recordings and fund-raisers, including events for trade unions and the ANC. Anne Pretorius (piano teacher and columnist) and I formed a do-everything kind of events company called Catalysts (we both like cats) and produced a couple of successful quasi-political conferences before she moved to Cape Town. Her marriage in 1994 to Alec Erwin was a joyous happening at the Jazz Centre, among other subsequent highlights, like the ball to celebrate Nelson Mandela's inauguration.

The more popular and patronised our regular Trios Plus sessions became, with attendance sometimes well over 300 people, the more we were able to improve facilities, create a proper stage and improve the sound system. This meant a higher profile and a huge increase in concerts and workshops by famous musicians. The number and variety of workshops included everything from how to write a biographical note and press release to instrument master classes. Foreign consulates and diplomatic missions wanting to fly their flags often sponsored projects and visitors. Here we were, in a relatively unknown part of the jazz world, benefiting from the crème de la crème. The CJPM became a springboard and resource for other ventures nationally, as we were identified with what Durban itself had to offer. It was listed in the *Rough Guide to South Africa*, popular national magazines and Durban's own diary of tourism highlights. It was now part of the character and image of the city just as the Jazz and Heritage Foundation in New Orleans keeps that city's distinguished past and present in focus.

Inaugural Ball band, CJPM, 10 May 1994. From left: Darius, George Mari, Chris Merz, Lex Futshane, George Ellis (photo: Cathy Brubeck; Cathy Brubeck collection).

After lots of correspondence, advisory committee meetings and consultation with NUDF, it was evident that businesses and individuals were unlikely to come in with further large gifts so the 'trio', as we (Darius, Glynis, and me) were known, became minor impresarios. The university continued to pay for the phone, utilities and building repairs and the rest was up to us. We were 'officially' part of the Music Department, but had the discretionary power to raise and distribute our own budget. In providing a community service, the Jazz Centre emphasised that jazz staff were both teachers and creative artists. This legacy continues. The Centre's thriving outreach programme was in keeping with the university's mission statement and we entered into significant musical and profitable partnerships – for example, we established relationships with many foreign embassies, in particular, the United States Consulate in Durban, as well as the South African government. The American Cultural Center hired our bands for their functions, helped facilitate Fulbright visitors and supported students who won Fulbright scholarships to study in the United States. We worked with successive ambassadors, cultural attachés and consul generals and this steady relationship often led to their funding guest teachers for the jazz course. Pamela Bridgewater, Liam Humphreys and Craig Kuehl were tremendously co-operative and full of ideas for us.

One of the temporary educators was Professor Larry Ridley of Rutgers University. The terms of the agreement were generous, with the Music Department contributing only a small portion towards the costs. CJPM structured the teaching programme, arranged performances and paid for local transportation. Professor Ridley taught bass students, gave special ensemble workshops and participated with staff in regularly scheduled classes and rehearsals. These visitors gave university lunch-hour concerts and played at the Rainbow with staff and students. In Ridley's case, he also appeared with South African guitar great Bheki Khoza. Memorable contributions were also made by Tom Smith (trombone), Butch Miles (drums) and Richard Syracuse (bass). Written reports were required by USIS as well as curriculum evaluations in accordance with the provisions of their contracts. These evaluations proved very helpful and kept our Jazz Studies course on the map. Tom Smith directed the big band and took part in SAJE performances as well. After we left UKZN, he recommended Darius for a Fulbright grant to teach in Romania (2010) and we overlapped, as he was about to return to the United States.

In the early years, we wanted and needed to justify our special status and dispensation, and this meant ensuring there were enough students studying jazz. We cared for their welfare and actively found housing, instruments and gigs and worked hard to break even. Distributing and sharing resources was a week-by-week response to individual circumstances. There were no precedents for this total involvement; an

Reception on 4 July 2001 at the residence of the United States consul general. From left: Darius, Jane Lucas, Craig Kuehl (consul general), Cathy, Glynis Malcolm-Smith, Liam Humphreys (photographer unknown; Cathy Brubeck collection).

academic department is not structured for this purpose, so we really made the most of our discretionary liberty, which was sometimes viewed with raised eyebrows from conservative academics. The advisory committee recognised that jazz student musicians' needs were immediate and often expensive, so Glynis Malcolm-Smith was allowed to keep a petty cash fund that could immediately pay for things like a bus fare from the township or guitar strings. Dealing with university red tape and long waits just didn't work for our multitasking centre. Employment for jazz students increased on and off campus, with more bands hired, and touring (domestic and international) became more frequent. The Jazz Centre, which had been an innovation by the University of Natal, is still unique in the world of jazz education.

Most entrepreneurship was extracurricular and placed more responsibility on the three of us. Glynis and I worked together daily and all of us did everything from physically moving chairs to moving the mountains of ideas that we drummed up at our regular brainstorming sessions. When income from a project was significant, I was paid a fee, but generally I was the unpaid fund-raiser, promoter, organiser and manager. Glynis, who also put in many unpaid hours, and Darius and I practically lived at the CJPM. We had begun ordering sweets in addition to the usual bar supply of potato chips and nuts, but soon abandoned this as the three of us ate all the stock and had to pay for numerous packets of fruit gums and chocolate bars instead of taking proper meal breaks. The rewards were many, however, and, as managers, chaperones and organisers, our experiences ranged from workshops in Maputo's dilapidated, bullet-holed and grubby buildings to high-grade sponsored hotels in New York City.

We visited unusual places, had adventures and fun in the company of highly amusing and talented people and, of course, there was always the music and the field experience for the students. Profits from the bar enabled us to enlist student help in exchange for free concert tickets, meals and often a small wage. Students also became effective leaders, sound engineers and bartenders, and this was usually funded event by event. Pianist John Edwards, who is currently a lecturer in Jazz at Nelson Mandela University, Gqeberha (formerly Port Elizabeth), and was a jazz student from 1998 to 2004, told us in an email response to our questionnaire on 6 May 2019:

> I tailored my bands to suit the gig and provided regular and occasional work for several musicians . . . including Philani Ngidi, Grant Emmerich, Daniel Wilson, Wesley Gibbens, Duane Nichol, Paul Kock, Bongani Sokhela and Debbie Mari . . . Some venues (Zacks especially) became so successful that more sessions featured additional jazz bands . . . led by Gerald Sloane, Evan Roberts, George Mari and a whole host of other sidemen were added. Soon we were all on rotation. It took quite a lot of negotiating to get the restaurants to pay us a reasonable wage, but such is the lot of gigging musos everywhere.

I played a part in how jazz became a standard feature at several trendy bars and restaurants in Durban in the early 2000s. This was something of a double-edged sword . . . 'Cafe jazz' was the descriptor we were given by some, something of a pejorative because the implication was that we only played a background type of jazz for the chattering classes in wealthy Durban suburbs and were not part of the real scene, which was apparently elsewhere. (For the record, we were in other places too, at Trios and at the Hilton 'serious' jazz sessions on Thursdays.) But those other gigs taught a lot of us plenty in real-world gigging experience. We all became better players and better friends – and, yes, I guess we played 'Girl from Ipanema' often, but hey, we also played 'Angola' by Bheki Mseleku and some original compositions too – I always tell my students, don't knock 'Girl from Ipanema' if you can't hold down that bossa nova groove (it takes a special kind of musical maturity in my view) . . .

Many of the Jazz Centre's high-profile projects involved the participation of Darius, as the director, as well as nationally known musicians, but the day-to-day work remained the creation and co-ordination of gigs for students and local musicians. This led to

John Edwards, Nelson Mandela University in what was then Port Elizabeth, 2013 (photo: Leonette Bower).

an informal advisory role, giving help to township-based youth, club owners, festival organisers and all those hoping to study jazz. All this activity on the part of staff and students simultaneously built the image of the Jazz Centre and expanded its operations and impact.

John Edwards further told us that studying jazz changed his life:

> The weekly Trios live jazz programme was an excellent initiative that provided a venue – and a community (bridge between university and the public) – also something to aspire to. Excellent professional training – you had to be on top of your game to play at Trios! Standards were high (pun intended)! Along with the diploma programme at the Tech (which was largely staffed by UKZN graduates), the university jazz programme was pretty much the core of the jazz scene in Durban . . . It played a role in promoting (and furthering) the South African jazz sound/s of the time/s (there was a significant political dimension to this in the earlier years, especially the 1980s/90s – South African jazz was a uniting force against apartheid) – so many young jazz musos (both established and aspirant) came from all around the country to study jazz at UKZN, which also meant that there was a wonderful melting pot of different South African jazz variants in Durban. So much in the way of new local jazz sounds grew from this.

Most days CJPM was abuzz with aspirant jazz students auditioning, jamming or just hanging out. In jazz education, as in performance, jazz musicians, whether professionals or students, learn from each other and this reciprocity was a huge factor along the road to achieving, in university terminology, 'centre of excellence' status.

Joining international jazz education organisations was an important move. Annual conferences of such organisations as IAJE, then later JEN (Jazz Education Network) and our own creation, SAJE, all featured top jazz artists from around the world. Certainly, the Brubeck name helped to open doors, but our success was also due to the consistently high quality of student performers. In 1992, the launch of a South African chapter of the IAJE was co-hosted by CJPM and the University of the Witwatersrand's School of Music and underwritten by SAMRO.

The 'trio' started organising biannual conferences around pertinent themes, built up a national membership and benefited from IAJE, the parent organisation. This activity was aided by SAJE committee members over the years and they facilitated conferences in Pretoria, Grahamstown and Cape Town. In 2007 the headquarters moved to Cape Town and Di and Mike Rossi took SAJE to even further heights by entering the web world and introducing a festival in off-years in addition to the conferences. Helped by elected committees, they created great exchange opportunities for students and teachers and ensured a positive and lasting influence on music education in South Africa.

With Music Department co-operation, we also supported teaching by South African musicians and this encouraged further community involvement. We approached local Durban jazz stars and high-profile musicians to spend time at the Jazz Centre and one of these was Hugh Masekela. He had always told us that he would love to do some teaching, so in August 1992 he came, and his work focused on the aural tradition of the township jazz bands of his youth. A student ensemble, led by Masekela, gave a concert to demonstrate the roots of South African jazz, which was overwhelmingly successful. Sadly, for us, the lure of the road overwhelmed his desire to stay full-time in Durban, although we were seriously talking about this possibility. CJPM's role in facilitating these visits was exactly the kind of contribution to student experience envisaged when it was established and these residencies worked well for both short periods and longer ones.

Over the years there was a significant increase in the number of overseas visitors performing in the Wednesday Trios sessions and at special concerts. Overseas visitors continued to be externally sponsored, but also involved costs that CJPM was obliged to cover and did. In many cases, we paid workshop fees, master class fees, for accommodation, catering, hospitality, publicity and local transportation, which included airport pick-ups and departures. A glance at the highlights listed in Appendix 2 shows the Jazz Centre as a global hub.[2]

More about money

Funds to run and develop the Jazz Centre itself were also needed because the university intended it to reach some degree of financial independence – unrealistic without an endowment. Operating CJPM as a club and venue for hire brought in revenue, but we were part of a university, not a commercial enterprise. Given this limitation, it is astonishing to recall what we did – and got away with. The current situation is more rule-bound, but CJPM still presents cutting-edge bands and high-level musicians. The directors and staff that succeeded us have not had the freedom we had – or a 'ghost worker', an unpaid, do-everything worker like myself!

As we grew in status and professionalism, we wrote more sophisticated letters, accompanied by elaborate motivations and lists of achievements. Enrolment had gone from 3 students in 1983 to 35 jazz majors in 1993 and we measured our success by the fact that some students had upgraded from diplomas to full degrees. Jazz students were among the most visible on campus. In 1993, nine bands included student performers. We encouraged students to raise money themselves by playing gigs, working at CJPM and other locations during vacations, as well as applying for bursaries. Centre support made students and guarantors less nervous about loan applications in the critical early months of the academic year. Once the students were in the system, life became easier. The active and supervisory role of CJPM had made it so, although not without drawing criticism from others over our 'spoon-feeding' system. Glynis carefully banked and distributed the money raised and became an angel figure to many, taking care of needs that ranged from instrument repair to new shoes. In the motivation document,[3] we were aiming to raise R126 880, which was the shortfall on R357 540, the amount needed for 25 students. Loans had already been taken out for R125 446 of this amount.

In the 1990s jazz students were the biggest cohort in the Music Department and got used to the concept of loans because we helped with negotiating these and with finding guarantors, where required. However, we still needed large donations to make sure new recruits could enrol and we also needed to support the returnees. The Jazz Centre continued its fund-raising role for students who didn't qualify for loans – a personal and unique endeavour, which meant we were still operating on an intimate Ma and Pa and Aunt Glynis configuration. The upside was a stable student population and the downside was the worry that inevitably we couldn't help everyone and the three of us were on overload.

In the bigger South African picture, ongoing protests by student organisations and others ensured a new Bill before Parliament that would widen the scope of student loans. Karen MacGregor (journalist with the *Times Higher Education Supplement*), writing in the *Mercury* on 14 March 1993, says:

> A major cause of South African student unrest – the inability of black students to afford a university education – is to be tackled by the government this parliamentary session and while loan schemes could be established privately, it is likely that a truly national student loan scheme will flow from this.

This did eventually happen. Our own dropout rate for reasons other than those financial was practically nil, which was excellent in a climate where the university accepted that approximately one-third of all registered students would not complete degrees. In 1993, which is almost the mid-point of our Natal University life, we had sixteen students registered for a degree and nineteen for diplomas, as well as four Master's students.

What are the lessons here? Paddle your own canoe? We set up a whole flotilla of passbook accounts. Glynis oversaw the following: a Jazz Outreach account (for musician and community needs), a Gathering Forces account (for off-campus band performances), a CJPM operating account, into which the substantial bar profits went, a Ronnie Madonsela Scholarship account and a NUJE account (specifically for the big band). Profits after paying musicians and gig expenses were reinvested in further gigs and used for CJPM improvements. Glynis was also, for a long time, the treasurer of SAJE and in charge of an independent SAJE account, which held membership dues and money specifically raised for SAJE expenses. These funds helped students attend the organisation's conferences.

Our relative financial independence worked and, in a small way, reduced the financial burden on the university. In so many ways we grabbed that liberal moment in time and, it was, as far I know, a one-off in academe. Obviously not many departments or centres within a university are able to run such a flexible operation or take responsibility for students individually. Tacitly, the university retreated from requiring total self-sufficiency as both Glynis's salary and an annual operating budget of R9 000 were covered centrally. In reputational terms, the university was getting a lot from hosting the CJPM. It seemed things couldn't get better than this. We had a good relationship with the IAJE, having presented both the Jazzanians and the NU Jazz Connection bands at their international conferences based in the United States. In turn, IAJE launched the Music Relief Campaign to provide instruments and printed music to schools offering jazz instruction throughout South Africa. The IAJE's president (Dennis Tini) visited schools in townships and was quoted in the *Jazz Educators Journal*: 'They have scores of dedicated teachers but no resources to

Two IAJE presidents, Ron McCurdy and Dennis Tini, outside CJPM, December 2000 (photo: Cathy Brubeck; Cathy Brubeck collection).

work with.' This immediately led to two drum kits being donated by the famous American drummer Ed Shaughnessy and further donations of music books from Jamey Aebersold, who had already donated music and CD playback equipment valued at several thousand dollars. With the help of USIS, the CJPM distributed these gifts and kept the more advanced music books for University of Natal jazz students.

We actively nurtured exchange opportunities with the United States, Scandinavia and Europe and students from these areas were partially our responsibility. One example of a literally far-flung exchange was that two of our jazz students were accepted as part of an inter-university agreement with Edith Cowan University in Perth, Australia. There were many of these productive exchanges that led to lasting connections and CJPM continued to receive donations of instruments, scores and books for our use or redistribution. Sometimes our students were recipients of instruments they couldn't dream of buying themselves.

The tradition of international co-operation continues under Neil Gonsalves's directorship and a spectacular example of this is the project with Virginia Commonwealth University. Neil's liner notes for the collaborative CD *Leap of Faith* with the VCU Africa Combo, directed by Professor Antonio Garcia, and the UKZN Jazz Legacy Ensemble, directed by Neil, point out 'our common Southern heritage of migration from serfdom to global citizenry'.[4] This was the basis for an easy understanding between the musicians involved. The project had many strands, jointly managed by Neil and Antonio, including obtaining grants in the United States, vital co-operation from both universities, commissioning new works, visits to Richmond, Virginia, by South African students and students from the United States visiting the Jazz Centre. As we all know by now, the music is the easy part.

During the 2000s, the university eventually reviewed all the centres on campus and took over most of CJPM's accounts. This reduced the administrative burden, along with some independence. I should point out, however, that we had been regularly audited and our activities were approved by the advisory committee. We remain hugely indebted to the chairs of the advisory committee, the deans of Humanities, Professor Andrew Duminy and his successor Professor Michael Chapman, for their tolerance, imagination and the long view they each took. The lasting effect was to establish the Jazz Centre as a unique and innovative entity on campus. To summarise, CJPM significantly supported individual students, which made the jazz course sustainable. It also provided space, a base (and sometimes even a bass) for students, and further supported staff, local musicians and the community, so that the Durban jazz scene continued to flourish. In our interview at the Market Theatre in Johannesburg in April 2019, Lex Futshane said that CJPM 'gave all the students a platform to experience the real world of being a musician, from forming a band to performing and composing music and playing for a paying audience'.[5]

Archives

CJPM became a repository of valuable documents, photographs, sound recordings and videotapes accumulated from the early 1980s onwards. These artifacts pertain both to our own history in South Africa as well as general jazz history and the development of jazz education. This archival material has been divided between the university's own archive in Pietermaritzburg, which includes internal university correspondence and documents, and DOMUS, Stellenbosch University. The latter holds the Darius and Catherine Brubeck personal archive, which contains many photos, newspaper clippings and various performance memorabilia. Dr Lizabé Lambrechts is managing our archives and other South African collections. Long after Darius, Glynis and I left CJPM, we successfully motivated for the university to hire Glynis to organise and rationalise the vast amount of material housed in CJPM. After all, there are wider interests than merely creating a chronological record of CJPM and jazz in the School of Music. The evolution of the jazz course during the 1980s and early 1990s was positively a precursor of transformational change; it brought in black students from around the country who would ordinarily have never gone to university.

Darius

Although it was colloquially known as the Jazz Centre, I wanted to make good on the full name we had chosen, the Centre for Jazz *and Popular Music*. Popular music did not mean pop, but rather music with community roots that wasn't supported academically. Ladysmith Black Mambazo, for example, was popular in every sense of the word and Joseph Shabalala (28 August 1940 – 11 February 2020), the leader, having an office at CJPM added to our prestige. He had approached the Music Department for help in establishing a Ladysmith Black Mambazo Academy in northern Natal and we had known each other for several years. Dynamic and bossy on stage with his group, he was soft-spoken and smiling in person. One could just tell that these were, as the Paul Simon song goes, 'the days of miracles and wonder' for him,[6] and understandably so. He was only officially appointed a fellow of CJPM in 1993 because he had been on the road so much in the years following Paul Simon's 1986 landmark hit album *Graceland*, which included their haunting, collaboratively composed hit 'Homeless'.

Ladysmith Black Mambazo was on the bill in 1990 at the New Orleans Jazz and Heritage Festival when Afro Cool Concept with Barney Rachabane and Lulu Gontsana played there, and Afro Cool was the opening act for Paul Simon when he came to Durban in 1992 on the Born at the Right Time tour. Joseph's brother, Headman, was shot dead in December 1991 by a white off-duty security guard and a tribute concert to raise money for Headman's family had been organised at the Playhouse for the day after the King's Park Stadium outdoor extravaganza. In order not to be inundated by fans who couldn't get tickets, the fund-raiser was a performance without Paul Simon, but all the jazz musicians who were in the show the previous day took part. World-famous tenor sax icon Michael Brecker joined our quartet on stage and when our set was over, he told me he had enjoyed it and I said, 'We should definitely make a point of getting together every twenty years'. (Michael had been on my first album, *Chaplin's Back*, which was a very early recording for him at the beginning of the 1970s.[7])

In 1994, Joseph and I collaborated on what is remembered as a significant concert of that period. Roots & Branches was held on the Durban campus at the Howard College Theatre, but it was broadcast nationally on SABC because Joseph was a major star. The line-up featured bassist Sipho Gumede, then an international artist and producer (leader of Peace at the campus concert the police broke up ten years earlier), and Sazi Dlamini (now lecturer in Music at UKZN). They both contributed different styles of Zulu music. Chris Merz, Geoff Tracey and Lulu Gontsana also participated in this exuberant mash-up of traditional and modern styles. We even closed the show with Shabalala's version of a James Brown yell at the end of 'I Feel Good'.

During the years that followed, members of Ladysmith Black Mambazo came around to do administrative work at the office from time to time and did some coaching of students who wanted to know more about their distinctive vocal style.

Roots & Branches, rehearsal at CJPM, April 1994. From left: Sazi Dlamini, Sipho Gumede, Darius, Joseph Shabalala (photo: Ted Brien; Cathy Brubeck collection).

They sometimes stayed for our shows but, for them, it was a different musical universe, a different vibe. Having an office and even a de facto assistant (Glynis) didn't result in our seeing Joseph very often, but when he was there, he breathed a kind of spiritual softness into the atmosphere.

Not long after the official opening of CJPM, the famous poet, dramatist, songwriter, painter and Afrikaner dissident Breyten Breytenbach attended one of the regular Wednesday evening jazz sessions. By this time, we had a baby grand piano and table seating like a real jazz club. We had deliberately kept the entrance charge very low and this drew a wide audience. Natalie Rungan, now a well-known professional with many recordings, was singing and as usual the accompanying musicians were advanced jazz students – black, white and Indian. The place was packed and the bar was doing a brisk trade.

Natalie Rungan, 2019 (photo: Val Adamson).

CJPM had a reputation for being a hip and happening place and the joyous atmosphere in the room was generated by both the music and the very mixed crowd. Breytenbach, who spent nine years in prison for his anti-apartheid activities, was deeply moved and exclaimed, 'It is amazing to think of the immense effort my people put into preventing Paradise'. This echoes a similar point in a letter that Victor Ntoni and I wrote to the United States ambassador Herman Nichol on 25 October 1985: 'Jazz will not solve South Africa's problems, but it offers a model of what South African life might look like without them'.

7

Some Remarkable People

Catherine

We went to South Africa for two years and stayed nearly a quarter of a century, meeting some of the most remarkable people one could ever hope to encounter in a lifetime. As a low-grade civil war raged, and South Africa was increasingly associated with political and personal danger, we often debated whether to stay or to go. Letters from Dave and Iola Brubeck contained attractive pleas for us to return. Refusing these didn't have anything to do with bravery because it was the music and the musicians that held us; the feeling that we could make a small difference, that jazz mattered and we could orchestrate some changes. We were very fortunate to have this chance and grateful for the lessons we learned about resistance and one of its resilient relatives, humour. Did the political climate make everything more remarkable or was the music good regardless? I think we have decided that the answer is both.

Allen Kwela and Sandile Shange

Allen Kwela (born in 1939) and Sandile Shange (born in 1944) were two jazz guitarists who, for us, are forever linked in music, life and death. Darius and Afro Cool Concept's *Still on My Mind* was Allen's last recording and two of Sandy's songs were also recorded in 2003, the year they both died, on Darius's album, titled ironically *Before It's Too Late*.[1] Their style of music was as different as their personalities, but one thing was common to both, exceptional talent.

Darius and I wrote a tribute to Sandile and Allen, which was published in the *City Press* newspaper on 12 December 2003. I am expanding on that tribute here, as we hope they will never disappear from the chronicles of South African jazz.

Much of Sandile's existence illustrated the many ways that apartheid distorted the flow of his life. His surname was not really Shange and nor was he a blood brother to the other Shanges, Claude (piano), Cyril (tenor sax) and Boise (drums). Musical kinship aside, he felt that he needed a local name to remain in Durban. It's difficult to recall the exact chain of events, but we were soon very much together as friends and

146

colleagues. Darius and Sandy started playing as a duo, then expanded into the Darius Brubeck Quintet, which included Marc Duby on bass, Nelson Magwaza on drums and, soon after, a very young Kevin Gibson replaced Nelson. (This group also backed Allen in some Durban appearances and on his still relatively unknown recording *The Unknown*.[2])

Sandile's songs became core material for the Darius Brubeck Quintet and he began rebuilding a career in his own right, often playing solo. Everyone who came to Durban wanted to use Sandy; stars like vocalist Busi Mhlongo and saxophonist Winston Mankunku. Sandy never had hits like Pat Matshikiza's 'Tshona!' or Mankunku's 'Yakhal' Inkomo',[3] but South African fans recognised and responded to numbers like his 'Ndabazita'. Its introduction is similar to neo-traditional *maskandi* guitar, an out-of-tempo 'tease' building up to the dignity of an imaginary royal march. The composition worked as jazz when the quintet played it. Combinations of the same basic group, which sometimes featured other musicians such as Johnny Mekoa, appeared under various band names, including the Brubeck/Shange Jazz Coalition, and this close association continued into the early 1990s when Sandy left to join Mbongeni Ngema's large stage productions. Ngema's musicals emphasised African popular music more than jazz or even Sandy's own signature South African jazz.

Allen Kwela, Bols Jazz Festival, Mofolo Park, Johannesburg, 1984 (photo: Cedric Nunn).

Darius and Sandy played quite often with Judy Joubert, a very good jazz vocalist who now lives in Thailand. This combination was quite in demand, although we saw the funny side of Judy belting out the words 'Hates California, it's cold and it's damp and that's why the lady is a tramp' for sunny South African audiences. The trio was billed as As Time Goes By and featured Judy's arrangements, reflecting her own anxious jazz journey from an award-winning teenage performer, and Sandile's 'I'm not in a hurry' attitude to most things, including recording. Judy eventually decided to try her luck in cold and damp England and supposedly, on her way to London, we ended up doing quite a few farewell concerts (Durban, Pinetown, Pietermaritzburg). I asked Darius if she was driving to England! Judy and Sandile had a special rapport and he was always up for her gigs, unlike the time he showed up at the Rainbow without his guitar and asked Ben Pretorius whether he could find it or another one. Ben firmly replied, 'Sandile, you are the guitar player, not me.'

Sandy composed and played the loveliest lyrical ballads, probably because these work so well for solo guitar. In the tribute published by *City Press* newspaper on 12 December 2003, Darius wrote:

> He instinctively found the inner connections between chords, creating threads of melody on the lower strings that sounded like a second guitar playing along

Sandile Shange, JPS Jazz Festival, BAT Centre, Durban, 1996 (photo: Rafs Mayet).

. . . the way he worked his choruses up into chord solos was amazing, as good as Wes Montgomery, one of the most influential American jazz guitarists, whom Sandy personally revered. The more you know about guitar playing, the more mysterious and impressive Sandile's quiet mastery seems.

Sandy made a significant contribution to student guitar playing and the general music scene, but whether he was in our home ironing his clothes in the most perfect way I have ever seen, discussing his efforts to sell Portuguese-made shoes in the township or revealing all he had learnt about Paraguay (from some obscure movie), his presence was always a lesson in beating the system and living on very little. The shoe-selling enterprise consisted of buying shoes wholesale in Johannesburg and reselling them as high-class, imported fashion items in the township. In those early years, he was family and I was so very touched when he asked to come with us to my mother's funeral in 1986.

Darius

Sandy loved playing standards, particularly tunes like 'My Foolish Heart'. The late George Nisbet, a Durban *Daily News* music critic, reviewing yet another trio format, this time with Marc Duby, said:

> The trio has two personalities; one fully equipped for jazz improvisation, the other dedicated to turning precious oldies into icily charming, immaculate clever performances . . . Sandile Shange supplied the opportunity for the trio to open up a bit and get their teeth into his 12-bar blues called 'Blues for Nuts', he fairly lit up the Hermit with his stylishly crafted solos.[4]

Allen Kwela's lifelong idol was the American West Coast guitarist Barney Kessel. Kessel was noted for harmonic logic, clarity of form and execution and swinging fluency. Kessel and Kwela were both originally country folk, a background that seems to endow guitar players with an appealing naturalness. Like Kessel, self-taught from Oklahoma, the deep essence of Kwela's playing was from his own background, originally the coast south of Durban. The *kwela* music craze in the 1950s provided some fortuitous hype for the reputation of a young guitarist coincidentally named Kwela, but it was really his dedication to the rigours of jazz and association with other modernists, like pianist and composer Gideon Nxumalo, that took him to Johannesburg.[5]

By 1983, the year we came to South Africa, Allen was an established performer with international experience, which was a major achievement given the political climate. Musically, he projected himself as a proud voice from the past, rather than the next big thing. He held to his chosen musical ground ('It takes years of work to develop real jazz phrasing,' he often reminded me) and said that he would keep at it until the rest of the world realised how good he was. He was very good, able to spin out long, horn-like lines and could relax at tempos that most musicians find challenging. As far back as the 1980s he seemed to be caught in a musical time warp, insufficiently rewarded when his kind of music *was* 'hot' and progressive.

Barely surviving in South Africa due to circumstances musicians and their close associates understand all too well, Allen was nevertheless a local star, at least an established 'name' with a repertoire of American standards and original African jazz compositions that brought in meagre but dependable royalty cheques. Reluctance to chase trends might have cost him along the way, but his integrity eventually brought him respect, tours and festival appearances and the relative stability he enjoyed in later years. His self-destructive drinking and histrionics were tamed by age and perhaps by an inner realisation that he really couldn't keep it up much longer. When we called him to do what turned out to be his last recording, we knew what we were getting and we were delighted when it turned out exactly right. Even the brief ritual argument over payment – he always claimed he *deserved* more – was pure Allen. We would sometimes regret having him on a gig, but with a few deliberately provocative and evocative chords he would make us forget the emotional strain.

Cathy and Sandile in Montreux, July 1987 (photo: Darius Brubeck; Cathy Brubeck collection).

Sandile, by contrast, was consistently on form and our association with him began on a very different footing. Sandy was the darling of a small coterie of (mostly part-time and white) Durban jazz musicians whose gigs were barely more than semi-organised Sunday sessions at a couple of venues in town. Willie Ellison, a well-known local bass player, told us that a group of white musicians that included one of South Africa's most gifted guitarists, Johnny Fourie, had tried to send him overseas because he was such an original jazz player, but Sandy didn't or couldn't embrace this opportunity. A near-fatal motorbike accident had interrupted his career and we perceived long-lasting effects on his ability to get organised. A combination of effects, which included a permanent diffidence and his own fluctuating attention, held him back. He could be very forgetful – song titles, arrangements and even the names of his seven children would sometimes elude him. Procrastination ruled Sandy's life and despite sporadic lobbying of promoters and record producers, he was always waiting for the right moment or the right band. Off the scene, as a regularly working musician for years, he supported his large family doing deliveries for a chemist who admired his guitar playing. As soon as we heard him (in 1983), I knew I wanted to play with him. In turn, he was stimulated and encouraged by access to some organisation (Cathy's) and creative collaboration with our band members. As related in Chapter 4, in 1987 Sandile came with us to the Montreux Jazz Festival, where we were favourably reviewed and broadcast over Swiss radio.

Despite this being his first trip overseas, Sandile was good at making his own way around, taking in the music, linking up with musicians from the other South African bands and zeroing in on press receptions and product or album launches, and collecting 'goody bags' to take home. When describing Montreux, some of his observations were quite revealing. Seeing lots of expensive Swatches on display in street-side market stalls led him to conclude that Swiss people must be rich because it would be so easy to walk off with the merchandise. He was very dismayed that there were no signs in English. 'People here must be very proud of their language,' he said, noting that some people he attempted to talk to didn't answer in English. He was put out by this apparent chauvinism. For him, English was clearly *the* sole international language of public discourse and official information, and the default medium of communication in polyglot urban townships. Afrikaans was also used this way in some parts of the country, but Afrikaans was, in Sandy's view, just another local language like Setswana or isiZulu. English – Sandy believed – was the main language of the world. He thought other European languages were local languages like Afrikaans and that everyone should be polite enough to speak English when spoken to in that language. This *idée fixe* was undoubtedly reinforced by encounters with Swiss people like Robert Trunz who *did* speak English. Cathy and I pointed out in various ways that French and German and Italian were languages of equal standing in the world, but generations of

English imperialism made this idea unthinkable. Cathy reminded him that there were Africans who didn't speak English. 'Yes, there are some who don't speak it well and we tell them, "Don't mess up the Queen's language",' said Sandy.

'Well,' she continued, trying another tack, 'there are Europeans who can't speak English because they never learned it or had to.' We thought we'd got through with this point but, as we parted at Louis Botha International Airport in Durban, he said that he was going to tell 'the brothers in the township that they needn't be ashamed of their English' because he had met plenty of *white people* who couldn't speak English either!

Catherine

I had met Allen before I went to America. He was a close friend of my brother's and the two played nothing by the rules except that Allen did have a strict and reverent approach to the history and development of jazz guitar. He was one of the first local musicians we got the university to employ as an instrument teacher and everyone thought we were mad to think this could work. He was enormously egocentric and never knew when to stop talking or playing. The part-time teaching didn't quite work, except for the lasting impression on students that Natal indeed had its own unique jazz masters.

Of the many South African musicians (around a hundred) who died during our time in South Africa, Allen is someone I keep thinking about and miss. Certainly, hanging out with him at G-128, an inherited matchbox house in KwaMashu, gave us both a more thorough understanding of the enormous gap in our fortunes and what it would take to attempt a level playing field at the university. A lot of people gave up on him because of his self-aggrandisement, especially when he was drunk, which is very understandable. I should add, however, that his fearlessness and tenacity also got him recognition that eluded other, equally good, musicians.

I asked him to join Darius and Chris Ballantine in Canada for the Third International Conference on Popular Music Studies in Montreal and found a way to cover his expenses. His role would be to demonstrate the influences of South African indigenous guitar music on jazz and vice versa, but it very quickly became the Allen Kwela show. As the conference was held in Montreal and our presentation was in English, there were many pauses while our remarks were translated into French. This annoyed Allen, so when he was invited to speak, he delivered his opening remarks in isiZulu, looked the bemused translator in the eye and said, 'So translate this'! Not all his fault though, because overzealous and politically correct whites at the conference were determined in 1985 to see him as captured for a 'Western purpose'. Not only would he not leave the stage and subsequently the auditorium when the programme was well over, he exploited the anti-colonial vibe and stayed far too long drinking at a house party, putting us in an uncomfortable caretaker and 'boss' role. Allen happened to be sitting near the phone when it rang and instead of handing it to our host, picked up the receiver himself. The caller must have said something in French and Allen, already three sheets to the wind, grandly replied, 'I do not speak your language, but I will learn it for the next·time I am here'. One couldn't stay angry with Allen for long, at least I couldn't. For this trip, we had had the whole Brubeck family looking for gigs in America for Allen and Darius's brother Dan got him one with the well-known alto player Lee Konitz. Lee commented on Allen being out of tune, which was quite ironic given that Konitz himself was infamous for his out-of-tune style. It was difficult to tell who was in and who was out, but certainly their performance was unique.

In other ways, Allen definitely had his act together and had joined SAMRO, so that radio transcriptions of his music brought in royalty cheques, however meagre. Before his brothers died, he had helped them to maintain a house in KwaMashu and stood by one of them whom we knew was in prison. Allen acknowledged that he had been the one favoured with more schooling. He could also read and write music and he placed great value on learning, as did Sandy. They both loved language and the intricacies of meaning and this made them both great company. Barney Rachabane was endlessly fascinated by Mr Rider, his name for Allen, which is a translation of the word 'kwela', and Lulu Gontsana would often mimic Allen's voice and gestures perfectly. One night during an annual Jazz Festival gig in Grahamstown, Allen stayed up drinking at the bar of the old Grand Hotel and ended up sleeping on the floor of a room belonging to two other musicians named Fekile (Arrived) and Vukile (Awake). The following morning, one of their band members came calling for Vukile and Fekile. Greatly annoyed by this disturbance, Allen shot back, 'Go away! *uVukile ulele, uFikile uhambile!*' (the one who is Awake is asleep and the one who has Arrived has gone). Allen relished this wordplay.

Allen the intellectual was really engaging, but his need to be the centre of attention would trigger the egocentric persona and his self-claimed 'shrinking from the limelight' would all be forgotten. Once, at a Sandy and Allen gig at the Hermit Restaurant, Sandile floored Allen for his continued carping and attempts to upstage him. We were astounded when, with just one quick decisive blow, the quiet, little one literally levelled the guitar playing field. The gig, friendship and respect all continued as though nothing had happened.

It's difficult to say why Allen was the more organised, but he was. They could both self-destruct, Allen with drinking and histrionics and Sandile with apathy, reticence or bewilderment. Sandile believed his boat would come in, but didn't do enough to spread the sails, while Allen made sure some kind of vessel reached the shore. Johnny Fourie told us that when he first knew and played with them both, Sandile was way ahead of Allen in concept and skill but, by sheer perseverance, Allen caught up and settled on a style that he was comfortable with. Sandile, on the other hand, was continually searching.

On 30 June 2003, a few days before we left on a three-month overseas trip, Allen died in hospital, quietly. We hadn't known he was there and had grown used to his coughing and laboured breathing. Years ago, in one of his dramatic moods, he said, 'Let other people die all they want. I don't believe in dying' and we kind of believed him, thinking that he would always be around in our orbit, making things difficult or delightful. Often, it was both at once. Allen Kwela was a lean, dominant, angry man and devilishly handsome despite a long, jagged scar on his face, a long jaw and a high forehead. He was tall, angular and square-shouldered, with long arms that reached beyond the full length of the guitar when he made one of his trademark gestures. Sometimes, after too much brandy, the performance was more gesture than genius.

In the violent and confusing 1980s, we were transported by his solo set at a shabby cinema in Umlazi. We've heard guitarists the world over, but Allen's concert that day was untouchable. He played signature pieces like 'KwaMashu' and 'The Unknown' and everything was 100 per cent right – the sound, the urgency, the form – and quite beautiful. Perfection eludes most of us and it is all too rare, but we want you to know that for that performance alone we will always be grateful for the 'broken strings of Allen Kwela' (this was a phrase he used as an album title).[6]

Sandile's death in a motorbike accident outside a jazz club on 4 October 2003 was a public one. This happened the day we arrived back from the United States, marking a sad symmetry between the two musicians we had known and worked with for twenty years. Sandy had always been full of surprises – musically, verbally and emotionally – and said things that made us laugh and cry. Like Allen, his language was quite poetic and precise and like Allen he knew that apartheid had really hurt him. Of course, millions of people suffered but, in Sandile's case, his gentle and compassionate view of the world was constantly challenged by the insensitivity around him. He could have been many things because he knew and absorbed so much, but somehow he couldn't clear a path through the undergrowth. Kevin Gibson remembers watching Sandy watching the rest of the band taking solos, so absorbed in their improvisations that he would forget to play himself.

His question 'When is April?' was a Sandile Shange classic. Funny, on the one hand, but at the same time deep and unsettling. (When did he have to do what?) Time and calendars were immaterial, but what is the essence here? It revealed a time- and boundary-free life, annoying to all those who were schedule-bound, but challenging in what for, who for and wherefore categories. On one occasion, we had a gig in Pietermaritzburg and planned to leave Durban at noon. We sent a message to Sandile to come to our house at twelve, but he didn't appear. We left and had to play the gig without him. At midnight he duly arrived with guitar and amp. Yes, jazz is usually played at night and yes, we weren't clear about which twelve and yes, Sandile was a dreamer and yes, everything got lost in translation.

After four years of ad hoc management and absorbing most of the expenses, which included buying Sandy a guitar amp, we tried to formalise our relationship as this is what we were used to in the US of A. In 1987 we were not wealthy and felt we had to get our relationship on a business level. Sandy signed all the paragraphs about percentages if we got him a recording and so forth, but all these attempts at professionalism failed and just made us seem opportunistic and we were pleased to let the contractual legalese drop, especially since we weren't successful at pulling off a recording of Sandile's music. It was uncomfortable explaining anything financial and particularly the finances of the trip to Switzerland, which we had subsidised. A wonderful story from that time illustrates both Sandy's charm and his take on the world. His disappointments were many on this trip. Firstly, the lack of immediate camaraderie on the part of black American musicians he encountered at the festival and on the streets of Montreux. To them, he was just another musician and all the race consciousness of South Africa had led him to think that the 'brothers' would automatically befriend him. Secondly, as Darius describes earlier in this chapter, the use of French, German and Italian by native speakers really bothered him. Somewhere in there, one senses the depths of the colonial experience.

After gigs, we often took Sandile home to Ntuzuma, a township about 40 minutes' drive from Durban, if one didn't get lost in the sameness of the houses and the roads. Sometimes we dropped him at the Blue Swan Cafe in town, where he could catch a bus to the township, which was created in the 1970s as an extension of the ever-burgeoning KwaMashu. 'Blue Swan' became the name (for us at least) of one his numerous unnamed tunes. As I have said, names and ages seemed of no consequence to Sandy and the more there were, the more eccentric he became about them.

Very tragically, his son Dumisane, who had been in the jazz programme at UKZN, died when a shower in a northern town, near Pretoria, poured out natural gas instead of water. We believe this may have been caused by illegal fracking. It happened a few years after Sandile's own death and after we had left for the United Kingdom. We stayed in touch with his wife Bongi, who has also since died, but one of Sandile's beautiful compositions, 'Sibongile', written for her, was one of the tunes we often performed.

In his final years, Allen Duma Kwela (his full name) accepted that he really couldn't keep the '*duma*' (thunder) part going, but recordings preserve his memory. Conversely, numerous uncollected Sandile Johannes (Shange) Dlamini, Mgwaba tracks exist, but there has never been a dedicated Sandile Shange album. He, too, was an original composer and musician and hopefully one day a posthumous CD will address this loss to South African jazz.

> South African jazz is the local understanding
> of the potential of a global art form.
> — Marc Duby

Darius

Marc Duby

Marc talks like this in real life. Sometimes you need to pause for a moment, then when you get it, you realise how much deep thought is compressed into one sentence. 'Cliché after cliché is what you'll get from me,' he adds cheerfully before moving on.[7] He bears a passing resemblance to the British actor-musician Hugh Laurie and has a similarly polished and charming manner that conveys self-confidence seasoned with self-deprecating irony. We go back a long way, having met shortly before I was hired at UND, but it is best to start in the present.

Marc, with the title of Professor Extraordinarius of Musicology at UNISA, has been a senior academic, heading music departments and programmes at (in reverse order) UNISA, Tshwane University of Technology and Rhodes University for the last ten years. He has supervised graduate students from several countries and has published articles on subjects ranging from Malcolm Lowry and Maurice Merleau-Ponty to the glory days of the Rainbow.[8] And yet, as he said in a recent interview, 'the purpose of my life was always wound up with jazz'.

We first connected in 1982 (the year before I was appointed to UND) as jazz musicians in Cape Town and performed at the People's Space Theatre. He felt then he was drifting, gigging at night while holding down a day job at Ragtime Records, a high-end record store. He claims that he moved to Durban 'without expectations', but I had enough for both of us, anticipating working together as musicians and how much it would help the overall mission if Marc got a foot on the academic ladder in the new field (in South Africa) of Jazz Studies. Given the busy jazz scene in Durban, he had nothing to lose by enrolling at the university for a Master's degree. Marc has kindly acknowledged the role I played in his life, referring to me as a mentor and father-figure and his excitement at playing with, as he humorously put it, 'a real American jazz musician'. I humbly accept all of this because he says so, but ours was a highly symbiotic relationship, where both sides benefited. It was a bit of a stretch for the Music Department to take on a graduate student in jazz and appoint me as his supervisor since I only had an Honours degree in Ethnomusicology and History of Religion from Wesleyan University, but it was a soundly practical decision that gave Marc a small stipend and access to everything on campus, and the department gained a top-class part-time teacher.

Victor Masondo recalls my arranging for Marc to tutor him in music theory for admission to the university: 'Bra Sandy told me to talk to Darius about study at university and Darius was very encouraging, but said I had to know theory'.[9] The minimal standard was Royal Schools Grade 5. Passing the grades meant sitting an exam administered by or on behalf of Royal Schools (ABRSM). I didn't believe that anyone with real musical ability should be disqualified by lack of formal education, but a minimum standard of music literacy and knowledge was a practical necessity, or they simply wouldn't be able to follow the lectures and lessons. A motivated and bright student could get through one grade per semester (per year was the expected norm), but I think the time span here was something like from August to January when enrolment at university began. Victor didn't believe he could do it, but Marc made it happen, even insisting that Victor stay overnight with him before the exam because township transportation was so uncertain in those days. Victor's being a student led to his being a Jazzanian, which led to an international career and, as Victor tells the story, none of this would have happened without Marc's teaching and his refusal to accept delays, excuses and practical problems as obstacles.

Meanwhile, I benefited by having an impressive bass player and, on the academic front, I had a chance to learn about supervision – once again learning the job by doing it. I was supposed to act as guide or at least point out pathways on the cerebral, discursive level that I had last glimpsed when I was a student at Wesleyan, fifteen years earlier. I have repeatedly mentioned how lucky I was in the early days. This feeling seems to be shared by Marc, who wrote, 'A combination of sheer luck and being at the right place at the right time enabled me to take part in this programme from its inception; this literally changed my life'.[10] Having Marc as my first graduate student is one of the best examples of my good fortune because he already had a Bachelor of Arts degree in English and French from the University of Cape Town (his military service had consisted of teaching French in the South African Navy). He already knew about evidence and argument and how to organise research and write.

My task – and this wasn't always easy – was to make sure he *did* write. Who can't find reasons *not* to write? (Even smoking counted as one, because he couldn't stay in the library for more than an hour without a cigarette break.) Marc's taste in jazz, a little reductively describable as ECM (Editions of Contemporary Music) and experimental,[11] contrasted with mine. He was a fan of the avant-garde German bassist Eberhard Weber. He also turned me on to a set of musicians he affectionately referred to as 'English loonies', which included Django Bates and bands like Soft Machine and Loose Tubes. Marc's independent projects as bandleader from Durban days until now have gone under the name More Garde Than Avant – or Moregarde, for short – reflecting his interest in Euro-jazz and the 'further-out' figures of the American canon. His 2007 doctoral dissertation was on an improvisational system known as 'soundpainting'.[12] Looking back, I see Marc as an experimenter and myself as a consolidator.

Given these contrasting yet compatible mindsets, his Master's thesis with me on the music of Thelonious Monk was perfect for both of us. Setting aside our intellectual call-and-response as his thesis, 'The Compositional and Improvisational Style of Thelonious Monk', developed, what I hopefully gave Marc was unwavering support, which is exactly what he gave to Victor Masondo. Victor was awarded the first diploma in Jazz Performance the same year that Marc Duby earned the first Master's degree in Music in Jazz Studies (with distinction) awarded by a South African university.

Three states of emergency were declared during the time Marc was in Durban. A politically motivated bomb attack killed three patrons and injured many more in a bar on the beachfront. I noticed certain SABC staff (not just security guards) carrying guns 'just in case' when I went in to record my radio shows. The smell of unseen, smouldering fires was often in the air and censored reports of 'unrest' were *on* the air. And here we were, fellow band members dropping off musicians in townships and getting lost late at night. This happened several times with me at the wheel and Marc in the car. Once, we were followed home by cops, who could have suspected we were

The Darius Brubeck Quintet outside the old Music Department, UND, 1984. From left: Marc Duby, Darius, Rick van Heerden, Kevin Gibson, Sandile Shange (photo: Ted Brien; Cathy Brubeck collection).

white saboteurs. I got out and spoke to them, playing a naive American. They accepted my explanation of why we were there, but I was sternly told that it was dangerous (true enough) and not allowed in the first place. 'Thanks, officer.' Of course, that warning didn't stop us.

Durban, while nominally under the same rules as the rest of the country, was where Marc met and worked with lots of black musicians, including Sandile and Allen and visiting artists from Johannesburg and Cape Town. Marc played bass on Allen's recording *The Unknown* and on a Pat Matshikiza album recorded by David Marks for Tusk Records. He realised that the jazz scene in Cape Town consisted of two worlds, but Durban was rapidly becoming a place of intersection and blending, and he was excited about taking part in this opening of musical and social territory.

The Darius Brubeck Quintet, with Marc on bass, had a very successful life in the 1980s and existed concurrently with Afro Cool Concept, which Cathy and I treated as Johannesburg-based since Barney Rachabane and Victor Ntoni lived there. The Darius Brubeck Quintet had started to surf a little wave of popularity caused by the release of 'Tugela Rail', which featured Marc's stunning fretless electric bass solo.[13] This became a highlight in all our live sets and Marc remembers to his astonishment that 'the audience began shouting encouragement and clapping during a solo when I performed (this) with Darius'. This happened for the first time at the University of Zululand, with Nelson Magwaza on drums. Marc further writes: 'This particular concert will remain in memory for another reason . . . I was very much in awe of him [Nelson Magwaza] having grown up listening to Dollar Brand's 1971 trio album *Peace* with Nelson and Victor Ntoni.'[14]

Nelson Magwaza's funeral, 21 April 1984, *City Press*.

Nelson died suddenly of an asthma attack in that same year, 1984. Cathy, Marc and I went to Agrippa Magwaza's house in KwaMashu, where Nelson's widow and little children (one a six-month-old baby) were staying for the customary week of mourning, and we sat in silence while Connie (Nelson's wife) gave what must have been the one hundredth account of his death. The ambulance hadn't come for hours, and hours and he was therefore 'dead on arrival'. Marc and I were pall bearers and we collected money for the family at our next gigs, both adding to it as well because, unsurprisingly, he had left absolutely nothing. This distinctly personal memory took place during a period of personal and political grief and anger around the country. I think Marc was more destabilised by all this than Cathy and I were. We had each other, living parents, a solid job, modest success and a home country to flee to – if it came to that. In comparison, Marc's future as a white South African who owned little more than his instruments and his beat-up VW Beetle looked precarious.

Kevin Gibson replaced Nelson Magwaza on drums and our quintet toured Namibia. It was also one of the first (possibly *the* first) jazz band to play at the Grahamstown National Festival of the Arts before the jazz festival component came into being a few years later. Although nobody foresaw this, the group dispersed in different directions in 1986. Kevin went to the United States to join a summer course at Berklee College of Music in Boston, Rick skipped across the border to avoid being drafted into the SADF and Marc committed to working regularly at the Cellar, a new venue within the Playhouse Theatre complex that featured cabaret and jazz. He also started teaching at the Natal Technikon (later renamed Durban University of Technology). These jobs provided regular income, but it meant giving up taking gigs here and there and going on the road with me. Sandy and I still played together, but my creative focus was now mainly on seeing what could be done with the cohort of outstanding students who were already lifting the level of jazz on campus.

There were ups and downs to come in our long friendship, especially during the brief period when I was simultaneously his thesis supervisor, bandleader and landlord. Marc was upset not to have been part of the triumphant Jazzanian adventure in the United States, which had so richly benefited the students who went. That Marc was no longer a student in 1988 didn't seem a compelling reason not to include him. Victor Masondo, too, had just finished his course, but in American eyes, Victor counted as a current student until May or June. To Marc, this was a thin technicality. Frankly, it *was*, but there were more decisive reasons for his omission, mainly the understandable expectation and insistence by USIS and NAJE that most of the South African group be black. As Cathy said, we had to be colour-conscious to do battle with racism. (These conundrums continue to exist today.) In any case, we didn't have the luxury of making decisions based purely on principle. Ever articulate, even in anger, Marc accused me of 'Crow Jim, inverted racism. Jim Crow, Crow Jim'. Things could only go up from this low point and fortunately they did.

From left: Darius, Marc Duby and Kevin Gibson, St George's Cathedral, Cape Town, 2015 (photo: Cathy Brubeck, Cathy Brubeck collection).

Marc left the Natal Technikon for a job at Pretoria Technikon in 1992 and, from then on, followed an ascending path that would lead to a PhD and a series of ever-more distinguished positions and an output of erudite articles and chapters in academic books.[15] He has far outdistanced me as a professional academic, but what matters is that we still play together when I'm in South Africa. It feels so right because we met as performing jazz musicians and that's what we do.

Victor Ntoni

Victor Ntoni (21 June 1947 – 28 January 2013) and I were born exactly a week apart and special circumstances brought us together when my father, my brothers Chris and Dan and I came to South Africa in 1976. Victor was the guest bass player with this New Brubeck Quartet as the family group was called and we all bonded as musicians and friends. We had many adventures in South Africa and Botswana and my parents thought of Victor as another son. They helped him to enrol and study at the famous Berklee College of Music in Boston, Massachusetts. He always referred to them as Papa Dave and Mama Iola.

While in the United States, he worked with Hugh Masekela and other exiled musicians until he moved back to South Africa in 1985. Musically, Victor was in touch with the deepest underground streams of tradition, yet he was also a polished and accomplished Quincy Jones-type figure. Victor was considered a very fine jazz bass player, but this alone hardly does justice to the range of his music projects and interests. His soundtrack work, TV appearances and arrangements of Xhosa and Zulu music all reveal talents as both curator and creator.

Subsequently, when I came to teach in Durban, Victor and I formed Afro Cool Concept, with Lulu Gontsana on drums. The three of us always appeared with a fourth musician. We featured tenor saxophonist Duke Makasi initially, then Winston Mankunku and Ezra Ngcukana, but the leading alto sax man Barney Rachabane became the permanent soloist after Afro Cool Concept released *Live at the New Orleans Jazz & Heritage Festival* in 1990.[16]

Victor was a good storyteller, one of the best I have ever known, and we were all captivated by not only that resonant bass voice, but also his tales of rural and urban life. He had a real understanding of what it meant to cross over into different worlds and this led to musical collaborations with great playwrights and producers. After moving permanently to Johannesburg, the centre of South Africa's media industry, 'Bra Vic' became a national celebrity, the personification of cool, urban, black middle-class aspirations, appearing on the cover of *Tribute* magazine with his wife Linda and their children.[17] He hosted a live music series on TV and appeared in commercials. All of this both helped and hurt. He was always overcommitted workwise and overstretched financially. I remember a lunch at the Market Theatre with Victor and the great theatre director Barney Simon. 'See these grey hairs,' said Barney, 'each one is called Victor Ntoni.' Despite the history

Victor Ntoni at the Music Department, University of Natal, Durban, in the mid-1990s (photo: Paul Weinberg).

of unreliability, missed appointments and deadlines that had given Barney Simon grey hairs, Victor was the go-to guy in many situations. His persona, like so much aspirational imagery of black life portrayed in the South African media, belied a precarious struggle to make ends meet while keeping up appearances.

Victor was politically shrewd and well connected. When we played at the first Afro-Jazz Festival in Harare, we met with the ANC Regional Cultural Committee over quarts of beer and endlessly discussed the role of music in the struggle and in the eagerly anticipated 'new South Africa'. Rather than being awed by articulate, militant comrades in exile, Victor attacked them for undervaluing the role of people back home and for exploiting musicians overseas by always expecting them to play for nothing.

Victor, Lulu and I were the house rhythm section for several consecutive editions of the Grahamstown Jazz Festival, which took place in July every year, starting in 1989. Cathy and I often arranged to bring Victor and Barney Rachabane down from Johannesburg to perform as Afro Cool Concept at the Rainbow and other Durban venues throughout the 1980s and 1990s. We even played an all-Brubeck programme of symphonic arrangements with the Natal Philharmonic Orchestra, conducted by Russell Gloyd, my father's conductor, who had flown over from the United States for this premiere event at the Durban Playhouse.

From left: Victor Ntoni, Darius, Russell Gloyd (guest conductor, NPO), Barney Rachabane, Playhouse Theatre, Durban, 1994 (photo: Cathy Brubeck; Cathy Brubeck collection).

Victor and Barney usually stayed with us and we always had a good time. I loved playing with Victor, but living in two different towns didn't make it easy to keep the same band of musicians going and this meant I only saw Victor a few times in the following decade. However, Afro Cool's story doesn't end there because Victor's replacement, Bongani Sokhela, picked himself. Afro Cool was scheduled to do a Monday lunch-hour concert at Howard College Theatre, the music auditorium right in the middle of the campus. The hall was completely full by the time we had set up and people were standing in the entrance and in corridors, spilling out into the rotunda. No Victor. It was not unknown for him to be late, especially since he hadn't come home to us the night before. He had plenty of friends in Durban. We had noticed he spent a lot of time talking to a pretty bar manager/waitress at the Rainbow when we were there on the Sunday. We always borrowed the department's string bass for Victor to use and Bongani Sokhela, a bass student, was tasked with delivering the instrument backstage for our concert, which he eagerly did, in part to spend more time with the famous Victor Ntoni. I waited for Victor until waiting was no longer an option, then decided to ask Bongani to suggest tunes he could play with us. He was a shy and diligent student, so he surprised us all by saying, 'I know all of your songs from the record'. (He was referring to *Live at the New Orleans Jazz & Heritage Festival*.) From then on, Bongani Sokhela was the Afro Cool bass player and he travelled with us to England, Denmark, Thailand and Italy during and after his time as a student. He really filled Victor's big shoes and enjoyed visiting Buddhist temples in Bangkok, the *Little Mermaid* in Copenhagen and, later, the sights of Istanbul as a bass player in the group Thusini, which I led and which featured two other students, Paul Kock (alto sax) and Chris Mashiane (drums).

The jazz scene is an intimate network and we heard about Victor's drastic ups and downs, heavy drinking and separation from Linda, but a few years later he was getting big commissions and they were back together. In January 2014, a year after his death, Linda invited me to write an introduction for *The South African Songbook: SA Folklore Music*.[18] I enjoyed reconnecting with Victor through his music and it was a great opportunity to learn about work I didn't know. It was exciting to find a 2005 version of 'Maxhosa' in the material Linda gave me. I was already very familiar with the first version, which was the title song of an Africanised *Macbeth* filmed in South Africa in 1975. The play was set in a Xhosa village and the score is appropriately traditional, using voices and local percussion instruments. Christian choral singing is adapted and invigorated by the Xhosa language with its complex accent patterns and clicks. This version of 'Maxhosa', performed as part of *Mzansi Sings a Tribute to Oliver Tambo*,[19] at an event at the posh Gallagher Estate Conference Centre, is elegantly urban, like smooth jazz or 'neo-soul'. Victor himself sings lead, trading off with other male voices. The globalised soundscape throughout this tribute programme is capacious, rich and

Some Remarkable People 165

Brubeck/Ntoni Afro Cool Concept, cover photo for *Live at the New Orleans Jazz & Heritage Festival*, 1990. From left: Darius, Victor Ntoni, Barney Rachabane. Front: Lulu Gontsana (photographer unknown; Cathy Brubeck collection).

Afro Cool Concept with Bongani Sokhela on bass, publicity photo for Sheer Sound, 2003 (photo: Jürgen Schadeberg; Cathy Brubeck collection).

sophisticated, although a little retro, evoking the struggle era. The music envelops the audience in a particularly South African emotion of joy tinged with gravitas; memories sweetened by reflection on how far we've come. Modern drums and glossy synth pads are *now*, while singers interjecting cries and ululations are *then*. The overall effect is indigenous yet urban, spiritual yet secular, respectful to the older generation yet irreversibly moving on. In short, this was *perfect* ANC mood music. Victor's musical craft, refined in theatre and television, was always right on message. However, one of the lyrics asks, 'Was it all for nothing?' Later, eGoli (Johannesburg) is referred to as 'city of death'. The original reference was to apartheid-era cops shooting protesters during the 1976 Soweto uprising, but here the city is still violent. The soliloquy continues with 'when did the song go sour?' and 'will our voices be heard again?' Victor was nevertheless genuinely behind the patriotic message of this music composed for the Tambo tribute.

For African musicians in Victor's generation, music literacy was a prized and rare accomplishment. In this context, it is truly remarkable that he didn't filter out the unwritable vernacular music of daily life – people singing at work, in church, at political rallies, at weddings and during village rites and rituals. He captured not just the chants and songs, but also the feeling of ancestral musical forces and he injected this sensibility into a show tune or a jazz arrangement. His impressive skill set as a composer-arranger-producer-showman draws from his professional experience – session work at the SABC, jazz, and the production of local-language segments for Disney's *The Lion King*.

Victor's lifelong association with jazz is a major influence on the rest of his work, yet somewhat apart from it. Anyone today hearing Dollar Brand's *Peace* or his *Blues for a Hip King* (as Abdullah Ibrahim) for the first time is bound to think, 'What a bass player!'[20] However, Victor was on a different quest, which is why he went to America to study composition and arranging. My father often told me that, originally, he just wanted to be a composer, but to realise this dream, he had to succeed as a performer first. So, for both Victor Ntoni and Dave Brubeck, formal study was a prerequisite to fulfilling their highest ambition. Applying what he learned at Berklee to South African music is what gives so much of Victor's work a national, modern-vernacular sound. His memorable and singable melodies do not follow the post-bop road the rest of jazz was on, but he nevertheless spiced his compositions with harmonic twists that came from his formal study. The performances were seldom as good as the charts, a problem that Charles Mingus and Beethoven allegedly had too.

The essential Victor Ntoni, the true expression of his heart and soul, comes through song. If Victor Ntoni had been born in Italy in the nineteenth century, he might have been Giacomo Puccini because his music is theatrical, with melodies that carry lyrics very naturally. Working with stage directors Clarence Wilson and Barney

Simon, his songs deliver knock-out punches in the scenes in which they appear – for example, 'Where Are the Children Now?' in *African Odyssey*. This is the opposite of 'incidental' music.

Music can be a force for national cohesion and celebration and Victor, at his best, achieved this. He truly knew and loved the music of his homeland and his influence on me was pervasive during my South African years. We often talked about getting back together. He would phone sometimes out of the blue and he and Cathy would make plans, but sadly they mostly evaporated. Victor's death felt as though the world had suddenly changed and it was not a good feeling. We had always been able to pick up where we left off and now that conversation about life and music is gone forever.

David Marks

David Marks, three years my senior, was our entry into the South African music business. He doesn't need us to memorialise him, but key parts of our own story won't make sense without telling some parts of his. He is best known for his songs from the 1960s, when his style of music was a fashionable expression of South Africa's counterculture (mostly whites). He was still working underground in a gold mine when he wrote 'Mountains of Men' and the international hit 'Master Jack'.[21]

Dave left the mines and surfaced as a musician on the folk scene in Johannesburg and then went to America for a spell, where he had the exceptional opportunity to learn about outdoor concert sound from Bill Hanley, joining his crew in time to work at the Woodstock Festival in 1969.[22] Practically everything Dave did from then on was, in his words, 'the house that Jack built'. When we met Dave, he was still a celebrity from the nostalgically celebrated folk era for his song writing and thereafter for his dashing ways with a sound system and mobile recording studios. He not only felt a compulsion to record literally everything, he *kept* everything. Shamefully, even the SABC didn't do this because of the cost of the magnetic tape, which could be erased and reused (although it shouldn't be). Dave accumulated tapes, documents and photos – seven tons' worth – as a producer and engineer for live concerts and studio albums. In 1990 he formed the Hidden Years Music Archive Project,[23] because he realised 'the value of what we were doing and saying and playing during those turbulent times and how we did it is important and makes for a great story'.[24]

I visited Dave several times on my recent trips back to South Africa. He and his wife Frances (who died in 2020) had moved out of Durban to Melville, 'down the South Coast'. Their tree-shaded, sprawling bungalow was still piled high with tape boxes and smelled of slightly damp paper. Seeing the open-reel tape machines and vintage equipment was like meeting old friends. When I asked in 2019, if he remembered how and when we met, he showed me a page from his diary – Friday, 19 August 1983, with 'Darius/Cathy Brubeck, 9.15 am' and our phone number.

Dave moved to Durban from Johannesburg the year we arrived. He said, 'I had a family and there had been threats' – meaning the Special Branch had dropped broad hints that his famous Free Peoples Concerts and association with suspected anti-government activists would have consequences. These legendary concerts, which presented musicians of all genres and races on the same platform, were held regularly on the University of Witwatersrand campus from 1972 to 1992. Attendance was *free* of charge, hence 'free' was arguably an adjective rather than a call to action, as in 'free Mandela', but the authorities weren't blind to the true meaning of such events.[25] Dave needed to leave town and Bill Hanley obligingly asked Dave to set up ProSound (a national sound reinforcement and sound equipment distributer company) in Durban. So, naturally, our paths crossed.

In addition to being an ace sound engineer, Dave knew all the main players in Johannesburg's record industry, which in those days consisted of Gallo with its many local sub-labels, and some internationals like WEA and Sony that in turn managed and

Dave Marks and Darius at Dave's house, South Coast, 2019 (photo: Jorne Tielemans; still from documentary *Playing the Changes*).

distributed other international labels in South Africa. There were a few independents too: Sun Records and Mountain Records for jazz and later Shifty Records, essentially a counterculture label featuring disaffected Afrikaner rockers with pseudonyms like Johannes Kerkorrel and Bernoldus Niemand, young singer-songwriters like Jennifer Ferguson, who later became an ANC Member of Parliament and jazzy, but unclassifiable, guitar-led bands like Tananas and the Genuines. It is a rich catalogue of engaged artists.

In conversation, Dave has a diffident, even vague manner, often pausing to ask if he is right, but he has a tremendous memory for people, names, concerts he has worked on, political events and who was working for which record company. I always tried to keep a toe in the music business, rather than snuggling down into academic life, so this was interesting talk. The problem for me and Cathy was that he assumed everyone was on a first-name basis with everyone else in the business: 'So I told Ivor that Ian would ask Lloyd if we could record Roger in Durban'. Although a self-effacing 'folky' when it came to his personal musicianship, Dave likes jazz and had recorded jazz artists Hugh Masekela, Spirits Rejoice and Malombo for his company Third Ear.[26] We collaborated on a few important projects that included putting on a music festival in Durban billed as 8/6/86, and he and Ron Selby recorded *We Have Waited Too Long*, the Jazzanians' one and only album.[27] Dave also recorded some of my earliest appearances in Durban with Sandile Shange, Allen Kwela and Evan Ziporyn at the Hermit, which is now part of the Hidden Years Archive of Music.

Dave was effectively the leader and point of contact for MANA and meetings were held at Dave and Frances's large house on a steep slope overlooking the city, or at Le Plaza Hotel, part-owned by our good friends, the architects Dennis Claude and Paul Mikula. Dave's wife Frances was welcoming and accustomed to a house of much coming-and-going. She had been the manager of the Market Cafe in Johannesburg's famous Market Theatre complex and usually wore soft-looking long dresses, sort of hippy pre-Raphaelite style. Dave was always in shorts and sandals. Frances's mother, who taught classical music and carried herself with an air of old-fashioned gentility, sometimes singled me out for a quiet word about teaching piano. There was a gentle, tie-dyed, Woodstockian atmosphere; posters on the walls, boxes of tapes, cassettes and LPs piled high on chairs and overflowing shelves, loosely coiled mic cables, a guitar on a stand, and young children and a dog and a cat wandering in and out. Music as Lifestyle meets Music as Profession.

Johnny Mekoa

Trumpet player Johnny Mekoa (11 April 1945 – 3 July 2017) graduated in 1990 as the first black student in Africa with a Bachelor of Music degree in Jazz Studies. Working through the American Consulate in Durban, Cathy, Glynis and I helped him to obtain a Fulbright scholarship to enter a Master's programme in Jazz Pedagogy at Indiana University under the premier authority in that field, David Baker. Three years later, Johnny became the first South African to complete such a degree. In 1994 he founded the Music Academy of Gauteng (MAG) in Daveyton township (near Benoni), where he grew up. Johnny spent the years between Indiana and opening MAG lobbying political connections as well as fund-raising. He kept us fully updated on progress and acknowledged Clive Mennell, late chairman of Anglo-Vaal, and the Coca-Cola Company in the United States as his main donors. MAG is currently on SAMRO's list of schools receiving support from the SAMRO Foundation. He also pursued donations of cash and in kind from anybody willing to help; items like chairs recycled from a local restaurant or second-hand instruments and sheet music were accepted with effusive gratitude. His presentation at a jazz education conference in Durban in 1993 included slides of children playing instruments in front of a building without a roof. 'All we need now is . . . [I can't recall the exact figure] and we'll have a roof over our heads.' He was unrelenting. Back on the East Rand, he did local fund-raising gigs using the street kids he had recruited and taught to play second-hand instruments. Many of these instruments were donated by jazz educators in the United States through the relationship with IAJE. Like the Centre for Jazz and Popular Music previously, he made use of diplomatic pouch deliveries to the United States Embassy, circumventing both tariffs and sanctions under the banner of Jazz Aid, which was created by Dennis Tini, the president of IAJE in those early years. All this activity was a spin-off from the celebrated Jazzanians' appearance at the Detroit conference.

'The little darlings', as Lulu Gontsana humorously called Johnny's child-musicians, got better fast and, under Johnny's leadership, started playing at ANC social functions, strengthening his political network and identification with the liberation movement. He would often exaggerate to make a good story better and sometimes Cathy and I wondered whether we could believe him completely. When Cathy and I interviewed Johnny at MAG in 2017, he described a recent battle with the municipality over non-payment of electricity rates:

> Me, I'm a fighter. One time, Ekurhuleni Metropolitan wanted to take [the school] to court. You know that I have surrounded myself with some heavyweights; Father Seya Themba, the bishop of the diocese of the Highveld. One day I cried. I said this is happening . . . we took the municipality head-on. The rates were cancelled! I don't pay rates, Cathy.

This is typical Johnny. He never went into battle alone – and this was a point of pride. He believed that he was watched over, protected and could expect help when he called for it. This confident assumption was rooted in a Tswana custom. He wore a necklace of tiny red and white beads, which signified that he was the youngest child of his parents, which meant all his relatives were obliged to look out for him. This family obligation somehow extended to his community and a Brechtian or Dickensian cast of memorable characters like Big Brain, who organised the systematic looting and resale of cargo at Johannesburg's Jan Smuts Airport. Johnny formally referred to influential people by name and title: Bishop this, Doctor that and, in third-person parlance, I was, of course, Professor Darius. People must know! In his world, politicians, intellectuals, millionaires, musicians, teachers, priests and gangsters all, to varying degrees, took a benign interest in his affairs. How much of this was elaborated in his super-charged imagination we'll never know for sure, but certainly some of it was true and very effective. The website Music in Africa says:

> The Music Academy of Gauteng is one of the few remaining community-based music education (NGO) schools. It is providing a much-needed arts education for youth coming from disadvantaged families and informal settlements . . . The school is grateful for the continuing support it receives from government, the corporate sector, and individuals both locally and overseas.[28]

Johnny always came out on top, navigating life under apartheid with humour, dignity, pragmatism and an air of invulnerability. As we witnessed on countless occasions, he was fluent in every language spoken in the country and certainly his English was eloquent, way beyond merely communicative. When Johnny told stories, they weren't mere conversational digressions, but well-plotted set pieces, acted out with skilful code-switching, mimicry of characters' voices and body language, always culminating in a punchline.

One of Johnny's bands, the Jazz Ministers, had been invited to the world-famous Newport Jazz Festival twice in the early 1970s, but weren't given passports.[29] They were finally allowed to go in 1976. This was the year of bicentennial celebrations in the United States, which included visits by warships from friendly nations, including South Africa. The Newport Festival was in New York City that year. The battleship *Paul Kruger* was docked in the harbour and the South African Embassy asked the band to perform a set on deck as part of an official reception. They refused, so members of the band were briefly detained by the Special Branch when they returned to South Africa, probably because, according to Johnny, 'the Boers' wanted to know if the musicians had been in contact with banned organisations overseas. Once satisfied that the Jazz Ministers' refusal to perform had been their own idea, there were no drastic reprisals, but their passports were confiscated. Somewhat later, Johnny was picked up again and taken to the notorious interrogation centre at John Vorster Square for further questioning. Two big cops led him into a bare room with one small window high up on a blood-spattered wall. 'This is the place of truth,' one of them told him in Afrikaans, glancing significantly at the wall. But Johnny already knew that they routinely threw meat from the butcher against the walls to set the scene for interrogations. He acted scared and said he'd tell them everything, which was fine because there wasn't anything to tell. They let him go. How did he know this was how to play the game? Perhaps his entourage of heavyweights included a security cop.

Johnny didn't see himself as a valiant hero, but he was never a victim. He triumphed as a wily Odysseus, aware of his opponents' blindness and vulnerabilities. In another story, he related with obvious delight, cops addressed him as 'Boesman' (Bushman) and allowed him to vouch for 'the natives' (black colleagues) who were in his car after curfew for blacks, the 'white-by-night' law. They had an acceptable excuse as musicians, but the cops could choose to believe them or not. 'You never knew where you were with these guys who could throw you in jail on a whim if they felt like it.' Johnny's light skin, self-confidence and command of Afrikaans allowed him a certain fluid racial status when dealing with officialdom. Rather than cringe and appease, he took charge of the situation, played 'Sarie Marais', a sentimental Afrikaans popular song, on his trumpet to prove they really were musicians and the police thanked him for the song and waved them through the checkpoint.

Johnny still didn't have a passport when we started planning the Jazzanians' tour, so during the Christmas break he applied for a new passport at the local Native Affairs Office in his township of Daveyton. He found reasons to go there often, inventing petty errands and making sure he always saw the same official. He observed him smoking Peter Stuyvesant cigarettes, so Johnny left an unopened pack on the counter after completing some petty transaction. The next time he was greeted with a brief smile of recognition and they moved on to exchanging pleasantries. On a further occasion, Johnny wordlessly handed over a whole carton of Peter Stuyvesant cigarettes. Following that 'gift', Johnny boldly greeted the official by name as he entered the office, calling out, 'I've got something for you'. The official ushered him to his private office where Johnny handed over a bottle of brandy. A passport was on the desk. This man had the power to restore Johnny's access to the world. He said, '*Ek sal dit vir jou doen, maar jy moet altyd onthou, ek is die baas, jy is die kaffer*' (I'll do this for you, but you must remember always, I am the boss, you are the kaffir). Johnny nodded, smiling, '*Ja, jy is die baas, ek is die kaffer*' (Yes, you are the boss, I am the kaffir). So that was it. To Johnny, a little racist abasement in a private office seemed a small price to pay. The official signed the form with a flourish, loudly stamped the passport and handed it to Johnny across his desk.

Mark Kilian, who was also from Benoni, joined the jazz course in 1987, the same year as Johnny. They met at the first Music Department meeting, instantly becoming friends. They managed to set themselves up in adjacent rooms in a student residence when Johnny moved to campus from our house on Peace Avenue. Neither of them could afford to pay for the full residence meal plan and so prepared their own meals over a little gas stove in Johnny's room. Mark's eulogy on Facebook after Johnny died reads in part:

> Johnny had endured a life of apartheid, and . . . I had just completed 2 years in the conscription apartheid army. My biggest excitement coming to a mixed university was to meet people from other ethnic groups. Unbelievable though it may seem, that had been denied to most of us up until that point. The very point of apartheid, I suppose. He never once judged me. He never once belittled me. He never once showed anger or resentment towards me or my tribe.

Jazz aficionados and teachers knew that Johnny was an exceptionally good musician. Music students and faculty at Indiana University told him they expected a beginner, 'a brother from the jungle', as one American student put it, but he wowed them, quickly moving up from an entry level to the top student big band. His sight reading

Johnny Mekoa with Lulu Gontsana and Zim Ngqawana, Carling Circle of Jazz Festival, City Hall, Durban, 14 November 1987 (photo: Cathy Brubeck; Cathy Brubeck collection).

174   Playing the Changes

went from okay to proficient and, thanks to further instruction, his trumpet range, already good, increased. He returned to South Africa hitting high notes with affected gun-slinger nonchalance and a lower register, especially on flugelhorn, that sounded like an affectionate hug.

In later years he was an emblematic and revered figure in jazz education. Visiting MAG was de rigueur for jazz celebrities on tour – for example, the Count Basie Orchestra and Wynton Marsalis with Lincoln Center jazz musicians, who wanted to connect with 'the community'. Visitors were always impressed with the learner-musicians they found and the moving story of how Johnny pretty much created the whole thing himself. The Jazz Centre in Durban also impressed visitors, but at least we started in a building on a university campus while Johnny literally started with nothing.

The Music Academy of Gauteng is located on a two-lane tarred road that runs past flat, sandy fields, shacks and small, down-market shops. It is not attractive country. Facilities at MAG include a good music library, an auditorium and a recording studio. The showpiece is the large, commercially equipped kitchen and dining room, proudly situated at the very centre of the school. 'If nothing else, these kids will get one good meal every day.' Johnny's large office was near the main entrance, with functional office furniture and a trophy cabinet displaying a collection of awards. Teachers were drawn from the local community, including some former UND students who originally came from the East Rand area. One of the formative incidents in Johnny's life was being taken as a boy by his older brother Fred, also a trumpet player, to the Murray Campbell School, a private music school in Johannesburg and being told, 'We don't teach blacks here'. He never wanted this to happen to anyone else. Consequently, anyone could come to MAG and learn as much or little as time and talent would allow.

Johnny did at times take a self-serving Africanist line when it suited him – for example, describing as 'racist' the criticism he received as president of SAJE for simply not doing enough for this organisation. (Not doing enough was hardly contestable and not very damaging compared to labelling those who complained as 'racists'.) He often played the race card whenever straightforward budgetary decisions related to the Grahamstown National Youth Jazz Festival or SAJE conferences didn't stretch to full sponsorship of his 'little darlings'.

Back in Daveyton, not all was sunny and there were rumours. Some MAG teaching staff felt they weren't paid what they were worth. We had no proof of this, but where else would they be paid at all? There were mutterings – nothing overtly alleged – about his famous new (in the mid-1990s) cherry wood kitchen and the fashionable wood-burning Jetmaster stove in his home, but he was still in Daveyton, not anywhere more glamorous. I noticed a vanity licence plate, MEKOA on the Mercedes sedan parked at the school when we visited in 2017. (Turns out the car was a present from his son, but not everyone knew this.) I look at it this way: who could be more deserving? I'm glad he had a comfortable lifestyle because Cathy and I know how much he did for others to achieve it. We were surprised and shocked to learn of his death not long after we saw him while doing research in Johannesburg. He was extremely obese, but seemed energetic and happy. At the time of his death, he held honorary doctorates from UNISA and the University of Pretoria and had received the Order of Ikhamanga for Achievements in Arts and Culture from President Jacob Zuma.

Ezra Ngcukana

Ezra Ngcukana (1954–2010) and I were on the front page of the *Daily News* of 13 November 1987, along with Dalton Khanyile and Merle McKenna, next to the Angolan war and other major news. We met as participants in the Carling Circle of Jazz in 1987. From then on, I played with Ezra whenever he visited Durban from Cape Town. During the 1990s he was able to take time off from his day job in marketing at BP to give workshops, particularly when the sax teacher at UND was on sabbatical. I noticed that he found my teaching style too lenient; he favoured drill and memorisation. Ezra claimed that music was 'just mathematics' and technique, but his playing was never less than soulful – overflowing with passion. He put it all down to skill, firmly shutting the door on alternatives. His creativity and versatility were such that it was hard to believe he truly felt that way. He was not formally trained, but he

Front page of the *Daily News*, 13 November 1987. From left: Dalton Khanyile, Darius, Ezra Ngcukana, Merle McKenna.

had learnt his technique from his renowned, saxophone-playing father, Christopher Columbus 'Mra' Ngcukana, a fabled jazz explorer, sometimes fancifully compared in jazz journalism to his navigator namesake. When he recorded *The Brothers* with Duke Makasi, Tete Mbambisa, Victor Ntoni and Lulu Gontsana, Ezra's compositions 'One Up' and 'Sexlessness' had an air of cerebral singularity, not unlike a conversation with Ezra himself.[30]

Ezra's nickname was Pharoah, after the American avant-garde saxophonist Pharoah Sanders, to whom he bore a slight resemblance. Ezra sometimes went in the direction of musical abstraction, 'playing all the sounds' (his description) at great length in his solos. This could sometimes be a problem at gigs, but usually he knew when he could get away with it. He might go on and on, which could get uncomfortable on stage, but he didn't run out of ideas and audiences found this exciting. When he wasn't experimenting, he could just as freely deliver funky disco jazz, then prevalent on the Cape Town club scene. He was impatient with what he called 'wiggle-waggle' music, music that makes no difference to anyone 'as long as you wiggle-waggle your ass'.

Ezra and Cathy were really good mates and watched many football matches together. Since childhood, Cathy has been a committed football fan and likes to say she measures her life in World Cups, which, (for the uninformed) happen every four years during the months of June and July. This means they coincide with the National Arts Festival in Grahamstown, which takes place in the middle of South African winter. The Jazz Festival within the Arts Festival was a good gig, but for many years it was no holiday. Performers stayed in houses that were rented out during the festival period or in Rhodes University dorms that were vacated during the winter break. July can be brutally cold in Grahamstown (now Makhanda) and the houses and dorms were never heated, as if those responsible had simply forgotten that winter was a predictable phenomenon. It was so cold in the house we shared in 1990, a World Cup year, that we left the oven door open to warm us up. Leaks in the roof caused puddles on parts of the floor and Ezra was nearly electrocuted on the way to the TV area to join Cathy watching Roger Milla of the Cameroon team defeat and astonish the England goalkeeper Peter Shilton. Incidentally, Allen Kwela absolutely refused to stay in 'such a house' and Henry Shields, the festival director was forced to find him a room in the Grand Hotel, which was popular but not grand. The rest of us battled on, but stipulated accommodation conditions for the future.

For World Cup years, I could count on finding Ezra and Cathy early in the morning huddled in coats keeping track of the tournament. And, in 2010, barely a month after they once again watched games, this time held in South Africa, Ezra died. He had looked unusually thin, but was still playing very well and we had no idea this would be our last time together. It was a very sad time indeed because Robbie Jansen, a legendary Cape Town alto player, band leader and singer also died following this festival. He played his final concert there with an oxygen tank next to his chair.

The inescapable cold and spartan accommodation, coupled with predominantly male musician camaraderie and late hours, encouraged drinking. This was a given. And yet, I was always astounded to see Ezra first up in the morning cracking ice cubes into a glass bowl. He would set the bowl on a table beside his litre of Coke and pint of brandy to accompany study for his Bachelor of Commerce exams. I knew that despite his prodigious alcohol consumption, he was very disciplined about certain things, two sides of his character operating concurrently. He was incisive and funny when criticising other people; he would tell it like it is, but without judgement or malice. 'Duke is a drag,' he said of his trumpet-playing schoolteacher brother because Duke Ngcukana never drank and 'takes himself too seriously'. According to Lulu Gontsana, Ezra and his other brothers diarised 'drinking appointments' with friends and each other. Ezra said that Victor Ntoni was 'sluggish' because he was a habitual procrastinator and didn't finish work. I wonder what he said about me . . . No matter – he remains, for Cathy and me, one of our favourite and most remarkable South African friends.

In his 'mathematical' world view, if two opinions were possible, it was likely that neither was right, so differences never became conflicts. For example, when discussing some political point with us, he reminded us that we were ANC supporters and he was PAC and simply left it at that, not unlike a Communist official ending a civil conversation with a Catholic bishop. In this way, he directed every conversation he took part in, stated his views in a way that was not only clear but absolute, and always with good humour, which I suspect was supported by a deep conviction that none of us truly knows anything.

Ezra presented to the world a bundle of well-managed contradictions, which he seemed ironically aware of and at peace with, so he is remembered as caring, popular, respected and friendly. He evidently loved helping his 'drag' of a brother teach music to kids in the community and took great pride in the Little Giants, the Gugulethu township youth band they founded together and organised. If ever a song could summon up his character – and this is a song he played often and brilliantly – it is trumpeter and former Blue Notes member Mongezi Feza's 'You Think You Know Me (but You'll Never Know Me)'.[31]

Catherine

Barney Rachabane

We have mentioned Barney Rachabane (1946–2021) throughout this book, but he deserves further acclamation. He was central to our lives as a musician and friend, and was a luminary in the South African jazz world. As South Africa's foremost alto sax player, he had a great career, which included touring and recording with Paul Simon and Hugh Masekela. One can hear his distinctive sax voice on the universally loved *Graceland*.

Barney became the permanent sax player with Afro Cool Concept in 1990 and in addition to numerous concerts around South Africa, he toured the United States, Thailand, Italy and Denmark with this group and met all the Brubeck family on a number of occasions. He arranged tickets for Dave and Iola and Darius's sister to see him with Paul Simon, Michael Brecker and Ladysmith Black Mambazo in New York City, and also stayed at the Brubeck home in Connecticut on a number of occasions. Touring with Afro Cool Concept, we visited all kinds of historic and 'holy' places, ranging from Graceland, Elvis Presley's house and shrine in Memphis, to the Vatican.

Afro Cool Concept was a featured group at the Celimontana Festival in Rome and I remember resorting to various subterfuges to keep a reporter from *Il Manifesto*, the communist newspaper, from interviewing Barney, who was railing against all things African. He was very impressed by the Italians who, as he pointed out repeatedly, speak their own language, eat their own food all the time and build things that 'will never fall down'. He demonstrated this by kicking a huge column in St Peter's. 'If God is coming again, it will be right here.' One of his favourite lines, and indeed our favourite Barneyism, was that the 'Italians didn't need the English to tell them what to do'. Colonial heritage runs deep! We could imagine a devastating headline, without context or humour, that would make our quartet seem like ambassadors for the apartheid regime.

Barney had a very strong and dominant personality and had no truck with political correctness. He always played just what he wanted and wasn't prepared to fulfil anyone else's agenda. To some degree he felt that the musicians returning from exile took over and undervalued those who had remained. He was one of the few South Africans who earned his living as a musician all his life, first playing penny whistle on the streets of Johannesburg. A Pedi by ethnicity, he was born and raised in Alexandra township, an extremely tough place by any standards. He was self-taught and his band, the Kwela Kids, was noticed in the late 1950s, along with other extraordinary penny whistlers such as Spokes Mashiyane and Lemmy Special. The Kids performed at township jazz festivals and for the African Jazz and Variety shows that played around the country. Barney later taught himself to play trumpet, clarinet, sax and flute, but the alto sax became his favourite, a choice that marked his virtuosic music identity.

In March 1984, Barney told Derek Malcolm – former film critic for the *Guardian* and *Evening Standard*, in South Africa for the Durban International Film Festival – that Darius had 'broken the egg', meaning that Darius had got jazz firmly into mainstream events. Barney was totally enthused because so many musicians of all races were taking part. After a gathering at our house, Barney, Darius and I went to Evan Ziporyn's

Some Remarkable People   179

Hermit gig with Allen and Sandile, which turned out to be fantastic, especially when Barney started jamming with them. The best music started after the audience had left and Darius and I enjoyed a concert where everyone was playing in top form. In a letter to Iola (31 March 1984) I wrote:

> I think you would have been really knocked out by the chaotic Mr Kwela and, I suppose like the Charlie Parker syndrome, one forgets the stuff he puts one through in those rare but superb moments. Needless to mention, no one had a cassette machine . . . Tonight, Darius has a Maitre Pers gig with Barney, Marc and the young drummer Kevin Gibson. Probably the Hermit contingent will show up for jamming later. As Darius said on the phone, he wants to cut down on the little gigs and just do the ones that matter either musically or financially, so, after Easter we really hope to have less running around.

Famous last words! In 2023 we are still on the road and Darius still plays tunes he played with Barney. Barney is on the very first recording of 'Tugela Rail'. In 1984, apartheid reached into unexpected places. At the RPM recording studio in Johannesburg, Barney, Sandile and Nelson were told they couldn't use the nearest toilet, so Darius asked for the key as if for himself and then, in full view, handed it over to Barney. 'I see you don't take any shit,' he said, which was pretty funny given the lavatorial context.

During a lecture at the Stellenbosch Institute for Advanced Study, Zimbabwean author Noviolet Bulawayo spoke about how humour humanises us and both Darius and I feel that this applies particularly to the jazz world. In heavy situations, using language like Lulu Gontsana's 'security cats' or trying his 'almost-best' served as good solo 'licks'. Jazz spawns an improvised insider humour of its own. We laugh at each other and the world and along the way enjoy the instant mythology of present and past players, fans and situations.

In Memphis, not especially known for its liberal attitudes, our friend and hostess Tommie Pardue, a former Miss Tennessee, took Barney with her to a white old-folks' home, which embraced traditional Southern etiquette. Tommie had to visit a resident en route to our rehearsal and when they got there, Barney just got out his sax and charmed everyone playing well-known songs. His respect for old people came to the fore and this charismatic visitor from Africa made a huge impression – so much so that there were requests for him to return. Adapting to his audience, he didn't unleash his great trademark octave glissando (Oh-wee-Oh), which can be heard in many of his solos and very notably on his own tune 'Kwela Mama'.[32] In New Orleans this lick really tore up the audience and was captured in a live broadcast on NPR (National Public Radio), subsequently released as Brubeck/Ntoni Afro Cool Concept, *Live at the New Orleans Jazz & Heritage Festival.*[33] Playing with Barney was a musical high that galvanised all in the quartet. It spurred them on to greater heights and, when I was in an audience, as I often was, the feeling was that the music really mattered to everyone there too.

Speaking on behalf of the Minister of Sport, Arts and Culture, the Hon. Nathi Mthethwa, on the occasion of the funeral of Barney Rachabane – 20 November 2021

What would jazz music be without the saxophone and what would South African jazz be today without Barney's contribution? In an interview in 2013 he (Barney Rachabane) said:

> My dad was a bus driver. He told me to get a job. He was a pianist. He asked how could I have a wife, children and a home as a musician. But I did. This is what I wanted. God gave me what I wanted. I only wanted to be a musician. Music makes me tick.

Much has already been said of the many years he toured with Bra Hugh Masekela and of his participation in the Graceland tours of Paul Simon. He collaborated with Abdullah Ibrahim, Darius Brubeck and younger musicians. But he was not affected or dazzled by the bright lights of other places and always longed to be back home . . . Perhaps this is why he did not flee into exile despite the hardships he experienced, for he was at one with his community and people . . .

He was known to be a walking musical encyclopaedia well versed in South African jazz music, and a professor through his own making. He was a musician of which it must be said that there is no other like him. His musical career spanned more than six decades. For him music emerged and emanated from his soul and 'music,' he said, 'is a gift from God'.

We shall treasure our memories of him and do all we can to preserve and honour his musical legacy. Our condolences to the entire Rachabane family.

Darius

We received an email from Lex Futshane with the information that Barney died 'last night', which was Saturday, 13 November 2021. Barney's much-beloved wife Elizabeth had died three months previously. We phoned his daughter Octavia to offer condolences and were consoled in turn by hearing that 'he was just sitting in his chair'. It sounded like an easy exit; no ambulance, no hospital time, which would have been grim in Soweto's vast Baragwanath Hospital complex; just a night at home, not followed by another day.

Barney and I shared many travels together over the years, which allowed opportunities for long conversations about life. His father was also a lay minister, so his upbringing was stable, anchored by firm adherence to religious beliefs. Barney was surprised that we didn't say grace the first time he had dinner at home with us. He did not go to church or follow any creed, but he often referred to God. His God was another figure of power, like the state or ancestors or township gangs, who might take sides in a conflict – you never knew what He would do, so it was best just stay on His good side. Barney had little formal education and yet when I asked him how many languages he knew, he started naming them, counting them off on his fingers. The answer was nine! He learnt to read music through a correspondence course – I think Royal Schools (ABRSM) – which he paid for with earnings from the Kwela Kids. He said he 'grew up under' Zacks Nkosi (1919–1978), who made hit after hit in the early 1960s with definitive recordings of original pieces in a slightly older style of township jazz or *mbaqanga*. This was Barney's apprenticeship, the old-school way of learning music in the jazz community. He carried Zacks's instruments (alto sax and clarinet), helped him set up and ran errands at gigs in return for being allowed to hang out with the band. From time to time, he was shown a scale fingering or a choice lick. What Barney learnt from Zacks, more than anyone else, was the importance of developing his own sound. What made Nkosi such an influence? Barney said, 'It was his tone.'

Apparently, Zacks's greatest vice was gluttony. According to Barney, once Zacks had money, he just ate all the time. 'You go to his house any time of day and he is at his table with every kind of food there – meat, sausages, chicken, desserts – everything. Zacks just ate himself to death.' (I remember that his son Jabu, who was the ace keyboardist with Sakhile, was also very overweight.) Afro Cool recorded Zacks Nkosi's 'Hoshhh Hoha' with Allen Kwela on guitar just to pay tribute to Zacks and his focus on tone.[34]

Barney was also drawn to the Charlie Parker-influenced modernism of Kippie Moeketsi, after whom the famous Johannesburg jazz club was named much later. Sadly, it has now gone. It is obvious that Kippie was also a big influence on Barney, but he wasn't so easy to hang out with. 'He was mad . . . he drank too much . . . he got into fights . . . he used to chase women – really chase them, I mean – *with his cock out*.'

Barney's opinions, as Cathy has indicated, needed a little filtering, but he expressed them firmly and with humour. He decried the cruelty of 'the Boer' and related some compelling incidents as examples, including the infamous raid in 1985 on a recording studio complex just across the border in Botswana where several musicians were murdered by 'Boer guys who were looking for Hugh', but strangely he had zero confidence that black people would ever successfully govern themselves. He told us about having his instruments confiscated while crossing back into South Africa at the Zimbabwean border, clearly a shake-down. He had to bribe officials to get them back. It was safer to live in South Africa because, 'if you go to a hospital in *real* Africa, you just die'. Unlike the Italians (and he added the Thai people, once he heard, while we were on a bus tour of Bangkok, that Siam had never been colonised), Africans, according to Barney, *did* need the English to tell them what to do.

We last visited Barney and Elizabeth in 2019. His home had been added to over the years and was a solidly built compound in his old neighbourhood, housing three generations of Rachabanes. It now had a double-storey annex at the back and a triple garage on the side. There was a music room with a drum kit, keyboard, amps and recording equipment upstairs. These additions and improvements must have been made during the Paul Simon years, when everyone on the road with Paul made good money. Some of them, like electric bassist Bakiti Kumalo moved to the United States; others stayed in South Africa, but migrated to the better suburbs of their respective cities. Not Barney. He made himself and his family comfortable where he had grown up, on the dusty streets of Alex (actually, Pimville, a subdivision of Alexandra). This was where he spent his last night, at home.

Zim Ngqawana

> It is time that the South African 'black' began to appreciate the value of aspiring toward the universal and then to live in it, to become a part of it, to add to it the cumulative value of the experience of being free in the specificity of their historical circumstances, where dream and effort are inseparable.
> — Njabulo S. Ndebele, 'It's Time to Shed Blackness'

We were involved with Zim Ngqawana (25 December 1959 – 10 May 2011), and Zim with us, for a major part of our lives. People like to talk about Zim and this is an important part of his legacy because talking about Zim inevitably means facing up to perennial questions about art and life. By word and deed, he problematised everything related to jazz, perhaps everything related to being an African 'aspiring toward the universal', which is among the more profound reasons that jazz exists. Zim and therefore 'Zimology' – his word for anything and everything he thought about – was a hot topic in South Africa on the tenth anniversary of his passing in 2011.[35] Catherine wrote the following after Zim died:

Zimasile Ngqawana was born on December 25, 1959, a special day, and a special year in music. 1959 was a milestone in the history of jazz because four momentous albums were recorded that year; Dave Brubeck (*Time Out*),

John Coltrane (*Giant Steps*), Miles Davis (*Kind of Blue*) and Ornette Coleman (*The Shape of Jazz to Come*). It is perhaps this last title that comes closest to representing Zim's persona and his drive for an original and profound music statement. Along with other special friends, we have great memories of living together during the politically challenging and transitional '80's and we are thinking particularly of former Jazzanians and of Zim's comrades Lulu Gontsana, Feya Faku and Lex Futshane.

In 2011, Cathy, Zim and I sat eating and talking for hours at the Ocean Basket in Rosebank, a northern Johannesburg suburb. This was not a pre-arranged meeting. Cathy and I had talked about trying to get together with Zim, but this was our last day in South Africa before returning to London and we still had a lot to do. We couldn't fit in the long drive to the suburb where Zim lived, but we did have time for lunch. When I looked up from the menu, he was standing in front of us, as if by magic. He was upbeat and talkative. He had been shocked and depressed by the destructive looting of the smallholding where he had set up his Institute of Zimology in 2010, but he seemed to have come to terms with it now. He loved punning and wordplay, softening the horror of finding two grand pianos with their legs sawn off by calling it 'vandalizim'.[36]

Over the years, we had watched him evolve from a focused and critical student of the mainly American jazz canon into a self-consciously authentic and impressively original Afrocentric version of himself. But the emphasis here is on 'version' because that day he seemed quite over that too. 'African' Zim had developed an international career and a powerful critique of the jazz world and post-colonial culture in general, but he didn't need to live within that any more than he needed to continue learning or even composing tunes. Musically, he was not one for playing the changes and when he did, once his student years had passed, he seemed like an adult taking some pleasure in playing a kid's game. At that last lunch he was universal Zim, cosmopolitan Zim, Zim the cosmonaut. As with many artists – Miles Davis and Picasso spring to mind – his restless questing resulted in episodes of egotism and selfishness that upset people closely involved with him, but I don't know of anyone who ceased to love him. I think it is this personal charisma even more than his music that makes Zim something of a cult figure now.

UND didn't have a jazz saxophone teacher when Zim arrived in 1986, but there was an extensive collection of jazz books and records in the music library, including some volumes of Jamey Aebersold's Play-Along series, and there was also the beloved Prac Block, where he could practise with the records or with fellow students. Zim said this was all he needed and he was an instant star in the jazz workshop classes and big band rehearsals. After some weeks, he asked for an appointment in my office. I was bracing myself for complaints about the (to me) obvious inadequacies of the programme, or perhaps a plea for more financial support. Instead, he told me about Feya Faku, a trumpet player in New Brighton, the township of Port Elizabeth. He concluded with the pronouncement, 'He deserves the same chance I have'. In fact, we got two valuable additions because bassist Lex Futshane, also from Port Elizabeth, came with Feya the following year. In effect, Zim was recruiting for us. If Feya and Lex wanted to give up whatever their chances might have been in their own community and move to Durban, Cathy and I would somehow make it possible. This was no casual decision because 'making it possible' included more fund-raising, finding places for them to live and navigating the currents and reefs of academic administration, as described elsewhere. But our efforts paid off big time.

Lulu and Zim went to stay with Helmuth and Leslie Holst, two very politically progressive friends we had met through Jürgen and Brigitte Bräuninger, and they were very supportive of the jazz programme. Later, after Marc Duby left our Peace Avenue garden flat, we had Feya, Lex, Lulu and Zim staying there. After the Jazzanians' tour, we sold the Peace Avenue house to live nearer campus. Between houses, we rented a spacious but dark, no-frills flat in MacArthur Street and all six of us moved there. As whites, Cathy and I could retain the lease and simply leave the others in place when we moved to Queen Elizabeth Avenue. We were camping, mattresses on the floor and minimal furniture, but it was fun and cemented a long-lasting spirit of togetherness.

It was interesting to observe the group dynamic. Zim assumed the role of *primus inter pares* – not the boss, but the owner of the final word in discussions ranging from music, politics, fashion (they cared more about clothes than we did) to daily plans. He tried to introduce regular meditation practice into the routine, but Lulu wasn't having it. He was quick to see that Zim was setting himself up as a sage, a stance already adopted by Bheki Mseleku and Abdullah Ibrahim. Lulu respected and worked with both these musicians, although he mimicked and mocked their self-important mannerisms, but he wasn't going to take it from someone he grew up with in the township.

Zim, as we have already mentioned, was offered a scholarship to study at the University of Massachusetts, Amherst, where the multi-reed player and composer Yusef Lateef was teaching. Max Roach's patronage allowed him to extend his stay and become familiar with New York City's creative scene. He did make it back to Durban in time to record the Jazzanian album and to play some wildly successful Jazzanian gigs. He then returned to Amherst and spent more time with Max Roach.[37] This was an exciting and formative period, as can be seen in this handwritten letter to us on Max Roach's letterhead from Central Park West, dated 27 October 1988:

I'm getting another perspective here. I'm studying Afro-American music with Dr Tillis. This is a deep course, and quite appropriate for the situation in SA, because as far as I'm concerned, SLAVERY is taking place in SA right now. I'm quite aware about the air of hope and am up to date with SA politics . . . Anyway, I'll be sending some stuff concerning teaching methods cause we can't discuss this in a short letter. I would appreciate it so much if you could send me my *Smithsonian [Collection of Classic Jazz]* records, sax stand, and my boots. It's cold here . . . I also go to Archie Shepp's 'Black Music' class. We played with him last week – just playing. He is great. Miles is coming to town next month. I'm studying Max's music and learning a lot from it. He is urging me to write some stuff. He keeps on telling me that he has big plans for me. Don't ask me what they are. I don't bother, I've come to the US to study. Period . . . I'll probably be seeing Dave and Iola soon, please keep in touch. Peace!!!
Zim

I managed to persuade Bobby Mills, who was then an assistant dean, that Zim's courses at Amherst counted as credits and that he could therefore remain on the books as a student, while staying in the orbit of the good and great in the United States, where he strengthened ties with the black avant-garde and Dave Brubeck. His second period at the university there resulted in the friendship with Chris Merz, who was finishing a Master's degree under Jeff Holmes, and this connection resulted in Chris applying for the saxophone job at University of Natal. Once again, Zim had successfully recruited for us. Chris and Zim were on campus together for a year or two and we sometimes played together in bands called Jazz Comrades and Double Vision because of the two-sax front line.

The photo on p. 186 was taken at a party at United States Ambassador Bill Swing's Pretoria residence in 1991, which shows Abdullah Ibrahim and Cathy bookending a line-up of musicians, including Zim and me with Ambassador Swing. I was playing a fairly straight-ahead South African and American repertoire at what was essentially a cocktail reception for diplomats and cultural VIPs, but Zim, whenever it was his turn, kept playing 'out' as if we were in an avant-garde music club in Berlin. I knew what he was doing and why. Abdullah was there and Zim was distancing himself from, in his view, trivial music-making, whiteness and *from me*. It worked. When I say, 'it worked', I mean I got the message and so did Abdullah. Zim moved to Johannesburg and started playing with him, going the full distance by later converting to Islam. Abdullah Ibrahim's name has long been synonymous with all that is great and unique in South African music, its compelling reconciliation of city and country, ancient and modern, licentiousness and spirituality, which for convenience might be called 'jazz', but in his case, it really is just music. His latest album, *Solotude*, recorded when he was 80, is a perfect example of his profound artistry.[38]

Zim reached a high level in the jazz world very quickly and now he was going to finishing school under a true master. Sure enough, when we saw him in the 1990s and early 2000s, he could turn on an air of aggrieved superiority just like Abdullah. Zim's attitude was never as pronounced, but he knew how to work it. He didn't last very long with Abdullah because he was determined to do his own thing.

In 1997, I put together a third version of the band Gathering Forces, which included Zim and Kevin Gibson, for a festival in Nantes, France, known as Les Rendez-vous de l'Erdre. The theme was 'Johannesburg à la Fin de Siècle', so my partnership with Deepak Ram and our Indo-Afro jazz music fitted the bill, as did Zim's own quartet, which now consisted of Andile Yenana on piano, Herbie Tsoaeli on bass and Kevin on drums. This was his magic quartet and Cathy and I were totally entranced by their concerts, which took place in a club after the Gathering Forces performances in the grand Theatre Graslin. Zim's wonderful contribution to Gathering Forces was a new arrangement of his composition 'Mamazala', an intriguing, almost Mozartian melody, set to the formulaic chords of African jazz.[39] (Lulu wittily referred to it as

At US Ambassador William Swing's residence in Pretoria, 1991. Back, from left: Abdullah Ibrahim, Darius, William Swing, Victor Ntoni, Chris Merz. Middle: Don Mattera, unknown, Zim Ngqawana, Cathy. Front: Lulu Gontsana, unknown (photographer unknown; Cathy Brubeck collection).

ECM *mbaqanga*.) Zim thought of 'Mamazala' as his juvenilia, but asked us to try two radical ideas that made it a highlight in the second iteration. First idea: slow the tempo down to a crawl, slower than anything you'd expect to hear in a jazz concert. Second idea: replace the four-chord African cycle with Charlie Parker changes during the solo section after the melody. Non-musicians may find this description hard to follow, so the best I can say is that both ideas are so counter-intuitive that no one in the world but Zim would have thought of them. The result was a cathartic fourteen minutes and ten seconds of music making.[40] After 24 years, I'll admit that I could have done without Zim's reed-biting squealing and squawking late in his solo and that I played too many choruses, but the energy level was too high to just get in and get out. (As pianists since the late Coltrane era know, horn players can ignore the form, but we can't.) He drove us all over a cliff, but to a soft landing, cushioned by the return of the sweet melody, gospel-plain chords, slow-drag tempo, and pianissimo coda. 'Mamazala' remains in my current quartet's repertoire and is a hit with audiences in all the countries we have played.

Seven years later (2004), Jazz at Lincoln Center in New York City was in the process of commissioning a full programme of new pieces under the rubric of 'Let Freedom Swing' for the opening of Rose Hall, the new auditorium designed for the Lincoln Center Jazz Orchestra, directed by Wynton Marsalis. All the commissioned pieces were to be settings of famous speeches advocating visions of equality – for example, Robert Kennedy's address to University of Natal students in 1966 (incidentally, Cathy had been in the audience). We happened to be in the United States in 2004 and were invited to a meeting with Todd Barkan and others involved in the project. I was asked if I knew a South African composer who could take on a commission to write music for excerpts of speeches by Nelson Mandela and Archbishop Desmond Tutu. The premiere would take place on 28–30 October, during the week before voting began in the George W. Bush versus John Kerry presidential contest. I didn't see myself as directly taking part because I'm not South African and they were looking for a black South African. When we returned to South Africa, we sent examples of traditional *marabi* and township jazz that could be re-orchestrated, and suggested contacting Caiphus Semenya, Bheki Mseleku or Abdullah Ibrahim. They had already considered them and rejected the idea on the basis that the focus should be on the band and the message and the only 'stars' involved should be the actors that did the readings. The South African speeches would be read by Morgan Freeman. So, we referred them to Zim's CDs, which were now available internationally, and sent examples of my arranging for orchestras. I was told when the piece had to be delivered in playable form – score and parts – given absolute deadlines and technical criteria that *had* to be met. In the end, it seemed the most satisfactory solution was a joint commission for Zim and me. Back in Durban, I had access to professional music-notation software on the university computer system, a logistics and communication team in Cathy and Glynis, plus the help of Music Department colleagues Jeff Robinson as editor/proofreader and Jürgen Bräuninger for technical support. I was very proud that our Jazz Centre would be involved in this project at Jazz at Lincoln Center. Zim made three sponsored trips to Durban, staying with us and working with me in my office. He was cheerful and confident at first, although I could see he wasn't as engaged as I was. In his view then, Wynton was 'a curator, not a creator'. I intended Zim to take the lead and we spent time noodling around on the piano (which he could also play well), but he couldn't or wouldn't decide on anything, so I started interpreting, sketching and composing and, as time was running out, orchestrating, and finally copying the parts. I nearly resigned when I found out that Zim had contacted Jazz at Lincoln Center between trips to Durban to say that our collaboration 'wasn't working out' and that he needed more time and money. (How would more money resolve a creative impasse?) I was really angry and said I wouldn't continue working with him, but Cathy and Todd Barkan convinced me I had to finish what I started. This was the closest I had come to not fulfilling a contract in my whole career. The last item on the checklist, so to speak, was a title. Surely, it was just a matter of selecting a phrase from one of the speeches. Well, that was too obvious for Zim, who harboured doubts about the Rainbow Nation ideals of 1994, so we settled on a neutral title suggested by Cathy, 'Commission 2004'. Zim was meant to be the main composer and I was meant to be merely the arranger/copyist and guarantor of punctuality and competence. I accepted the political necessity of Zim being credited as the lead composer and that was fine, but he didn't write down one bar of the music. However, if Zim had not participated as a sounding board, criticising my sometimes-dated ideas, and sometimes pitching good ones, 'Commission 2004' would have been a different and inferior piece. The fact that his name was on the composition gave him a veto and I paid attention to the effects and moods he wanted. It was more like a composer working with a film director than two composers working on a piece.

Cathy and I were in New York for the premiere and I helped a little with the final rehearsals. It all felt worth it on the night. Zim didn't attend, but Wynton wrote him a personal thank-you note, which we delivered. That same year Zim was holding concerts all over South Africa and being noticed at home and abroad and, somewhat unexpectedly, won Male Artist of the Year at the South African Music Awards.

As the inevitability of my retirement from UKZN came into view, I began thinking about succession scenarios. I persuaded Zim to apply for the upcoming vacant post and put in a big effort convincing the selection committee (of which I was not a member) to consider his application – a replay of the old days, but at a higher level. His academic credentials (if any, beyond diploma level) were incomplete and unclear. Anyway, I emphasised his creativity and proven artistry. He interviewed terrifically,

Some Remarkable People   189

tactfully leaving out any attitude towards institutions. He acknowledged the help he had received as a student and recounted his rewarding days in the Prac Bloc. I had argued that given his fame and visionary commitment to South African music and, given that there were no specific academic criteria for a jazz lecturer, he was appointable. He was appointed. In fact, the committee made what seemed to me to be a very innovative decision by appointing two people to take my place. The other appointee, also endorsed by me, was guitarist Mageshen Naidoo, a former UND student, then a doctoral candidate at University of Southern California (Los Angeles). This was affordable because I had reached a senior rank with a salary that could cover two new staff members.

Instead of the customary inaugural lecture, the Music School organised a concert titled 'Anthology of Zimology' on 22 April 2005 at the Howard College Theatre, followed by a reception at the Jazz Centre. This was with the magic quartet again and, along with the rest of the audience, we were enthralled. Zim had recently performed and recorded as universal Zim, but for this occasion he gave us the African Zim. His concert was a connected narrative consisting of pre-arranged pieces with titles and musically distinct themes performed seamlessly, rather than as a selection of tunes punctuated by announcements. His compositions referenced rituals, migrant workers, ancestors, orphans and so on, and the effect was pure, enveloping, wordless storytelling or, as Chris Ballantine put it, 'an amazing feat of musical architecture'. Lindelwa Dalamba, a graduate student at the time and a music critic for the *Sunday Tribune*, wrote an insightful review worth quoting in snippets here because, though duly appreciative, I think she really got his number:

Welcome to Brand Zim and . . . Please Remove Your Shoes
His is a universe structured by a spirituality (and gadgets, it seems) that ranges across humanity's attempt to be significant . . . We, the audience, were elect guests and surveyors of this music . . . With the kind of aura that surrounds Ngqawana himself, the audience arrived expecting a mystery . . . To the right: a shrine to old traditional instruments on a table set with black cloth. To the left were wind chimes and bells of some sort. Centre stage were four saxophones of various sizes and a flute.

We entered the dream world of Zimology . . . The gig was unapologetic about Ngqawana's relationship with music and the world; it was his account of it to us . . . Cathy Brubeck noted that we were 'privileged to be there' . . . Suspicious of anything that smacks of mysticism and depth, I remain ambivalent toward Zimology as a creed . . . though I would gladly welcome re-admission to the Magus' domain.[41]

Reviewing a similar concert during the 2004 Grahamstown Festival (same personnel), Gwen Ansell wrote, 'Ngqawana hit the perfect balance between righteous anger, jagged abstraction, melody and swing, in the expression of a uniquely South African voice'.[42] The same could be said for the Anthology of Zimology concert in Durban.

Classes taking place within the Magus's domain were another matter and Zim was often a polarising figure. Informed of the necessity of giving marks for credit-bearing courses, he told students to give themselves an assignment, then mark it themselves. This delighted his new acolytes, but exasperated others who thought they were being short-changed. He repeated sayings like 'jazz is dead' or intoned a litany of negatives like 'jazz is not a style' and 'jazz is not a repertoire' to bemused first- and second-year students, who were there to learn about jazz. He preached Zimology. 'Zimology is the study of the self,' he said. Also, the study of *himself*, it seemed. Lindelwa Dalamba remembers: 'Ngqawana's making of the self was playful, but not superficial. He also resisted the label "jazz", which he considered at once "too limiting and too all-encompassing" '.[43]

Zim and I taught separate undergraduate workshops, which featured improvisation and repertoire, in the Jazz Centre, where my office was located. His classes normally began with a quiet lecture with minimal lighting, students sprawled out meditating or dozing. Soon after the mystical homily, the building would be vibrating with the sounds of back-beat drumming, pounding percussion, one-chord bass vamps, a small female chorus, pseudo-angry rapping, horns squeaking and squawking, spacey synth washes and overdrive guitar. Sometimes I had no choice but to listen. Zim was indeed directing a kind of jam session, shaping it so that certain reference points stabilised, clear solo spaces emerged from the electric Milesian bedlam and eventually convincing moments of beauty did break through. Was the student experience one of self-actualising rampant creativity or just the lowest common denominator of what could still be called music? Kevin Gibson told us a funny story about working with Zim: 'He did a gig and recorded it and then wouldn't pay us . . . so one Friday he played back the recording and said, "Now listen to this. Do you think I'm going to pay for that?" '

Academic committees can set goals and outcomes, but it is a sacred and universal rule of academic life that one never tells a colleague what to teach or even how to teach. I tried talking to Zim privately about the expectations that went with the job. Part of me acknowledges the absurdity of teaching improvisation based on Broadway tunes from the first half of the last century. Fine, he didn't have to teach the canon, but what were students being taught? I recommended some conventional wisdom along the lines of preparation for classes always made them more worthwhile and that there was a certain etiquette to giving individual lessons and student evaluation was part of his job, and so on. I spoke as a friend, a former mentor and professor. I believed his presence as a South African artist would bring glory and credit to the university. He would be increasingly influential very soon because I had already given my notice.

He could be set up for life, but he still had to do some of the required work to justify his presence. It was ironic that I, the loose cannon of the 1980s and 1990s, was now explaining what was due to the institution. He listened carefully, even respectfully, and was not the least bit defensive. Everything I was telling him was constructive, correct and made practical sense, down to the fact that he could count on a pay cheque virtually forever but, I guess rightly in a way, he saw it as consenting to limits on his freedom. Finally, he said, 'But then I'm just a saxophone teacher.' I'm sure I plied him with reasons why staff *could be* and indeed *were expected to be* more than our official handbook job descriptions, but I got what he meant and I knew he would leave.

Zim honourably resigned, but finished the semester doing what he did. Some students met with me to say they thought he should take over the Centre when I left. They didn't know that this was also my wish, or part of it, and that things were much more complicated than that. Two students eventually followed him to the Institute of Zimology, which, as I heard from one who came back, was not an entirely successful experience for everyone who went there.

After the Lincoln Center experience, I knew that Zim wouldn't really take on lecturing, planning, committee work, curriculum development and directing CJPM. The important thing in my mind was that giving Zim a position at UKZN signalled a creative, even radical re-set. With Zim, UKZN could tack towards becoming a school noted for experimentation and launching new directions in South African music. But I had also been worried that the established programme could implode, if it only channelled Zim's subjectivity, mysticism and identity politics. It also needed someone with pedagogical and academic orientation. This is why I had supported the application by Mageshen Naidoo. I remember the words of Michael Chapman, when he was dean of Humanities and a little fed up with long searches for overseas candidates for jazz posts: 'Why can't we grow our own timber?' Well, at last, it looked like we had done that. Unfortunately, it became clear that Zim and Mageshen couldn't or wouldn't develop a co-operative relationship. One person doing two jobs works better than two people doing one job, no matter how demanding that job is. The grand plan for my departure and succession was my grand mistake.

I left for England, but Zim and I saw each other when I returned to South Africa, and notably in 2010 when we listened to each other's sets at the Grahamstown Festival. I still felt like we were all on a long and winding road to new horizons and would continue meeting up for years to come. And, as I stated earlier, the following year we did, at the Ocean Basket. Albert Einstein's famous remark, 'Coincidence is God's way of remaining anonymous', which Zim would have appreciated, certainly seemed to fit that occasion. More than the uncanny synchronicity, it was the emphatic way he told us that he 'could die happy' because of a recording he made with some American musicians in New York.[44] 'No rehearsal, no plan, just go on and play.' Universal Zim had peaked. His journey in music was already 'sufficient'. Less than a month later, Zim *did* die, having suffered a stroke during a rehearsal on the anniversary of Nelson Mandela's inauguration.

Zim's wife, Sarah Davids, was raised as a Muslim and, as next of kin, was responsible for the funeral arrangements, so he was buried almost immediately according to Muslim custom. Zim did have long-term Muslim friends, notably Zaide Harneker, who for many years supported all his endeavours and was a very close confidant. Cultural flexibility was part of life in modern, polyglot Johannesburg, but I heard that many regretted this hasty burial. Yes, he had converted to Islam (his complex, syncretic, personal version of it, mainly visible in his attire and unabashed, polyamorous lifestyle), but no amount of spiritual experimentation outweighed the self-evident, existential fact that he was a Xhosa who once sacrificed a goat on the balcony of his Johannesburg flat.

It rained as the body was interred, a sure sign that the ancestors had welcomed him after all. Zim's exceptionalism was far-reaching to the last – and beyond.

8

Off Campus and on the Road

I remember the student and professional jazz life of Durban, the many venues,
mostly fly-by-night places, the jazz scene's many esoteric and out-of-the-box
characters, friends, girlfriends, the liberation struggle . . .
it was hipper than now.
— Rick van Heerden

Catherine

There are so many road stories and songs. Real life is somewhat suspended while you engage with the music, each other and the audience. Being on the road is addictive and one is always ready for the next adventure. The students loved it too – the excitement of preparing a show, driving, or flying to a different destination and then hotels, often fancier than home and special meals and applause. Road stories are the usual, hilarious and frustrating components of a musician's life and our many hotel adventures illustrate the first- and third-world nature of South Africa and its jazz scene. The stories are anecdotes, randomly remembered, not chronological, so be prepared for a haphazard and bumpy ride, which is often the case with a jazz life.

I'll start in 1983 with hotels and recount our stay in downtown Villiers, roughly 160 kilometres from Johannesburg. We had overestimated the number of petrol stations on the old main road and found we had to drive into this *verkrampte* (Afrikaans word meaning 'rigid' or 'uptight') town in search of fuel. We checked at the police station, where the commanding officer was in uniform, but barefoot. He informed us that there wasn't any petrol to be had at that late hour and we would have to stay overnight and he gave us directions to a hotel.

The first mistake I made was to enter the bar/lounge, which was for men only. We were barely over the threshold and the hotelier was angry and horrified – even though there were no other customers present. From the doorway we explained that we needed accommodation for the night. Despite there being absolutely no evidence of other human beings or cars, the man said they had no accommodation. We figured

193

that this rejection was caused by prejudicial factors: woman entered bar, foreigners, English speaking and, to top it all, Darius looks Jewish. We played our trump card and said we were sent there by the commander at the police station (I spoke some Afrikaans as well) and so he told us that the only room he had was a very small room with a single bed. Fine, we'd take it as we couldn't press him any further. There was no supper and I can't remember the breakfast, but I think there was a bowl of congealed porridge.

Returning from Johannesburg on that same trip, we picked up a white hitchhiker and, after not too long, he realised that Darius was an American. He said we needed to watch out for the 'kaffirs' and how much he hated them. At first, we tried to reason with him and said we had many black American friends and that one can't make statements about people based on their skin colour. He replied, 'Your blacks are different' and words to the effect that the 'natives' in South Africa were totally inferior. Darius pulled over and said, 'Get out'; we didn't want him in our car. He was very surprised, but after these two experiences, Darius was more wary of casual contact and extreme racism. Could we even last the term of the two-year contract?

Taking the Natal University Jazz Ensemble, the seventeen-piece big band into Umlazi (a township south of Durban) for the first time proved more difficult than we thought. We had borrowed three university vehicles to take the band for its first appearance at a run-down stadium near some men's hostels. At that time, we didn't have enough students to fill all the chairs and we were dependent on and grateful to the local symphony orchestra for providing trombone and trumpet players. Not being familiar with Umlazi and its many unnamed rough roads seemingly leading nowhere, we got lost and at my request the drivers had to stop and turn around to retrace the written directions we had been given. When we stopped at some dead end in the apparent middle of nowhere, one of the orchestra musicians got out to shout at Darius and me for our lack of professionalism and planning, saying that something like this wouldn't happen where he came from – the United States. As the 'manager', I responded that he was behaving like a spoilt symphony orchestra player and that most of us felt we were there to put on a show and so what if it took us longer than we thought? This exchange exposed the difference in attitudes to pioneering gigs in hitherto little-known places. The jazz cats, who were used to townships, didn't think it was a big deal. The concert eventually took place in what was affectionately referred to as 'African time', actually in sync with the audience who showed up after we did. They were thrilled to have the first South African university big band playing its heart out on their sports ground. The band (including the detractors) played like we were in Carnegie Hall.

Mixed memories on the road with the NUJE include a huge band bus travelling to Johannesburg for a concert at the Linder Auditorium. On the way there, we were entertained by the outstanding mimics Victor Masondo, Johnny Mekoa and Lulu Gontsana. They could take off anyone, each other and all the music staff. Sometimes we felt they were in the wrong profession and could knock Pieter Dirk Uys (South African comedian) off his perch. The accents, the songs and subject matter were both hilarious and moving. Johnny could enact every detail of his encounters with the South African police and his humour and overview found its way into his music. At the back of the bus, there were students who also played in Zanusi, another band that included Sazi Dlamini, S'thembiso Ntuli and the late Madoda 'Bruce' Sosibo. Sosibo was a 'Malopoet' wordsmith who always wore a miner's tin hat on stage. He used it for percussive backing to their music making. I'm not sure why he was with us because he wasn't in the big band – maybe he was just hitching a ride to Johannesburg. These three sang traditional Zulu songs and their own compositions for practically the whole 570 kilometres.

On arrival at the Linder Auditorium, we discovered that the South African army was among the sponsors of this event and this was not acceptable, especially at a time of deadly invasions into Namibia, Swaziland and Botswana, where even Hugh

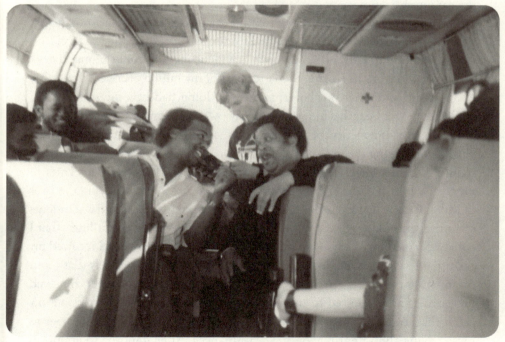

Victor Masondo and Johnny Mekoa singing on the bus to Johannesburg, with Mark Kilian (standing) and Bheki Mbatha and Vusi Sabongo looking on, 1987 (photo: Cathy Brubeck; Cathy Brubeck collection).

Masekela had been a target. Killing so-called terrorists and agitators was a military objective. Musicians like Johnny Mekoa were adamant that we shouldn't play. We had started to unpack our stuff but, after a quick poll of band members, we decided to bail out and forfeit the fee. We didn't want to be associated with the SADF in any way, so we all went to Bill Ainslie's house, played some music there and looked at his paintings. He was the founder and director of the Johannesburg Art Foundation, an art school bravely open to all racial groups. This misadventure reminds me of Mark Kilian's account, in his response to our questionnaire of 9 May 2019, of his military side-step and perception of political life on campus:

> The political climate was so pervasive on the campus at the time, it affected everyone in different ways. All the way from the muted indifference of white students who didn't want to realise their country was blowing up around them, to black students who had directly been affected by the police brutality that was beginning to spill over from the townships and into the cites and onto the campus. It was hard to separate studies and our student lives from this reality . . . Our music studies were awesome, but what was going on outside the campus was important.
>
> I was only nineteen when I started my studies at UND, and I might very well have been one of the least qualified students simply on a musical level. But I was a military intelligence lieutenant, having just completed the mandatory two-year conscription. During the latter part of my military service, the reality of apartheid and what our government was doing had become something I could no longer bear, having seen with my own eyes some of the darker sides of the 'state of emergency' of 1985 and 1986, the years I was in the military. As part of completing the two years conscription, one was expected to do either a month or even a three month 'camp' every year for the next ten years. Later in my first year at the university when my head was stuck into studying the likes of Miles, Coltrane, Stravinsky and the Beatles, and my friends and co-students comprised all colours of the rainbow, I was so far away from the military that I could not conceive of having to put on a uniform again. So, when I received my call-up orders for a camp during my first year of study, I did precisely that – put on my uniform and tucked my too long hair under my black beret, removed my earrings and reported to the local command post in Durban to state my claim that to do a 'camp' would effectively terminate my university career as I was relying almost entirely on my own finances. After standing to attention and being the subject of some scrutiny, my claim went surprisingly well and not only did I get excused for that camp of 1987, but I never received another

call-up for a camp again. I suspect they figured I was a lost cause. However, from that time on I was visited on occasion by undercover intel agents on the university campus and asked if I would be prepared to infiltrate and spy on various organisations at the university, in exchange for having my university fees paid for. I kindly told them to 'fuck off'. And, eventually, they did.

The band was able to play our other gig, which took place in an open-air space outside a sponsoring supermarket in Boksburg. The band performed in front of a giant display board showing the South African featherweight boxing champion Brian Mitchell. As mentioned in Chapter 3, this was when we had to purchase clothes pegs from the supermarket to hold the music down. A few shoppers, passers-by and band family connections thoroughly enjoyed this musical first.

Major George Hayden, a retired army officer and piano and saxophone player, had bought a famous old hotel in the Natal Midlands and we happened to book in there on one of our many trips back from Johannesburg to Durban. We hadn't met him and nor did we know that he now ran the Nottingham Road Hotel. 'Ran' is a

NUJE outside Boksburg hypermarket in 1987 – in front of a Brian Mitchell poster (photo: Cathy Brubeck; Cathy Brubeck collection).

rather fanciful word for what he appeared to do because our room registration was certainly calamitous.

The hotel reception desk adjoined a stable door where the top half was open and led through to a bar where people were drinking heavily and playing darts. One of these came zinging towards the stable door and barely missed Darius's face. Of course, he got a huge fright and exclaimed loudly with expletives. This brought the major to the reception area and he enquired who we were. When he heard the name 'Brubeck', he was effusively apologetic and yelled accusingly at the errant darts player, 'You know what you just did? You threw a dart at a very famous person!' We started muttering that this was hardly the case or the point and that we would like to register, but the major and dart thrower were now engaged in a battle of their own and it was escalating.

Dart thrower: 'My family could buy out you and your hotel and throw you out tomorrow.'

Major: 'I've got friends in the army that can kill your family in the middle of the night, before you even know it'.

He then presented his bald dome to the darter, then to Darius, 'See the teeth marks in my head? That's how tough I am!'

Much cursing ensued and although increasingly doubtful about our stay, we thought we had better register after the major's display of superiority. That evening, Major Hayden was on the lookout for us and, as we entered the dining room, he launched into 'Take Five' on the piano. After this tribute recital ended and we and others had applauded, he joined our table along with a few cats (the real kind) that had also adorned the piano. All during the major's performance, there was a continuous and almighty din in the kitchen and the cats seemed used to joining the tables as food appeared. In addition, we were having difficulty giving our order to the waitress, who was clomping loudly around the dining room. The major's wife, Rose, had by now joined our table as well. George, as we were entreated to call him, eventually went to check on the kitchen, but first played a rather good rendition of another Brubeck hit, 'In Your Own Sweet Way'. Rose shook her head and said to us, 'You are international people. You've travelled, but you see what's going on here – the cats are jumping on the table, we have a deaf waitress, there's a riot in the kitchen and that fool just plays the piano.' Clomp, clomp and the major shouting 'Menu!' at the waitress. We sympathised with Rose, feeling a little treacherous after all the welcoming fanfare and his rather good piano playing.

A couple of years later, George, no longer an innkeeper, was a sabbatical leave replacement for Darius and we received a telegram from the head of the department saying Major Hayden was a major success. As Fats Waller, the virtuosic stride pianist from the 1930s said in one of his comedic introductions, 'One never knows, do one?'.

Darius

8/6/86: *Jazz and Folk for Free*

MANA often worked with the Durban Publicity Association, usually via the Durban Arts Association, and although this created jobs for musicians, entertaining tourists was not our *raison d'être*. We wanted to set up a local festival featuring local musicians. Albert Park was a large, green space that separated an architecturally distinguished but dodgy 'grey area' of the city from the double-lane Esplanade highway on the harbour side of downtown Durban. This was a great location for many reasons. It was accessible on foot for the local populace, close to bus routes and taxi ranks and had easy access to electricity. We could aim the loudspeakers towards the harbour, making it easier to argue that this festival wouldn't be a nuisance for residents in the art deco apartment buildings on the town side. Close by was a 1950s-style drive-in diner that Cathy and I loved, called Tropicale. It was tucked under the elevated highway junction yet surrounded with dense foliage just off the green. The weather in Durban was reliable in June and Cathy saw a special date when we looked at weekends on the calendar, 8 June 1986. This gave us our poster logo – 8/6/86 – and hopefully a running theme uniting visual impact and date selection. Next year, 8/7/87 would be as good and the following year we'd hit the jackpot, 8/8/88. Dave Marks, with his certified Woodstock experience would be the overall producer. The Durban Folk Club enthusiastically supported the idea and Cathy booked the jazz musicians. The event was called Jazz and Folk for Free. It almost didn't happen because certain journalists naively wrote about our planning a concert of 'protest music'. This truly wasn't our intention, but predictably enough we found ourselves in danger of losing our carefully negotiated permit. Applications for outdoor gatherings were regarded with suspicion, but we did have a permit thanks to sponsorship by Durban Arts, which was backed by the City Council, and we had carefully avoided calling it a Free Peoples Concert. We protested the 'protest' label in the press and, as everyone knows, there's no such thing as bad publicity.

In contrast to ratcheting up expectations of 'protest', the press release drafted by Cathy said, 'the free concert completes the weekend of fun and reflection that began with World Environment Day'. It went on to say, 'Jazz and Folk music are seldom presented together, but both project strong identities as people's music, an alternative to the vastly capitalized commercial variety'. Sponsors were acknowledged and people were asked to bring old clothes to donate to the Red Cross.

Come the day and Cathy, Dave and I arrived early as the last sheets of plywood were screwed down to make the stage. Bheki Mbatha and Vusi Sabongo were my student crew, tasked with running cables on the stage and taping them down. It was dry and sunny, as winter days tend to be in Durban, and the morning air smelled fresh. I was almost 40, but felt half my age, climbing up and down scaffolding like a sailor

Prominent Durban musicians, Jazz and Folk for Free Concert, 8/6/86, Albert Park, Durban. From left: Simon Kerdachi, Basil Metaxas, Milton Johnson, Gerald Kerdachi, George Hayden, Peter David, Marc Duby (photo: Darius Brubeck; Cathy Brubeck collection).

Two members of the Keynotes – from left: Clarence Khumalo (drums), James Mbambo (guitarist), Jazz and Folk for Free Concert, 8/6/86, Albert Park, Durban (photo: Cathy Brubeck; Cathy Brubeck collection).

on a yacht, supervising the placement of amplifiers and mic stands. Cathy, dressed in a striped skirt and Ronnie Madonsela Scholarship T-shirt, stayed on the ground with her clipboard and checked in crew members and musicians as they arrived. She was responsible for paying everybody at the end of a long day. Dave, as the overall producer, mainly stayed out in the middle of the park setting up the sound.

The jazz line-up included the ever-popular Keynotes from KwaMashu and Chesterville, my group with Sandile Shange on guitar, George Hayden (formerly of SADF and Nottingham Road Hotel fame) with a seven-piece band of Durban musicians who often played hotel and restaurant gigs in town and there was another group, which included NPO members. There was a veritable parade of 'folkies', who were thrilled to be giving a truly public performance outside of their Folk Club meetings. Some of them were very good, including Dylan Meer, a name I remember for obvious reasons. If others were less so, it didn't matter because everyone's friends had come, the sets were short and this was a major happening. The atmosphere was friendly and, yes, free. People sat on the grass, listened and drifted in and out of the Tropicale, mingling and dancing on the way. The police stayed far away, leaning against their vehicles. The festival resembled neither a political rally nor a rock 'n' roll bacchanal, so watching us was like a day off for them, and I guess they enjoyed some of the music.

Cathy with Roger Lucey (left) and Dave Marks, Jazz and Folk for Free Concert, 8/6/86, Albert Park, Durban (photo: Darius Brubeck; Cathy Brubeck collection).

The change-over to the closing act, Tight-Head Fourie and the Loose Forwards, was covered by a stand-up comedian. One of his lines was, 'Durban audiences are so laid back they can't see beyond their hip bones'. Tight-Head Fourie was in fact the provocative Roger Lucey, who the Special Branch (secret police) had been trying to put out of business for his straightforward and unforgiving lyrics mocking the system. His ironic pseudonym and band name, evoking 'rugger-bugger' masculinity, was typical of outlaw folk-rockers of the era identifying as South African white while making fun of whiteness. The band, especially Roger, had a large following and recorded on the Third Ear label. The festival vibe went from laid back to 'stoked' when they took the stage. The Loose Forwards proved to be a well-organised country-rock outfit, complete with twangy lead guitar, backing vocals and a canvas backdrop of a desert landscape. The grand finale was 'No Easy Walk to Freedom' with lyrics praising the still-imprisoned Nelson Mandela. As a sign of solidarity, all the musicians who were still there joined in on stage. I strummed away on the spruce-top Washburn acoustic guitar presented to me years ago by Don McLean. During the Vietnam War era, I would have given anything to play a protest song like this at an outdoor festival. As planned, the 'protest' song came at the end and the authorities could not stop the concert because it was over.

One of the best days of our lives was followed by one of the saddest. The phone rang on 9 June. It was a neighbour of Cathy's mother, Dorothea Shallis, who told us that Dorothea had been taken to hospital. Dorothea herself had phoned early that morning saying she had a bad headache and Cathy had told her to take some extra strong aspirin and that we were going to visit the following Friday. However, when we arrived at Grey's Hospital in Pietermaritzburg that afternoon, we could tell immediately from the way the nurse approached us that Dorothea had died. There had been no warning, no lingering illness, no brave fight to the end and no goodbyes. Cathy, who was emotionally traumatised, filled out some forms and we went to Dorothea's small but comfortably furnished cottage in a retirement complex and she cried the whole night.

Dorothea's story is interesting: a child of the Raj in India, where she went to a convent for nine months of the school year high up in the Himalayas, an early adulthood in England before the Second World War and then sailing in a 1942 troop ship convoy to South Africa with five-year-old Catherine to join her Royal Airforce husband, who was sent out, as they said in those days, 'to keep an eye on the Germans'. Cathy's brother, Jo, didn't have a suit to wear for the funeral and I helped him get one in town. Our close friends Douglas and Colleen Irvine hosted a reception at their house. (At the time Douglas was teaching at the University of Natal on the Pietermaritzburg campus.) We were both deeply touched that Gerrit Bon and Sandile Shange attended the funeral in Pietermaritzburg.

Catherine

NU bands

The Jazzanians had spectacularly highlighted the availability of university-based national and international touring groups. Lex Futshane and Mark Kilian had some Jazzanian experience after Victor Masondo and Melvin Peters had graduated and, with other band members, they continued performing under this name for a while longer. Lex and Mark became core members in 1992 of the NU Jazz Connection, the band that succeeded the Jazzanians in representing the university. Three subsequent groups, NU Jazz Link (1994), NU Afro Jazz Band (1998) and the combination UKZN/UCT Ensemble (2005), which was co-directed by Mike Rossi, attended, and performed at international conferences in the United States. Later, Mike Campbell, head of the UCT Jazz Department also took a group to the United States. He had started the UCT jazz course under Gerrit Bon, who moved to UCT from UND in 1989. Mike Campbell, a North Texas State graduate, was very popular and influential in South Africa, particularly for big band arranging, composing and his many performances.

Independently, and very notably, the Indo-jazz group Mosaic, led by piano student Nishlyn Ramanna and flautist Stacey van Schalkwyk also represented Natal University.

Mosaic – from left: Bongani Sokhela, Magendran Moodley, Stacey van Schalkwyk, Nishlyn Ramanna, Mageshen Naidoo, publicity photo on Howard College Campus, Durban, June 1995 (photo: Gisele Turner).

They raised funds themselves, with additional help from Michael Chapman, who was the dean of Humanities at the time and from Betsy Oehrle's United States connections. The latter provided free accommodation at Morehouse College and the group played at the 1996 Atlanta conference of IAJE. They were so impressive that they were invited to play at the Royal Academy of Music in London by Graham Collier, who had seen their performance. Mageshen Naidoo (guitar), Bongani Sokhela (bass) and Magendran Moodley (*tabla*) were the other members of Mosaic.

With student groups, we visited New York City, Boston and Miami, as well as several cities in France and Germany and, indeed, many cultural sites, as well as sampling food ranging from crêpes to sushi. While our efforts at tour guiding must have palled at times, we were so fortunate to see things as if for the first time. I asked Lulu Gontsana why he hadn't joined the group taking a museum tour in Mainz, Germany, and he replied, 'I should think it's your typical European stuff'. (He missed out on the Gutenberg Bible, printed in 1455.) Durban had its share of wonders too. In his response to our questionnaire on 9 May 2019, Mark Kilian describes how, at one of his first lessons with Darius,

NU Jazz Connection at CJPM, publicity photo, 1992. From left: Mark Kilian, Lex Futshane, Chris Merz, Feya Faku, Darius, S'thembiso Ntuli, Sazi Dlamini (missing, Lulu Gontsana) (photo: Ted Brien; Cathy Brubeck collection).

a couple of vervet monkeys came to the window, which was open and started messing about with a few things they could reach. Without missing a beat or even smiling, Darius continued his speech on the blues form, casually got up and shooed the monkeys away and closed the window. He didn't even bat an eyelid, as though he'd done that a thousand times, but I'd never seen anything like it.

Fund-raising for all the groups that Darius and I organised got much easier, with large contributions forthcoming from the South African Department of Arts and Culture, Durban Arts, the university itself and USIS, which sponsored a Greyhound bus tour for the NU Jazz Link that included the current head of Jazz Studies at UKZN, Neil Gonsalves. Darius's parents continued to host the students in these bands and we certainly couldn't have done as much without all these willing, interested and generous partners. While not being complacent about fund-raising, we no longer had to go to friends and jazz fans with a begging bowl. Jazz was now considered an important discipline at the university and in Durban there were almost more jazz gigs available than musicians to play them.

In 1992, the United States government was still very intent on cultural diplomacy and organised an extensive tour for the NU Jazz Connection, which later recorded and played in Germany.

The NU Jazz Connection

Chris Merz	co-director, alto and soprano sax, voice
S'thembiso Ntuli	tenor sax, voice
Feya Faku	trumpet, voice
Sazi Dlamini	guitar, voice
Mark Kilian	keyboards, piano
Lex Futshane	bass, voice
Lulu Gontsana	drums, voice
Darius Brubeck	director/piano
Catherine Brubeck	concept and management

Darius

We aimed to attend IAJE conferences every time a new cohort of students was ready and commensurate with the extracurricular effort involved in organising such trips. This happened roughly every two to three years. Although we had a standing invitation to *attend*, we had to submit audition tapes like every other school or university to get a performance slot. Using CJPM as a base for organisation and rehearsal, we applied for a series of groups after 1988. The main beneficiaries of these efforts were the students themselves. However, we wanted and needed to follow the Jazzanians with another impressive group as soon as possible to establish a continuing presence on the international scene. Our goal this time was to perform at the Miami IAJE conference in January 1992 and we had very fine student musicians in place. Lex Futshane (who had taken Victor Masondo's place in recent Jazzanian gigs) and Mark Kilian (who had replaced Melvin Peters, who was now teaching full-time at the University of Durban-Westville), S'thembiso Ntuli and Sazi Dlamini (who had been working together in two successful neo-traditional music projects directly referencing Zulu popular music in a jazz context) and Feya Faku (an outstanding trumpeter, who was a member, along with Lex, of the Melvin Peters Quintet that won the Carling Circle of Jazz competition). Lex and Feya were also in Chris Merz's band, Counterculture. So, the aptly named NU Jazz Connection band consisted of a three-horn front line, a guitarist with a strong *maskandi* influence and Lex on electric and acoustic basses. They were all strong singers too. We didn't have a student drummer at their level and, as Lulu Gontsana was working in Johannesburg, I asked my brother Dan to play with the band while we were in the United States. This meant we were covered for a New Year's concert at the Congregational Church in Greenwich, Connecticut, which again had generously organised this warm-up gig for us.

As before, Cathy received financial help from the university (both Administration and the Students Representative Council) and the Durban Arts Association and she had also worked with the American Consulate in Durban and the Washington cultural desk to set up and fund sight-seeing and cultural opportunities for the students. A visit to Bra Johnny at Indiana University, one of the biggest and important music schools in the United States, was included. Johnny had nearly completed his Master's programme and was thrilled to show his 'home boys' around campus. He told us repeatedly that he was 'working his butt off' and Sazi finally said, 'I wish I had a butt to work off' – Johnny was huge while Sazi was skinny.

A two-page list Cathy handed out to the students titled 'Notes for USA Visit Jan 1st – 23rd 1992' included items needed, such as:

1 heavy coat
1 jacket – this jacket can be part of a suit, but you don't have to have a suit
1 warm dressing gown, but you can use your coat if you don't have one

and general tips such as:

Most American households don't have domestic workers and women *and men* do housework themselves. If you are in a private home, you should take your plate from the table and offer to help with the chores.

> Airport and hotel porters usually get $2 per bag they carry – so grab everything yourself!!

A December fax to my mother, who once more opened the Wilton home to us all as if it were the easiest thing in the world, assured her that 'only' five students (plus me and Cathy, of course) needed to stay. (Chris Merz already had accommodation with a good friend of his.) The USIS helped to fill in some of the days for the students in New York City while Cathy and I enjoyed being with family.

Once in Miami, we again witnessed the students' excitement at being under the same roof as so many world-famous musicians. Lex observed, 'It was striking to meet so many of these stars and find they were very humble people. One never felt intimidated – it was like talking to buddies from down the road.'[1] Besides several big-name artists, Jamey Aebersold, the doyen of jazz educators, came to hear us. He invited me for coffee the next morning and spontaneously offered to go to an audio store to buy a big ghetto blaster for us to take home for use in our practice rooms and promised to send a full set of his instructional Play-Along CDs and more books. Adding responsibility for managing these significant assets to her various duties made Glynis Malcom-Smith the Jazz Centre librarian, as well as administrative assistant, bookkeeper, bartender and student counsellor.

Reviewing the concert for the *Los Angeles Times*, veteran critic and jazz scholar Leonard Feather wrote: 'This music transcends the categories of African or American. As South Africa moves irrevocably toward integration, the contributions of these young Africans – all in their 20s – will be more fully absorbed into the mainstream of world music culture.'[2]

Back in Durban, I talked to music critic Anthea Johnston about our concert at the large Ashe Auditorium in the Miami Hyatt Regency:

> It was a good performance spot . . . and the group went over very well. The NU Jazz Connection is very different from the Jazzanians who had a lot of original material. We decided this time to takes tunes such as 'Ntylo, Ntylo', 'You Think Your Know Me', and 'Amabutho', tunes that are well known [in South Africa] . . . The Jazzanians were about style and this group is about repertoire.[3]

I was officially on leave during the first semester of 1992, but we were very busy arranging things for the group. Bernd Konrad, director of Jazz Studies at State University of Music and Performing Arts Stuttgart, who we had previously met through Jürgen Bräuninger, attended the Miami conference, and invited the NU Jazz Connection to appear at a student music festival the following May in Karlsruhe. He also set up an additional workshop and concert. When we returned, Cathy approached the ever-generous patron of South African arts, Paul Mikula, (Bartel Arts Trust) and other big donors like SAMRO and, together with the help of the university and the German Consulate, managed to get airfares and some cultural activities organised, such as a trip up the Rhine and a visit to Mainz of Gutenberg Bible fame. We considered these excursions as a real learning experience and personal and professional contacts were made that remained for many years to come. There were still too many hotel nights between paid engagements, so Cathy came up with the idea of recording the band in Germany.

Serendipitously, Cathy and I had planned to be in England for a friend's wedding and, remembering how enthusiastic Robert Trunz had been in Montreux, we called him for a chat and advice. At the time he was an executive at B&W an audiophile speaker brand. We didn't know then that Robert was both very successful and very bored with selling speakers and wanted to move up the signal chain to selling music. He had already decided he wanted to aggressively upgrade B&W's company record label, which had existed since 1986 for promotion purposes – basically a logo to put on demos and giveaways. He invited us down to his country house near Worthing in leafy, horsey Sussex, where it seemed most of the cars on the narrow lanes were Land Rovers or vintage Jags and MGs. (He had a red Ferrari parked by the barn that had been converted into a studio/showroom.) We joined him for a terrific dinner prepared by two glamorous Italian sisters, watched unreleased video footage he had of Miles Davis's last appearance at Montreux and went to bed in one of his guest suites, feeling privileged but outclassed. The next morning, we pitched the idea of recording the NU Jazz Connection in Germany and played him the cheap cassette tape recorded straight off the PA mix of our concert in Florida on his top-of-the-range sound system. He seemed only mildly interested until one of Sazi's guitar solos. 'What was that?' he exclaimed. 'Ah, now something I haven't heard before.' Trunz was an astute listener. We replayed the track and I explained that Sazi's tone and phrasing sounded unfamiliar to him because he was channelling traditional Zulu guitar in a jazz context. Robert listened again, asked a few practical questions and we made a deal.

In the next few years, B&W Music recorded Counterculture as well as *Gathering Forces II* (with Deepak Ram) and released my original *Gathering Forces* album made in the United States in 1980.[4] B&W also signed many more South African artists, including Sipho Gumede, Mabi Thobejane, Pops Mohamed and Madala Kunene. By expanding what was basically a one-off student project, the NU Jazz Connection tour, Cathy had helped to open a door to international exposure for quite a few South African musicians in our circle.

The NU Jazz Connection CD was titled *African Tributes* and for this recording we once again had the inspiring presence of Lulu on drums.[5] Staying in a rustic village in Bavaria, we had dinner and drinks every night in the little family-run hotel and were served fresh trout from a river that ran through the property. The bar was mainly patronised by locals and we all quite liked the Bavarian draft beer. After a long day in the studio, we would raise our glasses and say, 'Cheers', as South Africans often do. One evening we were joined by some friendly regulars and one of us asked what the equivalent toast in German was. He thought we were saying 'chairs' and translated accordingly, so when the next round came, Lex politely raised his glass and said, '*Stuhle*', the German word for 'chair'. For a while '*stuhle*' (like *stoele* in Afrikaans) was the toast used by members of the band. 'These foolish things' are some of the most memorable souvenirs of road trips.

Leonard Feather was right that these musicians would be 'more fully absorbed into the mainstream of music culture'. Mark Kilian is a successful Hollywood film composer. His credits include *Tsotsi*, which draws on South African material, as well as more mainstream films, such as *Official Secrets*, *Replica* and well-known earlier scores featured in *La Mission*, *Eye in the Sky* and *Before the Rains*. This last film was musically significant for bringing the sound of Deepak Ram to Hollywood. Sazi Dlamini, who much later earned a doctorate in musicology and lectures at UKZN, gave us an account of his university journey in his response to our questionnaire on 17 May 2019:

> From 1981 until 1987 I was registered at UND/UKZN as a medical student, and then as music student from 1989 (until 2009!). When I arrived at the blacks-only Alan Taylor residence in Wentworth to enter the [blacks-only] faculty of medicine at UND on 8 February 1981 I had a cowhide drum with me. The guitars were at home in Magabheni Township 40km down the KZN coast. I became friends with Mlungisi Conjwa [from Orlando East – Soweto] who was studying for BA Music Honours with Chris Ballantine . . . At the beginning of 1984 (in the 'gap' between my two stints of Med School), following my tentative telephonic enquiries with the Dept of Music Reception – Darius actually called me at home to ask if I wanted to study . . . If there is (a story to be told) and it is about music, it is yet to be told and I am possibly part of it.

Lex moved to Johannesburg, where he is a senior figure in the jazz scene, teaches at several institutions and manages the teacher training programme for the Johannesburg Youth Orchestra. In his response to our questionnaire on 17 May 2019, he recalled:

> Getting to play with almost all the great jazz musicians that came to perform in Durban is a memory that I will always have with me . . . also the trip of the senior students that Cathy organised, which culminated in the recording of *African Tributes* in Germany.

S'thembiso stayed in Durban, where he got a permanent job in the South African Navy band, but he still connects musically with those musicians he studied with. Lulu continued to be South Africa's 'house drummer' and to tour with Afro Cool Concept into the early 2000s.

In 2005, I was awarded a residency in Bellagio, Italy, by the Rockefeller Foundation to work on a piece to promote AIDS awareness in the jazz community. AIDS was rife in South Africa in those years. Cathy wrote the lyrics for the Bellagio composition and I called it 'Lulama' in Lulu's honour. Mike Campbell of UCT conducted a big band performance of 'Lulama' at Dan Chiorboli's Awesome Africa Festival in Durban in 2006. This took place in the beautiful City Hall, with Natalie Rungan singing the lyrics.

One late afternoon in April 2016, I was checking sound for a Brubecks Play Brubeck performance with my brothers Chris and Dan and British sax star Dave O'Higgins at Dizzy's Coca-Cola Club (Lincoln Center, New York) and Feya Faku walked in. He was checking out this famous venue because he was playing there with band leader and sax player McCoy Mrubata the following night. I wish someone had taken a picture of the two of us, dramatically silhouetted in front of the double-storey windows high above Columbus Circle. Here we were, almost a quarter of a century after NU Jazz Connection, and we felt we had made it to the top.

Catherine

Darius, Feya, Chris and all of us experienced a different kind of high 3 353 metres above sea level when a reconstituted NU Jazz Connection (there were so many bands we were running out of 'NU' names) was invited to play and give workshops in Peru. John Dixon, who was then running USIS programmes from Mexico City, arranged the invitation to Peru. This NU band now included guitarist Prince Kupi, bassist Piwe Solomon and drummer Lebohang Mothabeng, all students at that time. A music jam exchange took place with Peruvian musicians and, as well as Machu Picchu, we visited Cusco and the capital Lima. We had a shocking and funny dinner experience when Prince decided to order the speciality of the house – guinea pig. It arrived cooked, but in its full shape, standing on the plate! Most of us had to look away while he worked his way through it. Darius and I read Pablo Neruda's great work *The Heights of Macchu Picchu* while contemplating the heights to which our jazz life had ascended. Shortly after that, we found an Irish pub in Cusco that was showing the 1999 Champions League final between Manchester United and Bayern Munich for the second time. (This was the famous game that Manchester United won in the very last moments of extra time, with goals from Teddy Sheringham and Ole Gunnar Solskjaer.) Before this showing, Darius had heard an English-accented person say, 'I know the result and it's disgusting'. Darius kept this information from me, as he thought Manchester

Publicity photo for Peru, 1999. From left: Feya Faku, Prince Kupi, Lebohang Mothabeng, Piwe Solomon, Darius (photo: Ted Brien; Cathy Brubeck collection).

In Paris with Kwazuna, 2004. From left: Ayanda Sikade, Darius, Burton Naidoo, Paul Kock (photo: Logan Byrne; Cathy Brubeck collection).

United had lost. At the end of the game, one of the most exciting ever, he asked the Englishman why he had responded in this way, and he replied, 'I'm a Liverpool supporter'! We were elated our team had won and felt that all was right in the world; watching a game in Peru that was being played in Barcelona and this all made possible by South African jazz and the American government.

During the years from 1984 to 2005, we had staff and/or students play in the United States, Germany, Thailand, Peru, Turkey, Italy, Australia, Korea, Denmark and France, and in Africa had major performances in Namibia, Swaziland (now eSwatini), Mozambique and Zimbabwe.

There were mini-tours and major tours with new and spin-off bands featuring university staff, students and nationally known musicians. In addition to the Afro Cool Concept quartet, musicians such as Chris Merz and Zim Ngqawana were much in demand and, along with others, now formed their own bands offering both American and South African jazz. Counterculture's album *Art Gecko* earned high praise from Dr Yusef Lateef, quoted on the CD's sleeve notes: 'The music in this album is creative and intelligent in the highest degree. In other words, the musicians bring to this music their special qualities of thoroughness, intelligence, and deeply serious creativity.'[6]

Darius

A major change

Americans who were alive in 1963 can tell you exactly where they were when they heard President John F. Kennedy was shot. Similarly, I imagine many people in South Africa remember where they were when President F.W. de Klerk gave his historic speech at the opening of Parliament in Cape Town on 1 February 1990.

Cathy was in the ANC press office in Lusaka as the telex machine noisily typed out a transcription of the speech as it was delivered. Cathy's brother, Jonathan (Jo) Shallis, at the time an assistant producer for CBS News/South Africa and based at the Johannesburg bureau, had arranged for her to go as a freelance fixer, because of her contacts within the ANC. She had been sent to Lusaka to get interviews with the main protagonists and provide information on impending developments. An excited witness to history, she took the transcript to the nearby ANC headquarters while the exile operatives were still listening to it in real time over a telephone connection to Cape Town.

I was in a repurposed meat locker in an area of Johannesburg called Newtown with a group of musicians preparing to make an album. Mega Music, owned by two enterprising brothers from Pretoria, Derek and Dennis Woolridge, had converted an industrial wholesale meat market into a music business hub that included cold-storage rooms adapted for rehearsals (heavy doors and double walls made effective soundproofing), offices and storage and retail space for their sound gear. Roots

Records, a jazz label headed by Robin Taylor and part of the family of labels run by Rashid Valli, the owner of Kohinoor Records, the well-known jazz record store, had arranged this three-day rehearsal period. Cars and trucks could drive up to Mega, load in and out on Goch Street, a little service road behind the pedestrianised area dominated by the Market Theatre, known internationally for its critical protest dramas and brilliantly progressive productions. The Market Theatre faced the Yard of Ale, a long shed made into a bar-restaurant with a low overhang and outside tables. The Yard was a place where you could count on meeting people from the intersecting worlds of theatre, foreign NGOs and media. Kippies Jazz Club, housed in a replica of the original food market's ornately domed public convenience, stood between the Market and the Yard. So, Mega Music was conveniently placed in the funky, cosmopolitan heart of alternative Johannesburg and was always throbbing with hopeful bands (mostly black) managed by lefty entertainment business types (mostly white). It was grimy, but Mega's owners, who at first seemed to be a bit rough themselves, were smart and helpful. Taken as a whole, the Market Theatre, Mega Music, the Yard of Ale and Kippies was the centre of an evolving, hip counter-establishment; everyone was some kind of big fish in a seething small pond.

I took my transistor radio to Mega Music, so that we could listen to the opening of Parliament during rehearsals for *The Brothers*. The sudden quiet as other bands stopped to listen too was noticeable when we opened our steel door for some fresh air. Reforms were anticipated, but we'd heard that one before, notably when P.W. Botha established a Tri-cameral Parliament in 1983, attempting to co-opt coloureds and Indian people into implementing apartheid legislation, while excluding Africans. This was a mistake from any point of view and it led directly to the state of emergency of 1985. We all expected better from F.W. de Klerk as there had been frequent media reports and rumours about informal meetings (and even games of table tennis) between National Party grandees and Nelson Mandela in his recently upgraded prison accommodation. Political insiders expected something big, but no one expected what was to come.

President de Klerk in a crisp, lawyerly way announced the unbanning of the ANC, SACP (South African Communist Party) and the PAC, the abolition of the death penalty (a reprieve for many condemned freedom fighters) and the imminent release of Nelson Mandela. All of this was simply decreed, not presented as an agenda for Parliament. Except for Mandela's release, which would take time to organise, everything else would take effect immediately. Life would be different from now on. Neither the white electorate nor the suddenly unbanned liberation movements had anticipated such a dramatic and unconditional change of direction from the still-powerful National Party government. And yet, no cheers or shouts of 'viva' echoed down the halls and our own meat locker was completely silent. I remember Victor Ntoni's first words after the speech were 'I'm going to buy a gun'.

The calibrated handover of power from white minority to black majority might have become irrelevant if the country disintegrated into war between regional, political and tribal factions, not to mention a likely rebellion by the extreme white right, the AWB (an Afrikaner resistance movement called the Afrikaner Weerstandsbeweging). Knowing Bra Vic as well as I did, I am sure he didn't really buy a gun, but he was suggesting that the lid was off and there were plenty of reasons to be concerned. Racial reconciliation was the prevailing theme in international reporting, but deadly power struggles between black factions, in some cases supported by shadowy white forces, were wreaking havoc in the townships.

People of goodwill tend to think of the birth of the New South Africa, the Rainbow Nation, in terms of the triumphal narrative depicted in the Clint Eastwood film *Invictus* about South Africa winning the 1994 Rugby World Cup. This was reaffirmed by displays of national pride and collective euphoria during the 2010 Football World Cup, which took place in great stadiums all over the country. We were there and all that happiness happened, thanks to Mandela ably fulfilling his role as a kind of national saint – forgiving, kind, humble and steadfast in his 'one nation' belief. Cathy and I attended the rally in Durban at which Mandela famously commanded his followers to 'take their guns and their knives and their pangas and throw them in the sea', but attacks and reprisals continued. So, while my liberal soul rejoiced that a better nation was about to be born, Victor knew what to expect in the interim.

The Brothers

Duke Makasi, Ezra Ngcukana, Victor Ntoni, Lulu Gontsana, Tete Mbambisa and I were often together at events like the Carling Circle of Jazz so, by 1990, I had played with all the members of this quintet; even, on a single occasion, with fellow pianist Tete when two keyboards were required. *The Brothers* is the only album apart from *We Have Waited Too Long* that I produced without being involved as a player. The plan was to feature music by all four composers, Duke, Ezra, Tete and Victor. Despite appearing in various subgroupings and combinations, they had never recorded as a quintet. Tete had made two records as a leader in the 1970s,[7] but he lived near East London, which was out of the way, while Ezra now lived in Cape Town and the others in Johannesburg.

Zim, Lulu, Lex and Feya often talked about how they were all nurtured in a rich, non-commercial local tradition and regarded the 'brothers' as mentors. The Eastern Cape was already famous for producing modern, influential jazz musicians like Chris McGregor and the rest of the original Blue Notes, as well as Todd and Pat Matshikiza, whose music became widely known in the 1960s and 1970s. In fact, Todd's compositions were already known in the 1950s. When Cathy and I attended a jazz festival in Port Elizabeth (now Gqeberha) in 2019, we heard accomplished young players whose exciting, original music was a virile extension of this legacy. We had been invited by John Edwards, who is now in charge of Jazz Studies at Nelson Mandela University.

In addition to being part of a wider jazz family, what made the five musicians 'brothers' was their common Xhosa heritage. (Our in-joke name for the album was *Xhosa Nostra*.) Xhosa music and its presence in daily life in this fairly monocultural area had a deep influence. It is often said that Eastern Cape jazz is a fusion of John Coltrane and local music. The title of Mbambisa's composition 'Trane Ride' from one of his earlier albums and the music itself makes this connection.[8]

New Brighton made an extraordinary contribution to jazz, considering that it was a relatively poor area and lacked any semblance of a self-sustaining commercial music scene.[9] Almost no one outside of this area heard one of its finest bands, the Soul Jazz Men, but they deserve to have their names mentioned here: Dudley Tito, Pat Pasha, Buggs Gongco and Whitey Kulman. These musicians and others who came and went over decades of continuous involvement collectively created a scene, encouraging and mentoring teenagers in the township. Garages and backyards were transformed into

The Brothers album cover, taken outside the Market Theatre, Johannesburg, 1990. From left: Ezra Ngcukana, Duke Makasi, Tete Mbambisa, Victor Ntoni, Lulu Gontsana (photographer unknown).

jazz clubs and on weekends and holidays, thanks to them and their friends, music making was a local passion. Perhaps lacking viable opportunities for fame and fortune was a secret advantage because there was nothing to be gained by playing music you didn't believe in. Duke Makasi and the Ngcukana family, starting with Christopher Columbus (Mra), then his sons, Ezra, Duke, Fitzroy and Ray (and later Claude Gawe, another son) were raised to a high level of proficiency in this environment. Ezra and Duke left for Cape Town and Johannesburg, respectively, but returned often enough to take part in local jam sessions, reaffirming family ties and their place in this community. When in Durban, Ezra, always wanted to stay with the 'boys' (Zim, Lulu, Feya and Lex) when they were living in the flat attached to our house at Peace Avenue. We observed how deferentially they treated their elder (though far from elderly) guest.

Duke had lived in Johannesburg for a long time when we started working together and had been a member of the popular and pioneering Spirits Rejoice, an early, perhaps even the first, Afro-fusion band in the 1970s. Duke's personal life wasn't simple. He had documents for different official identities that helped him navigate apartheid bureaucracy. He was sought after for his straight-ahead, but still highly individual jazz playing. I heard him at Spats, an upscale restaurant-cum-jazz club in central Johannesburg, with the legendary Johnny Fourie. Knowledgeable jazz buffs sometimes compared Duke to Joe Henderson. (I heard from a New York friend that Joe Henderson had somehow heard Duke and agreed. The spread of esoteric information in the jazz sphere pre-internet never fails to amaze.) Personally, Duke was very likeable, introverted but warm. He spoke seldom and softly, getting on with things at a pace that resembled slow motion, compared to our hyperactive pace. He was sensitive and moody at times, but mostly charming in a thoughtful, reserved way. At the outset of one of our Afro Cool road trips, we were loading the rental van in my driveway and the handbrake took a slight knock and came loose. The van slowly rolled backwards, trapping Cathy's foot under the front right tyre. She yelled and I threw my full weight against the open door on the opposite side and Duke and Victor put their shoulders to the back. We all moved the van forward, releasing Cathy's foot and I reached in and set the brake. Lulu ran up the stairs from our house with a glass of sugared water, an all-purpose township remedy for shock. To our great relief, Cathy had been more scared than hurt. She was gratefully sipping the water when about five minutes later Duke quietly asked if he could stop holding the van. We all laughed and laughed at his reluctance to move without instructions.

Duke seemed always to be in a reverie, some paces behind us all and his beautiful ballad 'Years Ago' reveals this contemplative state. The challenging chord progression underpinning this lyrical melody seems to express how it felt to be him, an understated, serene melody floating over lots of changes. We all loved the tune when the group ran through it, so I asked him for the title. 'Oh, it's just something I worked out years ago,' he replied, looking down, so 'Years Ago' was what I put on the track sheet. It is a beautiful composition in song-form, comparable to great standards like 'Body and Soul'.[10] The performance on *The Brothers* album (with Ezra's astutely sympathetic improvised counter-lines) has the gravitas of any of the revered tenor sax ballads that have become canonical over time.

Jivey, swinging 'Zukile', also on this album, is by Duke and Tete and counterbalances Duke's ballad. Tete, the only surviving 'brother' is a co-credited composer because he 'found' the chords that worked with it on the piano.[11] Even when written down for copyright protection, songs like 'Zukile' were just a way to begin and end a freewheeling cycle of improvisations based on the *marabi* framework, like the blues in America. Cathy's favourite 'Zukile' moment took place during a beachfront festival in Durban, where she was organising the jazz and I was backing visiting artists. Winston (rather than Ezra on this occasion) and Duke performed some spontaneous choreography on the spot. The band just vamped for about a minute before the two tenors, who had hidden behind the speaker stacks, made their stage entrance together, playing, crouching and swaying to the music. The band dropped the volume and Duke and Winston played the first phrase, repeated four times, mezzo piano. The tension broke with a loud drum fill as they pivoted to face the audience, leaning back like rearing stallions, belting the second phrase fortissimo, one-two-three-four times! The approving crowd exploded with whistles, shouts and cries and a mighty horn battle began.[12]

Catherine

Hurry, hurry, jazz and curry!

We were fortunate to have close relationships with two outstanding Durban citizens, Ramoll Bugwandeen and Ben Pretorius, the owners of the Moon Hotel and the Rainbow Restaurant and Jazz Club, respectively. Neil Comfort and his wife Nicola, who bought out Ben's shares in 2001, live in Scotland, but against all odds, they booked many class acts for the Rainbow and kept the marvellous vibe going. Ben Pretorius and the Rainbow have been mentioned throughout this book, but we need to add more about Ramoll and the Moon Hotel in our jazz life. Both these impressive people deserve to be given the keys to the city, if such an honour still exists. Alternatively, they should be nationally acknowledged for their brave and enduring contribution to the arts. Architect Paul Mikula should also be honoured for his enormous cultural contributions; namely, his support of musicians and venues and founding the Phansi Museum in Durban, an absolute treasure house of mainly Zulu art and artifacts, and the BAT Centre.

Ramoll had a long history of supporting jazz and individual musicians long before we arrived on the scene and had hosted many famous stars, accommodating them and presenting them on stage with his amusing introduction, 'Fasten your seatbelts'.

Ramoll Bugwandeen, 9 April 2019 (photo: Jorne Tielemans; still from documentary *Playing the Changes*).

Jazz Jol at the Moon Hotel, 1992. Left to right: George Ellis, Sazi Dlamini, Lex Futshane, Sthembiso Ntuli, Feya Faku and Chris Merz (photographer unknown; Cathy Brubeck collection).

At first, he operated the Challenger Restaurant as a club before moving to the larger room that featured many groups from UKZN, including our seventeen-piece big band. The artists who played there included nationally known and local performers and given the many apartheid group area restrictions, it was remarkable that he staged big names such as Sakhile, Thandi Klaasen, Ronnie Madonsela, Allen Kwela, and Cape musicians Winston Mankunku, Robbie Jansen and Basil Coetzee (of 'Mannenberg' fame). Leading guitarists such as Gerald Sloan and Sandile Shange also performed at the Moon and George Ellis's father played there in the 1960s. Ramoll often told us that Indians and coloureds lived in perfect harmony in the old South Coast area that had everything from mosques to fishing-tackle shops. He offered 'Jazz and Curry' at a discounted price, so that as many people as possible had access to the Moon concerts. He supported and tolerated many difficult musicians whose demands could quite often stretch everyone's patience – for example, Allen Kwela who, despite having free lodging, would complain loudly about doors slamming. Certainly, the Moon Hotel had its rough edge and Ramoll says that at first it was very difficult to persuade whites to attend shows. This had changed a lot by the time we had our early Jazz Jols there and we are grateful to Ramoll for so many things besides the venue and the curry. Transportation of musicians and instruments was always a nightmare and Ramoll, when necessary, was able to organise huge liquor trucks to pick up the Natal University Jazz Ensemble and transport them back to campus. Two things that musicians always worry about are getting paid and getting something to eat. Ramoll always came through, regardless of audience numbers. His shows provided a very good learning experience for our students and we missed the Moon adventures once CJPM managed its own productions. When we were in Durban in 2019, Ramoll reminisced extensively about his own life in jazz and the Durban scene, and he sent us a written version:

> The black jazz scene popular venues in Durban were the Moon Hotel, known as the Home of Jazz, which has presented jazz since the sixties and featured some of South Africa's premier musicians . . . in the same period Thandi Klassen (vocals) appeared with African Jazz & Variety. Mackay Davashe & his band, the Jazz Dazzlers, played at the Moon Hotel in 1966 . . . The Moon Hotel attracted a cross-section of racial audiences, but it was illegal. Although Clairwood is situated on the south side of the Durban industrial area, it had a section of many racial groupings that regularly patronised the Moon Hotel, which was in a so-called Indian group area . . . Another popular Durban venue was a club called Star Point Five, which was in the Executive Hotel in the township of Umlazi, situated in the south side of Durban . . . Most progressive non-white people felt happy & comfortable visiting this venue as it had a reputation for good jazz.

Later the Rainbow Jazz Club in Pinetown was owned by a well-known progressive thinker Mr Ben Pretorius, who made a great contribution to jazz & is undoubtedly one of Durban's most popular jazz venues. Always had a homely welcome atmosphere and all races were welcome & most people could see the new South Africa beginning to take shape at the Moon Hotel & the Rainbow . . . The success of the Rainbow Jazz Club was due to its proximity to the township of Clermont, which in the eighties had the highest jazz following in Durban. If you walked on the streets of Clermont often one will hear the likes of Oscar Peterson & township jazz being played at many homes.

Darius played a great role in helping venues to attract cross-cultural audiences. In particular, he also assisted me at the Moon Hotel to move jazz at the hotel into a much bigger venue, which could seat 500. Together we founded the Southern Comfort Natal University Jazz Jol, which featured more than 50 musicians. This was an event not to be missed on the Durban Jazz calendar & it simply grew & gained momentum.

Another Durban stalwart is the legend Theo Bophela the pianist & his son Barney Bophela. Theo recently passed on & was associated with the band the Keynotes, which was responsible for keeping the jazz scene alive for well over 35 years . . . Roy Peterson (pianist) was well known & also kept the jazz scene alive for many years. He was extremely well respected & had no formal training. Bobby Timol too was a well-known drummer . . .

In the sixties & seventies the Goodwill Lounge in Victoria Street was thriving . . . It was also famous for jazz & the owner, the late Pumby Naidoo, discovered the vocal genius Sonny Pillay, who married Miriam Makeba. It was at Goodwill Lounge that Lionel Pillay (pianist) played with the great American clarinettist Tony Scott & they played the famous standard 'Tea for Two' for two hours . . .

Jazz has always had & will certainly play a political, economic & social role especially in South Africa where social cohesion is a relatively new concept. Society needs to look at the work done by the great social & cultural reformers like Louis Armstrong . . . he spoke out when blacks were turned away from job opportunities. Historically in South Africa & the rest of the world, jazz attracts a cross-section of people from various race groups & they function harmoniously without security staff in venues where jazz is played.

Darius

Gilbey's fallen hero

I recently discovered some handwritten notes I had prepared for a speech I delivered at the funeral of saxophonist Dalton 'Tony' Khanyile, a long-serving Gilbey's rep and a front man for the Keynotes. They are reproduced here, with some amplifications:

1. I am here representing students in exams and musicians from other places.
2. DK was one of the first musicians and first friends I met [in Durban].
3. The Keynotes was one of the very few organised groups in those days. I was proud to arrange some of his compositions six years ago for a musical tribute [performed as part of the Carling Circle of Jazz concert in Durban.] Dalton was pleased and it was fun.
4. Whatever we did was fun – he made the best of situations, e.g., playing to an empty stadium in PE and at his short-lived jazz club [in Durban].
5. Grand Opening of Tony's Jazz Club. I was a guest, but it turned out Dalton and I were the only musicians at the event. 'We don't need anyone else' [he announced]. Big sound. Big heart.
6. This is a sad moment, but Dalton was optimistic about death. 'So many have gone before me,' [he said].
7. Sincere condolences to Mrs Khanyile, their children, family and friends.

There is a little more to the third note. Dalton had given me some recordings and sketchy lead sheets to work with. The idea was to arrange his tunes for a 'little big band' comprised of the Keynotes plus the rest of the artists booked for the outdoor Carling Circle of Jazz concert on the Durban City Hall steps. Alfred Nokwe, who was a TV actor and a local celebrity, was the Master of Ceremonies.

I duly scored two or three numbers for the available instrumentation, mainly adding brass hits and sax harmonies to Dalton's lead-line, leaving plenty of space for solos. The written part was relatively short, but I had marked cues, so that the ensemble players would know when to come in and where to go next. For this to work, we all had to literally be on the same page(s), so I rewrote Dalton's part, adding rehearsal markings, so that he would be in sync with everyone else. I carefully made sure he only needed to play what he had played before. He found this really perplexing and inhibiting, so I stopped trying to explain how the chart worked and simply removed the part from his music stand, so that he wouldn't see his own music written out. We had a good laugh about that later.

Smirnoff, another jazz-supporting brand, decided to sponsor a jazz festival in Port Elizabeth featuring talent from all around the country. I forget the details now, but somehow, I ended up leading the Durban contingent, an honour that included driving the inevitable Toyota High Ace van – a twelve-hour drive – straight through. I'm shocked now at some of the things I eagerly accepted as long as a gig was involved. Members of Afro Cool were staying with us in preparation for the journey ahead. We set out early, going from house to house, picking up Keynotes, each stop adding a little delay as goodbyes and last-minute things were dealt with, until we finally arrived at Dalton's an hour late. He was waiting at the gate beaming. 'I'm ready,' he called to us,

'I just have to pack.' We all climbed out of the van and hung around his yard while he packed. What did he mean by 'ready'?

I was so exhausted by the time we got to Port Elizabeth, I don't remember what we did that night, but the next morning all the musicians assembled in the local stadium under brilliant sunlight. Everything was there – sound system, piano, drums already set up and ready to go – but no fans waiting to get in, no cars in the vast parking lot, not a single early arrival seated in the stands. By showtime, a handful of people had drifted in to see what was going on, but they didn't seem like part of an audience. Members of the African Inkspots and other bands milled around, pleased to be there at first, then worried. Was this a boycott? Would they be paid? Cathy and I worried that future sponsorship was in jeopardy. Corporate brands, mainly those owned by beverage conglomerates, underwrote most of the large-scale jazz activity in the country. Such money was allocated for marketing and promotion, not to support jazz as such. It could as easily be spent on fashion shows or boxing. Hentie Engelbrecht, the Smirnoff rep in charge, responded to gradually deflating spirits backstage by handing out his product mixed with orange juice. 'An Orange Blossom in the morning. Nothing wrong with that.' The mood lightened a little and we all agreed we might as well play. After all, we had everything we needed to make a joyful noise under clear blue skies, including plenty of free booze. Dalton led the party in every way. Hentie correctly assumed poor promotion and/or politics was to blame, rather than jazz itself. 'This is Africa,' he said, pouring another round for all, while the African Inkspots offered a cheerful rendition of 'Do I?', complete with choreography in the empty stadium. This was the first time I had heard that expression (later shortened to TIA). Each band played a set to an audience of musicians and Smirnoff employees. Hentie later invested in the Smirnoff Jazz Festival in Grahamstown, but he wisely contracted with Henry Shields, a Cape Town lawyer and jazz aficionado to organise it, rather than leaving it to his local brand managers. Henry Shields, in turn, approached Cathy for help. She had a lot more concert production experience at the time and thus began a long relationship, as well as the annual jazz festival in Grahamstown/Makhanda.

Organisation was lacking for the launch of Tony's Jazz Club too. It was situated in one of the public rooms in the badly run-down Butterworth Hotel near Durban's old train station and one of the main transport hubs, where several highways merged and ended at the edge of town. This wasn't a bad location in terms of accessibility from township and suburb alike, but the Butterworth was a seedy, unsafe firetrap. Tony's Jazz Club was up a flight of stairs (the lift was broken) and the hallway on the first floor was partly blocked by a pile of discarded mattresses. The room itself was just an empty room with an upright piano – no decor, no furniture, apart from a few randomly spaced unmatched chairs and a couple of card tables. Drinks, courtesy of Gilbey's, were served in plastic cups, replenished from a cardboard box full of bottles on one of the tables. Dalton's name had drawn a gathering of friends and fans, so he said we had to play. This is when he proclaimed, 'We don't *need* anyone else', to much applause, but Tony's Jazz Club closed the night it opened.

The final eulogy of the day on 5 November 1993 was delivered by a sombrely dressed Alfred Nokwe, looking like a different person without his usual natty nautical attire. He movingly evoked the sense of loss felt by many, offering consoling memories of Dalton's playing and playfulness, his humour and warmth, but now, he said, the time had come to 'bid farewell to Gilbey's fallen hero'.

Catherine

Glynis goes to Germany

In 2000, when we were in England, where Darius was completing a MPhil at Nottingham University, we encouraged Glynis Malcolm-Smith to tender for organising a showcase of South African music at the World Expo 2000 in Hanover, Germany. The brief from South Africa's Department of Arts and Culture and Department of Foreign Affairs was to present different genres of South African music and culture. She went to Pretoria, representing CJPM, and put in a successful bid for the contract. Glynis then organised this huge project, which included 38 musicians, with the help of Jürgen Bräuninger, Mike Rossi and Patricia Opondo (senior lecturer in African Music and Dance), but what a drama it turned out to be. Jürgen, chief sound engineer for all the acts, wanted to make a quick visit to see his parents in Stuttgart, a few hours' train ride away and, by the way, get some laundry done. He gave all the relevant technical instructions to Mike Rossi for the time that he would be gone. Well, Mike got ill with food poisoning and poor Glynis had a lot of tricky explaining to do to South African government officials, while trying at the same time to locate Jürgen and ask him to return immediately. For Glynis, it had been the worst and (in retrospect) most off-the-wall trip of her life, with people only showing up at the airport at the last minute and not having the correct documentation. In a conversation after our trip to South Africa in 2000, she recounted how

> some of the township musicians had never travelled outside of KwaZulu-Natal and the only mode of transport they knew were minibuses. The mother of two of the student dancers insisted they visit a bone-throwing *sangoma* [a diviner who communicates with the ancestors] to see if they would be safe to fly.

For Jürgen, it was the most expensive load of laundry ever.

Glynis's role had grown from dispensing bus fare to township-based students to convincing government departments to trust the Centre with a large budget and the organisation of a South African show for an important world stage. She did all this

Jazz band for World Expo, Hanover, Germany, 2000. From left: Moketsi Kgadi, Mike Rossi (director), Mageshen Naidoo, Brian Thusi, Bongani Sokhela, Mpho Mathabe (photo: Ted Brien; Cathy Brubeck collection).

Mike Rossi and Jürgen Bräuninger, World Expo, Hanover, Germany, 2000 (photo: Glynis Malcom-Smith; Cathy Brubeck collection).

with flair and grace, but had to deal with several problems. Firstly, she recalls that Brian Thusi (a senior jazz student at the time) 'found out that some of the artists were being paid a higher fee and he threatened to withdraw from the tour'. Glynis had to participate in frantic negotiations with Joan van Niekerk (Department of Foreign Affairs) and Themba Wakashi (Department of Arts and Culture) to resolve the matter. Joan found extra money to pay the musicians. Glynis told us that 'the boarding call for Lufthansa was called and two jazz students, Piwe Solomon and Xoli Nkosi were missing'. She then had to convince passport control to let them through. 'They had gone outside the airport complex looking for food and had left their tog bags and passports with friends who were now waiting to board.' She managed to find the friends and the passports, which were just sitting in a trolley on top of the bags. Other incidents included students riding on trams without paying (they were caught), Makosi hearing voices and not wanting to dance and Lebhohang (drummer) and Prince (guitarist) having a fight at 3 a.m. outside the hotel and smashing two chairs. Glynis quite rightly made them each pay for a chair! In a recent note to us describing some of this, Glynis ends with 'looking back at the good times!'

Our 'on the road' experiences ranged from VIP status in six-star hotels with every kind of service to mattresses on the floor. When we played our first concert at the University of Zululand, the proudly proclaimed new possession, a baby grand piano, was still in its shipping crate. An enormous sound system on the stage left no room for the band, so the performance got delayed for a couple of hours while the untuned piano was unpacked and all the enormous speakers and sound paraphernalia was more effectively and unobtrusively placed. The rapturous audience and everyone dancing to 'Take Five' made up for this uncertain start. It was on another trip to Zululand that Winston Mankunku and Sandile Shange engaged in a long and argumentative conversation about *ilobola*.[13] To our surprise, Sandile was by far the most conservative and said he would certainly expect a handsome payment for his many daughters. Winston pointed out that nobody had cows anymore and that in any case that was an archaic custom, whereupon Sandy said he wanted to be paid in imaginary cows and that he would do the imagining.

On one of our first tours out of South Africa, the Darius Brubeck Quintet (with Sandy, Rick, Marc and Kevin) gave three concerts and workshops sponsored by the Music Academy in Windhoek and the Rossing Foundation in Swakopmund in Namibia. Even with a war on its northern border, Namibia was more relaxed than South Africa – no formal apartheid evident except in race-designated government administration departments. Darius wrote to Iola on 5 May 1987:

Our Namibian Tour . . . was a now unusual chance to play the same 'book' with the same guys on consecutive nights and get into a groove. The Namib really does look like Lawrence of Arabia territory and some of our audience hadn't seen a live band of any kind in 12 years!

A year earlier, the same group had an engagement in Donnybrook (in rural Natal) and South African Breweries had arranged the transportation. The white farming community had not expected a mixed-race band, but jazz trumped apartheid and we were all allowed to stay at the same hotel and were cheerfully served by surprised black staff. It was a good 'playing the changes' moment and there were many of these in the years before 1994. We didn't think twice about black musicians staying with us in what was nominally a white area and we were not alone in simply ignoring the law. There were many individual jazz musicians, venue operators and restaurants doing the same thing. Our efforts were made easier by the younger black musicians we worked with. They were not as demoralised or wary as many of the older players, who often drank too much and had a more bittersweet and less trusting relationship with privileged whites.

Darius

Fin de siècle

Acceleration year on year finally reached escape velocity in 1999/2000 when I was offered a visiting fellowship at Nottingham University and was granted an extended sabbatical to read for a MPhil degree there. A shortened version of my dissertation '1959: The Beginning of Beyond' was published in the *Cambridge Companion to Jazz*.[14] Here, I will reconstruct some of the frenetic activity in the closing years of the twentieth century.

The first universal franchise election year of 1994 divides the decade. Cathy and I were honoured to be chosen as election monitors, part of a huge international effort to ensure its legitimacy. A detail I can't resist relating is that I was allowed to vote. The legal ramifications of citizenship in South Africa had become so qualified under apartheid that the Electoral Commission decided the simplest solution was to initially give the vote to everyone who lived in the country – a unique event in the history of elections.

Most of our many visitors came in the latter half of the 1990s, although the Centre was active from the start – for example, organising and promoting a 1991 Abdullah Ibrahim concert at Durban City Hall. This was also the year I was elected vice-chair of Natal Cultural Congress and Chris Merz joined the music staff. Paul Simon returned to South Africa in 1992 with his Born at the Right Time tour. Cathy, Anne Pretorius, Glynis and I organised the launch of the South African chapter of IAJE and this was also the year of the first Standard Bank National Youth Jazz Festival, an enduring national institution. The National Youth Jazz Band of South Africa is assembled annually from the pool of high school and university students, with a new director appointed every year. Hugh Masekela did a wonderful residency at the Centre in 1992, which gave students the experience of close contact with a charismatic celebrity and this entrenched the tradition at UKZN of emphasising the depth and worth of South Africa's own musical heritage. Joseph Shabalala, leader of Ladysmith Black Mambazo, was appointed a fellow of the Centre for Jazz and Popular Music in 1993 and CJPM was officially opened to the public that year. We started our long-running Wednesday Trios Plus concert series in 1994 and CJPM organised a concert to launch the Phil Harber Jazz Scholarship at the Playhouse. Saxophonist Mfana Mlambo was the first recipient.

Gathering Forces

Deepak Ram and I occasionally address one another as Deepak-ji and Darius-ji, riffing on the Hindi honorifics used in traditional Indian parlance, especially among musicians. It's a joke between old friends who have remained in touch over the years, but the respect is mutual and real. He has been a guest at my parents' home and played at my father's memorial service in New York in 2013. He stays with us when he is on tour in England. When Cathy and I met Deepak after his inaugural concert at UDW, I was pleasantly surprised by his recognition of the name 'Brubeck' and his interest in jazz. He told me his father (a yoga teacher) played an old 45-rpm record of Herbie Mann's 'Comin' Home Baby' every year on Diwali.[15] His older brothers, who are successful businessmen, are accomplished classical musicians too, but Deepak dared to make it his whole life. (It helps that his wife, Kitu Mistry, who played *tanpura* in his inaugural concert at UDW, is now an international authority in the field of paediatric phrenology.)

We started rehearsing together soon after we met, teaching each other how our respective approaches to improvisation worked on a technical level.[16] When we gave concerts on campus, we added players and used the name Gathering Forces. I had explored this kind of fusion under that name in the 1970s, but this was my first opportunity to work with a musician like Deepak. Deepak's life story is fascinating, taking in formative experiences in a South African settlement founded by Mohandas Gandhi, studies in India, migration to England and then to America, where he now lives. He is a disciple of Hariprasad Chaurasia and considered a global figure in Hindustani classical music in his own right.

The sound of the *bansuri* (bamboo flute) is intrinsically seductive (remember Krishna played it to get his Gopi girlfriends), but it was technically tricky to keep it in balance with louder instruments and stylistically even trickier to keep the jazz/Hindustani balance right as well. Indo-jazz had been an established but marginal sub-genre since the 1960s, but this was something new in Durban.[17] We were not influenced by Indo-jazz predecessors, but looking for our own style and level of fusion, something that worked for us and felt natural in Durban, and for the musicians we played with. We worked on this intermittently for three years and my goal all along had been to present the result on a bigger stage with a larger ensemble. The opportunity came in 1993 with the creation of the Durban International Festival of Music (DIFM), a project that built on the success and longevity of the Durban International Film Festival, which had already been going for five years when we first arrived. DIFM had significant support from the Durban Arts Association and other sponsors, who hoped that it would become an international attraction like the film festival.

Cathy and I were involved with DIFM from its earliest stages because the director was none other than Ann Ashburner, who had produced the Harare Jazz Festival in 1989 and was now married to ex-Jazzanian Rick van Heerden. The one and only time Cathy and I have ever seen a leopard in the wild was on the way to Harare in a band bus with Sakhile, Tananas and Afro Cool. It was night and the driver hit the brakes as he caught sight of the huge cat caught in the headlights lying on the black asphalt soaking up the warmth. She hesitated for a minute or longer, gave us a disdainful look and got up with body language that said, 'Well, I was about to go anyway' and padded into the surrounding blackness at a dignified pace. This trip north was also memorable for culminating in the night that Bra Vic 'socked it to the ANC', as Cathy often describes it, paraphrasing 'Harper Valley PTA', Jeannie C. Riley's 1968 country hit. Victor told the exiled politicos in no uncertain terms that they were not the only freedom fighters.

DIFM was going to be good. Ann Ashburner knew what she was doing and had a decent budget to work with. Cathy and I pitched Gathering Forces as a purpose-made creation that represented what was unique about Durban – not Africa, not South Africa, but *Durban*. Of course, there would be international headline acts, as the name of the festival promised, but Gathering Forces signalled both local *and* international. Robert Trunz arrived from England. His direct involvement was through Fourth World, a band already on the B&W Music label. It was fronted by the celebrated Brazilian couple Flora Purim and Airto Moreira.[18] Robert was interested in signing still more South African artists and establishing his brand in the South African market. He presented Cathy with a large bottle of Nina Ricci's perfume L'air du Temps when we went to meet him at the Royal Hotel. He wanted to record Gathering Forces for his label and suggested that Airto work with us too. Great! Gathering Forces would live up to its name. Building out from Deepak and me, Chris Merz was a second featured soloist, members of Mosaic (Stacey van Schalkwyk on flute and Bhisham Bridglall on *tabla* (Indian drums), an ideal South African jazz rhythm section of Concord Nkabinde on electric bass and Kevin Gibson on drums plus Airto on percussion as a 'special guest artist'. We could even afford a small *real* string section of violin (Candace

Whitehead) and my brother Matt (who came especially from California) on cello, supported and augmented by Mark Kilian on synths, providing fullness and various drones. We had the use of the stage and sound system at the Jazz Centre for rehearsals.

All this seemed thrillingly professional after years of adapting to low-budget circumstances. What could go wrong?

Well, for one thing, I could die just before the first rehearsal. Evidently, I contracted food poisoning from a single piece of tainted sushi at the new Japanese restaurant on the beachfront. This felt dire after an hour or so and I almost finished myself off the next day by mistakenly taking Julia Zondi's blood pressure pills, thinking they were for me. Our pharmacy had dropped off both of our prescriptions that morning and I was dehydrated, bleary and eager to get some medication in my system. Julia called Cathy when she found me semi-conscious, rolling on the floor of our bedroom. I don't know what happened next, but when I opened my eyes, I saw Glynis, who had been a nurse at one time, patting my hand in Entabeni Hospital. Cathy was very busy gathering new forces with all the logistics suddenly upended and arranged for Melvin Peters to take my place at the piano for rehearsal that night.

The album *Gathering Forces II* was recorded live before a full-capacity audience at the Playhouse Opera venue and subsequently mixed at the famous Bop Studios in Mmabatho, in what was then Bophuthatswana, an apartheid 'casino state' hundreds of miles from Durban.[19] My music department colleague Jürgen Bräuninger produced the CD and the recording aspect would have failed completely had he not been part of the team. We had planned to drive up to Bop together to do the remix in a state-of-the-art studio in the middle of nowhere, a vanity project of the 'homeland' government.

But first, we had to record the performance. The Playhouse had a recording studio control room with feeds from several performance spaces in the building, but were the channels on the desk really connected to the built-in mic points on

Jürgen Bräuninger (photographer unknown; Still from video, Jürgen Bräuninger and Sazi Dlamini, Electro-Acoustic Music Studio, School of Music, UKZN, 2017).

stage? The very question was almost dismissed as impertinent by the Natal Performing Arts Council's head soundman, Phil Audoire (Audoire sounds like O'Dwyer in a Durban accent, so that's what I thought his name was until I read it in the credits), but Jürgen insisted on testing every line. It turned out that the stage mic points were *not* connected to the studio control room, so at the last possible minute Jürgen took charge of running long cables to the stage, draping them over the opera box seats.

This Gathering Forces ensemble also went to Johannesburg on a band bus to perform at the Market Theatre as part of the Guinness Jazz Festival, which was broadcast on SABC TV. I am pleased to record that Don Albert, who had been quite critical of some of my previous projects and playing, really liked this performance.

The Durban jazz scene in the 1990s was perhaps the best it had *ever* been. Starting the jazz course had raised the profile of Durban as a jazz town, now indeed the 'Jazz Mecca'! With students playing at a high level (usually before finishing their degrees) and more overseas jazz stars visiting after the 1994 election, 'the joint was jumping' and Durban was the place to be. Younger people were going out to live jazz because it was cool and accessible, and because there were a lot of exciting young, local musicians on the scene. Venue operators took notice and opportunities to play burgeoned. Despite my allegiance to teaching jazz as a great musical tradition, I think the stimulating freshness and hipness about the live scene was in part due to the younger set *not* knowing very much about jazz history, its extensive repertoire and heroes. As a musician, you might as well play what you really want to play because an old standard and something you wrote that afternoon were equally acceptable to a young audience. Musicians from Johannesburg said they loved coming to Durban because the audiences were so receptive. There were hotels, bars and restaurants all over the city and beyond that wanted musicians for atmosphere and local colour, and real jazz clubs like the Moon, the Rainbow, Le Plaza Hotel, the Jazzy Rainbow and the brilliantly located BAT Centre (sponsored by Bartle Arts Trust, hence BAT) flourished.

The inspiration for this venue came from Paul Mikula, who had so readily and practically supported CJPM and the NU Jazz Connection's visit to Germany. He had redesigned the old, converted harbour master's office building right by the docks. At night the ambience was surreal; mercantile grit illuminated by lights high up on cranes and the superstructures of colossal freighters, giving the scene a Christmassy feel. The top level of the BAT Centre boasted an outdoor deck, with a Zulu/nautical-themed bar and restaurant (serving African delicacies like mopane worms) inside. Rising towards the skyline beyond the moored freighters was the boundless darkness of the Indian Ocean, bejewelled with the twinkling lights of ships waiting their turn to come in and unload. The Friday evening series Jazz on the Deck was a staple gig for student groups and those led by sax-teachers Bryan Steele, Chris Merz or Dusty Cox. Dave O'Higgins came as a guest member of Johnny Fourie and his keyboard-player son Sean's Short

Attention Span Ensemble to play there and on campus in 1994. Seasoned artists from the United States (Paul Winter, Butch Miles, Larry Ridley, Richard Syracuse) and Canada (Sundar Viswanathan) and talented European and Scandinavian exchange students all felt like staying longer in Durban for the vibe, the weather and, most of all, the many opportunities to play with local musicians. Compared with the limited prospects for young jazz musicians in most of the world's large cities, Durban was jazz heaven! Many international visitors told me that's what they felt.

Life at the Jazz Centre was, however, not only about prestige projects and international tours, nor were we inhibited by an idealistic art-for-art's-sake mentality. Our role was often enabling as much as creative and stoking the local scene was an important part of the overall mission.[20] There were many exciting student groups in which I wasn't involved at all. They found each other, rather than being picked and prepped for IAJE conferences. Some, like Del Segno, organised by pianist Fiona Hebrard, included very good musicians – for example Bongani Sokhela and Leonard Rachabane, Barney's son.

Pianist Andile Yenana also made guest appearances with Del Segno. He was later in Zim Ngqawana's quartet for over ten years and, since 2014, in charge of music at Gamalakhe Technical and Vocational Education and Training College, situated in Port Shepstone, down the South Coast. He has been quietly and steadily gaining an international reputation.

Del Segno, CJPM, 1993. From left: Bongani Sokhela, Leonard Rachabane, Fiona Hebrard (leader), Dave le Roux, Sydney Mavundla (photo: Ted Brien; Cathy Brubeck collection).

George Mari, publicity photo, 2021 (photo: Val Adamson; Debbie Mari collection).

Debbie Mari, publicity photo, 2021 (photo: Val Adamson; Debbie Mari collection).

Tenor man Mfana Mlambo turned an unfurnished recreation area of Jubilee Hall, one of the student residences, into a pop-up jazz venue. Mfana is unstoppably entrepreneurial in several areas outside of music, yet a serious proponent of the tradition of jazz as a spiritual and challenging music in a post-Coltrane way. George and Debbie Mari were versatile and polished entertainers. They are both central to Durban's music scene, teaching, performing and creating opportunities for other players.

In the 1990s, George mainly played trumpet in a Milesian manner, memorably partnering with Bryan Steele and in similar line-ups under the name of Error Nine. But on other occasions George and Debbie both presented themselves as good singers, who did cover versions and jazz standards with great charm and musicality. Glynis loved George's rendition of 'Mustang Sally', which she often requested loudly at party gigs. Twenty-five years ago, George and Debbie had a Methodist church wedding to satisfy her parents, then came to the Centre, which they had decked out in orange garlands, for an abbreviated Hindu ceremony, followed by a massive party. There was plenty of live music, but one of our fondest memories was Julia Zondi immediately and enthusiastically getting up to join other wedding guests to dance the 'Macarena',[21] a sexy and complicated Latin line dance of the era.

I haven't even attempted to mention all the ephemeral groups that played both routine and interesting gigs. When we took sabbatical leave in 1995, we left a thriving

Publicity shot for Error Nine, 1994. From left: Bryan Steele, George Mari, Lex Futshane, Jabu Dube (photographer unknown; Debbie Mari collection).

scene and it was thriving just as well when we came back. It was a time of optimism and new freedoms, so everyone was 'playing the changes'.

The Jazz Centre at the university was earning a reputation for reliability and competence that couldn't be matched in South Africa, so in the early years of the New South Africa, the government departments of Arts and Culture, Foreign Affairs and Trade or Tourism, as well as certain NGOs associated with the harbour or transport sectors or specific cultural initiatives, came to us for advice, which we gave freely and, as a result, we were often invited to participate in projects that paid well in money and adventure. One of these was accompanying a trade mission to Istanbul in 1996 with an ad hoc band that Cathy named Thusini (a Zulu name for the landmark Howard College building on campus). Thusini consisted of Paul Kock (alto sax), Bongani Sokhela (bass), Chris Mashiane (drums) and me (piano). We stayed in the luxury hotel where the trade promotion highlighting reciprocal landing rights for Turkish Airlines and South African Airways was being held and saw a lot of the ancient city by day. All we had to do was play mostly standards every night on a small stage set up near a stuffed lion in the main dining room.

That same year, Afro Cool Concept was one of South Africa's official participants in the king of Thailand's Jubilee Jazz Festival. Jonas Gwangwa's band, which included Johnny Mekoa and keyboardist Jabu Nkosi, formerly from Peace and Sakhile, was the other, so we saw a lot of one another in the hotel. (Incidentally, Dave O'Higgins was there too on a British Council sponsored tour.) We were all allowed rehearsal times in the hotel bar area and a band from Malaysia was waiting their turn while we ran our set. One of the musicians ran up to Cathy, very excited, crying, 'They're playing our music'. I'm not certain what we were playing at that moment, but what they thought of as 'their' music must have had some audible 'Malay' characteristics and a familiar groove. What a moment of jazz connection and communication. They were hearing an echo of music that travelled a long time ago with slaves from the Dutch East Indies, who were transported to South Africa in the seventeenth century.

The Thai government requested that all the bands play at least one piece by King Bhumibol Adulyadej, who attended Harvard University in the 1930s and was an avid jazz fan. We chose his ballad 'Still on My Mind', giving it a neo-soul ballad treatment and later recorded it as the title track of our next CD.[22] The package design is based on a photo I took of the famous *Reclining Buddha*. The four of us in the band and Cathy were avid tourists during our time off. We were dazzled by public spaces overcrowded with shrines and *stupas* decorated with fairy lights and garlands. We grew to love the song 'Loy Loy Krathong', which was on endless replay blaring from outdoor speakers and even the hotel's sound system. It celebrates the beautiful Loy Krathong festival with the ritual of floating ornate baskets of flowers in rivers. On the other hand, the sex-trade sleaze in the midst of all these public expressions of piety was just as inescapable. Henry Shields, now well used to seeing himself as a festival producer, had flown in from South Africa to check out this Thailand festival. He told us his airport taxi driver misunderstood his directions for the hotel and took him straight to an industrial-scale brothel. He had to insist, get angry and pay extra to go where he needed to be, which was not there. When Cathy and I took a tuk-tuk to the park where the jazz festival was held, the driver handed her (not me) a card with a list of 'tourist attractions'. I said, 'No thank you, we've seen everything.' (This wasn't true, but I don't like to be hustled.)

'No, we haven't,' said Cathy, handing me the card, which listed his 'attractions' in a clunky pentameter:

boy-girl-make-love-show
boy-boy-make-love-show
girl-girl-make-love-show (etc., etc.).

We played our music at the enormous and well-run festival and enjoyed listening to groups we never would have heard, such as the Fumio Itabashi Mix Dynamite Quartet from Japan, which was the usual piano-bass-drums trio plus a woman who played

Gathering Forces in Nantes, 1997. Standing, from left: Darius, Brendan Jury, Kevin Gibson, Zim Ngqawana, Mark Kilian, Chris Merz. Sitting: Manjeet Rasiya, Deepak Ram, Concord Nkabinde (photo: Cathy Brubeck; Cathy Brubeck collection).

koto and *samisen*, and sang, of all things, you guessed it, an ear-splitting Yoko Ono-ish version of 'Loy Loy Krathong'.

The 1997 Nantes version of Gathering Forces featured Zim Ngqawana, as well as Chris Merz on saxophones and violist Brendan Jury.[23] Our pitch to the French festival director, who was working closely with Robert Trunz, was essentially the one we made to Ann Ashburner and Durban Arts: Gathering Forces represented multicultural Durban, an African city on the Indian Ocean. Nantes was a wonderful experience of creative and thorough festival curation and production that involved different parts of the city, including rooms in the famous LU (LeFevre Utile) Biscuit factory done up in African fabrics. More importantly, Nantes is where Cathy and I saw Zim and his quartet with Andile, Kevin and Herbie play one of their finest concerts ever.

I returned to Nantes in 2004, marking the official twinning of that city with Durban, timed to coincide with this year's Les Rendez-vous de l'Erdre, which this time was mostly a straightforward jazz festival. It was great to bring yet another band, featuring top students, Burton Naidoo (keyboards), Logan Byrne (bass), Ayanda Sikhade (drums) and Paul Kock, and introduce them to the glories of France. At the official banquet, I got to sit between the mayor and Didier Lockwood (world-famous

Publicity photo for NU Afro Jazz Band in Jazz Centre T-shirts, CJPM, 1998. From left: Bernard Ayisa, Natalie Rungan, Darius, Paul Kock, Tulani Shezi (photo: Ted Brien; Cathy Brubeck collection).

French jazz violinist), which was held in what I think was a brandy distillery converted into an avant-garde art space.

Back to 1998, UKZN was once again invited to an IAJE conference, this time in New York City and Cathy managed to co-ordinate this with an invitation to Karlsruhe in Germany to have a guest spot with the Karlsruhe Uni Big Band. This student group, the NU Afro Jazz Band, featured a vocalist for the first time, Natalie Rungan, and Ghanaian sax student Bernard Ayisa. Natalie was a big success on this trip, a young Indian woman with a rich contralto voice singing jazz in African languages as well as English.[24] One of her admirers was famous jazz historian and critic Barry Kernfeld, who described her as having a 'wonderful instrument' when he invited me to breakfast. His main agenda, however, was to ask if I would provide South African entries for the next edition of the *New Grove Dictionary of Jazz*.[25] I said, 'Yes', having no idea how that would work out, but it did, because Cathy asked Chris Ballantine and Nishlyn Ramanna to join us in researching and writing short biographies and then she collated all our dictionary entries.

Bernard Ayisa went on to lead hotel bands in Abu Dhabi and other places in the Arab world. Years later, when Cathy and I were living in London, he helped organise a quartet tour in Saudi Arabia with me, Bernard himself on sax, Matt Ridley (bass) and Wesley Gibbens (drums). Matt and Wes, originally South African, are the rhythm section of the current Darius Brubeck Quartet. We experienced the wealth and dubious power of this kingdom. We stayed in a magnificent hotel and each of us had a private butler to take care of our needs, which apparently could include almost anything, but alas no alcohol. Alcohol was allowed, however, in foreign embassy domains where we played. Bernard is now in Accra, Ghana, where he is teaching and part of a circle of 'first-call' professional musicians. We are in touch regularly and I coincidentally saw his picture recently in an article about the thriving jazz scene in that city.[26]

As already described by Cathy earlier in this chapter, a second edition of NU Jazz Connection went to Peru in 1999. The trip was unusual in that it was co-sponsored by South Africa and the United States with the purpose of promoting south–south co-operation, which I gather was a briefly trendy policy in the late Clinton era. Lima, where we landed, is an attractive capital city, with the usual urban amenities and we were welcomed by staff from the American Embassy, introduced to our escort who then accompanied us to Cusco and we settled into a comfortable hotel.

Cusco is a city high in the Andes on the way to Machu Picchu. It has a music school, so NU Jazz Connection was there to play and give a workshop. We stayed for extra days because it was very interesting and cheaper than Lima. The Spanish colonial architecture, high nineteenth-century sidewalks and the startling clarity of the air felt like being on a movie set. The subtle buzz from drinking lots of coca tea, strongly recommended to fend off drowsiness and sickness at this altitude, might have added to the feeling. Indians in indigenous dress using llamas as pack animals shared the broad, shadowless streets with tourists and businessmen in cars. Cusco sits even higher than Machu Picchu, surrounded by a combination of unfamiliar landscapes – dense rainforest and steep mountains. Explorers from NGOs and research institutes often made Cusco their base, giving it a kind of frontier vibe – the place one downs a local beer after days of climbing peaks or hacking a trail through jungle in the Urubamba Valley.

I was about to cross one of the wide streets near the central Plaza de Armas, when I heard someone call my name. The voice belonged to Anton Seimon, a young South African geographer/explorer I had met through friends in Durban.[27] I couldn't get over the surprise of being recognised this far from anywhere I had been before. What's more, he had an urgent need to tell me something important in case he 'didn't make it back to the States'. Now I *was* in a movie, a script based on a John le Carré or Graham Greene story, but this was for real. Anton had just come out of the jungle. He had found a large, overgrown, partially submerged pyramid-shaped mound that probably contained an ancient temple and asked some Quechua-speaking Indians who, like him, knew some rudimentary Spanish, how long it had been there. '*Después el mundo*' (since the beginning of the world) came the reply, as I remember it. He logged his location using a newly minted piece of kit, a GPS that he wore on his wrist like a watch, which looked like a compass. It recorded his position and automatically relayed this information to a satellite, which beamed back map co-ordinates. He had wondered if there were other ruins in the immediate area and followed a faint trail in the dark rainforest until he found himself standing by the side of a logging road that wasn't on any map. It appeared to cut west to east through the jungle to transport lumber from Brazil to the Pacific coast of Peru. Security men at the site were on to him instantly, roughed him up a little bit and took the film out of his camera. He explained that he was a geographer from an American university, that he wasn't spying on them and what they were doing had nothing to do with why he was there. They went through his backpack, which was full of material that verified his story, and they relaxed a bit. 'They were curious about the GPS, so I *pressed the button*,' Anton said, smiling broadly. 'They were impressed by what it did, but naturally they didn't know my signal was being monitored at the University of Colorado.' Anton feared that an encounter with an 'Americano' (as they assumed he must be) in the jungle might get into a daily report and someone further up the chain of command might work out it was him. A road through the jungle had to involve people at government level and very likely the president, Alberto Fujimori, himself. Anton asked me to pass this story on to someone at the American Embassy as soon as I could. I suppose the idea was that once the secret was out, killing the *gringo* would only make things more complicated. I didn't have to go back to Lima to do this because our escort arrived later that day.

My embassy contact listened and then explained that an international treaty had specifically banned cutting through the rainforest to export timber from the Pacific coast of South America. Japanese companies imported most of their wood from Brazil. Obviously, corporate interests, in connivance with the Peruvian government, were ignoring the treaty to greatly reduce the cost of shipping timber from the Amazon via Atlantic ports. Foreign aid to the governments of Brazil and Peru would be withdrawn if they didn't comply with the treaty, so the road through the forest didn't officially exist.

Back in Lima and our next engagement was a party at the United States ambassador's residence. By now, I had played many similar functions in various countries. It would be a social evening for members of the diplomatic community and their partners, and a chance to conduct some business informally. Our performance as a band under diplomatic auspices provided an occasion and everyone would like us, if we didn't play too loud or too long. On stage, I would say something to the effect that jazz, while originally an American art form, had been adopted in many countries, including South Africa, and thanks to the USIS and the South African Department of Arts and Culture, here we were representing *both* countries, and so on. Our set was almost over when I sensed a shift of attention away from us. There was a little stir near an open door to an unlit adjoining room. Alejandro Toledo, an imposing man with dramatic Inca features, briefly stepped into the light of the main reception room, surrounded by people who seemed much smaller than him. He smiled at the band, gave a few high waves of the hand to the guests, paused for a few photos and slipped back into the shadows. When I hung out with our USIS contact during the following days as we looked around Lima and waited for our flight to Florida, I learnt that he was a very smart guy, fluent in Japanese as well as Spanish. Shortly thereafter, in 2001, Alejandro Toledo, a Stanford graduate who claimed to be a friend of newly elected George W. Bush, won a highly controversial run-off election and, to much acclaim from the United States, became president of Peru. Alberto Fujimori was charged with corruption and fled to Japan. It seems that, thanks to jazz, I've had unusual access to history-making moments ever since going to Poland with my parents in 1958.

The year 2000 was when the Jazz Centre provided bands for the Meeting of Commonwealth Heads of State, the World Expo in Hanover and three trumpet players for the Opening Ceremony of the Olympics in Sydney. When Durban was chosen to host the UN World Conference Against Racism in 2001, the South African Department of Arts and Culture invited us to tender for providing the official entertainment.[28] We successfully proposed yet another expanded Gathering Forces, which included African singers and dancers, and a theme song composed especially for the occasion. This event and the founding conference of the African Union in 2002, which was also held in Durban, will be described in the next chapter.

9

Continuum

Catherine

Some people and events are not sufficiently dealt with in these pages, for which we hope to be forgiven. Covering 23 years of organising jazz gigs and related educational events is a daunting task. When Darius, Glynis Malcom-Smith and I were running CJPM, there were sometimes around 250 gigs a year that featured guests (international and South African), staff and students.[1]

In the beginning, we underestimated the impact of the Brubeck name and the pressure on Darius to appear at music and other public events. He rapidly transitioned from 1970s' fusion and keyboards to mainstream jazz and played with anyone who asked. This raised the profile of jazz and of the university. Playing with students was refreshing and rewarding for Darius and the Brubeck name helped integrate them into the scene. There were critics who felt that there was an element of favouritism, and even exploitation, but more saw the ubiquitous Brubeck persona our way; that is, being a band leader and player was also a valid teaching role. We needed to emphasise performance when academic routes were too challenging for those students who had had an inferior school education. Performance levelled the playing field.

The problem of finding teachers was constant for many years and some students lost out for some of the time. Having lessons from an Allen or a Barney or a Sandy or an Ezra, although inspiring, was very different from having to adapt to a conservatory approach to playing an instrument, espoused by the classical musicians in the Natal Philharmonic Orchestra, who were also part-time teachers. There seemed to be numerous discussions and minor conflicts. For example, George Mari didn't want to give up his self-taught way of playing the trumpet, which had worked well for him for many years. Michel Schneuwly, a world-class trumpet player with the orchestra, insisted on George and others emulating his positioning, fingering and tone. We believe both sides moved an inch and that there were benefits to demanding the impossible. George is still one of Durban's finest jazz musicians, playing many instruments and

240

Michel, among other ventures, still runs the highly successful Baroque 2000 concerts that attain a beautiful level of precision and appeal. There is always room for a natural, improvising musician as well as a highly trained one.

There were conflicts and difficult issues during our 23 years in Durban. Bheki Mseluku, with whom we had been connected since 1976, would often have a go at Darius (never me, because I think he remembered how much I helped him in the United States). Bheki would say that *he* should be the one teaching at UKZN, not Darius, and get quite impassioned and ugly about it, despite Darius's efforts to have him on part-time staff. The problem, to a degree, was Bheki's serious diabetes and another part was simply not understanding how the university worked and that he needed to commit himself to a schedule and syllabus. He gave workshops, principally at the Natal Technikon (later renamed Durban University of Technology) and all who took part gained an enormous amount of knowledge about improvisation and being a creative musician with something to say. Sometimes these conflicts were racial, with resentment about Darius being white and an American, so there were personal political battles as well.

Inside Out, publicity photo taken on UND campus, 1991. From left: Concord Nkabinde, Lawrence Sale, Dumisane Shange, Mfana Mlambo, Andile Yenana (photographer unknown; Cathy Brubeck collection).

A somewhat amusing version of race consciousness arose out of an interesting discussion in 2019 with Mfana Mlambo. He and others apparently had the perception that Darius only taught and preferred piano students of Indian ancestry. There had been a long line of such pianists, starting with Melvin Peters and some others, including Neil Gonsalves, Nishlyn Ramanna, Chloe Timothy, Roland Moses and Burton Naidoo. We were mildly shocked at this observation, particularly as it had never struck Darius. Analysing it during this conversation, we noted that it was just a simple twist of academic fate. The reason was that the number of piano students and piano teachers had reached a point where Darius was primarily teaching third- and fourth-year students, who at the time happened to be South African Indians. Of course, there were other significant pianists – Andile Yenana and John Edwards, to name only two. Mfana then went on to point out another strange statistic that had been talked about among students, which was that almost all of Darius's main piano students were childless. This was true, but again an odd observation about his piano teaching. Not knowing what to make of this, we stored it in our funny story memory bank.

And, looking back there was even a race issue within the Jazzanians. Johnny Mekoa told Nic Paton that Nic couldn't write African music because he was white. Whether the music was *good* should have been the discussion, but in South Africa this was not always possible.

Way back in 1976, a trifling and funny incident set the tone for guarded behaviour where there were clear divisions between rich and poor, and black and white. The New Brubeck Quartet (Dave with sons Darius, Chris and Dan) were accused of stealing the water jug and glasses from the Nico Malan Theatre in Cape Town (later renamed Artscape Theatre Centre). The management was adamant that between their placing these articles in the dressing room and our departure after the concert they had disappeared, and that their staff was so trustworthy that it must have been our group. It took some convincing that, as we were staying in a five-star hotel, it would have been much easier to have lifted the hotel jug and glasses had we wanted them for our travels!

At the other end of the spectrum, we witnessed moments of awe and wonder when playing for people who had never seen a live jazz performance. Once a young African very politely, with the words 'Excuse me, Sir', came up to Darius to ask, 'What is that golden instrument?' He had never associated what he had heard on the radio with such a beautiful object as the saxophone. On another occasion we were informed by a radio host calling all the way from India that 'the best thing about improvisation is you cannot expect what's coming and that you have to prepare to be astonished'! He got that right and then his final observation about Darius's father was that 'it takes time to become a legend'!

United Nations World Conference Against Racism

Throughout our time in South Africa, we experienced a strong connection between jazz, internationalism and cultural diplomacy, which continued the theme that Darius writes about in the Prelude – jazz's global association with freedom of expression and struggle against oppression. This was dramatically and enjoyably demonstrated by our participation in the UN World Conference Against Racism in 2001. In a long letter to Dave and Iola, dated 8 September 2001, which I have abbreviated, Darius describes this major event.

The last month and especially the last five days have been completely dedicated to the World Conference Against Racism.

We just watched part of the closing speech on TV about 10 minutes ago, a full day later than originally planned. We were down at the International Convention Centre (ICC) earlier today to pick up a video tape of our 28-minute performance from the SABC broadcast area and delegates were still debating. We easily walked through what had been secure – almost 'No Go' – areas and picked up some left-over posters to give our musicians as souvenirs and other conference papers just to see if our 'Gathering Forces' presentation was even mentioned. It was. Also, the whole presentation was broadcast around the world! From the beginning it was clear that the SA government, who gave us a budget and some limited support inside the Conference Centre, wanted a little 'culture' in the programme and the UN was dead against it. I'm starting at the end because the biggest problem for us and I suppose other 'Service Providers' (this is what was on our passes that got us into the ICC) was knowing when the end – or any specific event – was going to be.

Our original brief had been to come up with music for a 'closing ceremony' and from early in the week it looked less and less likely there could be a definite schedule for such an event. We had fifteen musicians and technical support (including a piano tuner) amounting to twenty-two people living or staying in various parts of Durban and we had to move them all into the ICC and set up our show. Because of UN security rules, we all had to arrive simultaneously at 'checkpoint Charlie' to have our cars searched and everything checked and then proceed flanked and followed by armed motorcycle escorts to the loading docks at the ICC. We had to be in cars listed weeks ahead of time – registration numbers given into Foreign Affairs in Pretoria – we had to have our accreditation passes, we had in fact to be exactly the people, the equipment, instruments, and vehicles specified weeks in advance. But *they* could not tell us even a day in advance when to come to set up and sound check and when to do the show. This was the main problem Cathy, as producer, had to deal with for the duration of the exercise. And the other side didn't fully grasp how difficult this was with musicians coming from townships and down the coast and everyone having to alter their schedules numerous times.

We went to a meeting on Wednesday (5th) to discuss logistics and copyright (my music) and finally concluded the best thing was to just put our show on first thing in the morning on the last day, if the UN would accept that proposal. Any other time than first thing in the morning would have meant repeating the whole set up procedure from scratch before the performance and during the break in deliberations – i.e., at an unknowable time. A bright guy in the Dept. of Arts, Science, Culture and Technology (DACST) said we could call it a 'ceremonial closing' not a closing ceremony. (In the end it wasn't officially called anything because of all the uncertainties.)

Darius

Our regular Trios Plus series at the Jazz Centre happened on Wednesdays, so we advertised a public run-through of the 'show' that the conference delegates would see. This gave us an opportunity to have a dress rehearsal with sound and costumes – something we wouldn't get at the ICC. We had told the Department of Arts, Science, Culture and Technology weeks ago that we intended to do this and we were told to expect fifteen ministers and various government people. In the event, the run-through was only attended by one minister and some other officials we had been dealing with, who had been helpful. In their view, it was a late and final vetting of whether it would be suitable. Unfortunately, we were notified at show time (literally as people were lining up outside for us to open) that the public would NOT be allowed in for security reasons. Cathy arranged for some volunteers to sit outside to tell people to go away and come back later and we would do the show again after the government people had left. Glynis, at the Centre's bar, offered everyone who came back a free drink to compensate for the inconvenience (and we added the bar tab to the production budget from the ministry!). The minister and her attendants thought the show was great and left and then we did it all again. In the same letter to my parents, I wrote more about our experience of the UN Conference.

8 September 2001

Cathy had us all assemble on Thursday night at the Jazz Centre to wait for a call to come and set up and do a sound check for Friday morning. This meant organizing food, because we were stuck there until the call came and transportation and staying over at other people's houses for those who lived far away. You can imagine how much time was spent all day throughout the week working out shifting contingencies. People working for ICC, for Foreign Affairs and for the DACST were calling Cathy with different plans and she finally insisted that they all talk to each other and to the United Nations people who were the main organizers. We finally got the call to go down to town, went through security outside efficiently, and then were escorted to several wrong entrances. After a long time, we were taken to the right place and had to wait another long period for someone to let us in. By now it was getting late, and debates were still happening nearby while we were setting up on the stage and we weren't allowed to make any noise other than the piano tuning! This was all taking place at 10–11 p.m. Thankfully by doing a morning show we would be able to stay set up overnight and come in early for the soundcheck. Once again Jürgen Bräuninger was our excellent technical director.

Friday morning, we were up at 5 a.m. and left the Centre just after 6:00, the whole assembled Gathering Forces plus roadies, Cathy & Glynis and this time Security knew where to take us. Cathy estimates about 500 people of a possible 2,000 saw our show at 9:15 a.m. The people who did see it were enthusiastic and of course when I saw snippets on TV news last night, I was proud that we had done it.

A friend saw the whole show on TV 'live' and told us that there were some bemused commentators trying to make sense of this small, ethnically diverse army of musicians approaching the main platform imitating animal noises and playing percussion which was our choreographed way of getting on stage from the loading dock at the edge of the vast convention hall. The Conference TV crew hadn't received the press releases Cathy had both sent out and hand delivered to their bosses days in advance; but of course, they didn't know *when* and hadn't distributed the synopsis and description to the team on duty that morning. Later the pre-recorded and edited news did get it right. Anyway, the performance was fine except for a small technical screw-up on our joint composition 'Humanity Has No Colour' and, when it was over, we emerged blinking in the Durban sunlight at around 10:30 in the morning completely exhausted and wondering what we'd do for the rest of the day. Suddenly it was all over but what an incredible amount of work for not getting the best exposure for either the show or the South African government's cultural input. However, we were there!

I won't try to describe the music beyond saying it was meant to show all the cultures here cooperating. We had lots of percussion instruments, 4 Zulu traditional dancers in traditional regalia, Sazi (who was in the 1992 group that stayed in your house and is now a Ph.D. student) coordinating them and the drumming, a Maskanda guitar player in cowhides, a violinist and cellist with good singing voices and theatrical talent, a tabla and sitar duo, Barney, Lulu & Bongani and an extra keyboard player. So, it was visually as well as musically a Gathering of Forces.

15 September

Just a week and we now live in a different era. Obviously, I didn't finish the letter I started last week about our part of the Racism Conference. I'll try to get through the rest now. I also played a cocktail party hosted by the SA govt. for heads of delegations with a jazz quartet on the second day of the Conference. It was interesting to watch the interaction of some quite recognizable foreign and local dignitaries. No Yasser Arafat, Fidel Castro, or Thabo Mbeki (whose father had just died) but the next level down was there. I'm pleased to say that Foreign Affairs specifically wanted me but, as we normally do at the Centre, we included as many students as possible. In the event, the music really was important in terms of creating the relaxed, informal atmosphere which SA diplomats and officials – many of them former exiles and freedom fighters – prefer to the ceremonial protocol of typical state occasions. The foreign guests thought they were getting something South African (I doubt many of them knew an American was playing) and the SA hosts socialized easily and often talked to us while we were playing, like it was a private party in someone's house. Cathy and Glynis came as Manager and Sound Engineers and the food was 5 stars.

The next evening, we were guests of the US Cultural Affairs Officer, Amelia Broderick. The talking point was the American government only sending a low-level delegation. However, there had been many non-governmental American delegates in attendance, almost all African Americans, including Jesse Jackson and Congressman John Conyers who were at the party. Not only were we at the same party, but they actually sat at our table – their choice as it was outdoors and informal with no seating plan – and Cathy got a big hug from the Rev. J. and Dave got mentioned in the before-dinner prayer, which was in effect part of Jackson's quite incisive speech. Colin Powell phoned during dinner. Jackson, Conyers, and other Americans had really wanted him to come and Jesse told Colin that he should have just told the President he had to go and say, 'trust me'!

Dress rehearsal for UN World Conference Against Racism, CJPM, 5 September 2001 (photo: Cathy Brubeck; Cathy Brubeck collection).

Gathering Forces performing at the UN World Conference Against Racism at the Durban International Conference Centre, Durban, 7 September 2001 (photo: Cathy Brubeck; Cathy Brubeck collection).

Catherine

We were amazed and honoured by this sharing of privileged communication and there was a very touching and important (for jazz) speech to come. Congressman John Conyers rose to his feet and, acknowledging he was not officially representing the George W. Bush administration, he opened his remarks by grandly saying he was there at this world conference, 'on behalf of Miles Davis, John Coltrane and Dave Brubeck'. There was an appreciative moment of silence and he continued by saying that it was fitting that Darius was in South Africa 'spreading America's true greatness'. As the saying goes, jazz is an open sky. Our presentation at the UN World Conference Against Racism had emphasised the conference theme, 'Echoes of Hope', and the music portrayed the diversity that exists in South Africa by combining various styles of music – from traditional melodies to complex ragas and jazz. Local *maskandi* exponents traded sounds with the Western viola and the Eastern sitar and the totality projected an image of a world where humanity has no limit or colour. Again, I want to include another part of Darius's letter to his parents.

9/11

At the time of the attack on the World Trade Center, we were at work. Glynis' mother called first, and I thought she was reporting a 'normal' plane crash, then others started calling. Cathy's first thought was maybe it was related to the US pulling out of the Racism Conference. [The US had withdrawn in protest over anti-Israeli rhetoric in one of the resolutions.] When we finally got to a TV and saw more and heard more about the background and elaborate planning involved, it became clear that this wasn't done on behalf of Palestinians or to obtain a specific political end. It was not linked to demands for the release of prisoners or for Israeli withdrawal from the West Bank. However, I still think she has a point about the US being seen by many countries as contributing to many of the world's problems and not really participating wholeheartedly and open-mindedly in finding solutions.

Like everyone else, we're stunned, depressed and apprehensive about the immediate future. Hope Bush doesn't annihilate Afghanistan to get Bin Laden – this won't solve anything even if he is 100% the culprit. We feel that the New York we knew has gone and it can never really be the same. We're already exhausted by the coverage on the one hand and yet can't stop watching CNN, BBC and Sky as often as possible. Hope the term 'war' is figurative and legal rather than realized as practical fact. It also looks like the US had to take its own plane out – the one that crashed in Pennsylvania.

> I won't write much more in this letter. It's already long and I should spend the next leisure time I get working on my thesis again now that the Racism Conference is over. One thing more I'll say is how much the Racism Conference project was Cathy's. She submitted the proposal, pushed us all towards getting the programme right, organized complex rehearsal schedules, co-wrote the main song and worked more hours making it all happen than me or anyone else involved. Glynis was also a star so we have a great team, but it just wouldn't have happened without 'The Producer'.
>
> Love Darius

Darius's activities often took on an ambassadorial character and, with proposals that I generated, several professional and university-based groups played at the highest level in South Africa and overseas. As early as 1994, the Department of Foreign Affairs requested that CJPM tender for a student band to perform at a cultural exchange programme in Seoul, South Korea, and our proposal was accepted ahead of twenty other national bands. The quartet featured Neil Gonsalves, George Mari, Lex Futshane and Lulu Gontsana. Further official engagements for the new government followed – for example, playing for the Non-Aligned Movement luncheon hosted by Graça Machel in 1998 and another luncheon hosted by Zanele Mbeki for the Commonwealth heads of state.

In 2002, the Darius Brubeck Quartet was chosen to play at the banquet for the launch of the African Union and we were thrilled when Kofi Annan led Graça Machel onto the dance floor. However, the machinations before that high point were frustrating and politically remarkable. 'Brother leader' Muammar el-Qaddafi kept all the African heads of state in endless discussion and debate about his adamant desire and entitlement to the position of chairperson of this new body, which succeeded the Organisation of African Unity (OAU). Hours passed while the hot food cooled, and the cold food warmed, and the band wilted. We passed some of the time drinking gin and tonic with the then ANC Minister of Water Affairs and Forestry Ronnie Kasrils and his wife Eleanor, whom I had known as a schoolgirl. Although Eleanor Logan was at school in Durban and I was in Pietermaritzburg, we had a couple of boyfriends in common, mostly high school sports stars as opposed to the more revolutionary people we later admired. Anyway, we finally saw Nelson Mandela make a quiet and dignified exit, unlike Qaddaffi who, resplendently conspicuous in a bright green kaftan, made an angry, noisy one. Thabo Mbeki had been elected the first chairperson of the new organisation and very soon joined in the dancing. Meanwhile, Glynis and I were finally able to relax and have a meal. We gatecrashed a Namibian army general's table and he seemed to be delighted to meet those responsible for the entertainment.

It's the AU jive as Africa's leaders celebrate

JOHN BATTERSBY

WHAT do Robert Mugabe, Frederick de Klerk and Mangosuthu Buthelezi have in common?

Off the dance floor, probably not a lot.

But at a sumptuous private banquet hosted by President Thabo Mbeki at Durban's International Convention Centre on Monday night, they became masters of the African Union jive.

Gathered under a simulated night sky in a darkened banquet hall, African heads of state took to the dance floor to the accompaniment of the Darius Brubeck Quartet playing an up tempo version of Meadowlands.

After some prompting from Justice Minister Penuell Maduna, Zimbabwean President Mugabe broke into an awkward jive with his young wife Grace, Buthelezi, Maduna and several other dignitaries.

With the dance floor congested, clusters of heads of state began dancing alongside the long head table rather than trying to reach the dance floor.

Another enthusiastic cluster focused around former president de Klerk and his wife Elita.

The De Klerks were hosted by Speaker of Parliament Frene Ginwala, who showed she was up there with the rest of them when it came to the AU jive.

PICTURE: PURI DEVJEE

WHEN Africa's political leaders gathered in Durban this week for the historic launch of the African Union, it was not all serious talk; there was much partying too as shown by Deputy Speaker Baleka Kgotsisile-Mbete and Justice Minister Penuell Maduna who took to the floor to do the 'African jive' at the opening ceremony yesterday

African Union jive, featured in the *Natal Mercury*, 10 July 2002.

After all this name dropping, I need to return to some facts and figures showing that South African jazz and jazz education is still alive and well. Both the National Youth Jazz Festival (NYJF) and the SAJE have existed for 30 years and we are certainly proud that we can claim to have initiated the latter and been present at the first gathering of the former. Both organisations created great opportunities for students and teachers and will clearly have a positive influence on music education in South Africa into the foreseeable future.

South African Association for Jazz Education

When Darius and I established SAJE in 1992, we were inspired by the great music and educational expertise presented at IAJE's annual conferences in the United States. SAJE now has an international network and reputation with a history of outstanding conferences in South Africa. Credit is due to all those, especially Mike and Di Rossi, who, for many years, made SAJE an even more successful and multifaceted organisation. In addition to a biannual conference, the Rossis organised a SAJE festival every other year. We spent fourteen years at the helm and that was equalled by Di and Mike Rossi, who have now retired in Italy. 'Retired' is hardly the word because they continue to

Di Rossi running the SAJE conference, SA College of Music, UCT, Cape Town, 27 April 2018 (photo: Busiswa Damoyi; Di Rossi collection).

organise workshops and performances there and maintain strong links with the South African jazz world.

Debbie Mari took over a leadership and organising role in SAJE for a while, but now the organisation's president is Chantal Willie-Petersen from Wits University. Debbie first came to UKZN as a student in 1992 and is now a lecturer in Jazz Studies there. We love her vocal version of 'Before It's Too Late', the title song of Darius's last recording made in South Africa. I wrote the lyrics and Darius wrote the music. Lasting connections with former students create a continuum that demonstrates the success of the jazz programme and Chris Ballantine's enduring vision, which is now 40 years old. At last count, I can think of nearly 30 UKZN jazz graduates who became teachers and many of these have a significant playing career as well.

The founding SAJE conference that I organised with Anne Pretorius and Glynis Malcolm-Smith was held at Wits University, with major sponsorship from SAMRO, IAJE and the universities of Natal and Witwatersrand. Dr Dennis Tini, a wonderful jazz pianist and then president of IAJE, delivered the keynote address.

The SAJE backstory is related to our trip to the Montreux Jazz Festival in 1987 and experiencing the role of the NAJE in the United States. We decided that we needed a similar national organisation that could strengthen jazz education in South Africa. After a few years of targeted fund-raising and lobbying in my capacity as special projects manager for the Centre for Jazz and Popular Music, SAJE was launched with participation from eighteen educational institutions at all levels. This event at the Bozzoli Pavilion in Johannesburg featured music by Ladysmith Black Mambazo, Hugh Masekela, Dennis Tini (accompanied by Victor Ntoni and Lulu Gontsana), Marc Duby, Chris Merz and a host of others, including Darius. An abridged version of the programme in Appendix 2 from the last of these conferences organised by CJPM reveals the depth and breadth that jazz education had attained in 23 years.[2]

Mike and Di Rossi very successfully reconstituted SAJE as an independent organisation in 2010 when IAJE went into receivership due to financial mismanagement by the salaried executive director. In 2017, Glynis and I sent this message for SAJE's 25th anniversary:

> We remember well the founding of SAJE and the first eight conferences that we either organized or assisted in organizing. The joyous and difficult times with little money, great speakers, and significant musicians. We are thrilled that SAJE carries on and has expanded with such a major contribution to jazz education. Happy Anniversary to all.

The National Youth Jazz Festival

The NYJF (sponsored fully by Standard Bank until 2022) is one of the most important national jazz education activities in South Africa, and it has been directed by Alan

Webster of Stirling High School for 21 years.[3] Mike Skipper inaugurated the NYJF in 1992 and ran it until 2000.[4] We met with Mike when he came to Durban for an education conference and discussed his plans for starting his visionary venture. Glynis and I made sure that CJPM was able to raise funds for our students to attend year after year.

The NYJF now runs concurrently with the Makhanda (previously Grahamstown) Jazz Festival, which Alan took charge of in 2004, making the 'Jazz' and 'Youth' events into a single festival. In an email dated 7 November 2021, Alan said that combining the two is 'the most important aspect of the festival', as it 'brings together all facets of the jazz industry as well as introducing many SA jazz musicians to foreign musicians from around the world. It also introduces students from around the country to each other, to great SA musicians and internationally known musicians.' People come from 'all geographic regions of the country and this includes music teachers from community projects, secondary and tertiary institutions'. Since 2001, there have been more than 5 000 student attendees.

I attended many of these festivals and Darius performed at the first NYJF and several times thereafter, including playing a concert with his brothers, Chris and Dan, Mike Rossi and Barney Rachabane in 2004. He also directed student bands and gave lectures and workshops. Alan's collected data reveals that in the 1990s and early 2000s many of South Africa's leading jazz musicians attended the festival and it became a catalyst for bringing new styles into South African jazz. The NYJF was a bridge between high school and university programmes and a force in extending the number of schools and universities offering jazz. South Africa has gone from one university programme in 1983 to twenty in 2022.

Darius

Moving on

After twenty-plus years of jazz life in Durban, we were thinking that it was time to do something different and that it was politically and musically appropriate to leave the next phase of jazz education to South Africans. Life at CJPM was still great. There were sporadic experiments in administrative organisation affecting the Music Department, mainly renaming roles and changing terms like 'department', 'faculty', 'school' and 'division' that came from on high. However, I enjoyed the public-facing aspect of the directorship, especially hosting the shows on Wednesdays. It was rewarding to see former students doing well and contributing to the general cultural life, as well as being appointed as staff at other institutions. Cathy still did the door, Glynis ran the bar and I made sure everything was ready for the musicians and then went on stage to introduce them. I even enjoyed the physical work of getting the stage ready, but usually there was a student from Jürgen Bräuninger's Music Technology course to do this and to run the sound. There would be an hour or so of music and drinking, a clean-up by paid students under Glynis's supervision and the three of us might then go to Oscar's or one of the other nearby restaurants. These evenings overflowed with goodwill and fellowship because we had so many regulars who always came, as well as new people, who just couldn't believe their luck.

One fine evening, while we were having our last glass of wine and clearing the Centre, Cathy asked me, 'Why are we still here?' Personally, I wanted to compose and play more, and we also felt that we wanted to be nearer family. My parents were getting old and our grandchildren in the United States were growing up. England seemed a good mid-point geographically between South Africa and North America. Our ties with South Africa were strong and valued and we didn't want to break them completely. I was also aware of a growing age gap between myself and my students, which meant that future bands would relate to music in a new and different way.

When we first went to South Africa, our families worried about us, thinking of the risks involved in living in a distant country rife with pre-revolutionary turmoil. Relentless activity – whether playing music or working on committees – was exhausting, but there is an addictive sensation of momentum that comes from playing the changes, when it matters. But now, wasn't it sort of a case of 'mission accomplished', now that Jazz Studies was available at universities all around the land? Certainly, a major ongoing positive factor was the remarkable people that we encountered. We would always be protagonists in our own drama, but nowhere else would there be such an amazing cast.

Cathy and I were often asked if we felt safe and the answer is, 'Yes, and no'. South Africa can be a dangerous place. National statistics on crime and violence are perennially shocking and people we know have experienced muggings, break-ins, hijacking and assault, to varying degrees. Living in South Africa meant accepting as normal the hassles and mishaps attendant on setting alarms, locking and unlocking security gates, even hiring an armed response security company. People we knew and cared about had been murdered. Cathy and I didn't panic and run. We perceived crime as opportunistic, rather than politically or racially motivated. We certainly knew our burglary at Peace Avenue was not racially motivated because the name of the perpetrator on the police report was Martin van Ass. Van Ass made off with our wedding clothes as well as other stuff. A suit is a suit, but we were upset about losing Cathy's dress, which was irreplaceable and had been purchased in Bloomingdales in New York City.

I don't remember exactly why years later we sold our stylish architect-built modern house on Queen Elizabeth Avenue, with its panoramic views towards Westville, but the next house we owned in Durban was on Rand Road, way down on the inland side of the ridge. We were still in a 'white neighbourhood' with a small sportsground and a busy road between us and Cato Manor, still a contested territory.

Student demonstrations, which sometimes escalated into riots, especially near the start of term, were becoming almost commonplace. Organised demonstrations focused on public issues were not riots, but in addition to legitimate protests, there were sporadic disruptions that were never explained because their object was not to convince, but simply to prevail. Academics, as professional thinkers, tended to be forgiving, relating everything to a broader context of privilege versus inequality – as they say in French, '*Tout comprendre c'est tout pardonner*' (to understand all is to forgive all). The tides of disruption ebbed and flowed over the years, peaking in the Fallist movement more than a decade after Cathy and I had left.

Back in 1992, it was well known that a 'student leader' named Knowledge Mdladlose, who hadn't recently passed any exams, paid fees or bothered to attend classes, was busy organising various protests on his own behalf. He was not going to be readmitted as a student and therefore had no right to hold on to his dorm room. At the time, I was rehearsing the NU Jazz Ensemble in Shepstone 20, a large, unfurnished room at one end of the main concourse. I guess the sound coming from an over-twenty-strong jazz band attracted the protestors. My back was to the large, swinging double doors, so I didn't immediately know why the ranks of saxophones and brass I was facing fell silent. The crowd noise was suddenly very loud and within seconds the band was surrounded by slogan-chanting students. Heated exchanges in languages I didn't understand were taking place between some of the band members and the demonstrators. The latter were shaming my students for taking part in a class or activity while one of their 'brother students' (Knowledge) was being expelled. Someone tried to snatch Mfana Mlambo's tenor sax from its stand and he urged me to explain that they would be hurting fellow students if they damaged their instruments, which cost a lifetime of work to acquire and a lot of money to repair. I assumed the person standing closest to me was a leader and I appealed to him to ask for quiet, so that I could hear what they wanted. He demanded that we all leave immediately. I told him that we *had* stopped, but we couldn't just leave until the instruments were safely packed up. Mfana said the same thing in isiZulu. I pointed to a large closet where we stored equipment like drums, amps and music stands, and band members started packing their horns and putting things away. Seeing that we were indeed ending the rehearsal, the aggressive contingent got bored and left. Ezra Ngcukana, who was sitting in the sax section, later related this incident to friends we were having drinks with. He said he 'never thought he would see a white man stand up to a Zulu mob . . . when they see them *toyi-toyiing*, white men run away'. It would be ego boosting to turn this incident into a story of courage and leadership, but frankly, I *wasn't* brave; I just wasn't afraid.

One of my jazz performance classes was notable because it included members of a deservedly popular student band, Ba'gasane (Neighbours) that based its sound and style on Mozambican guitarist Jimmy Dludlu's music. The neighbours were two exceptional guitarists, Prince Kupi and Ranketsing Ramela, along with their bass player Piwe Solomon and drummer Chris Mashiane. The class also included Anna Mailula, who, unusually for a young woman at that time, played trumpet as well as piano. We met weekly in an empty storage room above the Jazz Centre that could only be accessed from the vast parking garage that took up most of this level. The class was playing something I had assigned when the sound of shots made everyone stop. I slightly opened the double door and saw the armoured car that picked up money every week parked near the stairs on the opposite side of the garage. The university cashier where students paid their fees was one level up. Shots echoed loudly in the garage again. I saw a man running full tilt for the exit ramp and two uniformed guards charging down the stairs, pistols in hand. It dawned on me that *I* was in charge; I was responsible for my students' safety! I locked and bolted the doors and ordered the students to crawl into a windowless cupboard in case stray bullets came flying in our direction. A few minutes slowly ticked by. I crawled to the door to peep outside. All clear. It seemed safe enough to carry on with the lesson to the end of the period. Everyone just picked up their instruments again. For township residents, this had been no more upsetting than a power failure or . . . an armed robbery, which is what it was. Ranketsing Ramela pulled a sad face and said, 'I didn't get to finish my solo.'

Ranketsing didn't get to finish his life either. It was cut off by a bullet early one morning in January 1997. Glynis, Cathy and I believed the motive was robbery but, according to Piwe Solomon, 'nobody knows why'.[5] I had phoned Piwe during the writing of this book. He was not actually there when Ranketsing died, so he got the story from Prince Kupi. He told Prince's version to me almost as if he had been a witness himself. It turned out to be different from what I expected. I recall that Glynis had just handed over a bursary (a scholarship set up by the UND/UK Trust Alumni Association) and Cathy had driven Ranketsing around to a few addresses that offered student accommodation. That night, Ranketsing went out on the town with Prince and some 'engineering guys' who were Ba'gasane fans, and their girlfriends, including a girl Ranketsing planned to marry. After spending some time at Mfana's concession at Jubilee Hall, they spent the rest of the night drinking at a club in the Workshop, a cavernous shopping centre built in the shell of the old railway station, right in the middle of town. Ranketsing, splashing a lot of cash, was a visible and vulnerable target for robbery. They left for the main bus rank a few blocks from the Workshop and, in Prince's version, someone shot Ranketsing along this route, but neither Prince (nor anyone else) had seen it happen. I wondered how this could be and asked questions around this point, but Piwe insisted that Ranketsing was behind them and that the group unwittingly kept walking while Ranketsing lay dying in the street. 'It was a lonely death; passers-by just thought he was drunk but he was still alive and suffering for a long time.' There is a lot missing here. Piwe's recollection of Prince's retelling contradicts a long-standing alternative account (possibly based on guesses) that we heard. This other version was that he was shot while attempting to board the bus just as it was pulling out, falling back into the street, and then was robbed. I asked Piwe if he knew what the police thought had happened. He replied that 'if you are not somebody who is well known, the police just want to end the case. The bullet went right through him and was not found, so they said there was nothing they could do.'

We received this terrible news at work because, as Piwe said, 'Glynis was the first person you would tell. She would know how to help.' Things moved fast from then on. Glynis went to the mortuary and identified the body. She had to sign for a plastic bag of bloody clothes and whatever else Ranketsing had on him and take it back to her office at the Centre. We were somewhat relieved when a mature student from the SRC named Musa Mhlongo came forward. He organised transportation for the body and helped Glynis with university and official paperwork. As a gesture of respect – but really because I was upset and needed to give the three of us at the Centre time to settle down – I cancelled tutorials that day. It was very quiet at the Centre, as it always was between semesters, but a small group of students showed up to pray in my office. In a few days, members of the Ramela family arrived to collect Ranketsing's guitar and other belongings on campus, and to meet with us. They asked to be left alone at the Centre and for access to be arranged to the places that Ranketsing had frequented on campus. Glynis made a short call to Security – she always knew who to call – and I told her she could go home. The family walked around a dark, empty CJPM and drove to the other locations calling Ranketsing's name softly and waving freshly cut branches so that his spirit would know that he had to leave the places he loved. We met the family again at the funeral in Johannesburg.

I hadn't called Piwe expecting to piece together evidence from a cold case as in countless TV dramas, but I felt I needed to remember Ranketsing here. Piwe paused at what seemed to be the end of the conversation and decided to reveal what he felt it was *really* about. He said:

> There was another thing. It was the curse. When Ranketsing was drinking with us, he would say, 'If anything happens to me, keep the band going all the time'. He told us there was a prophecy that someone in his family must die every year. I told him to never say that because what you say happens – *spiritually*. And that is exactly what happened.

The band didn't stay together. Piwe said, 'We all wanted to finish and get out of Durban as soon as possible. We didn't trust anything.' I hadn't noticed this at the time, but it is true that they didn't hang around Durban the way many others from out of town often did. Despite this tragedy, Prince and Piwe did finish with a special flourish of success. They were both part of the new NU Jazz Connection that went to Peru in 1999. Prince had an especially good run as a student, winning an expensive guitar in a competition and announcing his engagement to be married after graduation. He was also nominated for a SAMA for Best Newcomer. Piwe did very well in Johannesburg playing corporate functions and running the house band at the Sandton Sun. He now plays with Mduduzi (Clement) Magwaza, formerly of Mango Groove, and teaches at Central Johannesburg College, a job he has held for many years. Andile Yenana credits Piwe with encouraging him to get into teaching. Sadly, Prince Kupi was killed in a car accident in 2008.

Bongani Mthethwa, a distinguished ethnomusicologist and the first black academic to join the Music Department, rented an apartment Cathy and I had added to our Queen Elizabeth Avenue house. Except for infrequent visits by a teenage daughter or niece who was in boarding school somewhere, Bongani lived quietly and alone, but he went out a lot at night. I arrived home late one night after a gig at the Moon Hotel just as Bongani was locking his car in the driveway. As I put my car in the garage, he smiled slyly and said something like, 'I see you're getting around while Cathy is away.' Indeed, Cathy was out of town and I thought he was joking, but it later appeared that he was equating my nocturnal activities with his own. Music Department colleagues and students were shocked when we heard in June 1991 that his body was found in the burnt-out shell of his car near one of the townships. Why hadn't the car been taken? It was conjectured that there must have been a jealous husband or lover, a crime of passion. The main lecture hall in the new School of Music is named after him.

These stories are just an indication of the sorrow we experienced with unusual intensity in South Africa because as we have noted, there were many deaths during our time there. Piwe compared Ranketsing's murder to another homicide, that of a sax player we knew, Teaspoon Ndelu. 'They took everything from his flat, his sax, his gig clothes and I think he carried a gun, which was missing too. There was no investigation.' Gito Baloi, much-admired bassist and singer with Tananas, was found in his parked car after a gig in Johannesburg in 2004 with a bullet wound in the middle of his forehead. There was also a frighteningly high student mortality rate in the 1990s as the AIDS epidemic struck young people. During this period, I remember Jürgen Bräuninger talking about a largish Music History class and saying, 'Just keep counting – one, two, three – and the third person will be gone.'

One accepts mortality on a philosophical level and inevitably encounters personal loss, but friends and musicians dying throughout our time in South Africa affected us greatly and, indeed, has motivated our writing about some of them.

The too-long goodbye

In 2003 and 2004 I was still working more hours than ever just to keep on top of routine teaching and other staff work because there hadn't been a second full-time jazz lecturer for some years and there was little hope of getting one. I wasn't playing in town as much and I missed the psychological release as well as the opportunities to keep up my musicianship. Cathy and Glynis expressed dismay about my getting upset about stupid things at work, such as someone taking my parking space and similar territorial incursions. There was quite a row over male students from African Music and Dance using the women's toilet at the Centre because it was adjacent to their rehearsal area. I was cranky and defensive about demands on our space, time and energy and had less patience. There were systemic reasons for that, but less personal involvement with students changed how I felt about my job. Hadn't we completed our mission? I was nearly 60 and I had been a high-functioning teacher-artist-leader-committeeman-director for years and there were warning signs of burnout. However, university leave conditions were still generous and we travelled overseas regularly. Besides our family ties in the United States, we had a house (part of an inheritance) in Provence, France, good connections in England through the University of Nottingham, and close friends and music contacts in London. My parents and brothers came to England for Dave's birthday concerts with the London Symphony Orchestra in 2000 and 2005, for which I had composed original music. Participation in these events was an alluring taste of a different level of professional life. There were push and pull factors in favour of leaving and staying. Cathy and I didn't think we could or should abandon what was effectively our life's work.

I now realise that my inability to simply let go and move on caused a lot of unnecessary work for colleagues. Until then, I felt I had seldom made bad decisions about important things, but it was a mistake to signal my intention to resign in 2004 before doing so. There followed lots of memos and meetings to come up with a succession plan. Cathy and I thought I could continue as an 'international director' while a Music Department staff member remained the centre director on site. I floated proposals around this idea. A version of this plan (without invented designations just mentioned) was formulated by the dean and formally accepted by the Music Department and the faculty. I was to remain on staff with a 25 per cent contract, which meant returning to Durban for three months of active duty in 2005 and 2006 and this could even be renewed. This arrangement was not difficult to grasp as it related to teaching and postgraduate supervision and there had always been part-time staff. What was controversial and unresolved was my directorship. That designation represented *power* and the Centre for Jazz and Popular Music was now unanchored from my academic post and from me. In an elegantly written internal memo, Michael Chapman, as dean of the Faculty of Human Sciences, proposed splitting my academic post between

Neil Gonsalves rehearsing at CJPM, December 2019 (photo: Doug Mostert; Neil Gonsalves collection).

Mageshen Naidoo, a former UKZN student and PhD candidate at the University of Southern California (Los Angeles), and Zim Ngqawana, with Zim 'eventually' becoming director of CJPM. He foresaw that both would be 'mentored' into their respective roles by me during my orbital returns. As already discussed in Chapter 7, I supported the appointment of both Zim Ngqawana and Mageshen Naidoo. Mageshen, an excellent guitarist, had benefited from excellent jazz pedagogy courses at the University of Southern California, where he went on a Fulbright scholarship, upholding the canon, and Zim would be the radical voice and innovator. It didn't work. At the outset, Zim was just too free and neither of them saw their contrasting strengths as complementary. Zim resigned and Mageshen took over the centre.

In the long run, things at CJPM turned out for the best. Demi Fernandez, the dazzling Spanish guitarist, who headed the Natal Technikon music programme, Susan Barry and Neil Gonsalves joined the UKZN Music Division (note new terminology) when the technikon's Music Department was incorporated into UKZN. There were some experiments with collective leadership after Mageshen left,[6] but Neil has been the recognised director of CJPM for some years. He had been one of my preferred candidates anyway, but was fully employed at the technikon in 2004. He and I have been in frequent contact since I began working on this book. I admire the way he has always worked at balancing the established traditions of jazz education with a desire for innovation and adaptation to the dynamics of time, place and culture. Neil was in the group that went to the Boston IAJE conference in 1994 and holds a Master's degree in Music (Jazz Studies) from UKZN. In June 2021, *Eastern Eye Magazine* named Neil 'one of the top 50 influential personalities in South Africa'.

He wrote in answer to our questionnaire:

I was lucky to be a student when there was a strong live music culture on campus. I was a hapless Computer Science student in my first year on campus and remember rushing from the Science block to Howard College Theatre to watch the Jazzanians, only to have to listen from outside because the theatre was full. I'd also head off to UDW music department and concerts with Deepak Ram, Melvin Peters and the late Siva Devar elicited a similar buzz.

Also important in terms of 'playing the changes', he had been in close contact with Bheki Mseleku, by then the most acclaimed South African jazz pianist of his generation. Neil continues:

I remember playing gigs as a young jazz musician. The repertoire would invariably comprise our original compositions and American and South African standards, especially if people wanted to dance. Two separate things, and different approaches. Bheki's music consolidated those two worlds, the challenge of playing changes, but with township bounce and attitude. I spin that further by taking the American songbook into the township. You once used the term 'deharmonisation' to describe it. In any event, what Bheki does, or what I do, is not possible without American jazz and South African township music. It is a natural outgrowth and consequence, and a function of the traditions of the music. If only our formal institutions could cohere as nicely.

The album of one of Neil's former students, Nduduzo Makhathini, called *Modes of Communication: Letters from the Underworlds* was included with the Darius Brubeck Quartet's *Live in Poland* in *Downbeat Magazine*'s critics' list of best albums of 2020.[7] Makhathini's music is rooted in Zulu culture, even pre-colonial beliefs and practices, and he has an understandably critical take on formal Jazz Studies.[8] I am claiming that our simultaneous appearance on an internationally acknowledged honours list exemplifies generational torch-passing and 'glocalisation', a neologism coined by jazz scholar Stuart Nicholson to describe how artists incorporate their own national imagery and culture into the language of jazz.[9] Cathy says this is an awkward-sounding word, but it does describe how jazz continues to change and grow without abandoning its past and I'm all for it.

Coda

Darius

We did return to South Africa in 2005 and 2006 and I taught at UKZN as planned and, indeed, returned almost every year after that to visit friends and play music until I nearly died from Covid-19 in 2020 (that is another story). Before that watershed experience, Cathy and I were individually awarded grants from the Stellenbosch

A version of a Rolling Reunion Band in 2008, featuring Pamela de Menezes as vocalist. Left to right: Burton Naidoo, Pamela de Menezes, Darius, Paul Kock, Bruce Baker, Concord Nkabinde (photo: Cathy Brubeck; Cathy Brubeck collection)

Institute for Advanced Study, which covered residencies there to work on this book in 2017 and 2019. Saved concert programmes from the Jazz Centre, Grahamstown/Makhanda, the Cape Town International Jazz Festival, Cliff Wallis's concert series Jazz at the Nassau, and other individual performances record other South African visits since our move to England. We did a series of Rolling Reunion concerts with different UKZN alumni and staff, including an appearance at the Durban Fan Zone, organised by Dan Chiorboli, during the 2010 World Cup. Both Cliff (based in Cape Town) and Dan (based in Durban) supported jazz substantially by initiating and organising many live performances, which benefited both professionals and students.

While establishing a new career in the United Kingdom, I taught for one semester at Guildhall School of Music and Drama in London (2006) and was sponsored by the United States government to teach in Istanbul (2007) and Cluj-Napoca in Romania (2010) as a Fulbright senior specialist. I didn't know it at the time, but this was my last formal teaching job.

A couple of handwritten diary entries from early 2005 describe a party at Zim Ngqawana's house as, 'like a jazz festival without the hassle' because so many musician friends turned up. Another entry refers to 'stopping by Lulu's pad on the way to the airport'. This was the last time we saw Lulu Gontsana, who died in December of that year.[1]

Every trip to South Africa felt special, like a homecoming, spending time with lifelong friends. We often talked about how good it felt to be there. The weather, the friends, the good musicians to play with and the receptive audiences to play for, the comparatively low price of real estate, great food and the way routine processes like airport check-ins or buying a tank of petrol turned into friendly, personal encounters. It all appealed, but we fundamentally knew this was self-indulgent. We might return again and again, but we had emigrated and that was that.

A Mandela moment

On one of these trips, we were airborne and about to land when the pilot announced the death of Nelson Mandela on 5 December 2013 (exactly a year after my father died). We were on our way to the Mahiking Jazz Festival and some dates in Cape Town with the London musicians Matt Ridley and Wesley Gibbens and would be joined there by Mike Rossi. Our concerts were not cancelled, as might have been expected. Rather, in common with other music gatherings around the country, our concerts became joyful affirmations of respect for Mandela and allegiance to the ideals he stood for.

I shook hands with Nelson Mandela at Jan Smuts Airport in late 2000.[2] Cathy and I were on our way to London and, as usual, the Departures hall was massively overcrowded. Once we had checked in our luggage and were free to drift away from the crush, Cathy wanted to phone her brother to say goodbye, but it was just too noisy. We went down to Arrivals, which was a little better and I went scouting for a quiet place to have a conversation. There was a staircase between the levels and standing under it seemed to be the perfect spot, shielded from the general hubbub, not in or near a queue, a dead end not on the way to anything. There was a little shop nearby that sold newspapers and sweets and a door leading to underground parking. But that was *not* all! A hidden door suddenly opened in the wall under the staircase just as I was about to put in Jo's number and to my amazement, *the* man, with his close protection, two in front, three behind, was right in front of me. A frozen moment passed as my presence was as unexpected to his team as theirs was to me. Keeping my hands open and away from my body, I took a small step towards him and timidly said, 'Darius Brubeck'. I can't be certain that he knew who I was (he was reputedly a jazz fan, so there was a chance), but there was a flicker of recognition and he offered his hand. However, this is not the best part of the story.

A mother with her young, blonde, blue-eyed daughter was in the shop. The little girl turned around wide-eyed as if she had just seen a vision and pointed. Mandela stopped his entourage and went towards her. 'Do you know who I am,' he asked.

'You are President Mandela,' she replied.

'No,' he said, speaking very slowly and distinctly, 'I used to be President Mandela, but you can call me Mr Mandela now.'

He then added, 'And *you* could be president one day.'

What a generous vision for the New South Africa and the Rainbow Nation. The only witnesses were (I'll count them): the mother and daughter, the shopkeeper, Mandela's bodyguards, Cathy and me; ten individuals. No rolling cameras, no smart phones in those days. It was just real.

Name and fame

What's the point of being me? You need an answer for the inner critic more than for anyone else. This question didn't motivate our move to South Africa, but making that choice certainly gave my life new meaning and an unusual set of challenges and goals. I felt protected by the Brubeck name and I used this privilege to good effect when speaking out on sensitive issues. Being a Brubeck must have been a factor – not the total reason – in my getting the university job. People in the jazz and arts world were generally amazed that I was in South Africa at all when, in their view, I could be anywhere else in the world. A former colleague, Betsy Oehrle, likes to tell the story of meeting Chris Ballantine coming down the stairs of the Music Library, smiling broadly and saying, 'Guess who just applied for the jazz post?'

'A Brubeck,' she replied, as a joke, but when Chris said, 'How did you guess?' she realised it wasn't a joke.

I have been told countless times that it was an honour to meet me or, in the case of musicians, an honour to work with me; being able to claim an association with the

Brubeck name means something special for them, so why should I demur? My letters of recommendation are still sought after and still effective, so I'm happy to help. I'm not unaware that some musicians and critics, who expected more of me, felt let down. As I've said before, I never saw myself as an outstanding pianist. I know how to work with what I've got and my professional quartets, Gathering Forces ensembles and student bands express what I know about life and music. I take nothing for granted and no gig is unimportant if I've agreed to do it. Playing in public brings out my 'almost-best', to quote Lulu Gontsana again. I play for and to the audience, not to compete with other musicians – and not with my father.

Going to South Africa amplified my father's name while making my own relatively famous. My brothers, Chris, Dan and Matt, who are also musicians named Brubeck, haven't experienced as much 'celebrity' as I have, except perhaps for Chris. He is now far more productive and professionally active than I am. Recognition can be ego-boosting fun and it can often be silly, as in the Major George Hayden dart-throwing story recounted in Chapter 8. Cathy remembers the Durban Publicity Association booking my group in the very early days to play at their tourism promotion at an upscale hotel in Johannesburg. We were treated like bigshots night and day. Sandile Shange, who had never stayed in such a hotel before, talked a bartender into giving him a bottle of Red Heart rum, went out on the town with Count Wellington Judge, a jazz singer friend of his, lost his key and, sadly, ended up sleeping in the corridor instead of staying in a luxury suite like the rest of us. When I went to cash a cheque at the desk to pay the band, the hotel manager, without looking first, announced with snobbish servility, 'Of course we will cash Mr Brubeck's cheque', only to find they didn't have enough cash on hand. He had nevertheless shown the world that he knew who I was, which was the important thing – to him.

'Darius Brubeck' was even the answer to a question in the South African version of the game *Trivial Pursuit* and our beloved, well-known and characterful cat Schillaci (as in the Italian footballer) was the subject of a humorous article in the arts section of the *Daily News*. Years later, while working on this book at the Stellenbosch Institute for Advanced Study, I went to the travel agency on the Stellenbosch University campus. Craig, behind the desk, asked me what I was doing and I told him that I was working on a book about jazz in South Africa. He confided that there was a real legend at Stellenbosch University doing a project either about himself or his dad who started jazz at Natal. 'That's me,' I said, presenting my passport and credit card.

'Not trying to flatter you,' said Craig, extending his hand, 'but we don't often get legends in this place.'

General knowledge sometimes causes general confusion. Some people thought I was Dave Brubeck's father! They must have seen pictures of a younger Dave when he was at the height of his fame. I look a lot like he did, glasses and all, even more than any of my brothers do. I was sometimes asked why I had an American accent, with the implication that I was a local boy made good. Patrick Compton (himself the son of legendary England cricketer Denis Compton), reviewing *Ordeal by Innocence*, a film starring Donald Sutherland, noted in the *Daily News* in May 1985, 'the excellent jazz score by Dave Brubeck (father of Natal University's Darius) gives the film a suitably cool tone'. I sent that review home in a letter because I knew my parents would be amused by the inversion. When the Temptations came to South Africa in 1998, their leader paid a quick visit to the Jazz Centre, accompanied by the group's publicist, who just saw it as a local photo-op to promote their concert in Durban. The Temptations was one of my favourite groups in the 1970s, but they had gone through personnel changes, so I wasn't sure who I was meeting. I introduced myself and, hearing 'Brubeck', the Temptation (who seemed in a hurry to get it over with) thought I was putting him on. He extended his hand and said, 'Well, I'm Stan Kenton' (a famous American big band leader of the 1950s). I still don't know what his name was – and he didn't believe mine.

Ever since I was a child, interviewers have asked me, 'What is it like to be Dave Brubeck's son?' and they still do, even though I am 75 years old. I have no other way of being in the world. I learnt that what they wanted was a story, like my going to Poland with Dave in 1958, or sleeping under Cal Tjader's vibes in the Kaiser Vagabond car in the 1950s when the family used to travel together, but that's not really a deep answer. To quote Tolstoy, 'All happy families resemble one another . . . '. We were a happy family. Mom read stories to us; Dad and our 'uncles' played music. I was the eldest of five brothers and a sister. We had the usual family conflicts and fun together when our situation was economically precarious, as well as when we all had trust funds and our own cars.

It isn't unusual to be a second-generation jazz musician. Internationally, there are many examples – Joshua Redman, son of Dewey Redman; Ellis Marsalis's sons – Wynton, Branford, Jason and Delfeayo; Alec and Jacqui Dankworth, the children of Johnny Dankworth and Cleo Laine; and Thelonious Monk Junior spring to mind. In South Africa, there are examples, too: Bokani Dyer, son of Steve and all the Ngcukanas. But an inescapable fact is that very few jazz musicians were *as* famous as Dave Brubeck. His worldwide fame extended to the cover of *Time* magazine, White House dinners with presidents from Kennedy through to Obama, Kennedy Center Honours, a documentary produced by Clint Eastwood, countless music industry awards and honorary degrees and all kinds of education, diplomatic and civic honours. Since his death in 2012, he has been regarded as a 'cultural icon' and someone whose name evokes the best aspects of post-war American character. He was an important jazz ambassador whose playing made an impact at high levels – an example being his requested presence (by Mikhail Gorbachev) at the Reagan/Gorbachev summit meeting in Moscow for the Strategic Arms Limitation Treaty. It has always been a hard act to follow.

Being a Brubeck was ideal for fund-raising and getting press attention in America as well as in South Africa. It helped us take student groups to IAJE conferences and build tours around them. When I was much younger, I went out of my way to avoid trading on my father's name, which I equated with not deserving success myself, but in later years, when I moved to London as a full-time musician, I embraced my father's legacy as a significant heritage.[3] I play a lot more of my own music than I do of his, but his fame and 'Take Five' gave me a potential following to win over, if I could.

However, London is a later chapter in my life. Here is Dusty Cox's take (from an email of 13 October 2021) on my life as a local celebrity in Durban:

> The second evening I was there, Glynis Malcolm-Smith, the Centre for Jazz 'lynchpin' that did so-much-for-so-many-for-so-long drove Darius and I to the Rainbow Jazz Club in Pinetown to hear Winston Mankunku Ngozi and his band. To walk into that environment and see traditional Zulu dancers preparing to perform, to meet Ben Pretorius, his predominantly Zulu staff and learn a little about the history of the club while watching some burn a joint of 'Durban Poison' nearly as big as a human forearm and having a taste of homebrew 'white lightning' had my head spinning both figuratively and literally. People were calling Darius's name as we moved through the crowd

Darius, Victor Ntoni, Winston Mankunku and Kevin Gibson at the Rainbow, 1984 (photographer unknown; Cathy Brubeck collection).

and everyone wanted to say hello to him, to get his attention and to see how comfortable he was in this wonderful environment and all in it made me realise I was in for a very interesting time indeed.

When Winston came out to the vamp of his iconic 'Yakhal' Inkomo' with the crowd going nuts, jumping on seats, dancing, singing and to hear Winston play (and later to have the honour of meeting him backstage with Darius), I decided then and there I was 'home' and that I would never leave. It was a magical moment in my life and I am forever grateful not only for that moment, but for the many moments of wonder I experienced in Durban with the local players, former and current students of the day as well as with Cathy, Darius and Glynis. Alas, economics got in the way, and I left SA purely because of my US debt I couldn't repay.

In 2018, Cathy and I returned yet again to Durban to conduct on-the-spot research and interviews for this book. The nation was experiencing another prolonged crisis of transition, this time away from President Jacob Zuma's corrupt and disappointing misrule, but with hope for reform and better governance under Cyril Ramaphosa. Meanwhile, we shopped in supermarkets, ate in restaurants with friends, flew or drove between major cities and the world kept turning. We set ourselves up in a comfortable B & B apartment near campus where we could write and, with honorary research associate status, I also worked on campus.

There were some visible signs of neglect and dilapidation revealing that the university had been going through a bad patch, from which it has since recovered. I was pleased to see that, despite this, the Centre looked cared-for outside and in. Neil Gonsalves had improved the stage area and updated the tech infrastructure of sound and lights. Backstage, there were still boxes and boxes of unsorted documentary material from our time there, which we used for research and we successfully motivated for Glynis, who had retired two years after we did, to go through it all for the UKZN archives in Pietermaritzburg. I was dismayed when told by a colleague that admission policy was 'circling back to the way things were when you came', meaning only Bachelor's and Bachelor of Music degrees would be offered in music, no diplomas. This was due to a directive to all universities from central government – which I do not agree with, but I've come to realise now that this is less of a setback than I thought it was at the time.

As we've shown in these pages, student welfare had been one of our main preoccupations. For the first fifteen years, Jazz Studies was attracting active musicians who hadn't expected to go to a university and we needed to legitimise their presence by changing the rules. Now, students are completely funded from beginning to end and can be expected to meet minimum admission criteria. What we did back in the 1980s was right for the time, but conditions are different now.

When we were in South Africa in April 2018, Cathy and I decided that going on campus for a Trios Plus session on Wednesday would be a congenial moment to plunge into Durban life. Neil welcomed us at the door and invited me to play. Serendipitously, the programme that evening featured 'none other than the beautiful Melvin Peters', as Johnny Mekoa had so memorably introduced him in Detroit. (One time Johnny's announcement got all muddled and he announced a composition from 'the beautiful pen of Melvin Peters'.) Tonight, Melvin was leading a trio with Bob Sinicrope on bass and Bruce Baker, the excellent drum teacher.[4]

The Piano Passion concert, which six of my former students (named below) and I performed at Howard College Theatre on 6 April was the highlight of this visit.[5] This was a great thrill for us, a musical equivalent of a Festschrift. Howard College Theatre, with its two Steinway grands, was overflowing on the night. I played first, which allowed me to then sit in the front row with Cathy and luxuriate in the music, except when, at Melvin Peters' invitation, I took part in a two-piano improvisation on my composition 'October'. Each pianist introduced their numbers with short anecdotes about my piano teaching. Their stories were as different as their playing styles. Cathy and I were both very affected by this personal and soulful music. Chris Ballantine later excitedly claimed the concert demonstrated that there was a 'Darius Brubeck school' or a 'Durban school' even though each pianist was so individually distinctive.

Piano Passion line-up, 6 April 2018. From left: Burton Naidoo, Andile Yenana, Darius, Debbie Mari, Nishlyn Ramanna, Melvin Peters, Neil Gonsalves (photographer unknown; Cathy Brubeck collection).

Melvin's playing was very much in the jazz piano tradition he had always admired since discovering Oscar Peterson. Nishlyn Ramanna played his succinctly melodic compositions with wit and wonderful clarity. Burton Naidoo evoked Himalayan herders' bells and avalanches of sound (honouring his Nepalese ancestry) in abstract, gestural improvisations. Debbie Mari came on after interval and this was perfect programming for the second half. She sang a medley of standards and Cathy's and my song 'Before It's Too Late'. What really took me back was her rendition of 'What a Diff'rence a Day Makes'.[6] At Cathy's suggestion, we had performed this jazz standard at the Rainbow on the first Sunday after the election of Nelson Mandela as president of South Africa. Rainbow patrons recognised this was simultaneously humorous and respectful, an emotional cocktail. The rest of the concert tilted away from mainstream jazz towards the new and local, with Andile Yenana playing his modern African jazz compositions and one by Zim Ngqawana. And, finally, in the closing set, Neil Gonsalves delivered a superbly immersive experience in the form of a medley, mostly of his own original music, with titles like 'Indian Ocean Blue'. Neil describes his style as a personal synthesis of what he learned as a UND student, with me as his piano teacher, and what he later learned from Bheki Mseleku, as well as influences from a range of local communities. It is wonderfully eclectic and accomplished music. His former piano students, Nduduzo Makhathini and Sibusiso 'Mash' Mashiloane, who are also teachers, are counted among the most creative young musicians on the national scene.

Cathy and I had come full circle, with so many friends, colleagues and former patrons in the house. Ben and Pam Pretorius, Ramoll Bugwandeen and Paul Mikula were there. Rafs Mayet, one of South Africa's premier jazz photographers was also there and had taken photos of us all preparing backstage. Piano Passion affirmed that our 23 years of work still mattered.

This makes a good ending, but it wasn't the last visit. In fact, we returned a year later with a film crew making a documentary also called *Playing the Changes* and there were online iterations of the Piano Passion concept during two years of lockdown. One of these was a benefit for the Archbishop Denis Hurley Centre that provided food and shelter for people made homeless during the pandemic. I did not participate, but I am on the poster because it was promoted as a 'thanksgiving' event in honour of my survival. We were very moved by this.

I won't force a Hollywood ending focusing on music alone, but the special charm for us is that the music came from people we met when they were young students, who are now successful artists, raising successful children, touring the world, getting jobs at other universities and bringing their expertise into schools in their own communities. The journey that current students take is different, but there is clearly a continuum in the music and the values. I am proud of what we did. With no master plan, we pursued special goals and made a contribution. There is also no doubt that I gained immeasurably from my association with the exceptional students, musicians and intellectuals that I could only have encountered in South Africa. I am grateful for this transformational experience that remains the central chapter of my life.

And, to return to where I began, the liberation of Poland from Soviet domination and the liberation struggle in South Africa had little else in common, but both movements took jazz to heart. In both cases, jazz was *their* music. It was their music because it crossed racial, cultural, class and national boundaries, and concretely theirs because they (Poles and South Africans) could play it too. Cathy and I have had the privilege of witnessing and playing a small part in both stories.

Catherine

Darius often tells a story about Miles Davis visiting his father's California home in the 1950s. (Dave Brubeck and Miles Davis were later Columbia Records' best-selling jazz artists.) They knew each other from tours and playing at the Blackhawk Jazz Club

Piano Passion poster (poster: Daniel Sheldon).

in San Francisco. Miles had dropped by Dave's house, but instead of talking about new developments in jazz or the big picture surrounding their music, they simply talked about boxing and practised basketball goals in the yard where Dave had set up a homemade hoop. Darius, aged nine or ten, was somewhat disappointed. He had hoped for some jazzy conversation and revelation. Coincidentally, Ralph Gleason, one of the best-known critics on the West Coast, also came by and was astonished to see Miles in a social setting. Excited by this, he told Miles that he lived nearby and that Miles should come and visit him too. 'What for?' said Miles.

I used to enjoy this dark, amusing, quintessential Milesian moment – his determined self-centredness – but I've changed my view, realising how little we can predict what ultimately matters. Dave and Miles's time together broadened an understanding and bond between two very different people and this could also have occurred between critic and musician. So, a question, in conclusion: to whom are we addressing in this book and indeed, what for? We have replied by paying tribute to the musicians and students – and the university – that made our efforts meaningful.

The Darius Brubeck Quartet at a concert in Bishop's Stortford, England, 2022. From left: Darius, Dave O'Higgins, Matt Ridley, Wesley Gibbens (photographer unknown).

Appendix 1

Out-Takes

Don Albert (1931–2019)

You can have black waiters, black barmen, black cleaners and black American musicians who are regarded in South Africa as white, but not our black artists because of the liquor laws. Fortunately, we were able to ignore this ban and by and large the police did too.

Christopher Ballantine

I don't think one can overstate the importance of creating the jazz diploma – an almost illicit start – an under-the-radar way of bringing black students in – and how important that was – you know, important for everybody – important for the white students, for the black students, the staff – it was really a kind of a revelatory moment when that started to happen . . .

Initially other universities thought that everything we did was insane . . . with all these anti-apartheid ideas and looking at music in this funny way, but eventually they thought this was a good thing and jumped on the bandwagon. The performance opportunities that you created through the jazz programme – you know, playing in different parts of the world, I mean – was unprecedented.

Jazz's historic mission is huge. It still seems to me . . . that there isn't any music in South Africa that has worked beyond race in the way that jazz has done.

Karendra Devroop

I couldn't afford to stay in Durban, but hitchhiked every day on the N3 from Pietermaritzburg to Durban. My most important influences were the visiting artists that came to UKZN and access to world-class teachers such as Dusty Cox and Mike Rossi. Also being able to meet individuals such as Victor Ntoni and other legendary artists was truly inspirational and motivating. The off-campus concerts were really important because they offered me my first insights into the professional world of the jazz artist . . . I cannot emphasise just how much playing with the UKZN big band inspired me . . . I felt I could achieve anything I wanted. It just took hard work.

[Karendra is currently professor of Music and director of the Music Directorate at UNISA.]

John Edwards

I became more aware of jazz while I was in my twenties (not least because of the increased profile that jazz enjoyed in Durban due to the jazz programme and CJPM) . . .

Studying jazz changed my life . . . it was only when I took the plunge and became a full-time student at UKZN that I could fully immerse myself in the jazz 'experience' – this included having other musos around, there was a 'scene' as it were on campus . . . the UKZN jazz programme provided the focus, motivation, inspiration and goals that is/should be integral to any full-time (music) study programme . . . Jam sessions with various peers, the Jazz Centre Trios Plus sessions and the Jazz Jol were really important.

To some extent, my years of studying jazz (1998–2004) coincided with the emergence of a particular type of trendy restaurant/bar in Durban, which identified live jazz performance as a potentially lucrative component of their 'brand'. I was well placed with my past gigging experience (and new and growing jazz skills) to capitalise on this growing phenomenon and I put together several bands that played at a variety of these new and trendy venues – some venues were short-lived while others had more longevity. Such venues included Zacks (in Musgrave and at Wilson's Wharf – Umhlanga, Windermere and Hillcrest too as they rapidly expanded their footprint). There was Cuban Pete's and Soda Supra in Stamford Hill Road and there were also Sunday sessions at the Beverley Hills Hotel for a while. At some stage News Cafe added jazz to their menu as did Legends in Musgrave and there were many other places that pursued the golden jazz goose . . .

Hindsight is a wonderful thing. I think the programme fell short in terms of specialised modules that related to jazz improvisation that would enable students to better learn jazz patterns. This has always been a staple in Berklee courses, for example . . . American jazz was well covered and South African jazz was evident in history modules, but not so much in the repertoire of instrumental and ensemble classes. I think that the jazz programme was understaffed in the time that I studied, which meant that, at times, several of the jazz modules were taught by recent graduates . . . They got the job done, but obviously didn't have the experience and gravitas that a full-time lecturer would have had. On the converse, I was also appointed – once I'd graduated – as a part-time lecturer to teach those self-same modules and this provided an excellent grounding for my future career . . .

Feya Faku

Outside the classes, playing gigs and concerts was very important, like playing at the Rainbow on Sundays was very important because it was showcasing what you were learning in class. I wouldn't have done that without the help from the Jazz Centre's Ronnie Madonsela Scholarship and a bursary from the National Association of Democratic Lawyers. I make a living through music, I play worldwide . . .

Lex Futshane

The content of the Jazz course was not all that jazzy, so one had to do a parallel course of 'own' study from the library jazz collection of books and records . . . A module on music business would have made a huge difference in our lives as music students aspiring to making music a career . . .

Kevin Gibson

It's not so much the classes I remember because at that time there were so many gigs . . . we had to struggle with people who were sort of learning jazz, just trying to keep up. It was more the atmosphere I remember . . . the 'stories' about gigs.

Neil Gonsalves

I was part of the student group, NU Jazz Link, along with Nishlyn Ramanna, Zami Duze, Louise Marchant and Concord Nkabinde and led by Chris Merz that attended the IAJE conference in Boston in 1994 and enjoyed a jazz immersion week in New York City, in one of the coldest winters recorded on the East Coast. Dan Brubeck played drums with us. We spent a few days at Dave and Iola's place in Connecticut and my recollection is of lovely, caring and amazingly hospitable people. I roomed with Nishlyn and remember that we had a TV and video player in the room, and that the selection of videos featured predominantly jazz pianists. Such a nice touch and so considerate of the two young piano players. I also remember tobogganing down the hill down to the lake behind their house. And I remember seeing McCoy Tyner playing at Sweet Basil and Darius taking us to meet him after the show, and that he shook my hand. Life-changing stuff.

Chris Merz

Jazz was part of the struggle; it seemed that nearly every party I played was attended by major players in political activism. I think that the freedom inherent in jazz improvisation was a good metaphor for the political struggle. I would guess that is why the two were so intertwined in those days.

Nishlyn Ramanna

In retrospect I think I would have been grateful for the kind of rigorous training in bebop language that other guys got at UCT.

Di Rossi

Jazz clubs are merely surviving . . . Jazz festivals like Joy of Jazz and the Cape Town International Jazz Festival, and Grahamstown/Makhanda Jazz Festival provide steady work, but only once a year . . . SAJE (and others like the Cape Town Big Band Jazz Festival) provide free jazz workshops throughout the year, but sadly over the last few years the attendance has dwindled. Somehow, they seem increasingly irrelevant especially when you can find so much info on YouTube.

Mike Rossi

I would say jazz has grown in terms of more festivals/gigs and jazz-related teaching in the twenty years I've been here in Cape Town [since 2000] and since my first [five-month] trip to South Africa in 1989. Cape Town has always had a very active jazz scene for its size. Of course, places open and close all the time. The striking thing is how jazz education has attracted so many students, so more programmes and more teaching jobs, creating places to play – schools and university performance venues and clubs. Jazz is now a Matric subject . . . Students here really don't read books – quite sad.

I would say jazz has lost its special status and many young folks do not know the history of the music. It's the age we live in.

Rick van Heerden

The UCT Department subsequently established a reputation for rigour and, with hindsight, perhaps the UND jazz programme should have been more pedagogically intense. But I enjoyed the spontaneity and looseness of UND. There was freedom and conviviality. The UND programme basked in the benign warmth of Darius and Cathy's offbeat but determined custodianship.

Appendix 2

Documents

Chapter 2 (note 4)

University Racial Policy

If not always, then certainly for a long time now, it has been the firm and unequivocal policy of this university that the admission of students and the appointment of staff, should be at the discretion of the university, and that only academic criteria and individual merit should apply in exercising that discretion. Race, colour and creed should be of no account in admitting students and appointing staff. Despite this policy, over the years we have been subject to governmental controls regarding the admission of African, Coloured, and Indian students. In the last five years there has been some relaxation in the governmental control of our admissions policy. Although ministerial approval for admission of black students is no longer required, the Minister still has authority to define our admissions practices in relation to racial quotas. While we applaud the fact that he has elected not to exercise that authority, we continue to protest against the legislative potential for ministerial controls of the admission of our students. In practice, however, we now admit students of all races on academic merit. This policy is clearly stated in the University Mission Statement.

— Professor Prof. P. de V. Booysen, Speech, University of Natal, 1989

Chapter 3 (note 7)

In Defence of Our Freedom

On 19 October 1987 the South African government, through the office of the Minister of Education and Culture, issued a directive to universities of South Africa calling on them to enforce a series of highly contentious security laws, which allowed for state control of political activities both on and off campus. The document was clear in its indication that non-compliance could lead to the withdrawal of state subsidies.

The University of Natal declared its opposition to the ministerial conditions. Professor P. de V. Booysen, vice-chancellor and principal, stated that the laws the university is required to enforce seriously affect basic rights vital to the proper functioning of a university.

Public officials must not be given powers to suppress political dissent. 'I oppose the notion of investing public officials with vast unchecked powers while encouraging the suppression of political dissent and the abolition of hallowed procedures and safeguards for the protection of citizens against injustice,' said Professor Booysen.

'It is clear that in future the criteria on which the University is to be judged, is not based upon the success in educational objective and fiscal responsibilities, but rather on the willingness to enforce these contentious laws.'

The university responded immediately and an extraordinary meeting of the university assembly was convened on 28 October 1987. The meeting was addressed by Professor P. de V. Booysen, vice chancellor and principal, Mr G. Cox, chairman of the University Council, Mr Angus Stewart, Students Representative Council president, (Howard College), also representing the National Union of South African Students, Miss Gugu Ndebele for the South African National Student's Congress and Professor C.O. Gardner, chairperson of the university's Joint Academic Staff Association.

Unanimity

It is not often that all participating bodies of a university, i.e., students, staff, Senate and Council, agree on an issue. But in this instance, all are united and fully concur with the contents of the following statements issued by the University Senate.

In the grave circumstances that now face the university, Senate REAFFIRMS its commitment to

- the dissemination and advancement of knowledge through free enquiry, and free exchange of information, opinions and ideas; and
- the maintenance of the good order that is essential for free educational and intellectual endeavour.

Since these commitments are fundamentally threatened by the conditions imposed on the university by the minister,

SENATE SOLEMNLY DECLARES ITS REFUSAL AND INDEED ITS INABILITY, TO ACQUIESCE IN THOSE CONDITIONS, AND CALLS UPON THE UNIVERSITY COUNCIL TO USE EVERY MEANS AT ITS DISPOSAL TO RID THE UNIVERSITY OF THIS WHOLLY UNJUSTIFIED AND UNACCEPTABLE IMPOSITION.

The university challenged the Ministry of Education in the Supreme Court and won on 14 March 1988.

Appendix 2   279

Chapter 3 (note 10)

Letter from Prof. Duminy to Prof. Parker, 28 March 1989

Beverly Parker succeeded Gerrit Bon as head of department.

Mr Brubeck felt it is necessary for persons who are not registered students to attend some of the departmental courses. I have agreed that in some instances such attendance is to the benefit of the department as well as to the students. If, for example, no registered student plays the drums, it is of benefit to the other students if a drummer who is not registered as a student is allowed to join those courses that consist of practical music making. An additional consideration in 1989 is that I am reluctant to eject aspiring musicians from those practical courses in which they have already been participating since the beginning of the term. I believe that the persons who were asked to leave would feel that something that they had been promised was being taken away from them.

Therefore, if you and the principal agree, I would like to allow these persons who are already attending departmental courses in 1989 to continue to attend those courses . . . Once all these matters have been discussed I believe Mr Brubeck and I will be able to compose a document paralleling the one that exists for the Institute for Plasma Physics.

I have asked Mr Brubeck to submit to the department his suggested rule change concerning the registration for the diploma of students who do not possess matriculation exemption. He is hoping to submit this to a departmental meeting which is scheduled for the 25th of April.

Chapter 6 (note 2)

Special Events with CJPM Participation

Written for an advisory committee report.

1989   Sponsored workshops with Victor Ntoni and Duke Makasi at Waterford College Swaziland, plus Ezra Ngcukana in Durban.
Staff and students at first-ever Jazz Festival at the National Arts Festival in Grahamstown, including performances in Nolutandu Hall.
Benefit concert in Port Elizabeth for Dorkay House.

1990   Afro-Jazz Festival (Harare) performance and meeting with ANC Cultural Committee
Barbara Masekela (ANC Arts & Culture) addresses Durban musicians

1991   Darius Brubeck elected vice-chairman of Natal Cultural Congress

1992   Abdullah Ibrahim concert in aid of Ronnie Madonsela Scholarship Fund

1993   NU Jazz Ensemble for Nelson Mandela honorary doctorate graduation
Durban International Festival of Music

1994	UND Jazz bands at Guinness Johannesburg Jazz Festival
1998	Performance at Non-Aligned Movement Summit for guests of Graça Machel
2000	Performance – Commonwealth heads of government luncheon hosted by Mrs Thabo Mbeki
2001	Darius Brubeck Quartet – State banquet for heads of delegations attending the UN World Conference Against Racism, Durban Closing Ceremony: Darius Brubeck and Gathering Forces, Humanity Has No Colour (Department of Arts and Culture, DAC) broadcast worldwide
2002	Darius Brubeck Quartet, State banquet for African Union Summit, International Conference Centre, Durban (DAC)
2003	Research, co-ordination of SA entries for *The New Grove Dictionary of Jazz*
2004	*Brubecks Play Brubeck at* uShaka Marine World, SAJE Cape Town
2005	Create UKZN/UCT band for IAJE Conference, Long Beach, California
2006	UKZN Jazz Bands, Awesome Africa Festival, Durban
2007	Cape Town International Jazz Festival: UKZN Rolling Reunion Band

International Festivals & Conferences with Jazz Staff and Students

1990	New Orleans Jazz & Heritage Festival, USA
1992	IAJE, Miami, USA *African Tributes* records in Germany
1994	IAJE, Boston, USA Costa do Sol, Maputo, Mozambique Sekunjalo (student band) performances in Korea for South African Dept of Foreign Affairs' trade mission
1995	Darius Brubeck & Deepak Ram, Jazz & Indian Music, Royal Academy of Music, London and University of Southampton, UK
1997	Celimontana Jazz Festival, Italy Fin de Siècle, Nantes, France International Jazz Festival, Thailand Darius Brubeck & Thusini (UND students) perform in Turkey for South African Dept of Foreign Affairs' trade mission
1998	IAJE, New York University of Karlsruhe, Germany
1999	Peru (US & South African embassies joint project) UK Trust Benefit Concert, South Africa House, London
2000	38 (staff/student musicians) perform at World Expo 2000 in Hanover, Germany (DAC/DFA) Sydney Olympics, Australia UND/UCT students in opening ceremony (DAC)

2002	Darius Brubeck exchange concerts with Swedish musicians, University of Gothenburg (Sweden International Development Agency)
2003	National Youth Jazz Band plays North Sea Jazz Festival, Den Hague, Holland
2004	Memphis in May (Celebrating 10 Years of Democracy in South Africa attended by South African ambassador, Barbara Masekela, USA
	Les Rendez-vous de l'Erdre, Nantes, France (Durban Metro & Alliance Français)
	Commission 2004, Darius Brubeck & Zim Ngqawana – Lincoln Center Jazz Orchestra directed by Wynton Marsalis (Let Freedom Swing: A Celebration of Human Rights and Social Justice)
	Darius Brubeck & Afro Cool – Celebrating 10 Years of Democracy in South Africa, SA Embassy, Copenhagen
	Darius Brubeck & Afro Cool – Inauguration of UKZN Alumni Association, South Africa House, London (NUDF & South African Embassy)

Note: Attendance at all IAJE conferences made possible by CJPM fund-raising

Scholarships for Overseas Study (Includes Fulbright and SAMRO)

Karendra Devroop (University of North Texas); Kevin Gibson (Florida International University); Mark Kilian (University of Southern California); Moketsi Kgoadi (Edith Cowan University, Australia); George Mari & Sydney Mavundla (Florida International University); Johnny Mekoa (Indiana University); Mageshen Naidoo (University of Southern California); Zim Ngqawana (University of Massachusetts); Brian Thusi (University of New Mexico).

More than 100 international musicians and educators from Australia, Brazil, Canada, Cuba, Denmark, England, France, Germany, Holland, Ireland, Norway, Portugal, Scotland, Sweden, Switzerland, Turkey and United States of America visited the Centre between 1989 and 2005. CJPM organised master classes, workshops, performances in South Africa.

A selective list includes the following world-famous artists and institutions:
Butch Miles
Jasper Van't Hof
Kenny Wheeler
The Thelonius Monk Institute Ambassadors
Paul Winter
Chucho Valdez
BuJazzO (28-piece big band directed by Peter Herbolzheimer)
Rene McClean
Milton Academy Jazz Band directed by Bob Sinicrope
Julian Joseph

Patrick Bebelaar
Gold Company (vocal ensemble directed by Stephen Zegree)
Louis Moholo
US Jazz Ambassadors

Chapter 6 (note 3)

Abridged Fund-Raising Letter from 1993

Dear _____

At present we have 35 students who are in various stages of registering for Jazz Studies and I am enclosing a schedule illustrating the individual status of these students. 16 are studying for a Music Degree with a Jazz Major, which implies good potential and a future for jazz education, and 15 are aiming at the Jazz Diploma, which is mainly performance oriented. In addition, we have 4 students at the Master's level.

While we are excited by the sensational progress and the growing numbers choosing music and in particular jazz as a career, it also means that all our sources of financial aid are depleted.

Students helping themselves & loans

Every year we insist that students (although are extremely poor) raise money themselves and a whole range of effort has produced results. They play gigs, work in vacations, apply for every possible relevant bursary and when all else fails they take out loans (if they meet the loan requirements). As you know the life of an artist, especially a jazz musician, is financially precarious, so we turn to loans very reluctantly. Furthermore, the Centre tries to pay back some amounts on these loans (as democratically as possible across the board) if and when we manage to raise money after the loan has been applied for and granted. This practice makes the students and guarantors less nervous about applying for *large* loans in the first emergency months of the academic year.

The Centre for Jazz & Popular Music

In addition to fundraising and administration, the Centre also acts as a Student Support service and helps with accommodation, meals, and counselling, this all while trying to encourage and initiate projects, keep standards high and jazz artistically alive by presenting visiting artists. The Centre itself is stretched to the maximum.

To put you in the overall picture, the Centre has, through concert production, overseas touring, promoting South African jazz and recording it, been responsible for the reputation of the University of Natal as an important and growing jazz institution, attracting a lot of attention nationally and of course more students. Since we started in 1983, the University of Cape Town, Pretoria Technikon and various other less major institutions have followed our lead. I am telling you all this so that on the one hand you can appreciate the enormity of the task, but on the other see that our very success has caused near financial collapse.

Fees for 1993

Jazz Diploma Tuition	R4 610
Jazz Degree Tuition	R6 700
Residence & Expenses	+/- R9 000
Total	R13 610
1993 Shortfall	R126 880
Loans applied for over and above shortfall	R125 446

We would also like to reduce the loan amount considerably so that 1994 isn't an even bigger crisis. To summarize, we have an emergency situation as well as a long-term problem to address. I am up against deadlines in so far as registration is concerned and thereafter balances need to be paid by the end of June.

Our students are among the most visible on campus, often playing for university and student functions. There are 9 bands in Durban that consist of either all or some jazz students.

Our 'dropout' rate for other than financial reasons is practically nil. (The university incidentally accepts that approximately 1/3 of all registered students probably won't complete degrees.)

Chapter 8 (note 28)

Centre for Jazz and Popular Music Tender DFA 4 01/02

Personnel and musicians

Music Director:	Darius Brubeck (Director of the Centre for Jazz and Popular Music and jazz pianist)
Musicians:	Sazi Dlamini (*Maskanda* guitar, indigenous leg rattles, kudu horns, bells and vocal)
	Vevek Ram (traditional Indian sitar)
	Barney Rachabane (penny whistle, flute and saxophone)

284   Playing the Changes

Lulu Gontsana (Western drum kit, African percussion and *amanqashela*)
Shiyani Ngcobo (*Maskanda* guitar)
Joyce Mogoloage (indigenous *umakhweyana* bow, drum & vocals/dance)
Makhosi Mbatha (indigenous *umakhweyana* bow, vocals/dance)
Thandiwe Mazibuko (indigenous *umakhweyana* bow, vocals/dance)
Delile Mbhele (indigenous *umakhweyana* bow, vocals/dance)
Ellis Pearson (cello)
Brendan Jury (viola and vocals)
Haren Thana (traditional Indian *tabla*)
Bongani Sokhela (bass and vocals)
Roland Moses (electric keyboards with indigenous sound samples)

Sound Engineer: Jürgen Bräuninger
Project Manager: Catherine Brubeck (Centre for Jazz and Popular Music)
Administration & Finance: Glynis Malcolm-Smith (Centre for Jazz and Popular Music)

* In the event that any of the musicians above are unavailable, they will be replaced by musicians of similar standing and ability.

Chapter 9 (note 1)

CJPM Highlights

CJPM organised master classes, workshops, performances and, often, accommodation and travel arrangements for roughly a hundred international players and groups between 1984 and 2005.

Significant visiting teachers not mentioned in text
United States: Bart Marantz (trumpet), Dave Frank (piano), Clay Jenkins (trumpet), Rene McClean (saxophone)
Sweden: Henrik Gad (saxophone), Bjorn Cedegren (saxophone), Joel Sahlin (guitar), Sara Hedman (voice), Markus Ahlberg (trumpet)
England: Ian Darrington (trumpet), Julian Joseph (piano), Kenny Wheeler (trumpet)
Germany: Patrick Bebelaar (piano), Peter Herbolzheimer with BUJAZZO
Australia: Jim Chapman
Holland: Jasper van't Hof
Switzerland: Andy Brugger (drums)

Partnerships with
Alliance Française
American Embassy
Bartel Arts
British Council
Danish Cultural Institute
Durban Arts Association
Goethe Institute
International Association of Jazz Educators
Institut Français d'Afrique du Sud
Pro Helvetia
Natal University Development Foundation
South African Music Rights Organisation
South African Breweries
Swedish International Development Agency
United States Information Services

Chapter 9 (note 2)

The 8th South African Association for Jazz Educators Conference, 29 September – 1 October 2006

Jazz: The Original World Music
Performances in Collaboration with Awesome Africa Sponsors: University of KwaZulu-Natal, BASA (Business & Arts South Africa) and Centre for Jazz and Popular Music
Organised by Cathy Brubeck
With special thanks to Awesome Africa Music Festival, Darius Brubeck, IAJE, Royal Hotel, Saints Hospitality Centre and especially Glynis Malcolm-Smith

Papers & Workshops

Dr Michael Blake, Principal trumpet CTSO, teacher UCT & Bishops
Professor Michael Campbell, Head of Jazz Studies, South African College of Music, UCT
Dr Chats Devroop, Assistant professor, Department of Music, University of Pretoria
Marc Duby, Head of Department, School of Music, Tshwane University of Technology
Richard Haslop, Radio presenter, music writer, blues singer, guitarist & lawyer
David Marks, Director Third Ear Music & The Hidden Years Project
Concord Nkabinde, Bassist, composer, part-time teacher
Professor Chuck Owen, Head of Jazz Studies, University of South Florida, USA
Andrea Parkerson, Director, iKhaya leJazz, SA-Jazz.co.za

Dr Nishlyn Ramanna, Post-doctoral researcher, School of Music, UKZN
Henry Shields, Promoter, club owner, lawyer & festival producer
Janusz Szprot, Director Jazz Studies, Bilkent University, Ankara, Turkey
Keith Tabisher, Music curriculum advisor, Western Cape Education Department
Tarnia Van Zitters, Logistics manager, audience development & education, Artscape
Professor Sundar Viswanathan, Jazz Studies, York University, Canada
Gareth Walwyn, Lecturer, Rhodes University, DSG & St Andrews

Participating Institutions, Organizations & Additional Guests

Artscape Theatre Centre (Cape Town)
Awesome Africa Music Festival (Durban)
Bilkent University (Turkey)
Centre for Jazz & Popular Music (Durban)
Diocesan School for Girls (Grahamstown)
Hilton College (Hilton)
Ikhaya Le Jazz (Cape Town)
International Association for Jazz Education (USA)
MAG (Music Academy of Gauteng) Benoni
Michaelhouse College (Balgowan)
Mmabana Cultural Foundation (Mmabatho)
Rhodes University (Grahamstown)
SAMRO (South African Music Rights Organisation) Johannesburg
Siyakhula Music Centre (Umlazi)
St Anne's College (Hilton)
Third Ear Music (Durban)
TUT (Tshwane University of Technology) Pretoria
UCT (University of Cape Town)
UKZN (University of KwaZulu-Natal)
UP (University of Pretoria)
USF (University of South Florida, USA)
University of Göteborg (Sweden)
Alan Webster, Director, National Youth Jazz Festival (Grahamstown)
Anne Barr, Producer, Cape Town Big Band Jazz Festival
Jason King, South African Woodwind & Brass Specialists
Peter Tladi, TC Musicman (Johannesburg)
Rashid Lombard, Director, Cape Town International Jazz Festival
Tom Smith, Fulbright senior professional specialist, USA

Programme (abbreviated)

Friday 29th September

14h00 Make Your Licks Easier (Brass Workshop) – Michael Blake
14h45 Venue and Social Meaning in Contemporary South African Jazz – Nishlyn Ramanna
15h15 The Occupational Aspirations of Students Majoring in Jazz Studies in South Africa – Chats Devroop
16h00 Releasing CDS Independently and a Purpose-Driven Music Career – Concord Nkabinde
16h30 South African Jazz Syllabus – Gareth Walwyn
18h00 Welcome – Professor Sihawu Ngubane, Deputy Dean, Faculty of Humanities, Development & Social Sciences, University of KwaZulu-Natal (CJPM)
18h10 Official Opening – Mrs W.G. Thusi, MEC for Arts, Culture & Tourism, KZN
19h45 Public Concert in Howard College Theatre
The Mageshen Naidoo Ensemble
Mike Rossi and Saxology (including compositions by Ulrich Süsse & Jürgen Bräuninger)

Saturday 30th September

09h30 Whose World Is It Anyway? World Music: What's in a Name, and Does It Really Matter? – Richard Haslop
10h00 The Easy Part Is the Gig – Henry Shields
10h45 Expanding Implementation of the Blues Sound in Jazz Pedagogy – Michael Campbell
11h15 Signifyin(G) and Identity Politics in Jazz – Marc Duby
11h45 Deconstruction, Reconstruction and Revision: Insight into the Creative Process of a Jazz Composer/Arranger – Chuck Owen (President of the International Association for Jazz Education)
15h30 Rehearsals
17h00 Performances at Zulu Jazz Lounge (a venue within the Playhouse)

Sunday 1st October

09h30 Third Ear's Hidden Years Music Archives Project – David Marks
10h00 Do You Know What It Means . . . To Be a Polish Musician Teaching Jazz in Turkey? – Janusz Szprot (CJPM)
10h30 Artscape Youth Jazz Project – Andrea Parkerson, Keith Tabisher & Tarnia van Zitters
11h15 Advanced Concepts In Jazz Improvisation – Sundar Viswanathan

Venue City Hall
13h30 University of Cape Town Big Band directed by Mike Campbell (includes premiere of 'Lulama Gontsana' by Darius Brubeck)
14h40 SAPO/UKZN Rolling Reunion Band with 20 musicians
16h10 Andile Yenana Quintet
17h10 Feya Faku Five

Zulu Jazz Lounge
19h00 Zim Ngqawana & The Zimology Institute Band

Message from the President
(printed in the SAJE Newsletter)

Dear Members,
I am appealing to all members, old, new, and potential to come to Durban at the end of September for our conference and enjoy the Awesome Africa Festival at the same time. The weather will be great, and the cats are cool, and we just need you to complete the picture. I am very proud to announce that my wife has recently become the Minister of Arts and Culture for KwaZulu-Natal, so we certainly know that someone will have heard of our efforts in jazz education and performance!

I am in touch with Cathy Brubeck, our conference organizer, and with Glynis Malcolm-Smith at the Jazz Centre and will be overseeing their input from now until the big event.
Sincerely,
Brian Thusi
SAJE President

Discography

Recordings cited in the text are listed in alphabetical order below.

African Jazz Pioneers, *African Jazz Pioneers* (Gallo, 1989).

Dollar Brand, *Mannenberg 'Is Where It's Happening'* (The Sun Records, 1982).

Dollar Brand + Two [Nelson Magwaza and Victor Ntoni], *Peace* (Soultown Records, 1971).

The Brothers (Duke Makasi, Ezra Ngcukana, Tete Mbambisa, Victor Ntoni and Lulu Gontsana), *The Brothers* (Roots Records, 1990).

Darius Brubeck, *Before It's Too Late* (Sheer Sound, 2003).

Darius Brubeck, *Chaplin's Back* (Paramount Records, 1972).

Darius Brubeck and Afro Cool Concept, *Still on My Mind* (Sheer Sound, 2003).

Darius Brubeck and Dan Brubeck – *Gathering Forces 1* (B&W Music, 1992).

Darius Brubeck and Deepak Ram, *Gathering Forces II* (B&W Music, 1994).

Darius Brubeck and the NU Jazz Connection, *African Tributes* (B&W Music, 1993).

Darius Brubeck featuring Barney Rachabane, *Tugela Rail* (RPM, 1984).

Brubeck Ntoni Afro Cool Concept, *Live at the New Orleans Jazz & Heritage Festival* (Roots Records, 1990; B&W Music, 1993).

Darius Brubeck Quartet, *For Lydia and the Lion* (Gathering Forces Music, 2008).

Darius Brubeck Quartet, *Live in Poland* (Ubuntu Music, 2020).

Darius Brubeck Quartet, *Two and Four/To and Fro* (Gathering Forces Music, 2011).

Darius Brubeck Quartet, *Years Ago* (Ubuntu Music, 2016).

Dave Brubeck Trio, *Dave Brubeck Trio, Vol. 1* (Fantasy Records, 1949).

Miles Davis, *E.S.P.* (Columbia Records, 1965).

Miles Davis, *Kind of Blue* (Columbia Records, 1959).

Bill Evans, *Spring Leaves* (Milestone, 1976).

Fours Jacks and a Jill, *Fours Jacks and a Jill* (RCA Victor, 1967).

Abdullah Ibrahim, *Blues for a Hip King* (Kaz Records, 1989).

Abdullah Ibrahim, *Solotude* (Gearbox Records, 2021).

The Jazzanians, *We Have Waited Too Long* (Umkhonto Records, 1988).

The Jazz Ministers, *Zandile* (Gallo Records, 1975).

Allen Kwela, *The Broken Strings of Allen Kwela* (Sheer Sound, 1998).

Allen Kwela, *The Unknown* (Music for Africa, 1985, cassette tape only).

Nduduzo Makhathini, *Modes of Communication: Letters from the Underworlds* (Blue Note Records, 2020).

Malombo (Philip Tabane, Gabriel Thobejane), *Pele Pele* (Warner Elektra Atlantic Records, 1976).

Mankuku Quartet, *Yakhal' Inkomo* (World Record Co., 1968).

Herbie Mann, *Herbie Mann at the Village Gate* (Atlantic Records, 1961).

Pat Matshikiza and Kippie Moeketsi, featuring Basil 'Mannenberg' Coetzee, *Tshona!* (The Sun Records, 1975).

Tete Mbambisa, *Did You Tell Your Mother* (The Sun Records, 1979).

Tete Mbambisa, *Tete's Big Sound* (The Sun Records, 1974).

Chris Merz and Counterculture, *Art Gecko* (B&W Music, 1992).

New Brubeck Quartet, *Live at Montreux* (Tomato, 1977).

Ezra Ngcukana, *You Think You Know Me* (Jive Records, 1989).

Zim Ngqawana, *Zimphonic Suites* (Sheer Sound, 2001).

Zacks Nkosi, *Our Kind of Jazz* (Skyline (EMI), 1964).

Piano Passion Project (featuring Darius Brubeck, Melvin Peters, Nishlyn Ramanna, Burton Naidoo, Debbie Mari, Andile Yenana and Neil Gonsalves), *Piano Passions* [double album] (Centre for Jazz, UKZN, 2018).

Barney Rachabane, *Barney's Way* (Jive Records, 1989).

Paul Simon, *Graceland* (Warner Brothers, 1986).

UKZN Jazz Legacy Ensemble and VCU Africa Combo, *Leap of Faith* (Virginia Commonwealth University, 2013).

Notes

Foreword

1. For some revealing insights, see the 1988 programme on CBS News in which Billy Taylor talks about the Jazzanians. Darius and members of the band are interviewed and videos clips of the band's performances are shown. https://www.youtube.com/watch?v=8V6B8XvxX_c.
2. This research culminated in a number of publications. See, for example, Christopher Ballantine, *Marabi Nights: Jazz, 'Race' and Society in Early Apartheid South Africa* (Pietermaritzburg: UKZN Press, 2012).
3. See Carol Muller and Janet Topp, 'A Preliminary Study of Gumboot Dance' (Honours thesis, University of Natal, Durban, 1985).
4. Crucial to the success of the Centre for Jazz and Popular Music was Glynis Malcolm-Smith, its only paid employee. After the establishment of the Centre, Glynis became its tireless administrator; working alongside Cathy, she matched her role and activities.
5. Most of these papers will be housed in the UKZN Archive; the remainder (personal papers) are in the Hidden Years Music Archive, Africa Open Institute, Stellenbosch University. Importantly, the Dutch film-maker Michiel ten Kleij will soon be releasing, for international distribution, a documentary about the Brubecks' years in Durban.

Prelude

1. Its proper name in English is National Museum in Szczecin (Centrum Dialogu Przełomy).
2. Kelsey A.K. Klotz, 'Dave Brubeck's Southern Strategy', *Daedalus: Journal of the American Academy of Arts and Sciences* 148(2), 2019: 52–66; Carol A. Muller, 'Why Jazz? South Africa 2019', *Daedalus: Journal of the American Academy of Arts and Sciences* 148(2), 2019: 115–27.
3. I also have an ancestral connection with Poland through my father's maternal grandmother, who went to the United States from a region that is now part of eastern Poland.
4. The Blue Notes was made up of Chris McGregor (piano), Mongezi Feza (trumpet), Dudu Pukwana (alto saxophone), Nikele Moyake (tenor saxophone), Johnny Dyani (bass) and Louis Moholo-Moholo (drums). Miriam Makeba, Hugh Masekela and Jonas Gwangwa were in the London cast of *King Kong*, with music by Todd Matshikiza, first produced in Johannesburg in 1959 and transferred to the West End in 1961. The story is about a South African boxer named King Kong, who tragically killed his lover.
5. Giovanni Russonello, 'Jonas Gwangwa, Trombonist and Anti-Apartheid Activist, Dies at 83', *New York Times*, 28 January 2021.

Chapter 1: The Mission

1. Soweto uprising: Protests led by black schoolchildren in South Africa in June 1976 in response to having Afrikaans as the medium of instruction. It is estimated that 176 people were killed by the police. The day 16 June is a public holiday in South Africa, named National Youth Day.
2. Father Trevor Huddleston was a famous English anti-apartheid activist and author of *Naught for Your Comfort*.
3. During our 2017 visit to Durban, Cathy asked Christopher Ballantine to talk about what motivated him to hire me and recorded the conversation. The jazz post was Ballantine's vision, to which he was unwaveringly dedicated, and he encouraged me to apply for it.
4. Later, Evan Ziporyn joined the faculty at Massachusetts Institute of Technology and is the Kenan Sahin Distinguished Professor of Music.
5. Gwen Ansell, *Soweto Blues: Jazz, Popular Music, and Politics in South Africa* (New York: Continuum, 2005).
6. Peter Brown was the national chairperson of the Liberal Party and author Alan Paton was the party president. Archie Gumede was a prominent ANC member from the 1950s onwards. Chief Albert Luthuli was president of the ANC from 1952 to 1967. Dr Chota Motala was a leading light in the Natal Indian Congress.
7. The ANC, the South African Indian Congress, the South African Congress of Trade Unions, the Coloured People's Congress and the South African Congress of Democrats made up the Congress Alliance. They developed the document known as the 'Freedom Charter' and planned the Congress of the People, a large multiracial gathering held over two days in Kliptown, Soweto, on 26 June 1955.
8. Malombo (Philip Tabane, Gabriel Thobejane), *Pele Pele* (Warner Elektra Atlantic Records, 1976).

Chapter 2: The Scene

1. Cato Manor 'is known for the large-scale forced removals which took place there in the 1950s, destroying a multi-racial community of Indian and African residents. Although zoned for white residence, Cato Manor remained vacant until the 1980s, when it became a haven for refugees fleeing violence in the Natal countryside'. E. Jeffrey Popke, 'Violence and Memory in the Reconstruction of South Africa's Cato Manor', *Growth and Change: A Journal of Urban and Regional Policy* 31(2), 2002: 235.
2. See, for example, Carol Ann Muller, *Focus: Music of South Africa*, 2nd edition (New York: Routledge, 2008); Janet Topp Fargion, *Taarab Music in Zanzibar in the Twentieth Century: A Story of 'Old is Gold' and Flying Spirits* (London: Ashgate Publishers, 2014).
3. 'If you try to say what the whiteness of a white person or the blackness of a black person actually means in scientific terms, there's almost nothing you can say that is true or even remotely plausible. Yet socially, we use these things all the time as if there's a solidity to them . . . I do think that in the long run if everybody grasped the facts about the relevant biology and the social facts, they'd have to treat race in a different way and stop using it to define each other.' Kwame Anthony Appiah, quoted in Hannah Ellis-Petersen, 'Racial Identity is a Biological Nonsense Says Reith Lecturer', *The Guardian*, 18 October 2016.
4. See Appendix 2: University Racial Policy (1989).

Notes to Chapter 2   293

5. Christopher Ballantine, Michael Chapman, Kira Erwin and Gerhard Maré (eds), *Living Together, Living Apart? Social Cohesion in a Future South Africa* (Pietermaritzburg: UKZN Press, 2017), p. 40.

6. See https://www.dlalanje.org (accessed 20 July 2020).

7. The International Defence and Aid Fund, with headquarters in London, and founded by Canon John Collins, secretly sent money into South Africa when support for anti-apartheid causes was illegal. Cathy also briefly worked for Canon Collins and the umbrella organisation Christian Action in London in 1960.

8. African Jazz Pioneers, *African Jazz Pioneers* (Gallo, 1989).

9. Township jazz is a fair description of the African Jazz Pioneers' style because the Western instrumentation and presentation (musicians in matching band attire seated behind music stands) is influenced by American jazz. The music, however, is unmistakably a blend of American big band with Zulu, Xhosa and other local music, rather than the Western big band repertoire. The term *mbaqanga* fits less comfortably because it also refers to music that has no connection with jazz. Although liked by many for what it is, *mbaqanga* was sometimes denigrated by Africans themselves as 'cornmeal porridge' – food for plebeian, rural folk; not unlike what Americans mean by 'corny'.

10. 'New Mecca for Jazz', *Natal Mercury*, 18 March 1983.

11. Dave Brubeck Trio, *Dave Brubeck Trio, Vol. 1* (Fantasy Records, 1949).

12. 'Darius Brubeck and Quartet Get Ready', *Daily News*, 20 April 1983; Nelson Magwaza died of acute asthma in 1984.

13. Themba Blose, 'Jazz Fundis Rejoice', *Africa Today*, 6 May 1983. 'Fundi' is a colloquialism for an expert or teacher.

14. A shortened, solo version of 'Tugela Rail' was on the Royal Schools of Music 2019–20 Grade 6 piano syllabus.

15. Darius Brubeck, featuring Barney Rachabane, *Tugela Rail* (RPM, 1984).

16. The Hermit's owner/manager, Tam Alexander, was politically active. (The security police concealed a bomb in a computer that was delivered to Tam's other business, a computer repair shop, killing his business partner.)

17. George Nisbet, 'Jazzmen Light Up the Hermit', *Daily News*, 14 February 1984.

18. The UDF was an internal front for the ANC in the 1980s. This non-racial coalition of about 400 civic, church, student, worker and other organisations was formed in 1983. It was an organisation of organisations and 'rolling mass action' became its main strategy.

19. Other NUJE musicians included Dennis Sparrow (trumpet), who had been a professional big band musician in the United Kingdom before getting his current job in the British consulate and Peter David, an ex-pat Welsh accountant, who was a top-notch clarinettist and also a good alto sax player.

20. Our documents and photographs are with the Hidden Years Music Archive, Documentation Centre for Music (DOMUS), Stellenbosch University (later referred to by Cathy and me as 'Africa Open'). Material pertaining to the Music Department and the establishment of the Centre for Jazz and Popular Music is in the archives of UKZN, based in Pietermaritzburg.

21. SAMA was very much mass democratic movement and UDF-oriented. SAMA would repurpose itself as an organisation after apartheid was officially 'over' in 1994, becoming MUSA (Musicians Union of South Africa), bequeathing its excellent acronym to the glitterati South African Music Awards (SAMAs).

22. *Maskandi*: Zulu traditional music played on Western instruments, predominantly on guitar in a complex finger style comparable to flamenco.

23. These concerts were the Jazzanians, inaugurating the Loft Theatre in 1990; Gathering Forces, featuring Deepak Ram on *bansuri* (North Indian flute) and a special ensemble of Western and Indian instruments performing in the Durban International Festival of Music (1993) and Afro Cool Concept (plus saxophone lecturer Bryan Steele) with the Natal Philharmonic Orchestra, conducted by my father's conductor/producer, Russell Gloyd in 1994. These were all considered 'experiments' by management, but drew sell-out crowds.

24. A boomslang is a deadly, green South African tree snake. This magnificent taunt comes from Herman Charles Bosman's short story 'The Music Maker', which both sympathises with and makes fun of rural Afrikaners' longing for high culture. Herman Charles Bosman, *Mafeking Road* (Cape Town: Human & Rousseau, 1969), p. 39.

25. See https://playhousecompany.com (accessed 20 July 2020).

26. Njabulo S. Ndebele, 'Good Morning South Africa: Whose Universities? Whose Standards?', in *Fine Lines from the Box: Further Thoughts about Our Country* (Cape Town: Umuzi, 2007), p. 15.

27. Albie Sachs was appointed to the Constitutional Court of South Africa by Nelson Mandela in 1994. He was part of the group of exiles who returned with the unbanning of the ANC and the principal author of the South African Constitution, having played an active role in negotiating the transition to democracy.

Chapter 3: Improvising Education

1. The ledgers are at Africa Open as part of the Darius and Catherine Brubeck archives.

2. Bill Evans, *Spring Leaves* (Milestone, 1976).

3. From the album Dollar Brand, *Mannenberg 'Is Where It's Happening'* (The Sun Records, 1982).

4. The expansion, reorganisation and renaming of Natal University as the University of KwaZulu-Natal in 2004 changed the two-campus structure and UKZN now has five campuses, including the former University of Durban-Westville.

5. Address by Prof. P. de V. Booysen, 'Opening Ceremony', 1989.

6. *Natal Convocation News* No. 5, July 1983.

7. See Appendix 2: In Defence of Our Freedom.

8. The National Association of Jazz Educators became the International Association for Jazz Education (IAJE) and in 1992, a South African chapter (SAJE) was formed. When IAJE collapsed in 2008 due to financial mismanagement, SAJE was able to reply to a worldwide appeal for bail-out funds. (Darius was on both boards at the time.) IAJE fell apart completely just before money was transferred from SAJE, which is still operative.

9. Nowadays the term 'Third World' is problematic or at best dated, but in 1988 'Jazz in the Third World' was the theme of the upcoming jazz educators' conference. What I wrote in 1987 reflects the way many people situated South Africa in global terms. University students came from homes lacking basic amenities and this needed emphasising for an American audience. This article was very effective in motivating support from jazz educators overseas. 'Third World', while referring to poverty and lack of infrastructure, didn't carry the connotations of misgovernance and failure it does today. My statement that 'South Africans know and understand enough about jazz to be original' was meant to be a compliment, but it sounds condescending today. I met South African jazz musicians of every colour who were more advanced in their craft than I was.

Notes to Chapters 3, 4 and 5   295

10. See Appendix 2: Letter from Prof. Duminy to Prof. Parker, 28 March 1989.
11. Miles Davis, *Kind of Blue* (Columbia Records, 1959).
12. Miles Davis's mononym is an indication of high prestige and accepted usage, even in peer-reviewed academic journals.
13. Mark C. Gridley, *Jazz Styles: History and Analysis* (Englewood Cliffs, NJ: Prentice-Hall), first published 1978 has gone through six editions. I was using a later edition.
14. In a BBC radio interview in 2020, I said that Miles's *E.S.P.* album (Columbia Records, 1965) was life-changing for me because it showed there was 'open road ahead'.
15. The SABC and Southern African Music Rights Organisation (SAMRO) divided music broadcasts, awards and scholarships into 'serious' and 'light' categories.
16. Our interviews with former students often refer to interracial encounters as revelatory and liberating.

Chapter 4: Durban to Detroit

1. Darius Brubeck, 'Okay. I'll Do the Jazz without Too Many Oohs', *Weekly Mail*, 31 July – 8 August 1987.
2. New Brubeck Quartet, *Live at Montreux* (Tomato, 1977).
3. Paul Simon, *Graceland* (Warner Brothers, 1986).
4. '*C'est dans une ambiance très club (décidément le Platinum est un endroit délicieux pour écouter de la Musique!) . . . dans le cadre du New Jazz Festival . . . et le merveilleux musicien sud-africain Sandile Shange, véritable découverte de cette 21e édition . . .*' (It was in a very club atmosphere (decidedly the Platinum is a delicious place to listen to music!) as part of the New Jazz Festival . . . and the marvellous South African musician Sandile Shange, a real discovery of this 21st edition . . .).
5. There were other specific models of multiracial co-operation in the arts, such as the Space Theatre in Cape Town and the Market Theatre in Johannesburg, an internationally known performance initiative and the Johannesburg Art Foundation, founded by Bill Ainslie. (Ainslie was a University of Natal Fine Arts graduate, who later became internationally recognised as a painter and teacher.)
6. John Conyers Junior founded the Black Caucus in 1969, served in Congress for 50 years and sponsored the Bill that made Martin Luther King Day a public holiday. Cathy and I met Conyers in Durban in 2001.
7. Ron Aronson is Distinguished Professor Emeritus of the History of Ideas, Wayne State University and author of several books on Jean-Paul Sartre.
8. Chris Ballantine interview with Catherine Brubeck, Durban, 29 March 2018.
9. https://www.youtube.com/watch?v=8V6B8XvxX_c (accessed 20 January 2023).
10. For example, the Dakar Conference held in Dakar, Senegal, 9–12 July 1987, which was not officially governmental. It led to South African government talks with Nelson Mandela, who was still in prison.
11. The Jazzanians, *We Have Waited Too Long* (Umkhonto Records, 1988).
12. Brubeck Ntoni Afro Cool Concept, *Live at the New Orleans Jazz & Heritage Festival* (Roots Records, 1990; B&W Music, 1993).

Chapter 5: The Jazzanian Effect

1. A militant political party, AZAPO, the Azanian People's Organisation, popularised the name Azania in the 1980s.

2. I recently played a concert with Kevin Gibson on drums. Nic Paton and I sat in on a Mike Rossi gig with Kevin at the Crypt under St George's Cathedral in Cape Town. Melvin Peters and I performed together at the 2018 Piano Passion concert. We interviewed Johnny Mekoa, Victor Masondo, Melvin Peters, Nic Paton, Kevin Gibson and Rick van Heerden for this book and some direct quotes are transcribed from these interviews, conversations and answers to a questionnaire Cathy sent out between 2017 and 2019.
3. Lionel Pillay, alias Lionel Martin, is mainly remembered as the pianist on the Mankunku Quartet's iconic album *Yakhal' Inkomo* (World Record Co., 1968).
4. After retiring from directing the Defence Force Entertainment Corps big band, Major George Hayden took over the Nottingham Road Hotel, where we first encountered him. Hayden acted as my leave replacement when Cathy and I took advantage of a trip home to settle our affairs, paid for by the university.
5. Jürgen Bräuninger, during a departmental staff meeting, suggested we create a position of 'jazz drummer' to keep Lulu there, rather than continue to condone a student who could not pass elements of the basic curriculum. Lulu helped everyone else pass by accompanying them. He was essential to the programme until other drummers registered.
6. Led by Chucho Valdés on piano, Irakere included Paquito D'Rivera (clarinet and saxophones) and Arturo Sandoval, a trumpet virtuoso, who greatly influenced Johnny Mekoa. The group visited the United States a few times in the 1970s and D'Rivera became a life-long friend of my father's and played at his memorial service. D'Rivera and Sandoval (but not Valdés) eventually defected to the United States to play their own music.
7. Darius Brubeck, *Before It's Too Late* (Sheer Sound, 2003); Darius Brubeck Quartet, *For Lydia and the Lion* (Gathering Forces Music, 2008); Darius Brubeck Quartet, *Two and Four/To and Fro* (Gathering Forces Music, 2011); Mike Rossi and Darius Brubeck, *Odd Times: Uncommon Etudes for Uncommon Time Signatures: Developing the Ability to Play and Improvise in Uncommon Time Signatures* (Los Angeles: Alfred Music, 2016).
8. Chris Merz and Counterculture, *Art Gecko* (B&W Music, 1992).
9. See https://bryansteele.net/bio (accessed 28 September 2021).

Chapter 6: The Jazz Centre and Drinks at Five
1. Pioneering jazz trumpet and cornet player and band leader King Oliver played an important role in popularising jazz outside of New Orleans.
2. See Appendix 2: Special Events with CJPM Participation.
3. See Appendix 2: Abridged Fund-Raising Letter from 1993.
4. UKZN Jazz Legacy Ensemble and VCU Africa Combo, *Leap of Faith* (Virginia Commonwealth University, 2013).
5. Monde 'Lex' Futshane was the bass player with the NU Jazz Connection.
6. This is from Paul Simon's song 'The Boy in the Bubble', off his album *Graceland* (Warner Brothers, 1986). See https://www.paulsimon.com/track/the-boy-in-the-bubble-6/ (accessed 17 January 2023).
7. Darius Brubeck, *Chaplin's Back* (Paramount Records, 1972).

Chapter 7: Some Remarkable People
1. Darius Brubeck and Afro Cool Concept, *Still on My Mind* (Sheer Sound, 2003); Darius Brubeck, *Before It's Too Late* (Sheer Sound, 2003).

2. Allen Kwela, *The Unknown* (Music for Africa, 1985, cassette tape only).
3. Pat Matshikiza and Kippie Moeketsi, featuring Basil 'Mannenberg' Coetzee, *Tshona!* (The Sun Records, 1975); Mankuku Quartet, *Yakhal' Inkomo* (World Record Co., 1968)
4. George Nisbet, 'Jazzmen Light Up the Hermit', *Daily News*, 14 February 1984.
5. *Kwela* is an isiZulu word that means to climb or get moving. It is used as an invitation to dance. Police vans were called kwela vans – people had to jump into them when arrested.
6. Allen Kwela, *The Broken Strings of Allen Kwela* (Sheer Sound, 1998).
7. Director Michiel ten Kleij interviewed Marc Duby for the film version of *Playing the Changes* in 2019, and I interviewed him for this book in the previous year. Direct quotations are from these unpublished sources, except where otherwise indicated.
8. Marc Duby, ' "Reminiscing in Tempo": The Rainbow and Resistance in 1980s South Africa', *South African Music Studies* 33(1), 2013: 83–103.
9. Interview with Michiel ten Kleij.
10. Duby, ' "Reminiscing in Tempo" '.
11. ECM (Editions of Contemporary Music), 'the next best sound to silence' is the German record label founded in 1969 by Manfred Eicher, known in the 1970s mainly for spacious and contemplative productions of European and American artists.
12. Mark Duby, 'Soundpainting as a System for the Collaborative Creation of Music in Performance' (PhD diss., University of Pretoria, 2007).
13. Darius Brubeck featuring Barney Rachabane, *Tugela Rail* (RPM, 1984).
14. Duby, ' "Reminiscing in Tempo" '; Dollar Brand + Two, *Peace* (Soultown Records, 1971).
15. See, for example, Marc Duby, ' "A Unique Way of Being": Music and Merleau-Ponty's *Phenomenology of Perception*', in *Performance Phenomenology: To the Thing Itself*, edited by Stuart Grant, Jodie McNeilly-Renaudie and Matthew Wagner (New York: Palgrave Macmillan, 2019), 111–31; Marc Duby, 'Affordances in Real, Virtual, and Imaginary Musical Performance', in *Oxford Handbook of Sound and Imagination, Volume 2*, edited by Mark Grimshaw-Aagaard, Mads Walther-Hansen and Martin Knakkergaard (Oxford: Oxford University Press, 2019), 96–114; Marc Duby, ' "Fanfare for the Warriors": Jazz, Education, and State Control in 1980s South Africa and After', in *Jazz and Totalitarianism*, edited by Bruce Johnson (London: Routledge, 2016), 276–93; Marc Duby and Paul Alan Barker, 'Deterritorialising the Research Space: Artistic Research, Embodied Knowledge, and the Academy,' *SAGE Open* 7(4), 2017.
16. Brubeck Ntoni Afro Cool Concept, *Live at the New Orleans Jazz & Heritage Festival* (Roots Records, 1990; B&W Music, 1993).
17. 'The Black Family', *Tribute Magazine*, June 1988.
18. *The South African Songbook: SA Folklore Music*, scored and arranged by Victor Ntoni (Pretoria: National Heritage Council, 2012).
19. *Mzansi Sings a Tribute to Oliver Tambo* is available to watch on YouTube: Part 1: https://www.youtube.com/watch?v=mQY1j5ShKNk and Part 2: https://www.youtube.com/watch?v=N-fhWdU_erw (accessed 20 January 2023).
20. Dollar Brand + Two [Nelson Magwaza and Victor Ntoni], *Peace* (Soultown Records, 1971); Abdullah Ibrahim, *Blues for a Hip King* (Kaz Records, 1989).
21. 'Master Jack' was recorded by Four Jacks and a Jill on their eponymous album (RCA Victor, 1967).

22. Bill Hanley was the sound designer for the Woodstock Festival in 1969 and he sent part of the Woodstock sound system to David Marks in 1971. See Lizabé Lambrechts, 'The Woodstock Sound System and South African Sound Reinforcement', *Herri* 4, https://herri.org.za/4/lizabe-lambrechts/ (accessed 20 January 2023).
23. For an overview of the Hidden Years Music Archive Project, see: http://www.domus.ac.za/content/view/85/5/ (accessed 20 January 2023).
24. David Marks, 2012 interview in Lizabé Lambrechts, 'Letting the Tape Run: The Creation and Preservation of the Hidden Years Music Archive', *South African Journal of Cultural History* 32(2), 2018: 1–23.
25. Derek Davey, 'Dodging the Sjambok: A Glimpse of How South African Musicians Defied Apartheid', *Music in Africa*, 7 April 2020. For more about David Marks and Johnny Clegg in relation to this scene, see https://www.musicinafrica.net/magazine/dodging-sjambok-glimpse-how-south-african-musicians-defied-apartheid (accessed 20 January 2023).
26. See https://www.discogs.com/label/1069304-3rd-Ear-Music (accessed 20 January 2023).
27. The Jazzanians, *We Have Waited Too Long* (Umkhonto Records, 1988).
28. See https://www.musicinafrica.net/directory/music-academy-gauteng (accessed 20 January 2023).
29. The Jazz Ministers formed in 1968 with Aubrey Simani (alto sax), Furnace Goduka (tenor sax), Duncan Madondo (tenor sax), Johnny Mekoa (trumpet), Fanyana Sehloho (bass), Boy Ngwenya (piano) and Shepstone Sothane (drums). Victor Ndlazilwane joined in 1970. As former leader of the Woody Woodpeckers, Ndlazilwane was a kind of mentor with more professional experience. In 1975 Gallo Records released *Zandile*, with Nomvula (Victor's daughter) on piano. Ngwenya switched to bass. Two hits, 'Zandile' and 'Sekumanxa', raised the already popular Jazz Ministers to headliner status at festivals in the 1970s, leading to the booking at the Newport Jazz Festival. The Jazz Ministers, *Zandile* (Gallo Records, 1975).
30. The Brothers (Duke Makasi, Ezra Ngcukana, Tete Mbambisa, Victor Ntoni and Lulu Gontsana), *The Brothers* (Roots Records, 1990).
31. Ezra Ngcukana, *You Think You Know Me* (Jive Records, 1989).
32. On the album Barney Rachabane, *Barney's Way* (Jive Records, 1989).
33. Brubeck Ntoni Afro Cool Concept, *Live at the New Orleans Jazz & Heritage Festival* (Roots Records, 1990; B&W Music, 1993).
34. Zacks Nkosi, *Our Kind of Jazz* (Skyline, EMI, 1964); Darius Brubeck and Afro Cool Concept, *Still on My Mind* (Sheer Sound, 2003).
35. In 2021, commemorations of the tenth anniversary of Zim's death included intercontinental discussions with musicians and scholars hosted by the Durban International Film Festival and Radio Metro.
36. Tsepang Tutu Molefe, 'On the Prowl for New Sounds, This Afronaut Is a Perpetual Student', *Business Day*, 15 September 2017. Zim's love of wordplay is also evident in his album name – *Zimphonic Suites* (Sheer Sound, 2001).
37. Zim wrote several letters to my parents and to Juliet Gerlin, their personal assistant, filled with excitement at learning new things. Max Roach's all-percussion ensemble M'Boom was a model for Zim's 100-drummer 'Drums for Peace' performance at Nelson Mandela's inauguration ceremony in Pretoria in 1994.
38. Abdullah Ibrahim, *Solotude* (Gearbox Records, 2021).
39. The ubiquitous cyclic harmonic pattern I – IV – I 6/4 – V, with each chord lasting one measure, is comparable to the blues in American jazz and is found in every style, be it *marabi*,

mbaqanga, kwela or simply 'jazz'. For an in-depth history and foundational discussion of the roots of South African jazz and its relation to American jazz, see Christopher Ballantine, *Marabi Nights: Jazz, 'Race' and Society in Early Apartheid South Africa* (Pietermaritzburg: UKZN Press, 2012).

40. Darius Brubeck, *Before It's Too Late* (Sheer Sound, 2003). The Gathering Forces line-up in Nantes was Brendan Jury (viola), Chris Merz (soprano sax), Zim Ngqawana (alto sax), Darius Brubeck (piano), Mark Kilian (synth), Concord Nkabinde (electric bass), Kevin Gibson (drums). I still play 'Mamazala' with The Darius Brubeck Quartet and it's on our album *Years Ago* (Ubuntu Music, 2016).

41. Lindelwa Dalamba, 'Welcome to Brand Zim and . . . Please Remove Your Shoes', *Sunday Tribune Magazine*, 1 May 2005.

42. Gwen Ansell, 'Sonic Africa's Many Stylistic Skins', *Cue*, 4 July 2004.

43. Lindelwa Dalamba, 'Remembering Zim Ngqawana 10 Years On: A Singular Force in South African Music'. *The Conversation*, 8 May 2021, https://theconversation.com/remembering-zim-ngqawana-10-years-on-a-singular-force-in-south-african-music-160570 (accessed 20 January 2023).

44. This recording was never issued, but Seton Hawkins and Lex Futshane believe that Zim was referring to a Vision Festival concert with himself as nominal leader, Matthew Shipp (piano), William Parker (bass) and Nasheet Waits (drums) that took place in New York City in 2009.

Chapter 8: Off Campus and on the Road

1. Rafs Mayet, 'NU Jazz Connection Makes US Jazz Connections', *Two Tone* 1(3): 11; *Vrye Weekblad*, 21–27 February 1992.

2. Leonard Feather, 'Darius Brubeck Finds a Home in Africa', *Los Angeles Times*, 8 March 1992.

3. Anthea Johnston, 'NU Jazz in Miami', *Sunday Tribune*, 19 January 1992.

4. Chris Merz and Counterculture, *Art Gecko* (B&W Music, 1992); Darius Brubeck and Dan Brubeck – *Gathering Forces 1* (B&W Music, 1992); Darius Brubeck and Deepak Ram, *Gathering Forces II* (B&W Music, 1994).

5. Darius Brubeck and the NU Jazz Connection, *African Tributes* (B&W Music, 1993).

6. Chris Merz and Counterculture, *Art Gecko* (B&W Music, 1992).

7. Tete Mbambisa: *Tete's Big Sound* (The Sun Records, 1974) and *Did You Tell Your Mother* (The Sun Records, 1979).

8. Tete Mbambisa, *Did You Tell Your Mother* (The Sun Records, 1979). Winston Mankunku Ngozi and Victor Ntoni came from Cape Town, the Western Cape. As with similar taxonomies in jazz (West Coast jazz in the United States, for example) the term 'Eastern Cape jazz' describes music sharing certain characteristics as much as territorial provenance. The black population of the entire Cape region is predominantly Xhosa.

9. Influential Eastern Cape musicians must at a minimum include Todd and Pat Matshikiza from Queenstown, Chris McGregor from Blythswood in the deep hinterland, his bandmates Nikele Moyake (Addo), Mongezi Feza (Queenstown), Dudu Pukwana (Walmer, near Port Elizabeth) and Johnny Dyani, a bassist with an impressive range of international credits from New Duncan, near East London, where Tete Mbambisa was born. Andile

Yenana came to UND from King William's Town (now called Qonce), where he became a close associate of the New Brighton musicians, especially Zim Ngqawana.

10. Dr Michael Rossi ranks 'Years Ago' with 'Giant Steps' and 'In Your Own Sweet Way' for its challenging harmonic progression. I recorded 'Years Ago' with Afro Cool Concept (*Still on My Mind*, Sheer Sound) in 2003, with Barney Rachabane on alto, and in 2016 as the title track of a Darius Brubeck Quartet CD (Ubuntu Music) with Dave O'Higgins on tenor.

11. Typical township jazz pieces were structurally and harmonically alike, which made many new and previously existing melodies unavoidably similar. This led to much wrangling once musicians became aware of royalties as an income stream. For example, many musicians claim that Abdullah Ibrahim's hit 'Mannenberg' is *really* Zacks Nkosi's 'Jackpot'. But couldn't 'Jackpot' have just as *really* been something else?

12. A version of 'Zukile' is on the NU Jazz Connection's *African Tributes* (B&W Music, 1993).

13. An isiZulu word, *ilobola* is payment to the bride's family, traditionally paid in cattle.

14. Mervyn Cooke and David Horn (eds), *The Cambridge Companion to Jazz* (Cambridge: Cambridge University Press, 2002).

15. Herbie Mann, 'Comin' Home Baby' from the album *Herbie Mann at the Village Gate* (Atlantic Records, 1961). This was a jazz hit in the 1960s, featuring Mann on flute, hence the attraction for Deepak.

16. Deepak's discovery that the Rogers and Hart standard 'My Funny Valentine' can be performed as a raga with or without accompanying 'jazz chords' is a good example.

17. Albums by John Handy, John Coltrane, Alice Coltrane, Dave Liebman, Charles Lloyd, John McLaughlin's Mahavishnu Orchestra and his Carnatic-influenced Shakti, are historic examples of give-and-take between musicians taught to play the raga and those taught to play the 'changes' in their respective traditions.

18. Moreira and Purim were members Chick Corea's original Return to Forever group in the 1970s.

19. Darius Brubeck and Deepak Ram, *Gathering Forces II* (B&W Music, 1994).

20. An example: Glynis was charged with signing out our sound equipment, drums and the electric keyboard as long as a staff member was in charge. Many gigs simply would not have happened otherwise.

21. Released in 1995, 'Macarena' by Los Locos was a huge dance hit in South Africa.

22. Darius Brubeck and Afro Cool Concept, *Still on My Mind* (Sheer Sound, 2003).

23. Robert Trunz recorded the version of 'Mamazala' referred to in our section on Zim. It comes from this concert.

24. Natalie Rungan, currently director of the Chris Seabrooke Music Centre at Durban High School, has released many CDs, mostly recordings of her own songs, and performs frequently.

25. Barry Kernfeld (ed.), *The New Grove Dictionary of Jazz*, 2nd edition (New York: Oxford University Press, 2002).

26. Laura Kiniry, 'How Louis Armstrong Shaped the Sound of Ghana', *Atlas Obscura*, 7 December 2021, https://www.atlasobscura.com/articles/louis-armstrong-jazz-highlife-ghana (accessed 23 January 2023).

27. Dr Anton Seimon's biography on the website of Appalachian State University in North Carolina reads: 'A native of South Africa, I am a geographer with research experience

on a broad variety of themes in atmospheric and environmental science. These include monitoring climate change impacts on high alpine watersheds in the Peruvian Andes.'

28. See Appendix 2: Centre for Jazz and Popular Music Tender DFA 4 01/02.

Chapter 9: Continuum

1. See Appendix 2: CJPM Highlights.
2. See Appendix 2: The 8th South African Association for Jazz Educators Conference, 29 September – 1 October 2006.
3. Alan Webster is a jazz saxophonist, educator and administrator and has also been the director of the Standard Bank Jazz Festival in Makhanda/Grahamstown since 2004. In 2012 he received a Jazz Honour for Lifetime Achievement in Jazz from the minister of Arts and Culture, Paul Mashatile. He has a Master's degree in History and is the deputy headmaster of Stirling High School in East London.
4. Mike Skipper was educated at Rhodes University and was director of Music at St Andrew's College and DSG in Grahamstown/Makhanda from 1990 to 2003. He then became director of Music at Denstone College in the United Kingdom for twelve years, before returning to St Andrew's for a further four years. Since September 2019 he has been the head of Academic Music at Shrewsbury School in Shropshire, United Kingdom. A conversation with Darius resulted in the formation of the National Youth Jazz Festival in 1992. The very first teachers were Darius, Lex Futshane and Lulu Gontsana.
5. Direct quotes come from two long phone conversations with Piwe Solomon in early 2021.
6. Dr Mageshen Naidoo is now an associate professor and director for Jazz Studies, University of Pretoria.
7. Nduduzo Makhathini, *Modes of Communication: Letters from the Underworlds* (Blue Note Records, 2020); Darius Brubeck Quartet, *Live in Poland* (Ubuntu Music, 2020).
8. Nduduzo Makhathini, 'Jazz in Postcolonial South Africa: Tracing the Politics of "Formal" and "Informal" ', *Jazz & Culture* 4(1), 2021: 1–32.
9. Stuart Nicholson, *Is Jazz Dead? (Or Has It Moved to a New Address)* (New York: Routledge, 2005); Stuart Nicholson, *Culture in a Global Age* (Boston: Northeastern University Press, 2014).

Coda

1. See Darius Brubeck, 'Honouring Lulu . . .', *IOL*, 21 December 2005, https://www.iol.co.za/entertainment/whats-on/durban/honouring-lulu-935940 (accessed 25 January 2023).
2. Jan Smuts was the official name of the Johannesburg international airport until it was renamed OR Tambo International Airport in 2006. It was remodelled for the 2010 FIFA World Cup, which was held in South Africa.
3. I am currently president of the board of directors of Brubeck Living Legacy, a registered charity, and have contributed to numerous research and media projects related to Dave and Iola Brubeck.
4. In 1992 Bob Sinicrope brought a group of Milton Academy students, including Aaron Goldberg, later a highly regarded jazz pianist in New York, to Durban. CJPM organised a performance at the Centre and other plans including a braai in Umlazi at Brian Thusi's house, so the American students could take home a sense of township life. We visited Milton Academy in 1994 with a student group, which included Neil Gonsalves. Sinicrope

brought Milton Academy groups to South Africa eleven times, bringing with them around $219 000 worth of instruments and other teaching materials to distribute.

5. Piano Passion Project (featuring Darius Brubeck, Melvin Peters, Nishlyn Ramanna, Burton Naidoo, Debbie Mari, Andile Yenana and Neil Gonsalves), *Piano Passions* [double album] (Centre for Jazz, UKZN, 2018).A recording of the live Piano Passion concert is available in digital formats and CD at https://pianopassionproject.bandcamp.com/album/piano-passions-double-album.

6. Dinah Washington's 1959 Grammy Award-winning version of the Maria Grever song with English lyrics by Stanley Adams was familiar to jazz fans worldwide.

Bibliography

Ake, David. *Jazz Cultures*. Berkeley: University of California Press, 2002.

Ansell, Gwen. 'Sonic Africa's Many Stylistic Skins'. *Cue*, 4 July 2004.

———. *Soweto Blues: Jazz, Popular Music, and Politics in South Africa*. New York: Continuum, 2005.

Ballantine, Christopher. *Marabi Nights: Jazz, 'Race' and Society in Early Apartheid South Africa*. Pietermaritzburg: UKZN Press, 2012.

Ballantine, Christopher, Michael Chapman, Kira Erwin and Gerhard Maré (eds). *Living Together, Living Apart? Social Cohesion in a Future South Africa*. Pietermaritzburg: UKZN Press, 2017.

Blose, Themba. 'Jazz Fundis Rejoice'. *Africa Today*, 6 May 1983.

Bosman, Herman Charles. *Mafeking Road*. Cape Town: Human & Rousseau, 1969.

Brubeck, Darius. 'Honouring Lulu . . .'. *IOL*, 21 December 2005. https://www.iol.co.za/entertainment/whats-on/durban/honouring-lulu-935940 (accessed 25 January 2023).

———. 'Okay. I'll Do the Jazz without Too Many Oohs'. *Weekly Mail*, 31 July – 8 August 1987.

Cooke, Mervyn and David Horn (eds). *The Cambridge Companion to Jazz*. Cambridge: Cambridge University Press, 2002.

Dalamba, Lindelwa. 'Remembering Zim Ngqawana 10 Years On: A Singular Force in South African Music'. *The Conversation*, 8 May 2021. https://theconversation.com/remembering-zim-ngqawana-10-years-on-a-singular-force-in-south-african-music-160570 (accessed 20 January 2023).

———. 'Welcome to Brand Zim and . . . Please Remove Your Shoes'. *Sunday Tribune Magazine*, 1 May 2005.

'Darius Brubeck and Quartet Get Ready'. *Daily News*, 20 April 1983.

Davey, Derek. 'Dodging the Sjambok: A Glimpse of How South African Musicians Defied Apartheid'. *Music in Africa*, 7 April 2020. https://www.musicinafrica.net/magazine/dodging-sjambok-glimpse-how-south-african-musicians-defied-apartheid (accessed 20 January 2023).

Duby, Marc. 'Affordances in Real, Virtual, and Imaginary Musical Performance'. In *Oxford Handbook of Sound and Imagination, Volume 2*, edited by Mark Grimshaw-Aagaard, Mads Walther-Hansen and Martin Knakkergaard, 96–114. Oxford: Oxford University Press, 2019.

———. '"Fanfare for the Warriors": Jazz, Education, and State Control in 1980s South Africa and After'. In *Jazz and Totalitarianism*, edited by Bruce Johnson, 276–93. London: Routledge, 2016.

————. '"Reminiscing in Tempo": The Rainbow and Resistance in 1980s South Africa'. *South African Music Studies* 33(1), 2013: 83–103.

————. 'Soundpainting as a System for the Collaborative Creation of Music in Performance'. PhD diss., University of Pretoria, 2007.

————. '"A Unique Way of Being": Music and Merleau-Ponty's *Phenomenology of Perception*'. In *Performance Phenomenology: To the Thing Itself*, edited by Stuart Grant, Jodie McNeilly-Renaudie and Matthew Wagner, 111–31. New York: Palgrave Macmillan, 2019.

Duby, Marc and Paul Alan Barker. 'Deterritorialising the Research Space: Artistic Research, Embodied Knowledge, and the Academy'. *SAGE Open* 7(4), 2017.

Ellis-Petersen, Hannah. 'Racial Identity is a Biological Nonsense Says Reith Lecturer'. *The Guardian*, 18 October 2016.

Feather, Leonard. 'Darius Brubeck Finds a Home in Africa'. *Los Angeles Times*, 8 March 1992.

Gridley, Mark C. *Jazz Styles: History and Analysis*. Englewood Cliffs, NJ: Prentice-Hall, 1978.

Johnston, Anthea. 'NU Jazz in Miami'. *Sunday Tribune*, 19 January 1992.

Kernfeld, Barry (ed.). *The New Grove Dictionary of Jazz*, 2nd edition. New York: Oxford University Press, 2002.

Kiniry, Laura. 'How Louis Armstrong Shaped the Sound of Ghana'. *Atlas Obscura*, 7 December 2021. https://www.atlasobscura.com/articles/louis-armstrong-jazz-highlife-ghana (accessed 23 January 2023).

Klotz, Kelsey A.K. 'Dave Brubeck's Southern Strategy'. *Daedalus: Journal of the American Academy of Arts and Sciences* 148(2), 2019: 52–66.

Lambrechts, Lizabé. 'Letting the Tape Run: The Creation and Preservation of the Hidden Years Music Archive'. *South African Journal of Cultural History* 32(2), 2018: 1–23.

————. 'The Woodstock Sound System and South African Sound Reinforcement'. *Herri* 4. https://herri.org.za/4/lizabe-lambrechts/ (accessed 20 January 2023).

Makhathini, Nduduzo. 'Jazz in Postcolonial South Africa: Tracing the Politics of "Formal" and "Informal"'. *Jazz & Culture* 4(1), 2021: 1–32.

Mayet, Rafs. 'NU Jazz Connection Makes US Jazz Connections'. *Two Tone* 1(3): 11; *Vrye Weekblad*, 21–27 February 1992.

Molefe, Tsepang Tutu. 'On the Prowl for New Sounds, This Afronaut Is a Perpetual Student'. *Business Day*, 15 September 2017.

Muller, Carol A. *Focus: Music of South Africa*, 2nd edition. New York: Routledge, 2008.

————. 'Why Jazz? South Africa 2019'. *Daedalus: Journal of the American Academy of Arts and Sciences* 148(2), 2019: 115–27.

Muller, Carol and Janet Topp. 'A Preliminary Study of Gumboot Dance'. Honours thesis, University of Natal, Durban, 1985.

Ndebele, Njabulo S. *Fine Lines from the Box: Further Thoughts about Our Country*. Cape Town: Umuzi, 2007.

————. 'It's Time to Shed Blackness'. *Sunday Times*, 13 April 2014.

'New Mecca for Jazz'. *Natal Mercury*, 18 March 1983.

Nicholson, Stuart. *Culture in a Global Age*. Boston: Northeastern University Press, 2014.

————. *Is Jazz Dead? (Or Has It Moved to a New Address)*. New York: Routledge, 2005.

Nisbet, George. 'Jazzmen Light Up the Hermit'. *Daily News*, 14 February 1984.

Popke, E. Jeffrey. 'Violence and Memory in the Reconstruction of South Africa's Cato Manor'. *Growth and Change: A Journal of Urban and Regional Policy* 31(2), 2002: 235–54.

Rossi, Mike and Darius Brubeck. *Odd Times: Uncommon Etudes for Uncommon Time Signatures: Developing the Ability to Play and Improvise in Uncommon Time Signatures*. Los Angeles: Alfred Music, 2016.

Russonello, Giovanni. 'Jonas Gwangwa, Trombonist and Anti-Apartheid Activist, Dies at 83'. *New York Times*, 28 January 2021.

'The Black Family'. *Tribute Magazine*, June 1988.

The South African Songbook: SA Folklore Music, scored and arranged by Victor Ntoni. Pretoria: National Heritage Council, 2012.

Topp Fargion, Janet. *Taarab Music in Zanzibar in the Twentieth Century: A Story of 'Old is Gold' and Flying Spirits*. London: Ashgate Publishers, 2014.

Index

9/11 (2001) 248

Abbey Theatre (Durban) 36, 37
Adulyadej, Bhumibol *King* 234
Aebersold, Jamey 94, 142, 183, 207
Africa Arts Festival (Umlazi) 37
African American Music Appreciation
    Society (Pietermaritzburg) 16
African Inkspots 222
African Jazz & Variety 219
African Jazz Pioneers (AJP) 31
African Music and Drama Association
    (Johannesburg) 9
African National Congress (ANC) 13, 55,
    212, 213
African Odyssey 167
African Tributes 208–9
African Union launch (2002) 239, 249
Afrikaner Weerstandsbeweging (AWB) 214
Afro Cool Concept 43, 74, 93, 96, 111, 123,
    143, 146, 159, 162, 163, 164, 178,
    179–80, 181, 210, 212, 216, 221, 228,
    234, 294 n.23
Afro Jazz Festival (Harare, 1989) 96, 163
Agrippa and the Alcoholics *see* Keynotes
Ahlberg, Markus 284
AIDS epidemic 210, 258
Ainslie, Bill 11, 196, 295 n.5
Albany Hotel (Durban) 31, 32, 33, 111
Albert, Don 9, 12, 230, 273
Albert Park (Durban) 199
Alexander, Monty 88
Alexander, Tam 38, 293 n.16

Alexandra (Johannesburg) 182
Alliance Française 285
'Amabutho' 207
Amandla Cultural Ensemble (ANC) 6
Amato, Rob 63
American Cultural Center 134
American Embassy 285
'Angola' 137
Annan, Kofi 249
Ansell, Gwen 14
'Anthology of Zimology' 189
Archbishop Denis Hurley Centre (Durban)
    270
Armstrong, Louis 3, 16, 220
Aronson, Ron 92, 295 n.7
Art Ensemble of Chicago 91
Art Gecko 122, 212
As Time Goes By 148
Ashburner, Ann 228, 235
Ashe Auditorium (Miami) 207
Assemblies of God 106
Associated Board of the Royal Schools of
    Music (ABRSM) 68, 157, 181
Audoire, Phil 230
'Aunt Ann' 110
aural perception 22, 28
Awesome Africa Festival (Durban, 2006) 210
Ayisa, Bernard 123, 237
Azania 295 n.1

B&W Music 78, 208
'(Back Home Again in) Indiana' 33
Ba'gasane (Neighbours) 131, 255–6, 257–8

Baker, Bruce 269
Baker, David 170
Ballantine, Christopher 6, 7, 11, 12, 18, 19,
    45, 58, 68, 69, 72, 81, 83–4, 92, 94,
    114, 128, 152, 237, 270, 273
Baloi, Gito 258
bansuri (North Indian flute) 227, 294 n.23
Barkan, Todd 187, 188
Baroque 2000 concerts 241
Barry, Susan 260
Bartle Arts Trust (BAT) 131, 208, 230, 285
BAT Centre (Durban) 217, 230
Bates, Django 157
Baxter Theatre (Cape Town) 96
Bebelaar, Patrick 282, 284
Bedford, Don 39
Before It's Too Late 146
'Before It's Too Late' 252, 270
Before the Rains 209
Benfica 18
Benn, Beryl 9
Bergonzi, Jerry 117, 118, 122
Berklee College of Music 29
beverage companies 34; *see also* individual
    brands
Beverley Hills Hotel (Durban) 274
Bhekuzulu Hall (UZ) 37
Biko, Steve 18
'Black and Blue' 3
'Black, Brown and Beige' 3
Black Caucus (United States Congress) 83,
    87
black university students 19, 29
Blackhawk Jazz Club (San Francisco) 271–2
Blue Notes 5, 214, 291 n.4
'Blue Swan' 155
Blues for a Hip King 166
'Blues for Nuts' 149
'Body and Soul' 33, 217
Boksburg 52, 197
Bolden, Buddy 16
Bon, Gerrit 20, 57, 71, 73, 74, 84, 99, 105,
    128, 202, 203
Booysen, Peter 62, 128, 131, 277–8
Bop Studios (Mmabatho) 229
Bophela, Barney 220

Bophela, Theo 34, 220
Born at the Right Time tour (1992) 143, 226
Bothma, Noel 32
Brand, Dollar *see* Ibrahim, Abdullah
Bräuninger, Brigitte 184
Bräuninger, Jürgen 184, 188, 207, 223, 229,
    230, 245, 258, 284, 296 n.5
Brecker, Michael 78, 144, 178
Breytenbach, Breyten 145
Bridgewater, Pamela 134
Bridglall, Bhisham 228
British Council 285
British Musicians Union (BMU) 41
Broderick, Amelia 246
The Brothers 176, 213, 214, 217, 298 n.30
Brown, Clifford 109
Brown, Peter 14, 292 n.6
Brubeck, Catherine (née Shallis)
    administrator and fund-raiser (UND) 17,
        19–20, 22, 27, 52–3, 56–7, 69, 70,
        80–3, 85–6, 93, 95, 111, 129, 132, 133,
        136, 139, 188, 206, 252, 284
    background and early life 3–4, 16–17,
        20–21, 293 n.7
    and Durban homes 25–7, 184, 254–5
    and election (1994) 226
    and football 49, 176
    as journalist 212
    marriages 13, 21
    at Montreux Festival 77–9
    music entrepreneur in USA 10, 18, 21
    political activist 3, 8, 15–16, 49
    return to South Africa 14
    road trips 193–6, 197–8, 221–2, 225
Brubeck, Chris 9, 11, 119, 161, 210, 242,
    253, 265
Brubeck, Dan 119, 153, 161, 206, 207, 210,
    242, 253, 265
Brubeck, Darius
    as academic (UND) 6, 7, 12–13, 19, 53,
        58, 69, 96, 125, 226
    ancestry and family name 264–7, 291 n.3
    Bellagio residency 210
    as broadcaster 19, 22, 40, 48, 50, 58
    and Centre for Jazz and Popular Music
        118, 129, 137, 253–4, 259–60, 283

citizenship 49
as composer 187–8
and Durban homes 25–7, 184, 254–5
education 7–8, 157
and election (1994) 226
health 66, 85, 229, 262, 270
as journalist 77, 78, 111
marriage 13
at Montreux Festival 77–9
and National Arts Council 48–9
as performer 31–2, 33, 35–7, 38, 40, 50,
    60, 68–9
in Poland 1–3, 266, 271
as political activist 40–2, 43–4, 45, 46,
    47–8
press publicity, criticism and reviews 12,
    230, 265
relationship with South Africa 270–1
retirement 188–9, 191–2, 254, 259, 262,
    263
road trips 193–6, 197–8, 221–2, 225
teaching and supervision 28, 73, 75, 96,
    125, 156, 157, 190–1, 263
US tour (1988) 84–93
visits to South Africa (1976, 1982 and
    post-2006) 9, 10–12, 242, 262–3, 268
Brubeck, Dave
    as cultural icon 166, 266–7
    death and memorial service (2013) 227,
        263, 296 n.6
    and the Jazzanians 83, 89–90, 94, 100
    in Poland 1–2
    South African connections 9, 21, 132,
        161, 178, 242, 275
Brubeck, Howard 41
Brubeck, Iola 83, 89, 94, 112, 117, 132, 161,
    178, 207
Brubeck, Matthew 89, 229, 265
Brubeck, Michael 1, 2
Brubeck, Schillaci (cat) 265
Brubecks Play Brubeck 210
Brubeck/Shange Jazz Coalition 147
Brugger, Andy 284
Bugwandeen, Ramoll 8, 217, 219, 270
BuJazzO 281, 284
Bulawayo, Noviolet 179

busking 42, 107
Buthelezi, Mangosuthu 60–1
Butterworth Hotel (Durban) 222
Buxton, Mr 22
Byrne, Logan 235

Campbell, Mike 203, 210
Cape Town Big Band Jazz Festival 276
Cape Town International Jazz Festival 276
Carling Circle Competition 96, 175, 206,
    214, 221
Carlton Hotel (Johannesburg) 130
Carnegie Hall (NYC) 18
Carter, Nic 12
Carter, Ron 75
Catalysts 133
Cato Manor (Umkhumbane, Durban) 25,
    292 n.1
Catt, Ann 110
CBS (Columbia Broadcasting System) 92
Cebekhulu, Cyprian 53
Cedegren, Bjorn 284
Celimontana festival (Rome) 178
Cellar (Playhouse, Durban) 160
Centre for Jazz and Popular Music (CJPM,
    UND)
    archives 143, 268
    and festivals and conferences 97, 280–1
    foundation and naming 128–37, 138, 143
    funding and administration 139–41, 142,
        205, 253, 282–3
    participation in special events 48, 240,
        279–80
    personnel and musicians 240–1, 283–4
    students 96, 126–7, 139, 142
    tours 203–4, 211–12, 249
Chaplin's Back 144
Chapman, Jim 284
Chapman, Michael 142, 191, 204, 259–60
Chaurasia, Hariprasad 227
Chiorboli, Dan 42–3, 47, 210, 263
Christian Action 293 n.7
Civil Rights Museum (Memphis) 2
Clarence, Desmond 71
Claude, Dennis 43, 129, 169
Clegg, Johnny 27–8, 41, 77, 78–9

Index

Clermont (Durban) 220
'The Click Song' (Qongqothwane) 5
Coca-Cola 170
Coetzee, Basil 219
Colby, Vince 48
Coleman, George 75
Colepepper, Janet 56, 116
Collier, Graham 204
Collins, John 293 n.7
Coltrane, John 10, 48, 75, 126, 183, 215
Coltrane, Ravi 2
Comfort, Neil and Nicola 217
'Comin' Home Baby' 227, 300 n.15
'Commission 2004' 188
Commission to Restructure Arts in Natal
    (CRAN) 45, 47
Commonwealth Heads of Government
    meeting (2000) 239, 249
Compton, Patrick 266
Concert for Academic Freedom (Durban,
    1983) 60
Congregational Church (Greenwich,
    Connecticut) 90, 206
Congress of South African Trade Unions
    (COSATU) 42
Conjwa, Mlungisi 209
Conyers, John 87, 246, 247, 248, 295 n.6
Cook, Allen and Jasper 31
Corea, Chick 52, 100
Coryell, Larry 11
Count Basie Orchestra 174
Counterculture 122, 206, 208, 212
Cousineau, Phil 39
Cox, Dustan (Dusty) 122, 123, 125, 230,
    267-8, 273
Cox, Mitos 123
Cresswell, Christopher 128
Cuban Pete's (Durban) 274
cultural activism 47-8
Culture and Working Life Project
    (University of Natal) 43

Daily News Goldpot 52
Dalamba, Lindelwa 189, 190
Danish Cultural Institute 285
Dankworth, Alec, Jacqui and Johnny 266

Darius Brubeck Jazz Ensemble 12
Darius Brubeck Quartet 2-3, 37, 237, 249,
    262, 299 n.40
Darius Brubeck Quintet 51, 78, 101, 104,
    147, 159, 160, 225-6
Darrington, Ian 284
Davashe, Mackay 219
Dave Brubeck Quartet 1, 100, 120
Dave Brubeck Trio 33
David, Peter 293 n.19
Davids, Sarah 192
Davidson, Hamish 95
Davidson, Peter 18
Davis, Miles 5, 74, 75, 103, 112, 183, 208,
    271-2, 295 n.12
'The Day the Music Died' 11
De Klerk regulations (1987) 63
De Klerk speech to Parliament (2 February
    1990) 212, 213
De Lucia, Paco 78
De Menezes, Pamela 262
Del Segno 231
Delew, Joe 33, 34
Department of Music (University of Natal)
    11, 24-5, 28, 57-8, 59, 67-8, 71-2, 73,
    75, 76, 108; see also Centre for Jazz and
    Popular Music; Jazz Studies programme
Desmond, Paul 101, 120
Detroit 90, 92
Devar, Siva 261
Devroop, Karendra 273-4, 281
Dirty Dozen 91
Dixon, John 86, 210
Dizzy's Coca-Cola Club (Lincoln Center,
    NYC) 210
Dlamini, Sazi 144, 195, 205, 206, 208, 209,
    246, 283
Dludlu, Jimmy 256
Documentation Centre for Music (DOMUS,
    University of Stellenbosch) 143
Dolly, Les 32
Donnybrook (KZN) 226
Dorkay House (Johannesburg) 9, 31
Double Vision 185
Drake, John 33, 34
D'Rivera, Paquito 296 n.6

Dube, Jabu 233
Dube, Wallace 26
Duby, Marc 12, 27, 28, 36, 38, 51, 70, 72, 96, 106, 147, 149, 156–9, 160–1, 179, 184, 225, 252
Duminy, Andrew 72, 73, 128, 129, 142, 279
Dunscombe, Richard 79
Durban 23–4, 41–4
Durban Arts Association 41, 42, 43, 113, 119, 131, 199, 205, 228, 285
Durban City Hall 210, 221, 226
Durban Folk Club 42, 199, 201
Durban International Festival of Music (DIFM) 228, 294 n.23
Durban International Film Festival 21, 54, 228
Durban Publicity Association 265
Durrant, Geoffrey 20
Duze, Zami 275
Dyani, Johnny 291 n.4, 299 n.9
Dyer, Bokani 266
Dyer, Stephen 108
Dylan, Jakob 2

Eagle, Andrew 89, 90, 91, 92, 107–9, 111, 116
Editions of Contemporary Music (ECM) 157, 297 n.11
Edwards, John 136–7, 138, 215, 242, 274
Eicher, Manfred 297 n.11
Ellington, Duke 3, 16, 18, 20, 74
Ellington, Mercer 2, 18
Ellington is Forever Concert (1976) 18, 21
Ellis, George 118, 219
Ellison, Willie 32, 33, 151
Emmerich, Grant 136
End Conscription Campaign (ECC) 38, 51, 107
Engelbrecht, Hentie 222
Engelbrecht, Rika 17
Entertainment Corps band (SADF) 28
Environmental Panelling Systems 129, 131
Episcopal Church 18, 21
Error Nine 123, 233
Erwin, Alec 133
ethnomusicology 67, 68

Eusébio 18
Evans, Bill 51–2
Evans, Gil 75
Evita 44
Executive Hotel (Umlazi) 37, 219
Eye in the Sky 209

'Fables of Faubus' 3
Faku, Feya 46, 109, 122, 184, 205, 206, 210, 214, 216, 275
Fassie, Brenda 41
Feather, Leonard 207, 209
Ferguson, Jennifer 169
Fernandez, Demi 260
Feza, Mongezi 177, 291 n.4, 299 n.9
Filiatreault, Serge 39
Foglar Sound 83
Football World Cup (2010) 43, 49, 214, 263
Fourie, Johnny 34, 151, 153, 216, 230
Fourie, Sean 230
Fourth World 228
Frank, Dave 284
Frankfurt School 105
Frank's Coats 86
Free Peoples Concerts (Wits) 168
Freeman, Morgan 187
Fujimori, Alberto 238, 239
Fulbright scholarships 134
Fumio Itabashi Mix Dynamite Quartet 235
Futshane, Monde (Lex) 76, 109, 122, 142, 180, 184, 203, 205, 206, 207, 209, 214, 216, 249, 275, 299 n.44, 301 n.4

Gaborone raid (1985) 181
Gad, Henrik 284
Gallo Africa 83, 168
Garcia, Antonio 142
Garcia, Russell 73
Garden Restaurant (Johannesburg) 35, 111
Gathering Forces 208
Gathering Forces I and II 8, 9, 11, 121, 140, 186, 208, 227, 228–9, 230, 235, 239, 243, 245–6, 265, 294 n.23, 299 n.40
Gathering Forces II 229
Gawe, Claude 216
Genuines 169

Gerlin, Bob 84–5, 105
Gerlin, Juliet 84–5, 89, 105, 112
Giant Steps 183
Gibbens, Wesley 136, 237, 263
Gibson, Kevin 28, 33, 76, 89, 103–4, 107, 111, 116, 147, 154, 160, 179, 186, 190, 225, 228, 235, 275, 281, 299 n.40
Gilbey's 34, 222
Gillespie, Dizzy 75, 78, 107
'Girl from Ipanema' 137
Gleason, Ralph 272
Gloyd, Russell 163, 294 n.23
Goduka, Furnace 298 n.29
Goethe Institute 285
Gold Company 282
Goldberg, Aaron 301 n.4
Gongco, Bugs 215
Gonsalves, Neil 28, 100, 122, 127, 142, 205, 242, 249, 260–1, 268, 269, 270, 275, 301 n.4
Gontsana, Lulama (Lulu) 10, 22, 72, 74, 75, 86, 88, 90, 96, 97, 109, 110–11, 112, 116, 143, 144, 153, 162, 163, 170, 176, 177, 179, 184, 186–7, 195, 204, 205, 206, 208, 210, 214, 216, 246, 249, 252, 263, 284, 298 n.30, 301 n.4
Goodwill Lounge (Durban) 220
government departments *see* South Africa
Graceland 42, 78, 93, 107, 143, 178, 180
Graceland (Memphis) 178
Grahamstown Jazz Festival *see* Makhanda Jazz Festival
Grahamstown National Festival of the Arts 160, 176–7
Grahamstown National Youth Jazz Festival *see* National Youth Jazz Festival
Grand Hotel (Grahamstown) 153, 176
'Grazing in the Grass' 5
Greer, Sonny 74
Grey's Hospital (Pietermaritzburg) 202
Grimshaw, Mark 95
Gross, Izio 35, 111
Guinness Jazz Festival (Johannesburg) 230
Gumede, Archie 14, 292 n.6
Gumede, Sipho 34, 51, 144, 208
Gwangwa, Jonas 6, 234, 291 n.4

Hancock, Herbie 75
Hanley, Bill 167, 168, 298 n.22
Harare Jazz Festival (1989) 228
Harari 41
Harber, Anton 56
Harber, Phil 32, 34, 54, 56, 130; *see also* Phil Harber Scholarship
Harber, Rodney 129
Harber, Zara 56, 130
'Harlem Air Shaft' 74
Harneker, Zaide 192
'Harper Valley PTA' 228
Hawkins, Seton 299 n.44
Hayden, George 28, 105, 197–8, 201
Hayden, Rose 198
Hebrard, Fiona 231
Hedman, Sara 284
Henderson, Joe 216
'Herbie Mann at the Village Gate' 300 n.15
Herbolzheimer, Peter 281, 284
Herman, Woody 117
Hermit Vegetarian Restaurant (Durban) 38–9, 78, 149, 153, 169, 179
Hersov Trust 83
Hexagon Trust 132
Hidden Years Music Archive Project (DOMUS) 167, 169
Hlatshwayo, Mi 42
Holiday, Billie 3
Holmes, Jeff 121, 185
Holmes, Richard (Groove) 111
Holst, Helmut and Leslie 184
'Homeless' 143
'Hoshhh Hoha' 181
Hotline 41
Howard College Theatre (Durban) 164, 189, 261, 269
Hubbard, Freddie 109
'Humanity Has No Colour' 245
Humphreys, Liam 134
Hunter, Malcolm 16; *see also* Malcolm Hunter Collection

'I Feel Good' 144
Ibrahim, Abdullah 5, 6, 7, 34, 107, 159, 166, 180, 184, 185, 186, 187, 226, 300 n.11

'In Your Own Sweet Way' 90, 198
Indian community 8
'Indian Ocean Blue' 270
Inkatha Freedom Party (IFP) 55, 60
Inside Out 241
Institut Français d'Afrique du Sud 285
Institute of Zimology 183, 191
International Association for Jazz Education
    (IAJE)
    conferences 205, 267, 280–1: Atlanta
        (1996) 204; Boston (1994) 275; Miami
        (1992) 206–7; New York (1998) 235
    in receivership 252
    and South Africa 63, 86–7, 94, 138, 141,
        170, 285
International Conference on Popular Music
    Studies (Montreal, 1985) 152
International Convention Centre (ICC,
    Durban) 243
International Defence and Aid Fund (IDAF)
    293 n.7
International Jazz Day (30 April) 3
International Jazz Orchestra 107
Invictus 214
Irakere 112, 296 n.6
Irvine, Colleen and Douglas 202

'Jackpot' 300 n.11
Jackson, Jesse 246–7
Jansen, Robbie 176, 219
Jarman, Joseph 91
jazz
    and apartheid and segregation 33, 226
    bands 51, 117
    Cape Town 276
    characteristics and styles 105, 121
    clubs 276
    conferences 138–9
    Durban 32–3, 230, 231, 233–4
    Eastern Cape 299 n.8, 299 n.9
    education 64–5, 96, 120
    and freedom 3, 34–5, 64, 93, 243, 275
    and humour 179
    Indo- 227–8
    in Poland 2, 3, 271
    road stories 193

in South Africa 2, 3, 4–6, 14, 16, 50,
    64–5, 83–4, 96, 138, 156, 220, 248,
    273
    township see mbaqanga
Jazz Aid 170
Jazz and Folk for Free (Durban, 1986) 199,
    201
Jazz and Heritage Foundation Festival (New
    Orleans) 97, 133, 143
Jazz at the Nassau 263
Jazz Centre see Centre for Jazz and Popular
    Music (CJPM, UND)
Jazz Comrades 185
Jazz Dazzlers 219
Jazz Education Network (JEN) 138
Jazz Jols 56, 119, 132, 219, 274
Jazz Ministers 109, 171, 298 n.29
Jazz on the Deck (BAT Centre, Durban) 230
Jazz Outreach 140
Jazz Studies programme (University of Natal)
    content 5, 7, 108, 116–17, 274, 275, 276
    examinations 74–5
    foundation 3–4, 11, 18, 21–2
    scholarships 53–4, 55–6
    staff 125–6
    students 19, 50–1, 62, 65–6, 69–71, 72–3,
        268, 273, 279
    see also Jazzanians
Jazzanians
    foundation and name 79, 99
    legacy 93–4, 95, 204
    members 38, 160
    recording 113, 114
    US tour (1988) 81, 83, 85–6, 87–93,
        94–5, 100, 105, 141, 170
    see also Leftovers; Natal University Jazz
        Connection
Jazzy Rainbow 230
Jenkins, Clay 284
Johannesburg 166
Johannesburg Art Foundation 196
Johannesburg Jazz Club 9
Johnson, Milton 32
Johnston, Anthea 207
Jones, Hank 88
Jones, Quincy 78

Jordan, Stanley 78
Joseph, Julian 281, 284
Joubert, Judy 148
Joy of Jazz 276
Jubilee Jazz Festival (Thailand) 234, 235
Judge, Count Wellington 265
Juluka 27
Jury, Brendan 235, 284, 299 n.40

Karlsruhe music festival 207–8
Karlsruhe Uni Big Band 235, 237
Kasrils, Eleanor (née Logan) and Ronnie 30, 249
Kelly, Art 31
Kenton, Stan 117, 266
Kerdachi, Des, Gerald and Simon 32
Kerkorrel, Johannes 169
Kernfeld, Barry 237
Kessel, Barney 149
Keynotes 34, 201, 220–1
Kgoadi, Moketsi 281
Khanyile, Dalton (Tony) 34, 175, 220–3
Khoza, Bheki 135
Khumalo, Clarence 34
Kilian, Mark 57–8, 75–6, 172–3, 196–7, 203, 204–5, 206, 209, 229, 281, 299 n.40
Kind of Blue 74, 75, 183
King Kong 5, 291 n.4
Kings Park Stadium (Durban) 41, 143
Kippies Jazz Club (Johannesburg) 120, 213
Kirkwood, Michael 63
Kitchen, Syd 41
Klaasen, Thandi 9–10, 219
Kock, Paul 123, 136, 164, 234, 235
Kohinoor Records 213
Konitz, Lee 153
Konrad, Bernd 207
Kuehl, Craig 134
Kulman, Whitey 215
Kumalo, Bakhiti 107, 182
Kunene, Jerry 34, 55
Kunene, Madala 208
Kupi, Prince 210, 256–7, 258
Kuralt, Charles 92

'KwaMashu' 154
KwaMashu (Durban) 106, 152, 153, 155, 160
Kwela, Allen Duma 5, 29, 38, 40, 146, 147, 149–50, 152–4, 155, 159, 169, 176, 179, 181, 219, 240
Kwela Kids 178, 181
kwela music 149, 297 n.5

Ladysmith Black Mambazo 44, 143, 144–5, 178, 252
Laine, Cleo 266
Lambrechts, Lizabé 143
The Last of the Blue Devils 54
Lateef, Yusef 121, 184, 212
Le Plaza Hotel (Durban) 169, 230
Le Roux, Dave 231
Leap of Faith 142
Leftovers 94–5
Legends (Durban) 274
Lemmy Special see Mabaso, Lemmy (Special)
Lennon, Sean 2
'Let Freedom Swing' 187–8
'Let it Roll Mr Brubeck' 90
Liberal Party 16
Liberian Suite 18
Lincoln Center Jazz Orchestra 2, 187, 188
Linder Auditorium (Johannesburg) 194, 195
The Lion King 166
Lion Lager Road Show 40–1
Little Giants 177
Live at Montreux 78
Live at the New Orleans Jazz and Heritage Festival 162, 164, 179–80
Live at the Plugged Nickel 103
Live in Poland 261
Lloyd Webber, Andrew 44
ilobola 225, 300 n.13
Lockwood, Didier 235
London Symphony Orchestra 259
Loose Tubes 157
'Loy Loy Krathong' 234, 235
Lucas, Jane 135
Lucey, Roger 202
'Lulama' 210

Mabaso, Lemmy (Special) 178
Mabuse, Sipho (Hotstix) 41
'Macarena' 233
Machel, Graça 249
Madondo, Duncan 298 n.29
Madonsela, Ronnie 32, 33, 37, 54, 55, 219;
    see also Ronnie Madonsela Scholarship
    for Jazz
Magubane, Peter 11
Magwaza, Agrippa 34, 160
Magwaza, Connie 160
Magwaza, Mduduzi (Clement) 258
Magwaza, Nelson 36, 51, 52, 147, 159–60
Mahikeng Jazz Festival 263
Mailula, Anna 256
Maitre Pers (Durban) 31–2, 33, 104, 179
Makasi, Duke 10, 96, 111, 121, 162, 176, 214,
    216, 298 n.30
Makeba, Miriam 5, 6, 93, 106, 220, 291 n.4
Makhanda Jazz Festival 83, 96, 163, 253, 276
Makhathini, Nduduzo 261, 270
Malcolm, Derek 178
Malcolm Hunter Collection 17
Malcolm-Smith, Andrew 130
Malcolm-Smith, Glynis 96, 120, 129–31,
    132, 136, 140, 141, 143, 145, 169–70,
    188, 207, 223, 225, 226, 229, 244,
    249, 252, 256, 257, 267, 268, 284
Malcolm-Smith, Gregory 130
Malombo 9, 10, 18, 43, 169
'Mamazala' 186–7, 299 n.40, 300 n.23
Manana, Stompie 34
Mandela, Nelson 30, 53, 93, 121, 133, 187,
    202, 213, 214, 249, 263–4
Mangosuthu Technikon 37
Manhattan Transfer 123
Mankunku, Winston 12, 34, 96, 113, 147,
    162, 217, 219, 225, 267, 268, 299 n.8
Mann, Herbie 18, 227
'Mannenberg' 53, 219, 300 n.11
Manor Gardens (Durban) 24
Mansfield, Peter 41
marabi 4, 217
Marantz, Bart 284
Marchant, Louise 275
Mari, Debbie 123, 136, 233, 252

Mari, George 123, 136, 233, 240–1, 249, 281
Market Theatre (Johannesburg) 213, 230
Marks, David 40–1, 42, 43, 159, 167–8, 169,
    199, 201, 298 n.22
Marks, Frances 167, 169
Marsalis, Branford, Delfeayo, Ellis and Jason
    266
Marsalis, Wynton 113, 174, 187, 188, 266
Martin, Lionel see Pillay, Lionel
Martin, Lloyd 12
Masekela, Barbara 42, 97
Masekela, Hugh 5, 6, 11, 18, 78, 109, 139,
    162, 169, 178, 180, 227, 252, 291 n.4
Mashiane, Chris 164, 234, 256
Mashiloane, Sibusiso (Mash) 270
Mashiyane, Johannes (Spokes) 178
maskandi competitions 42, 293 n.22
Masondo, Victor 76, 90, 92, 95, 105–7, 114,
    116, 156–7, 158, 160, 195, 203, 206
'Master Jack' 167
Mathabe, Mpho 224
Matshikiza, Pat 147, 159, 214, 299 n.9
Matshikiza, Todd 25, 214, 291 n.4, 299 n.9
Mavundla, Sydney 281
'Maxhosa' 164
Mayet, Rafs 270
Mazibuko, Thandiwe 284
Mazzoni, Mike 33
Mbambisa, Tete 176, 214, 215, 217, 298 n.30,
    299 n.8
Mbambo, James 34
mbaqanga 31, 181, 293 n.9, 300 n.11
Mbatha, Bheki 95, 132, 199
Mbatha, Makhosi 284
Mbeki, Thabo and Zanele 249
Mbhele, Delile 284
M'Boom 298 n.37
McClean, Rene 281, 284
McCurdy, Ron 141
McFarlin, Bill 79
McGregor, Chris 5, 214, 291 n.4, 299 n.9
McKenna, Merle 175
McLaughlin, John 78
McLean, Don 11, 202
Mdladlose, Knowledge 255
Meer, Dylan 201

Mega Music 212, 213
Mekoa, Fred 174
Mekoa, Johnny 22, 57, 73–4, 76, 89, 90, 92, 94, 96, 108, 109, 110, 111, 112, 116, 132, 147, 169–75, 195, 196, 206, 234, 242, 269, 281, 296 n.6, 298 n.29
Mekoa, Margaret 109
Melvin Peters Quintet 206
Members of the Original Jazz Organisation (MOJO) 35, 44, 57, 119
Memphis (Tennessee) 179
Mennell, Clive 170
Merz, Chris 53, 112, 117, 120–2, 144, 185, 205, 206, 207, 212, 226, 228, 230, 235, 252, 275, 299 n.40
Merz, Jill 120
Metaxas, Basil 32
Mhlongo, Busi 147
Mhlongo, Musa 257
Michigan Coalition for Human Rights 92
Mikula, Paul 169, 208, 217, 230, 270
Miles, Butch 135, 231, 281
Milhaud, Darius 112
Millar, Stephanie 56
Mills, Bobby 185
Milton Academy Jazz Band 281
Mingus, Charles 3, 18, 166
Minor, Ron 39
Minter, Bobby 32
La Mission 209
Mistry, Kitu 227
Mitchell Park (Durban) 40
Mkhumbane 25
Mlaba, Obed 131
Mlambo, Mfana 120, 227, 233, 242, 255, 256
Mmabana Cultural Centre (North West) 53
Modes of Communication: Letters from the Underworlds 261
Moeketsi, Kippie 181
Mogoloage, Joyce 284
Mohamed, Pops 208
Moholo, Louis 282, 291 n.4
Monk, Thelonious 74, 158
Monk, Thelonious (Junior) 266
Monteregge, Mario 32

Montgomery, Wes 149
Montreux Jazz Festival (1987) 77–9, 151, 155, 252
Moodley, Magendran 204
Moon Hotel (Clairwood) 8, 118, 132, 217, 219, 220, 230
Moore, Tony 12
More Garde Than Avant (Moregarde) 157
Moreira, Airto 228
Morello, Joe 2
Morgan, Russ 121
Morphet, Alexandra 12, 21, 26, 29
Morphet, Mick 132
Morphet, Tony 21
Morris, Mike 128
Morton, Jelly Roll 16
Mosaic 8, 123, 203–4, 228
Moses, Roland 242, 284
Motala, Chota 14, 292 n.6
Mothabeng, Lebohang 210
Mountain Records 169
'Mountains of Men' 167
Moyake, Nikele 291 n.4, 299 n.9
Mr Q's 78
Mrubata, McCoy 210
Mseleku, Bheki 10, 18, 137, 184, 187, 241, 261, 270
Mthembu, Billy 14
Mthethwa, Bongani 258
Mtshali, Thami 57, 74
Mtshali, Thembi 11, 18
Muller, Carol 28
Murray Campbell School (Johannesburg) 174
Music Academy (Windhoek) 225
Music Academy of Gauteng (MAG) 170, 171, 174
Music Action for People's Power (MAPP) 43
Music Association of Natal (MANA) 41, 42, 43, 45, 46, 47, 57, 169, 199
Music Relief Campaign 141
Music Unlimited 32
'Mustang Sally' 233
My Fair Lady 45
'My Foolish Heart' 149
Mzansi Sings a Tribute to Oliver Tambo 164

316 Playing the Changes

Naidoo, Burton 235, 242, 270
Naidoo, Mageshen 189, 191, 204, 260, 281,
    301 n.6
Naidoo, Pumpy 220
Namibia 225–6
Narunsky, Mel and June 20
Natal Cultural Congress 226
Natal Cultural Council (NCC) 42, 45, 46,
    47, 57
Natal Performing Arts Council (NAPAC) 42,
    43–5, 46, 47, 52
Natal Philharmonic Orchestra (NPO) 21, 39,
    42, 46, 47, 70, 74, 123, 163, 194, 201,
    294 n.23
Natal University Afro Jazz Band 203, 237
Natal University Development Fund
    (NUDF) 52, 53, 129, 134, 285
Natal University Jazz Connection
    in Peru 210, 212, 237, 239, 258
    recordings 57, 208–9
    US tour 205, 206, 207
Natal University Jazz Ensemble (NUJE) 20,
    39–40, 52, 70, 72, 119, 121, 126, 140,
    194–6, 197, 219, 255
Natal University Jazz Link 203, 205, 275
Natal University/UKZN Voices 123, 132
National Association of Democratic Lawyers
    (NADEL) 275
National Association of Jazz Educators
    (NAJE) 79, 160
    conference (Detroit, 1988) 52, 80–7, 90
National Broadcasting Company (NBC) 88
National Union of South African Students
    (NUSAS) 60
National Youth Jazz Band of South Africa
    226–7
National Youth Jazz Festival (NYJF) 174, 226,
    251, 252–3, 301 n.4
'Ndabazita' 147
Ndelu, Teaspoon 258
Ndlazilwana, Nomvula 298 n.29
Ndlazilwana, Victor 109, 298 n.29
New Brighton (Gqeberha) 109, 215–16,
    299 n.9
New Brubeck Quartet 9, 10, 43, 93, 97, 161;
    see also Afro Cool Concept

New Brubeck Quartet 9, 78, 242
New Brubeck Quintet 78
New Orleans Jazz and Heritage Festival
    (1990) 97, 143
New York City (NYC) 88
New York Cosmos 18
Newport Jazz Festival 18
News Cafe (Durban) 274
Ngcobo, Shiyani 284
Ngcukana, Christopher Columbus (Mra)
    176, 216
Ngcukana, Duke 177, 216–17
Ngcukana, Ezra (Pharoah) 34, 96, 121,
    126, 162, 175–7, 214, 216, 240, 255,
    298 n.30
Ngcukana, Fitzroy and Ray 216
Ngema, Mbongeni 147
Ngidi, Philane 136
Ngqawana, Zimasile (Zim) 57, 73–4, 76, 86,
    89, 95, 96, 107, 109–10, 111, 112, 113,
    114, 116, 120, 182–92, 212, 214, 216,
    231, 235, 260, 263, 270, 281, 298 n.36,
    298 n.37, 299 n.40, 299 n.44
Ngwenya, Boy 298 n.29
Nichol, Duane 136
Nicholson, Stuart 261
Nickel, Herman W. 145
Nico Malan Theatre (later Artscape Theatre
    Centre, Cape Town) 242
Niemand, Bernoldus 169
Nisbet, George 149
Nkabinde, Concord 28, 122, 228, 275,
    299 n.40
Nkosi, Jabu 234
Nkosi, Xoli 225
Nkosi, Zacks 181, 300 n.11
'No Easy Walk to Freedom' 202
Nobs, Claude 78
Nokwe, Alfred 221, 223
Non-Aligned Movement 249
Nottingham Road Hotel 197–8
Nowotny, Norbert 101
Ntoni, Linda 162, 164
Ntoni, Victor 9, 10, 18, 25, 34, 41, 43, 96,
    106, 109, 112, 113, 145, 159, 161–7,

176, 177, 213, 214, 216, 228, 252, 274, 298 n.30, 299 n.8
Ntuli, S'thembiso 195, 205, 206, 210
Ntuzuma 155
'Ntylo, Ntylo' 207
Nxumalo, Gideon 149

'October' 269
Oehrle, Elizabeth (Betsy) 126, 132, 204, 264
Official Secrets 209
O'Higgins, Dave 210, 230, 234
Oliver, Joseph (King) 16, 296 n.1
'One Up' 176
Opondo, Patricia 223
Ordeal by Innocence 266
Oude Meester Foundation for the Performing Arts 83
Oyster Box (Umhlanga) 32

Pacific Express 109
Pan Africanist Congress (PAC) 13, 83
Papineau, Sarah 88
Pardue, Tommie 179
Parker, Beverly 129, 279
Parker, Charlie 75
Parker, William 299 n.44
Pasha, Pat 215
Paton, Alan 14, 21, 25, 62–3, 292 n.6
Paton, Jonathan 105
Paton, Nic 25, 28, 29, 71, 90, 91, 92, 94, 105, 107, 111, 112, 114, 116, 242
Paul, Allen 57
Pavitt, Vince 122
Peace 51
Peace 159, 166
Pearson, Ellis 284
Pelé 18
Pele Pele 18
People's Space Theatre (Cape Town) 12, 156
Perkins, Edward Joseph (Ed) 86
Peru 237–9
Peters, Melvin 28, 29–30, 92, 94, 96, 99–101, 107, 111, 112, 113, 114, 116, 122, 125, 203, 206, 229, 242, 261, 269, 270
Peters, *Reverend* 132

Peterson, Oscar 100, 220, 270
Peterson, Roy 220
PG Glass 131
Phansi Museum (Durban) 217
Phil Harber Scholarship 54, 56, 227
Piano Passion concert (Durban, 2018) 269–70
Pietermaritzburg 16, 20
Pikey, Austen 33
Piliso, Ntemi 31
Pillay, Lionel 100, 220
Pillay, Sonny 220
Playhouse Theatre (Durban) 9, 43, 45, 47, 56, 143–4, 160, 227, 229–30
Playing the Changes (documentary) 3, 270
Pop Voice ensemble 123
Pope John Paul II 2, 21
Powell, Colin 247
Pretorius, Anne 133, 226, 252
Pretorius, Ben 14, 34–5, 55, 83, 119, 148, 217, 220, 267, 270
Pretorius, Pam 35, 270
Prince, Bill 84, 91, 104, 117
Pro Helvetia 285
ProSound 43, 168
Pukwana, Dudu 291 n.4, 299 n.9
Purim, Flora 228

el-Qaddafi, Muammar 249
Quota Bill *see* Universities Amendment Act

race and racism 29–30, 91, 172, 242, 292 n.3; *see also* United Nations (UN) World Conference Against Racism (2001)
Rachabane, Barney 22, 35–6, 40, 93, 97, 108, 143, 153, 159, 162, 163–4, 177–82, 240, 246, 253, 283
Rachabane, Elizabeth 180, 182
Rachabane, Leonard 231
Rachabane, Octavia 180–1
Radio Port Natal 20, 22, 50, 51
Rainbow Restaurant and Jazz Club (Pinetown) 14, 21, 34–5, 54–5, 66, 113, 118, 119, 135, 148, 156, 163, 217, 220, 230, 267, 270, 275

Ram, Deepak 8, 9, 121, 122, 186, 208, 209, 227, 228, 261, 294 n.23, 300 n.15
Ram, Vevek 283
Ramanna, Nishlyn 203, 237, 242, 270, 275, 276
Ramela, Ranketsing 256-7
Rasiya, Manjeet 236
Rathebe, Dolly 34
Redman, Dewey and Joshua 266
Reed, Rufus 90
Renaissance Center (Detroit) 90, 92
Les Rende-vous de l'Erdre (Nantes) 186, 235
Replica 209
Reveille with Beverly 20
Ricker, Bruce 54
Ridley, Larry 91, 134-5, 231
Ridley, Matt 237, 263
Riley, Jeannie C. 228
Roach, Max 112, 113, 114, 184, 185, 298 n.37
Roberts, Evan 136
Robeson, Paul 21
Robinson, Jeff 126, 188
Robinson, Richard 28-9, 71, 106
Rockefeller Center (NYC) 88
Rockefeller Foundation 210
Rolling Reunion concerts 263
Rollins, Sonny 75
Ronnie Madonsela Scholarship for Jazz 53-4, 55-6, 97, 111, 132, 140, 275
Roots & Branches 144
Roots Records 212-13
Rossi, Di (née Vlotmann) 35, 118-19, 120, 138-9, 251-2, 253, 276
Rossi, Michael J. (Mike) 91, 96, 117-20, 138-9, 203, 223, 251-2, 263, 273, 276
Rossing Foundation (Swakopmund) 225
Royal Academy of Music (London) 204
Royal Schools of Music *see* Associated Board of the Royal Schools of Music (ABRSM)
RPM studios (Johannesburg) 179
Rumours 31
Rungan, Natalie 123, 145, 210, 237, 300 n.24
Russell, Bertrand 16-17

Russo, Bill 73
Rypdal, Terje 78

Sabongo, Vusi 95, 132, 199
Sachs, Albie 49, 294 n.27
Sahlin, Joel 284
Sakhile 51, 181, 219, 228
Sale, Lawrence 241
sanctions and boycotts 13, 41, 42, 43, 97
Sanders, Pharoah 176
Sandoval, Arturo 296 n.6
'Sarie Marais' 172
Sarkin, Ros 41
Saudi Arabia 237
Sayer, Rob 39
Scard, Dennis 41
Schlemmer, Laurie 130
Schneuwly, Michel 46, 240-1
Schoenman, Ralph 16
Scott, Tony 220
segregation 20, 51
Sehloho, Fanyana 298 n.29
Seimon, Anton 238
'Sekumanxa' 298 n.29
Selby, Ron 169
Semenya, Caiphus 187
'Sent for You Yesterday' 90
Setlotlo, McDonald 52-3
Seventh Avenue South (NYC) 11
'Sexlessness' 176
Shabalala, Headman 143-4
Shabalala, Joseph 77, 78, 129, 143, 144, 145, 227
Shallis, Dorothea 11, 202
Shallis, Jonathan (Jo) 30, 202, 212
Shange, Boise, Claude and Cyril 146
Shange, Bongi and Dumisane 155
Shange, Sandile 29, 33, 37, 38, 51, 78, 101, 146-9, 151-2, 153-5, 156, 159, 160, 169, 179, 201, 202, 219, 225, 240, 265
The Shape of Jazz to Come 183
Shaughnessy, Ed 142
Shezi, Thulani 236
Shields, Henry 83, 176, 222, 235
Shifty Records 169
Shipp, Matthew 299 n.44

Short Attention Span Ensemble 230-1
Shorter, Wayne 75
'Sibongile' 155
Sikhade, Ayanda 235
Simani, Aubrey 298 n.29
Simon, Barney 11, 162-3, 166-7
Simon, Paul 42, 44, 107, 143, 144, 178, 182, 226
Sinicrope, Bob 269, 281, 301 n.4
Skalkie, Aubrey 52-3
Skipper, Mike 253, 300 n.4
Sloan, Gerald 136, 219
Smirnoff 221, 222
Smith, Tom 135
Soda Supra (Durban) 274
Soft Machine 157
Sokhela, Bongani 136, 164, 204, 231, 234, 236, 284
Solidarity Museum (Szczecin) 2
Solomon, Piwe 130-1, 210, 225, 256-8
Solotude 185
Sono, Jomo 18
Sony 168-9
Sosibo, Madoda (Bruce) 195
Sothane, Shepstone 298 n.29
Soul Jazz Men 215
South Africa
    apartheid years 63-4, 273
    corruption and factionalism 49
    crime 254, 256-7
    Department of Arts and Culture 205, 223, 234, 239
    Department of Arts, Culture, Science and Technology 244, 245
    Department of Foreign Affairs 223, 234, 245, 249
    post-apartheid 214
South Africa House (London) 107
South African Association of Jazz Educators (SAJE, now South African Association for Jazz Education) 120, 135, 138, 141, 174, 226, 251-2, 285-8, 294 n.8
South African Breweries (SAB) 131, 226, 285
South African Broadcasting Corporation (SABC) 48, 58, 88, 144, 158, 167, 230, 243

South African Defence Force (SADF) 101-2, 103, 160, 195-7
South African Musicians Association (SAMA) 27-8, 41, 293 n.21
South African Police (SAP) 195, 257
Southern African Music Rights Organisation (SAMRO) 83, 138, 153, 170, 208, 252, 285
Southern Comfort Natal University Jazz Jol 220
Sparrow, Dennis 293 n.19
Spats (Johannesburg) 216
Spencer, Michael 129
Spirits Rejoice 111, 169, 216
Spring Leaves 51
Stable Theatre (Durban) 45
Standard Bank National Youth Jazz Festival
    see National Youth Jazz Festival
Star Point Five (Exclusive Hotel, Umlazi) 219
states of emergency 40, 63, 64, 158-9, 196, 213
Steele, Bryan 122-3, 230, 233, 294 n.23
Still on My Mind 146, 234
Stitt, Sonny 35
'Strange Fruit' 3
Stravinsky, Igor 74
Stuart, Bill 39
student loans, national 140
Sun Records 169
Süsse, Ulrich 20
Sutcliffe, Mike 41
Swedish International Development Co-operation Agency (SIDA) 132, 285
Sweet Basil (NYC) 275
Swing, William Lacy (Bill) 185
Swiss Air 77, 83, 93
Sydney Olympic Games (2000) 132, 239
Symphony Hall (Boston) 100
Syracuse, Richard 135, 231
Szczecin (Poland) 1, 2

'Take Five' 2, 21, 37, 198, 225, 267
'Take the "A" Train' 2, 20
Tambo, Oliver 6, 166
Tananas 169, 228
Taylor, Adrienne and Mike 31

Taylor, Barry 33–4
Taylor, Billy 92
Taylor, Colleen (née Cook) 30–1
Taylor, Robin 213
'Tea for Two' 220
Temptations 266
Ten Kleij, Michiel 3, 120
Terry, Clark 88
Thabane, Philip 9
Thailand 234–5
Thana, Haren 284
Thelonious Monk Institute Ambassadors 281
Themba, Seya 170
Third Ear 169, 202
Thobejane, Gabriel (Mabi) 9, 37, 208
Thusi, Brian 33, 34, 132, 225, 281, 301 n.4
Thusi, Mpumulelo 118
Thusini 164, 234
Tight-Head Fourie and the Loose Forwards 202
Tillis, Fred 112, 185
Time Out 182
Timol, Bobby 220
Timothy, Chloe 57, 242
Tini, Dennis 141, 170, 252
Tito, Dudley 215
Tjader, Cal 33, 266
Toastmasters Association 21, 50–1
Toledo, Alejandro 239
Tony's Jazz Club 221, 222–3
Topp, Janet (later Fargion) 28
Tracey, Andrew 109–10
Tracey, Geoff 144
'Trane Ride' 215
transformation 46–7
Transkei 10, 14
'Tributes' 57
tri-cameral parliament 213
Trinder, James 129
Trios Plus sessions 131–2, 133, 137, 138, 139, 227, 244, 269, 274
Tropicale (Durban) 199
Trunz, Robert 78, 151, 208, 228, 235, 300 n.23

'Tshona' 147
Tsoaeli, Herbie 186, 235
Tsotsi 209
'Tugela Rail' 37, 108, 159, 179
Tutu, Desmond 187
Tyner, McCoy 10, 275

UKUSA Performing Arts Programme 132
UKZN/UCT Ensemble 203
Umkhonto records 99, 113
Umlazi (Durban) 33, 37, 194, 301 n.4
Union Carbide 132
United Democratic Front (UDF) 38, 83, 293 n.18
United Nations (UN) World Conference Against Racism (2001) 239, 243–8, 249
United States Information Service (USIS) 2, 83, 84, 85, 86, 93, 111, 117, 131, 135, 142, 160, 205, 207, 285
Universities Amendment Act (1983) 63
University Forum (UND) 60
University of Durban-Westville (UDW) 8, 62, 99, 113
University of KwaZulu-Natal (UKZN) Jazz Legacy Ensemble 142
University of Natal (later University of KwaZulu-Natal, UKZN)
  academic freedom 60, 277–8
  armed robbery at 256
  campus protest 58, 60–1, 63
  campus spies 197
  Department of Music *see* Department of Music (University of Natal)
  student admissions 62, 64, 128, 268, 277
  student unrest 255
  Students Representative Council (SRC) 51, 60
University of South Africa (UNISA) 68
University of the Witwatersrand School of Music 138
University of Zululand (UZ) 21, 37, 62, 225
The Unknown 159
'The Unknown' 154
US Jazz Ambassadors 282

Valdés, Chucho 112, 281, 296 n.6
Valli, Rashid 213
Van Ass, Martin 254
Van Dyk, Bruno 129
Van Heerden, Connie 116
Van Heerden, Rick 28, 51, 71, 76, 101–3,
    106, 107, 116, 160, 193, 225, 228, 276
Van Niekerk, Joan 225
Van Schalkwyk, Stacey 203, 228
Van't Hof, Jasper 281, 284
Vaughan, Sarah 18
VCU Africa Combo 142
Villiers (Free State) 193–4
'Vincent' 11
Viswanathan, Sundar 231
Voice of America 2
Volans Dry Cleaning (Pietermaritzburg) 20
Volans, Kevin 20

Waits, Nasheet 299 n.44
Wakashi, Themba 225
Waller, Fats 198
Wallis, Cliff 263
Walton, Ruche 57
Warner Elektra Atlantic (WEA) 18, 79,
    168–9
Warwick Triangle (Durban) 24
Washington, Salim 127
Waterford Kamhlaba College (Eswatini) 96
We Have Waited Too Long 95, 98, 111, 169,
    214
Weaver, Carol Ann 132
Webb, Gyles 12
Weber, Eberhard 157
Webster, Alan 252–3, 301 n.3
Wellington Hotel (NYC) 87–8
'West End Blues' 74
Westin Hotel (Detroit) 90
'What a Diff'rence a Day Makes' 270
Wheeler, Kenny 281, 284
'Where are the Children Now?' 167
Whiplash 94
Whitehead, Candace 228–9
Williams, Johnny 32
Williams, Tony 75, 104

Willie-Petersen, Chantal 252
Wilson, Clarence 166
Wilson, Daniel 136
Wilton (Connecticut) 88–9, 105, 207, 275
Wind Band (UND) 73, 74
Winter, Paul 231, 281
Woolridge, Dennis and Derek 212
workshops 48
World Expo 2000 (Hanover) 223, 225, 239
World of Music, Arts and Dance (WOMAD)
    festivals 42
Wright, Graham 9

Xhosa Nostra see The Brothers

'Yakhal' Inkomo' 147, 268
Yard of Ale (Johannesburg) 213
'Years Ago' 10, 216–17
Yenana, Andile 122, 186, 231, 235, 242,
    258, 270, 299 n.9
Yeoville (Johannesburg) 30, 31
'You Think You Know Me (but You'll Never
    Know Me)' 177, 207

Zabalaza Festival (London, 1990) 57
Zacks (Durban) 136, 274
'Zandile' 298 n.29
Zanusi 57, 195
Zegree, Stephen 282
Zimphonic Suites 298 n.36
Ziporyn, Evan 11–12, 29, 38, 169, 178–9,
    292 n.4
Zondi, Julia 25–7, 55, 229, 233
Zucker, Anita 32
'Zukile' 217
Zwane, Henry 74
Zwerin, Michael 79

Darius Brubeck is an American jazz pianist, bandleader, composer, broadcaster, educator, and former director of the Centre for Jazz and Popular Music at the University of KwaZulu-Natal. He is the son of legendary jazz pianist and composer Dave Brubeck.

Catherine Brubeck, a South African, has worked in events organization, publishing, and artist management (specializing in jazz) in America, South Africa, and the United Kingdom. She was the project manager at the Centre for Jazz and Popular Music, initiating and organizing extracurricular projects and events throughout Darius's term as director.

The University of Illinois Press
is a founding member of the
Association of University Presses.

University of Illinois Press
1325 South Oak Street
Champaign, IL 61820-6903
www.press.uillinois.edu